CW01239338

MERE

Danielle Giles

MERE

MANTLE

First published 2025 by Mantle
an imprint of Pan Macmillan
The Smithson, 6 Briset Street, London EC1M 5NR
EU representative: Macmillan Publishers Ireland Ltd, 1st Floor,
The Liffey Trust Centre, 117–126 Sheriff Street Upper,
Dublin 1, D01 YC43
Associated companies throughout the world
www.panmacmillan.com

ISBN 978-1-0350-5122-9

Copyright © Danielle Giles 2025

The right of Danielle Giles to be identified as the
author of this work has been asserted by her in accordance
with the Copyright, Designs and Patents Act 1988.

All rights reserved. No part of this publication may be reproduced,
stored in a retrieval system, or transmitted, in any form, or by any means
(electronic, mechanical, photocopying, recording or otherwise)
without the prior written permission of the publisher.

Pan Macmillan does not have any control over, or any responsibility for,
any author or third-party websites referred to in or on this book.

1 3 5 7 9 8 6 4 2

A CIP catalogue record for this book is available from the British Library.

Typeset in Janson by Palimpsest Book Production Ltd, Falkirk, Stirlingshire
Printed and bound by CPI Group (UK) Ltd, Croydon, CR0 4YY

This book is sold subject to the condition that it shall not, by way of
trade or otherwise, be lent, hired out, or otherwise circulated without
the publisher's prior consent in any form of binding or cover other than
that in which it is published and without a similar condition including
this condition being imposed on the subsequent purchaser.

Visit **www.panmacmillan.com** to read more about all our books
and to buy them. You will also find features, author interviews and
news of any author events, and you can sign up for e-newsletters
so that you're always first to hear about our new releases.

For Kerri, Mark, Margaret and Harry,
who are always with me.

Prologue

The mere has fingers, the boy's mother told him. Clever fingers that reach up through the marsh and wrap around little ankles, strong arms to pull poor sinners downwards, and a great gaping belly that can never be filled. That is why men dig the ditches and tame the water. Let a mere be and it will devour all of Christendom.

Every night for a year after, he'd dreamt of it. An unending hunger reaching out for him. Sometimes he'd wake, the blanket wet with piss, and his mother would feel its damp warmth spreading to her and she'd sigh and go to wash it, again. The older boys saw this and named him loosebowel, mouseling, trembler.

So he learnt to ignore his mother's warnings. When she talked of elves with their arrows, he told her he would raise a shield and fend them off. If revenants came wailing through the gloom, he would strike their heads from their bodies and banish their souls back to hell. Be it foul beast or wicked spirit, he would meet it with glorious battle.

Now, though, he wishes he had listened more closely.

The boy stands in the darkness, water to his ankles. The ground is not ground here, only hollows and yielding. Like walking along a riverbed, like walking on flesh. The only light is the sliver of moon above but even that is weak, as if it comes from beyond the edge of the world. It turns the reeds to silver seax, raised and sharp. It unpicks the trees and sky and water, knots them into strange tangles through which he can see no way out.

He had not meant to wander off the path. But the boy's legs had ached and he only wished to rest a little where he would not be scolded for it. It had been a long week on the road, him on foot the whole time, and when he was not walking he was setting fires or feeding the horses, or fetching water. Even sleep was but a few moments, stolen on top of itchy hay or damp earth.

So he'd lingered a while behind the party, let them walk a dozen or so paces ahead. Enough for him to slow, to truly watch what was about him, and that was when he'd seen it. A break in the reeds and beyond it stones blushed yellow and white by lichen. The last of the daylight was with him and he thought he would wait there a while, until at least the others saw he was gone and called for him.

And then the daylight faded and with it the path back.

Now, the boy takes a step into a tussock of reeds. It crumbles beneath his foot like old bone. He trips but catches himself just in time. He must keep walking. They will be looking for him.

He had been so grateful to leave Gipeswic. It's only now that he understands how safe he had been there in the great hall of Thegn Theodred, in the kitchen with its strong walls and full stores. The giant ovens, filling the air with the smell of baking bread. The yule boar, turning on its

Mere

spit, the fat dripping down onto the flames and raising hissing, burning fire-snakes. His mother's strong, warm arms, which fussed and pinched and protected.

He wipes at his eyes. He passed his thirteenth summer this year and is a servant to a great, learned man. He's even earned the trust of the thegn's wife. He is too old for fear.

But not too old for hunger, nor for cold. He can feel both settling on him, pinching the feeling from his fingertips and the strength from his legs. He puts his hand on his belt, feels the knife there. Not a warrior's seax, but if some mere-beast comes he will raise the blade like a hero of old and strike, but no, he always wept to see even the chickens killed and

trembler

mouseling

that was why his mother sent him away not pride but shame

He walks on and then cannot remember how long he has been walking. It might be no time at all or half a day. The fog is now so thick that he cannot see more than a step in front of him, so thick he might reach out and clasp it in his hand like so much wool. He can smell green and the rich rot of mere-pools. He does not like looking in them, so dark and deep that they steal even his reflection. There is far-off birdsong but he cannot tell where it comes from or if he has dreamt it.

He begins to sing. He hears how small his voice is, how it cracks and deepens as if he is only half a man, but he sings anyway. It is a stout song from the kitchens on the days before feasts, when every soul was damp with sweat and soft-limbed with weariness and still they had to work through the day and night to prepare a great meal for the thegn and his guests. A song for long hardship and just reward.

He sings it a dozen times and a dozen more. And then, when his throat grows hoarse and each breath feels as if it is full of embers, he sees something pushing out of the ground ahead.

A post. A sign of a path, something crafted by a man's hand in this forsaken place. He stumbles, not caring that the water reaches his knees, his waist, for there is first one post and then another and ahead a stretch of wooden slats, all of different woods and hues, leading him onwards and in the air there is warmth and comfort, too.

A dwelling ahead, maybe, or even just a fire would be enough and he can see it now, boar-skin crackling with fat, the easy flesh of its cheek, a slice of bread and he would take even the burnt bottom crust that his mother would feed to the chickens and it is there he is sure right ahead of him but then he stumbles once more and

fingers grasping

his ankle caught

and there is water in his eyes in his mouth soaking his lungs winding about his throat and he kicks out but nothing yields and he feels it beneath him the great maw the empty belly and it will take him this mere will devour him just give him one more breath just

one more

Chapter 1

I slip from the convent just after Vespers, my lungs still filled with holy smoke. The evening is bitter, ponds and washbasins illuminated silver with ice. It's barely a week into November in the year of our Lord 990 and here, hidden not far from the coast of East Anglia, the first cold of winter comes and turns water to bone.

Hurrying across the bridge that separates the higher land of the convent from the farmland that surrounds it, a few souls lift their heads and watch me pass. Some are in fields, sowing overwintering wheat and digging ditches. Others in swift little boats, pulling eel traps from the water with one hand, eel-spears held in the other. They give a fifth of all they farm to us, year after year: apples, wool, sometimes girls.

There are over a hundred souls out here to the convent's fifty or so, drawn from a great multitude and deposited in this place. Some of them Anglisc, come from across the sea in centuries past, some northmen whose ancestors came to settle when this place was still under Danelaw. Still others

Wealh, from the stubborn lands to the far west, most of them enslaved and then brought from the market at Gipeswic. And some who have been here since before all others, cutting the reeds and fishing the pools as they always have.

No matter who, they still call their greetings to me, which so often hold within them seeds of worry.

'Some sickness, Infirmarian?'

'Are you searching for some herb? I saw late hellebore, not far from here.'

I wave them off with thanks, telling them I have everything I need. I wish they would not shout out to me. The abbess may still be away in Gipeswic but she has plenty of souls keeping watch for her. I am into my fourth decade now and still I must creep about like some disobedient oblate.

It is a difficult path across the farmland to the very edge where tilled soil falls to marsh. My leather boots are sodden through and I can feel silt between my toes. A few times I step thinking there is solid ground in front of me and trip into water that reaches my shins. I wish I could turn around and return, set my feet in front of the fire in the infirmary and find myself some honeyed wine.

But Sweet has asked for me and she will not be ignored.

So I only reach down and pull the hem of my habit up, rolling up the hose beneath them so that my legs are bare from my knees down. Shameful if I were to be caught. Whore, Jezebel, Eve and all her passions. But I am far from the convent now and there are not many out to see me. Besides, if the abbess learns I have visited Sweet again, my clothing will be the least of any sins.

I continue on, cursing and spitting and wading through

Mere

silt and bog and reeds. Over the four decades that this convent has been here, generations have fought the same battle: cutting ditches, pushing the water back and turning it to where it might be of use. Here they admit defeat and the marsh pours in. I am surrounded by frothing sedge and saxifrage, by ferns heavy with growth and greenery so thick it tangles even sound.

And, at the edge of it all, a small hut. The walls made of packed mud and reeds like many of the poorer dwelling-places about. Wood is only used for the walls of the richest of the ceorls and those buildings that belong to the convent.

There are fish and eels drying on a rack outside, fox and rabbit skins stretched out beside them, fellows in death where they never were in life. A bucket of urine to be used for tanning and a pile of dirty rushes that have not yet been swept back into the earth. Herbs and tiny charms made from delicate bird bones swing from the doorway.

A place of power, despite its smallness. It is enough to make me stop and take a few steadying breaths.

Then, I lift my shoulders and go to meet Sweet.

Inside, I press my hands against Eluned's belly. She does not flinch, only stares into the fire that Sweet is tending. It is our only light in this dark place and sets shadows climbing up every wall. There is the rich smell of brewing pottage and the peat that burns beneath it, turning the air warm and damp as breath.

'You said you felt it quickening?' I ask Eluned.

She nods, once. Eluned is so young, with loose black hair and an undyed wool dress. There is a stillness about her that many in the convent think slowness. This is how Eluned wishes it.

'When did you first know?'

'A week,' she says, softly.

'She came to me yesterday,' adds Sweet. She spoons the pottage into a bowl, passes it to Eluned. Then, one for herself.

'Your monthly bleeding?' I ask Eluned.

'I did not have it,' says Eluned. She lifts some of the pottage to her mouth but does not eat. Sweet has given her a gift of a bowl, filled with eel and sheep's meat and crab.

I sigh and lean back on my haunches. Sweet has only two stools and she is already sitting on the spare one, her head bent over her food. She eats in quick, snapping bites, as if she expects it to be knocked from her hands if she does not finish it quickly enough.

'Well, it is the old problem,' I say. 'Is it Sybba?'

Sweet reaches and pulls a fish bone from her teeth, then spits onto the pressed-earth floor. 'Who else?' she says. 'The only woman he can have these days are those that already belong to him.'

'Have you thought of telling the abbess?' I ask Sweet. 'The penitential says that if a slave bears the child of her master, there are punishments. The father should fast and the child should be freed.'

Sweet and Eluned look at each other over me and I know what they think. I have spent too long in the convent and have swallowed entirely all the talk of mercy and kindness. Both of them wear a cross about their necks, Eluned's wooden and Sweet's bone, but their faith is not one that follows the convent's pattern. Eluned came from Wealh full

Mere

of belief, but her years as a slave have taken much of that from her. As for Sweet, she wears other charms besides the cross on her neck, ones that are older, full of power.

Sweet is not alone in this. Many of the ceorls take Christ as their Lord readily, but He is often busy and so they pray to others, too: Woden and Frig and older powers that were never given a name. Christ may be king but He is the greatest of many.

When the gods do not answer, the ceorls turn to Sweet. The women who cannot bear living children, the men who wish to have their fates read, the households who are raising a new building and wish for a blessing for the threshold.

Many go to her before they would come to me for help. It is only for the worst that she calls down the convent's infirmarian – or if she feels I should know of an illness or problem.

Sweet does not need me now. She could mix together a potion to kill the babe in Eluned's belly in the time it takes most women to braid their hair.

It pricks at me, this lesson of hers. It is as if she thinks I am a child, innocent of all the sin about me. But I have been infirmarian for longer than I have been anything else, starting my learning when I was not even nine winters. I have seen bitter wounds and screaming death and I do not need her to tell me that Sybba is cruel and that the abbess does nothing as long as he pays his tithes.

'Our priest is returning soon,' I say. 'Coming back from Gipeswic with the abbess. He might listen, where the abbess will not. I could—'

'Leave it be,' Eluned says. 'The priest will only make it worse.'

'As you wish,' I say, standing. I wait for Eluned to

continue, but it seems she has come to the end of her words. Beside me, Sweet has almost finished her bowl of pottage.

'Is there none for me?' I ask. 'I have come all this way down.'

'The abbess would say that good deeds are their own reward,' says Sweet.

'Well, the abbess is away still,' I say. 'And I find meat and wine also suffice.'

I meet Sweet's gaze. She does not know her own age, but she must be well into her sixth decade, her narrow face deep-lined and watchful. She is small and thin, a knife that has been honed by age and use to nothing but edge.

'The cure first,' says Sweet, 'and then you can eat.'

We prepare the drink together, mixing dittany and wild carrot into hot water and honey. Sweet makes a show of cutting the right amount, feigning that she did not know what Eluned's trouble was all along, as if this is not the third time the girl has come to her in the last two years. She rolls up the sleeves of her dress, revealing constellations of bee-stings on her arms. She does not produce enough of worth to pay tithes and so spends any spare time in service of the convent tending the hives.

'If you had come to the infirmary, we might have this with wine,' I say to Eluned as I pass it to her.

'I would be marked by the others,' she says, shortly. 'They would know me and my sin.'

'It is no sin,' says Sweet, walking across to take Eluned by her shoulders. An odd grip it is, gentle and tight all at once. She lowers her head and begins to murmur instructions to Eluned, ones that will teach her how to curse a

Mere

man so that he cannot raise any part of him. They move from Anglisc to other tongues, words of British and Wealh that Sweet knows I cannot comprehend.

I only know British from songs and no Wealh at all, so I look instead to Sweet's herbs. I keep mine in our infirmary storeroom, in close-packed boxes and tight-knotted bunches. Sweet hangs hers wherever she can find space: from posts driven into the wall, from thread pulled tight across the room. That which cannot be hung is placed in covered bowls arrayed on the floor against walls. I stand and begin to search through these, opening half a dozen before I find what I need.

'A gift for you,' I say, passing it to Eluned. The small brown seed is about the size of her fingernail. 'Heartwort seed.'

'What will it do?' asks Eluned.

'I use it for fevers,' I say. 'It removes heat, of all sorts.'

She runs her finger over the ridges of the seed. Beside me, Sweet snorts. 'It will take more than a seed to quell Sybba's lusts.'

'But it is a start,' I say. I press Eluned's hands together. 'Crush it and place it into his wine with other spices to mask the taste. Do you understand?'

She nods, sliding the seed into the pouch about her girdle. Then, she takes the cup of dittany and wild carrot and drinks deeply from it. Sweet and I both watch in silence, intent as two old crows over carrion.

After we have made sure that she will not vomit it up, Eluned leaves. Sweet gives her a handful of berries and herbs to place in the basket that she has brought with her, so that she might tell the others she was out foraging.

'A mercy, to give Eluned heartwort,' says Sweet when she is gone.

'It was from your supplies,' I say. 'No great kindness.'

'Well, next time I am by the infirmary I shall come and take from your stores, then.'

'You would be welcome to it,' I say. 'If you ever came to see me.'

Sweet stares at the fire, which is beginning to dwindle. Eluned's visit has set darkness threading through her, old memories and wounds.

'If you ask me, the only way to stop Sybba is five coins of henbane in his beer,' says Sweet. 'And a quick burial.'

She lifts herself upwards, tosses a clod of peat onto the flames. It spits, then settles. There are rushlights hanging from the walls, their cores soaked in tallow fat, but Sweet has not lit them. Perhaps it is to avoid waste, but I think Sweet wishes to talk of this in a half-light.

'If she asked,' says Sweet, 'would you give it to her? The key to her freedom?'

'It would not work,' I say. 'Even if she was not caught, she would still be a murderer. That is a sin and—'

Sweet shakes her head. She looks at me as if she has found rot in her wheat after a damp summer. Sadness and worry in her eyes, but it is no sudden blow.

'You have been there too long,' she says. 'You are like the rest of them. Too bound by what is good to see what is right.'

She wears a headdress knotted with thick thread that she has woven herself, beneath it pale blonde hair that is now mostly grey. Her dress is thin but well kept, the yew-dyed green faded through years of long use. The only sign of wealth is the beads of antler and pearl she wears around her neck beneath her cross and other charms. To any who

Mere

might pass her, they would see a free woman, not rich but not yet starving.

It is a falsehood, of course. I know she has cooked meat because Eluned and I were coming. I know that she would rather have a belly empty than trade any of her treasures, scarce as they are.

And it is this, more than anything, that needles me. I am not the only one of us who clings to something half-false.

'I came here,' I say. 'I might be whipped for breaking the abbess's rule.'

'And I know how much love you hold for her,' says Sweet. 'It is not much, to disobey one you hate.'

'I have never said I hate her,' I say, quickly.

'No,' says Sweet, 'you have been careful not to.'

Sweet is always so, drawing me into words against the abbess. She collects them, I think, gathers them and waits for a day when they will be useful. But I will not be easily baited today.

'I came to help,' I say, 'because you called. Nothing more.'

'You come here to learn,' says Sweet, 'to gossip, to ask me where you might find this herb or that flower.'

'I do not need that any longer,' I say, 'I know this marsh nearly as well as you.'

I wait for the laugh, the insult. There is none who knows the surrounding bogs and pools as Sweet does. But she only tilts her head.

'Yes,' she says, in a low voice, 'you do. Half of the convent, half of the mere. But this place is not kind to border-walkers.'

Outside, I hear birdsong. The chatters of sparrows beneath eaves, the cry of a marsh harrier high above the reeds. Eels will be emerging to hunt, men and women will be laying down their tools and in the convent we will be preparing for our evening service of Compline. I should return to the infirmary soon or I will be missed.

'You look thin,' says Sweet. 'Are you fasting, repenting some sin?'

'No,' I say, 'the whole convent is hungry. The abbess hides it, but our stores grow low. She is in Gipeswic to sell what she can of our relics and tapestries and to beg her cousin for gold and supplies.'

'Abbess Sigeburg begging,' says Sweet, 'I wish I could see that.' She begins to spoon pottage into a bowl, this time for me. 'And here I thought these last few years of poor harvests had hurt us alone. But it seems the holy women suffer alongside us on that hill of yours.'

Although the sisters of the convent are set apart from the ceorls by holy vows and high ground, in truth this is less a chasm and more a single handspan. We take their tithes and in return offer mass and whatever else the convent has in charity. The portress, or sometimes the abbess herself, will come and judge some dispute on who owns land or cattle or a slave. We draw on them for girls to become novices and when they are full grown these sisters often find a reason to pass by their former families. Many of the women are paid for duties that the sisters cannot or will not do, often cleaning or cooking before returning to their own homes. We may seem as two separate rivers, each with its own flow and course, but in truth we share the same source, the same end.

The same troubles, too. I watch Sweet finish her serving of the pottage, a knuckle of glistening gristle setting my mouth watering. The tug of it between my teeth, salt and fat to be savoured for days afterwards.

Mere

Then she stops, spoon in hand. 'Oh,' she says, mockery in her face, 'but you are forbidden from meat, are you not?'

'And far more,' I say. I reach out to take the bowl, meat and all, when there is a sudden sound at the door. A knock, heavy and full of power.

Sweet and I both flinch, turn to each other. After years of unsteady peace, the northmen raids began again a decade ago with attacks in Kent. The stories came to us slow and heavy. Churches ravaged and razed, ports set ablaze and the souls in them raped and killed or carried off slaves. Our fear makes us twins; the same wide grey eyes, the same tight face.

It is Sweet who moves first. She unsheathes her knife, as if that might defend against a northman's axe, and treads towards the door. I follow and grasp for Sweet's spindlestick. I could laugh, for I would not trust it to keep away a wrathful goose, let alone a raider.

Sweet pulls open the door and steps into the doorway. Then, a half-bow as she hurries to place her knife back in her girdle. Sweet shows deference only when she must and I feel a different fear, now, that the abbess has returned and has come to find me in my disobedience.

I move forward, peering out. For a heartbeat there is only the marsh, its dark mere-pools grown black.

And then I see her. Not the abbess, but a woman, standing in the shadows beneath the eaves. She has her hands clasped tight together and I wonder who else would be out here at such a time, think of elves tricking children from their mothers and revenant ghosts coming to steal souls. But she cannot be either, for as my eyes grow used to the darkness, I see in this stranger's face no signs of malice, no wickedness. Only resolve, and somewhere deep within that a great fear.

Chapter 2

She steps into the hut without waiting for Sweet's say-so. It is so quickly done, her tread so easy, that neither Sweet nor I find the words to tell her no. It marks her as one who has spent her life walking through a realm of open doors and this room is but another.

She is unlike any other woman I have seen. Tall enough to stand alongside most men and large with it, her limbs thick and broad. Her face is plump and pale, her eyes so dark they are almost black. In a show of modesty, she is wearing a rough, undyed wool dress, similar to the habit that is given to all sisters. Yet her veil gleams, rich with embroidery of flowers and woodland, so that wherever she steps, water and earth step alongside her.

There is a burn on the right side of her face, running from her ear across her cheek and down her neck. Long ago healed, but still red and deep. She shows no shame at it, bears it as proudly as any thegn wears his arm ring.

Her head brushes the bones that hang from the roof and

Mere

sets them dancing, rabbits and eels and foxes brought back to whispering life once more.

'I am looking for a child,' she says, 'Father Botwine's new servant. Eadwig, he is called.'

The stranger's eyes search every shadow as if by the force of looking she might pull this child from wherever he hides. Sweet and I glance at each other. Ours is a small convent, and so though children stray they tend to be found quickly enough.

'We know Botwine,' says Sweet, carefully. Both of us are unsettled by this newcomer, her lost child. But she is of high rank and so Sweet must be deferent. 'He is our priest. But neither of us know this Eadwig. What does he look like?'

'Small, thirteen winters or so. Dark hair.'

This woman still has not given us her name, nor asked ours. There is a bluntness about her, thinking only of what must be done next and then what must come after. It is something I know myself, from those days in the infirmary when it seems as if every plague comes with its fellows.

'I am sorry,' I say, not without feeling, for though this woman is prideful and shows no heed for us, her worry for this Eadwig is plain. 'I have seen no child like that on convent grounds.'

'He was not on convent grounds,' says the woman. 'We lost him on the path here. We did not see he had gone, for he was always a quiet boy.'

For the first time, her words falter.

Beside me, Sweet stills. 'In the marsh?' she asks. 'He was lost there? Alone?'

The woman frowns at us, as if it is we who are slow to

understand, rather than she who is not telling us what is needed.

'Yes,' she says, 'as we travelled with the abbess and Father Botwine, back from Gipeswic.'

I look to Sweet, who still does not move. Something about this tale scares her. Sweet, who is so often about our convent lands with her rushlights aloft that the others mistook her for a ghost-light. Sweet, who taught me all the marsh's hidden paths and secret magics, how to pick woundwort and aster and dittany. And yet, she has always warned me against walking the mere alone and I have always obeyed. I thought it only good sense, for it is easy enough to lose bearings in the mist and stumble into a slow drowning.

I feel fear, then. Not my nightmares of wolves and raiders, blood and axes. Deeper, as if there lies a great giant beneath us, sleeping and waiting and hungry.

But when I look to Sweet, seeking comfort, seeking explanation, I see that she is no longer listening. Her gaze is beyond us both, through the open door and out to the marsh.

'You are a pilgrim, then?' I ask, for I do not like this silence and what might fill it.

'A sister,' she says. 'Or, one to be. I am Wulfrun.'

I know the name. The abbess went to Gipeswic seeking gold and land for us and has returned with this woman instead.

'You are Thegn Theodred's wife,' I say.

'I was once, yes,' she says. 'He is dead now.'

'They talk of you,' I say. 'The other sisters. They say you are a seer.'

But she has no time for even holy visions now. 'We can talk of this when we have found Eadwig,' she says, shortly.

Mere

'Tell me, are there no more dwellings on this side? This is the closest to the marsh?'

'Aye,' says Sweet, spreading her hands as if it is a kingdom beneath her and not a wilderness. 'Thanks to the abbess's gift. This hide of edge-land, all for me.'

Wulfrun nods. 'Well, if I ask one more kindness from you. A few of your rushlights.'

'No,' says Sweet.

Her refusal comes so sudden, so sure, that both the woman and I turn to her. Sweet may not own much, but I have never known her to refuse aid to any in need and a few rushlights is no heavy ask.

Wulfrun frowns. 'What is your name?'

'Sweet,' she says.

'Not a Christian name.'

'No,' says Sweet.

In the fire, the peat spits, hisses. Not long and it will burn down, leaving us all cold and dark.

'Well,' says the woman, fumbling at her purse. That worry at her heels again and she meets it with her shoulders straight and her chin high. Her only true shield an authority that has already passed. 'Sweet, I might pay you for them, if you would—'

'What will you do with them?' asks Sweet.

'I will light them and go to the marsh to search for the boy myself.'

'No,' says Sweet. 'We do not go alone to the marsh.'

Wulfrun watches Sweet, her hands still rested on her girdle. I see the pleas, the threats, the soft words and the hard all on her lips. But she remains silent, for Sweet's face tells her that there is no use in any of them.

Then, at last, she turns to me. For the first time, in the

dimness, she sees that I wear the convent's habit. Sees that I am far from its bells and candles, with this distant woman and her spells. Her gaze deepens and I feel as if I am being picked apart and set aside to be used later.

'You are a sister here?' she asks.

'Infirmarian Hilda,' I say. 'Also called Hilda the Wise.'

'The Wise?' she says, a small smile on her lips. It pulls at the scar on her cheek, creates new shadows in the burn.

'Every infirmarian is called so,' I say. I do not tell her that none in the convent have started using it yet though I ask them to.

'You do not look like the healers I have seen at home,' she says.

Many think I will be large and ruddy with good health and bright eyes. She finds me sharp-featured, thin-shouldered. An infirmarian half in need of cures herself.

'I have all the skill for it,' I say, 'and most of the good Christian spirit needed.'

'Well,' she says, 'if I cannot go alone, would either of you come with me in that spirit? You know the ways through, yes?'

She speaks gently enough, but there is a tightness to her voice. Slowly, she finds that paths are closed to her that she once thought open. That whatever power she held as a thegn's wife does not hold in this watery place. I feel pity, then. For this child lost in the marsh. For Wulfrun's desperate search.

'We know the ways, but would not take them at night,' I say. 'Even with rushlights.'

'Our faith might guide us,' she says.

'It will guide you straight into a bog,' I say. 'I have seen

Mere

sheep die there, pulled into the mere over the days. Too far for any rope to haul them free again.'

'I am no sheep,' she says.

'No, men and women are heavier and only sink faster.' I gesture at the jewels. 'And those would pull you down all the quicker.'

'You are telling me there is nothing to be done?' she says. Disbelief in her voice, outrage. 'That you stay warm beside your fires and leave him lost and alone, calling out for us and finding no answer?'

'It is not out of comfort,' I say, 'but safety.'

'No,' says Wulfrun. 'No, I will not have it.' She takes a step back towards the door. 'I have made the journey once and I might do it again. Look, the moon is strong tonight. The clouds have grown less heavy and I am sure that they will clear soon. You will both go with me then, in bright moonlight and good fellowship.'

Not a question but an order and yet neither Sweet nor I move. She looks between us. And, at last, there are no more paths to her. No more cunning words or heavy authority. She is only a woman, cast aside to die here.

'Surely,' she says, as if speaking might make it other than it is, 'surely there is something that we might do.'

But before we can reply, there is a call at the door. A torch lifted to make shadows of us all and another woman's weary voice.

'Come, Wulfrun,' she calls, 'we have done what we might today. We will find him tomorrow, with the light, I am sure of it.'

I know the voice. It guided me here all those years ago, brought me over water and across thresholds and into service and duty. Told me I was wicked but that I might not always be so, that I was slow but that I would learn in time. Ordered me to be whipped and starved and praised, sometimes all in the same day.

'Not yet,' Wulfrun calls out. 'I am talking here with Sweet, who warns me against the mere. Infirmarian Hilda is here also.'

Done without thought, without knowledge. She cannot know that the abbess has forbidden me from this meeting. Sweet flinches and Wulfrun's eyes widen as she understands she should not say my name. Her hand twitches outwards, as if to take mine, a supplicant gesture that I would not expect from her. Seeking forgiveness, maybe, but as soon as I mark the movement it is gone.

Whatever her meaning, it is done now and so I walk to the doorway to greet our abbess.

'I am here, Abbess Sigeburg,' I call out, giving our Mother Superior a small bow.

The abbess is small, in her eighth decade. The last four have been spent at the convent and where any other sister might retire to a few years of comfort, she holds on. She speaks softly, in a way that others might think kind. But Abbess Sigeburg has a piety that creeps around a woman like a vine. She will strangle you with scripture and punishment and insist that you thank her.

She is wearing her travelling clothes today, so much of her finery is hidden. But wealth hangs about her still. Her Pater Noster cord swings from her girdle, each pearl a prayer. And, about her head, the sign of her office. A single square ruby set in gold, fastened about her wimple with a cord of gold-spun thread.

'You must be tired after your long journey. I have mugwort to ease any pains. Or—'

Mere

She raises her hand to silence me.

'We have looked all we can for this boy,' she says, to Wulfrun. 'Return with me to the convent, find a bed, and we will renew our search tomorrow.'

'By then he might be dead,' says Wulfrun. 'Drowned.'

'Or he lies, just beyond our borders,' says Sigeburg. 'Waiting for the dawn. Who knows, he may even find his way back himself and what a welcome for him.'

For all her faults, our Mother Superior has always been able to gather hope to her. It let her raise the convent out of this sodden earth four decades ago, let her bully and trick gold and tithes and relics from whoever would pay, so that once we had nearly a hundred pilgrims come to stay with us each year, the whole convent alive with their worship. Last summer we had but a handful. We have sold too many relics, offer too cold a welcome, are too far down dangerous and fog-knotted paths. Many make pilgrimage, instead, to Ely, where they hold the uncorrupted body of Saint Etheldreda and will bear any pilgrim to the abbey by boat and ask no payment for it.

Yet still the abbess believes, even as the convent begins to sag and rot, that she might save us all with a gift or two from her Ealdorman cousin.

But Wulfrun is still not swayed. 'We will gather men now,' she says, 'with Father Botwine's help, for I know the care he has for Eadwig.'

Wulfrun does not understand the fogs. They fall heavy here, enough so that some days you cannot see even past your own hand, let alone some distant holy house.

The abbess begins to shake her head, but Wulfrun says, 'And this Sweet here, she knows the ways through.'

'Is that so?' says Sigeburg. She does not look at Sweet,

who has stepped into the doorway. 'I would not tell any soul to follow the paths she takes.'

Here, her eyes flicker to me. Sweet does not answer. She cannot. She exists here at the abbess's pleasure alone. I think our Mother Superior likes to keep her down here as a shrike leaves behind butterflies it snatches from the air.

'Is it true?' asks Sweet. 'The boy was left alone?'

The abbess is not a woman of raised hands or loud words. Joy or sorrow, wrath or terror, all of it she keeps fettered within her. But I have known her long enough to see what she cannot always hide. The clench of her fist, the small turn of her lips downwards. She is not stopping Wulfrun's search because she wishes to be back, in front of a fire and with honeyed fruits at her fingertips. She is as scared as I have ever seen her.

'What do you both speak of?' I ask.

Both women are still for a while, so still that they might be figures in some tapestry, hanging always in the middle of their tale and never moving onward. Something passes between them that I do not understand.

'Hush,' Sweet says to me, gently. 'It is not a tale for now.'

She presses at my back, pushes me ahead to join the abbess and return to my rightful place. I have a hundred protests, but I know neither woman will hear it and so I only stumble forward and make my careful way over to the abbess.

'Come, Wulfrun,' she says, holding out her hand. She is always so with women that she woos for this place. It will only be once Wulfrun has taken her vows that these kindnesses will sour.

Wulfrun pulls her veil tight around her once more. A

Mere

wind picks up, brings with it the smell of salted fish, of far-away smoke and damp greenery.

'It seems that all here have cast their vote against me,' she says.

I do not think this will be the end of it, for Wulfrun does not seem like a woman used to defeat. But I am glad that we will not go searching tonight, for to lose a child is strange and worrying and I do not want to be out there, in the darkness and cold. A wicked thought, unchristian and uncharitable.

And, as we begin to pick our way back up the hill, the abbess turns to me. 'I will see you at Compline,' she says. 'You will fast, for your current dress. You are a bride of Christ, not a whore.'

My habit and hose are still pulled up, showing my knees. I pull the hem down quickly. Wulfrun and the abbess return to the cart at the head of the procession loaded with supplies, though not as much as we would hope, and are drawn along. I walk behind them, every pool and puddle spreading dampness further up my skirt.

I barely feel it. The abbess has been threatening me with a whipping for the last year should she find me with Sweet, but today she rebukes me only for my dress. I do not think it mercy. It is the punishment of a woman who thinks too much of other matters to pay me much mind. And whatever lies heavy on the abbess might one day crush the rest of us.

Chapter 3

I sit in the infirmary the next morning, pulling leaves from rosemary. The fire burns strong, fresh-hung fennel shrouding the usual smell of blood and piss and bile. My patients drowse or else pray. It is how my infirmary should be, a place of quiet and rest not only for the ill but for those who tend to them.

The abbess would call it sloth if she saw me at my ease. I do not court her visits and she has not the stomach to stay here long. For all her praise of the miracle of man, his inner workings are too bloody for her.

I chew on a scrap of eel that one of my patients did not finish. I am meant to be fasting as punishment for last night, but it is an infirmarian's gift to eat meat and fish that is otherwise kept from us.

This gluttony is the only thing that the abbess might find fault with here. Otherwise, I keep a fine healing-house, the rushes on the floor tumbled with lavender and sage, a half-dozen straw mattresses laid out in rows. Our sheets

Mere

washed with lye against the fleas, though that is a battle that I think I will never win.

Though we traded away our tapestries last year to pay debts, the plaster walls shine still with paintings of miraculous cures: lepers dancing in jubilation, the blind with eyes flashing bright as kingfisher feathers, Lazarus waking from his death as if he is but a novice who has slept too long.

There is the sound of footsteps behind me and I start, swallow the eel so I will not be caught in this little sin. But it is only one of the ceorls, Oswy. A small, thin man, who always looks as if he is waiting for a blow, he serves in Sybba's household as a freeman.

He has a belly complaint that loosens his bowels and takes the joy from his every mouthful. Though he has visited Sweet and me many times, neither of us has been able to ease it. Even so, he returns every few months with a new cause. Last time, it was a punishment for eating meat on a saint's day. The time before, he told Sweet that one of the other women must have cursed him. In truth, I think he is afflicted with a long life at labour and that the only cure is an ease that he will not find in his current service.

'Today, I think I have it,' he says, sitting down to face me. 'It is a water-elf.'

I know better than to tell him otherwise, though from what I have seen the water-elf disease pales the nails and dampens the eyes, none of which afflicts Oswy. Instead, I do what I always must, which is fuss and question and nod kindly when he tells me of his woes. With Oswy, it is less the cure itself and more the skill and time behind it.

And so I gather together the needed herbs, mixing them with ale and holy water and singing over them a charm.

This seems to please him well enough, for after he has finished drinking he is in such good cheer that he smiles up at me and says, 'Fair Alfred was asking after you.'

'For a cure?'

'I do not think so,' says Oswy. 'Even so, he bade me greet you.'

He sits, waiting. But I know Fair Alfred of old and to give that man even a nod is to invite far more. I lean towards him, lower my voice.

'Do you know much of the marsh?' I ask. 'Sweet has always warned me not to go alone. The ceorls obey this rule also. Why?'

Oswy's face pales.

'It is dangerous,' he says, 'the paths—'

'Please,' I say, 'I would know, if there is some other threat to us.'

But pleading will not draw it from him, any more than threat. I must be cunning.

'It is only,' I say, 'Sweet is always talking of you. Of how you are wiser than many about. How you are able to recall what many others would forget.'

I do not think his name has been in her mouth for anything other than complaint. But Oswy, his chest held a little broader, his eyes a little brighter, does not need to know this.

'It was before I was born,' he says, slowly. 'There are not many left alive who remember.'

Careful, half-false words, for he knows as well as I do that stories do not die with their speakers.

'But you have heard?' I ask. 'From your father, perhaps, or others?'

Oswy watches me and then slowly shakes his head. 'I

Mere

cannot tell you,' he says. 'Only that you should listen to Sweet. Do not go alone to the marsh.'

He stands, his earlier cheer gone. 'I will ask Tiw to give us strength.'

'You might pray to a saint instead,' I say.

He considers this. 'Both,' he says. 'For if one does not help, the other might.'

I cannot tell him to give up his gods, for he will not heed me. And so I only say, 'Do not let the abbess hear you speaking of such things. I would not see any of you punished for idolatry.'

But as he leaves, it seems as if the abbess is the least of what worries at him. I begin to tidy away the pestle and mortar and the emptied ale-cup. I have barely started before there is another at my side. Not a patient but my helper in the infirmary, Mildred. She has just finished letting blood and holds the basin of red to her chest, ready to take it to the garden to pour on our herbs and crops.

'Is all well with Oswy?' she asks, watching him leave.

This will be Mildred's fifteenth winter and her sixth year studying under me. I have seen her grow from girl to maid and how with every passing year her limbs grow longer and more clumsy. She is already taller than me and may grow even taller still but she walks always with her shoulders hunched and face turned downwards. A meek girl.

And so this foolish question, for she knows that he is never well and cannot rouse the courage to ask what she really wishes.

'No,' I say. 'He believes himself King Alfred born again.'

'King?' Stunned, her fingers loosen on the bowl. If she is not careful, she will drop it and turn our rushes blood-soaked as a battlefield.

'Yes,' I say. 'Did the other sisters not tell you? We are to find him a crown.'

It is too far. For all her youth, she is a serious soul, with more of the novice mistress about her than the novice.

'You are being cruel,' she says.

I sigh. 'Yes,' I say, 'I am sorry. I did not sleep well last night. This boy, he preys on me.'

Wulfrun and Father Botwine set out this morning and have not yet returned. There are tales of kingdoms out in the marsh, places for elves and old gods, where a man might think he has spent a day in pleasure, only to come back to find an entire century has passed. Perhaps Eadwig has stumbled into some such place. Perhaps that is why none of us should venture there alone.

At Eadwig's mention, Mildred tenses. 'I wished to ask you,' she says. 'The other sisters say that a devil has woken in the marsh, taken the boy for his own.'

How quickly a lost child becomes something else. Because we cannot bear it, I think. The thought that it was only our own slowness that allowed him to wander away from us, rather than some terrible creature.

'I have not heard of this,' I say.

The infirmary is apart from the rest of the convent. We have our own toilets and kitchen and go to the stream for our water instead of the well. Most nights I sleep on a spare mattress here, for I long ago grew tired of the farts and snores and bickering of the main dormitory, a small building higher up the hill and closer to the church. But it is useful to know what tales are being told.

'And what else do they speak of?' I ask.

'They call me Littlevoice again,' she says, scowling. An

Mere

unkind nickname that trails after my apprentice like a dirty hem.

'And what do they say of me?' I ask.

She blushes. 'Only the usual.'

Byblow. Bastard. Adultery made flesh and appointed beyond her birth. I have heard it all before and it glances off me now. Most of my sisters have not the wits to think of new insults but Mildred is loyal enough to feel the rawness for me.

'So you do not think him devil-taken?' she asks.

'It has only been half a day,' I say. 'If the Devil has dragged him to hell, he will still only be halfway. Time enough for him to find his way back.'

I should not speak such words lightly, for Mildred pales. In truth, it worries me, too. I have not been able to return to Sweet's yet, for the abbess checks for me at every meal and holy office. Whenever I have gone out to gather herbs, I have looked for her. I even went to the beehives, but she was not there. If Sweet does not wish to see someone, she is skilled at making it so.

'He will return,' I say. 'I have faith.'

Mildred is still looking doubtful and so I ask, 'How are the other patients?'

It is much as it always is. One sister is afflicted with a lump in her throat that is growing ever larger, another has recovered from her gutrot but is lingering in bed, unwilling to return to her duties in the kitchen.

'They complain, also,' she says. 'They say the meals here are almost as small as those in the refectory. They say we keep back the best meat and fish.'

'If that were so, we would both be far fatter and happier than we are,' I say. 'The abbess came back from Gipeswic with far less than she wished and we are all being given less.'

The abbess has not said as much, but it is plain to see. Before she left, she ordered a tightening of our meals, telling us that it would be lifted on her victorious return. But she is back and nothing has changed. The beer we drink is still more water than anything else and the bread so rough that I am sure one day I will bite into it and find it pure grit. Our harvest this year was poor and the next few months will only be hungrier.

'Tell them that we must endure until spring,' I say.

'I would rather you spoke to them,' says Mildred. 'Tove only believes a thing if she has heard it from you.'

Tove is in her eighth decade and has been in the infirmary three years, for her bones and joints ache too much for her to walk more than twenty paces at a time and she cannot work full duties in the convent any longer. Every few months, death will hold out a hand that she knocks away. When Revelation comes, I am sure that she will be the only living soul left, clinging to her blankets and scorning the angels that come to fetch her.

And yet, I think that if she truly wished to leave our infirmary, she might. There is much that she is still able to do, from mending our habits and blankets to helping our portress, Ava, make her tallies. Ours is a slow sort of life, one that would allow her to take whatever rest she needed. But Tove has stayed here, nonetheless. She would rather be king of a single hide of land than a subject in another's kingdom. And, in truth, I would not wish to see her gone. I take some pride that she prefers the fellowship of my infirmary to the abbess's rule.

'I will talk to Tove,' I say. 'You go and speak to the sisters in the bakery, see if they have any spare for us. Even the burnt crusts might be softened in water.'

Mildred's face twists. 'We should not have to beg.'

'Let us all go hungry, then,' I say. 'I will tell Tove it is your pride keeping the food from her plate.'

I wonder if I should worry that Mildred fears Tove more than me, for she quickly bows and goes to do as I ask.

My helper is a strange beast. In some ways, she is a maid like many others, for I have seen her preening in basins and cups, trying to gather her features into vanity. But she can be stout, too. She has been with me as a man's guts spill out from him like a bowl of tipped pottage, as childbirth tears a woman and takes her lifeblood from her. I worry that I have turned her into the sort of maid that prefers to bleed a sister than to speak to one.

But we have made our pact and so I go to Tove. I have a salve for her joints and in truth enjoy talking with her above all other patients. Sometimes, if her mood is right, she tells stories of her ancestors, who she says came here from Afric to trade then stayed in Jorvik, growing over time into one of the wealthiest households there.

'So,' she says, as I rub her knee. 'Half the convent is sure that the Devil himself will come crawling out the bog to claim us.'

'I think he has far sweeter meats elsewhere,' I say. 'He would not start with a servant child.'

'True enough,' says Tove. She looks well today, her brown skin glowing and her movements easier than they have been for a while.

Tove observes the changes of this place as others do the passing of the seasons. She plans, too, as a farmer might. Where the right seeds might be sown, where she might find friendly soil. I am fortunate that she took a liking to me early on. In me, she has grown half an Eden.

'And what of our newest sister?' she asks. 'This Wulfrun?'

I have not been able to attend any of the holy offices last night or this morning, nor do I eat many meals in the refectory, and so I have only seen her in glimpses as we travelled back last night. Her face turned skywards in prayer. A single finger, pulling down the sleeve of her habit.

'I have not spoken with her,' I say.

Tove laughs. 'You should be thankful. They tell me she acts like she was the wife of King Aethelred himself, not some withered thegn. Do you know, she refused to take off that veil of hers when she came in? Portress Ava ordered it, but she would not be moved.'

'She refused Ava?' I say. 'That is some tale.'

'And there is more,' says Tove. 'That burn, they say it was not some fall or trip, but her own husband that did it to her. Held her face to the fire, for she was being disobedient.'

'How have you heard all this?' I ask. 'It has been less than a day.'

Tove smiles. 'This convent holds a secret about as well as a sprinkle-pot holds water. And many remember hearing tales of her from Gipeswic, before they became sisters here. I wonder if old Abbess Sigeburg will regret bringing such a flame to this dried-up place.'

Tove has never had to worry much about her speech. She is a poor Christian, but a rich woman. Without her family's gifts, we would have starved long ago.

'She is new-come,' I say. 'We are called to be kind.'

'I am kind,' says Tove, 'I have spent decades being kind.

Mere

Leave me to my idle talk.' She winces as I press on a tender spot. 'You press me like a millstone,' she says.

'I am being as gentle as Christ Himself,' I say, as I rub against knotted muscle. 'And I would wager that you and this Wulfrun will be as close as any, after some time. You share much, I think.'

'I thought that about me and Abbess Sigeburg, long ago,' says Tove. 'It is not always easy to tell these things.'

Tove speaks rarely of the abbess, of their ended friendship. All I know is that they have both lived through all the winter fluxes and summer agues that took away the others. They are bound by memories more than any goodwill, for the abbess has risen and risen while Tove has retreated to the infirmary.

'Do you know why Sweet would warn us against going to the marsh alone?'

'Because she did not wish you to drown, I would think,' says Tove.

'That is not all,' I say. 'When I asked Oswy, he would not tell me what he knew. You have been at this convent the longest of us all. Have you not heard anything, from the others, from the abbess?'

'And you ask me because you know the abbess and I gossip as maids before our wedding nights?' asks Tove.

'I only wondered if there had been talk of it.'

'Well, there has not,' she says.

I pat her hand. 'Do not worry if you have forgotten,' I say. 'It is easily done in old age.'

'Do not try to bait me. You are not cunning enough for it.'

'Bait you?' I say. 'I was only being kind.'

Tove laughs then, sudden and wicked. 'Insolent girl. Oh,

what wakes we would have left behind us, if we had met in our youth. Cunt-struck men and women, duels fought for our favour.'

'There is still plenty of time for that,' I say. 'Though, they will have to come to you now. And no duels, I have enough injuries to treat as it is.'

Tove lowers her voice.

'I do not know, exactly, what the abbess fears,' she says. 'But this has not always been a house of God. I have heard tales. Ghost-lights in the night, travellers snared in the bog. You have seen how the ceorls will sometimes spit as they walk, though the abbess dislikes it?'

'She forbids it,' I say. Not that they obey her.

'A few years before I arrived, there was a great battle of wills. The abbess wished to stop some gross idolatry they were all committing. I know not what, for she never spoke of it.'

'And the others?' I ask. 'You never heard anything of this from them?'

Tove shakes her head. 'They do not speak of it. You know how little they trust us.'

It is true enough. For every devout Christian, there is another who sees all that we take in tithes and finds holy salvation a poor reward.

'But attend to me no longer,' says Tove. 'There is somebody waiting for you at the door.'

'If it is Mildred—' I say, turning. But it is not my helper, not a patient. It is Wulfrun.

Chapter 4

*J*ust as before in Sweet's home, she steps through without asking any leave. She has kept her jewels, her glimmering wimple, but her habit is spattered with mud and damp nearly to her waist from what must be her search through the marsh. She is willing, at least, to do what she would ask of others.

She has learnt a little humility and understands that she should not disturb the ill, so she bows her head and treads across the infirmary towards us both. Patients crane their heads to watch her pass.

When she reaches us, she gives me a nod and then bows low to Tove and says, 'I have not greeted you yet, sister, but I have heard your name spoken in the hall of my husband. My sister married your uncle Lief in Jorvik, not six winters ago.'

'Is that so?' asks Tove, pushing herself upwards. Nothing stirs her like hearing of her family. 'The old boar has life in him still, then.'

'They have five children,' says Wulfrun, 'all boys. And I hear that it is like Ragnarok when they are at play.'

'Well, Lief's blood did always run strong,' says Tove. She lives on what she can in the convent, all our tiny sins and sorrows. But she is meant for great halls, not our little home. 'Five sons, eh?'

With Tove chewing over this good fortune, Wulfrun turns to me. Another lesson learnt, that she should make her greetings before her demands.

'I am sorry,' she says, 'that the abbess punishes you for visiting Sweet. I did not know there was a rule to be broken.'

'Well, it is a rule for me and me alone,' I say.

'Is that so?' she asks. I know what she will be thinking. How Sweet and I have the same grey eyes, the same pale, thin hair though Sweet's is more grey now. But whatever her thoughts, she does not say anything. I am grateful, for I do not want to have to tell her the whole, long tale.

She watches me through dark lashes. She seems all softness and welcome, round cheeks and lips half-parted as she considers me. But I know how cunning she might be, if she wishes. I understand why the thegn chose her for a wife, for even though she is weary and dirty, I cannot look away.

'They tell me,' she says, 'that besides Sweet, you know the paths in the marsh best.'

It is praise with claws, but I feel pride nonetheless.

'So it is said,' I say. 'I go there to collect my herbs, though always with Sweet, for neither us will walk there alone. If you need a guide, I am sure she will help you.'

'The abbess has forbidden it,' says Wulfrun. 'I do not know what has passed between her and this Sweet, but it sours them both.'

Mere

'And you would obey the abbess in this?'

'You would not?'

'Of course,' I say. 'It is only that you seemed half-ready to turn on your heel and take to the marsh yourself last night.'

'Well, as kind sisters have told me, I would surely stumble like some dull-witted sheep and drown myself.'

She brushes her habit, sending dried mud splintering from her. It seems that she has stumbled plenty this morning already.

'And,' she says, 'I cannot find the woman anyway. She hides from us all.'

Not wanting to be caught between the abbess and this newcomer, no doubt. Still, I feel a hope thwarted. Of course Wulfrun would not come to me first. She has no reason to.

'I cannot help today,' I say. 'I must go out to the fields with Botwine for his blessing-charm. And there is too much for me to do in the infirmary.'

She looks around her, at the patients dozing, at the dust falling like snow from the eaves.

'Yes,' she says, 'it is like Gipeswic on a market day here.'

Many souls have laboured for a long time to win this quiet. Just because it is calm does not mean that there is not much to do.

'I am sorry,' I say. 'If I left now, those under my care would suffer.'

It is not the only reason. If Sweet fears the marsh, then I should follow her in that fear. She is not often wrong.

Wulfrun sees this as well, I think. But she only bows to me, her voice a little weaker than it should be.

'You should know,' she says, 'that he is a good child – brave.

The other boys mocked him for a coward, for a mouseling, but they were always wrong. If that makes you feel any kindness towards him.'

I stare at her, a sourness in my mouth. I do not know what to say. She must have pleaded a hundred ways already for this child's safety. But he is only a servant boy and I have seen well how little they are worth, no matter their obedience, no matter how hard they work.

'This Eadwig,' I ask. 'Why do you do so much for him?'

She looks around, at the slumbering patients, their closed eyes. I would bet half of them listen to our every word.

'His mother was good to me,' she says, shortly. There is more there, far more, than she is willing to tell me. 'Will that sway you?'

I shake my head, my belly twisting. I do not like refusing help, but I must do what is best for the entire convent, not just one boy.

'A shame,' she says and I believe she means it and my belly grows even tighter.

Then, she gestures to the rushes on the floor beneath her. 'These are old,' she says. 'I can help you fetch some more if you wish, if you are so busy.'

'That is kind,' I say, 'but I will have Mildred fetch some. I would not keep you from your search.'

'No,' she says, watching my face. 'I would not be kept from it either.'

Then, she is leaving, passing through the doorway to rally more sisters to her side, her wimple flashing as bright as the sun itself. I have no doubt that she will charm half of them to her cause before the day is done.

'Well,' says Tove, swinging her legs to the side. She holds out her hand so that I can help her up from the

Mere

mattress. 'That is our new seer, it seems. Did she seem holy to you?'

'I think she could believe herself so,' I say, slowly. I think on Sweet's words of the other night, wondering whether I should have agreed to lead Wulfrun through the marsh after all. It is good that I stay in the infirmary, tending to all those who need it. I do not know if it is right.

But Wulfrun is already long gone and so I fetch Tove's cane. We often walk together after I have massaged her, a loop or two around the infirmary with plenty of rest, so that she might feel the sun on her face.

Today, though, I only take her to the threshold. The wind strips the warmth from us, sends the flags above each building in the convent whirling and twisting.

'Call for me if you need me,' I say.

'Why?' she asks. 'Where will you be?'

'I go to change the rushes,' I say. 'I would not say so to her face, but Wulfrun was right.'

I see Wulfrun again that evening when Father Botwine performs the Field-Remedy. He comes and stays with us twice a year and blesses the earth each time. It is always a solemn charm, but this year more than ever I feel the hunger about me. We cannot have another year of poor harvests and so Botwine has taken the time from his own search for Eadwig to perform the ceremony.

We should be at Vespers, but the abbess has given us all leave to come and pray with Botwine, if we wish. In truth, the abbess should conduct the ritual alongside our priest, but after her return from Gipeswic she has remained in her own rooms as much as she can.

The crowd today is the largest it has ever been, gathered

in a field near the bridge that separates the convent from the land around it. Even Tove is here, sitting on a stool that Mildred and I brought with us. She wraps her cloak tight around her, for the daylight is dying and we are far from fire and hearth. Above, the sky is smudged grey and blue, the stars smothered. It will be a shrouded night. I do not like it, for I need the stars and their signs to guide me in my work and tell me when one leechdom might heal and another might harm.

In this half-gloom, our priest walks the four corners of the field, his acolyte behind him carrying a basket filled with sods of earth. They are smeared at their roots with a poultice of yeast, honey, oil and milk, and all the finest herbs I keep. My hands ache still from preparing it earlier this morning. Each sod of earth has also been blessed and is marked with a small cross, woven from softened reeds. All told, that dirt is likely holier than most of my sisters combined.

They are a strange pair, Botwine and his acolyte, walking together. Botwine is a huge man, so strong that in his youth he could pull a plough with his bare hands alone. But for all his size, he is gentle. Always he would take the blow and forgive, always he finds a middle way and a kind word.

This new acolyte of his, Alwin, has much to learn. Some sisters have told me that his family wishes for him to one day become a bishop. A year or so under Botwine's steady tutelage and then he will be sent to a monastery and begin this hoped-for rise to glory. I cannot see it happening. He looks, always, as if he awaits a hunt – his face unmarked by disease or ill-favour, his tonsured hair thick and dark. A youth meant for glorious battle, not prayer.

In the corner closest to us, we watch as Alwin flings down

Mere

the earth and presses it in with his foot. Too forceful, for he has upset the cross and must crouch to right it.

'If that is how he treats holy earth,' says Tove, 'I fear for us penitent souls.'

'Botwine should warn him,' I say.

'Aye,' says Tove, 'but he is elsewhere, I think. That Eadwig of his still has not been found.'

'Perhaps he ran?' I say. Such things happen, when young boys and girls see the frame of their lives ahead of them, how it binds as much as it protects. But not many brave the winding paths of the marshes.

Tove shakes her head. 'He came from Gipeswic. Why not flee there, where some household might take him in, change his name for him?'

It is strange. It has been a day since he first became lost along the path from Gipeswic and the longer he is gone, the darker his fate. Bandits, cold and hunger: any of these might have taken him.

The last corner blessed, Botwine passes us and walks to the centre of the field. Now that he is closer, I see the weariness in him. There is a smile on his face, a foundation of comfort and good cheer with nothing built atop it. Tove is right. Our priest's thoughts are not with us, but with this lost Eadwig.

I wonder what binds Botwine and the child. Our priest is a caring man but he has never overturned a whole convent for a servant before.

Behind me, several of the ceorls hurry away to fetch the ox and plough, some more familiar to me than others. At their head is Fair Alfred, broad, full of the understanding of his own beauty. Even as he strides ahead, he glances back at the crowd, so that all might see the strength of his legs and yellow of his hair and beard, turned all the brighter by the lye that he washes it with every week.

Sybba is among the ceorls, also, walking a little slower than the others, clutching at his belly when he thinks others are not watching. The heartwort I gave Eluned, I think. I am glad she has found use for it so quickly and she seems glad, too, when I see her across the crowd.

In the centre of the field, Botwine faces to the east and calls out a charm, bidding the mighty Lord, bidding the great ruler, the holy mother and the blessed rood. As he does so, there is a rumble behind us. Two oxen, yoked together and bearing behind them a plough. The beasts look half-dead, ribs pushing out from sore flesh. But they pull anyway to the first corner. Botwine, his charm done, goes to meet it and calls again for blessings on the plough. Erce, Erce, Earth-Mother, and we all say Erce, Erce, Earth-Mother, bright barley and white wheat and endless abundance and please, please no more hardship.

Wulfrun's voice sounds out the loudest here. She has the magic to make it ring, I think, as some scops do, tales and songs cutting through halls that shake with laughter and brawls.

'Ah,' says Tove, beside me, 'so we know now that she is the most pious of us all.'

And it is true for we do not look at Botwine any more, or the plough, but instead to Wulfrun. She feigns that she does not see it, keeps her eyes closed and her hands clasped. A perfect supplicant. Even Botwine slows, watches her. It is the first thing that has cut through to him today.

So, we are all looking at Wulfrun when the oxen first throw off their yoke.

The bellows shake the earth, rattle through my bones. I

Mere

had thought the beasts half-dead but they are full of such fire, eyes wide, necks corded as if it is the Devil himself that shackles them and not a few soft men.

The yoke, old wood, half-rotted in our damp air, splinters down its middle and the plough falls from it to the ground, heavy as a millstone. There are ceorls shouting, running for eel-spears and hoes and ropes to bind the oxen but it is too late, both oxen are free and the other sisters scatter as they buck and scream.

I cannot move. My hand on Tove's shoulder, for if I run I will leave her here and if I stay I will be trampled.

But the oxen are confused. A lifetime of shackles and then this sudden freedom. They press their hooves into the earth, stare about as if waiting to be told what to do. Sweat beads down their golden hides. Their horns are very white. Very sharp, even now.

Then, the air is filled with a sudden animal weight. I stumble backwards and I smell sweat and blood and fear as one of the huge beasts charges past us, only a few inches from knocking us all down. It is a loosed arrow, leaping over the ditch and beautiful, almost, and then it is gone, charging towards the marsh.

The other ox, though, is circling. Snorting, bowing its head, the wrath of a thousand whip-stings and the daily yoke returned all at once. Men surround it, hopping back when it steps forward, pressing in when it turns, a net opening and closing but tightening, always tightening. There is an eel-spear in its haunch, scrapes along its hide where the children throw stones at it.

I shout to Mildred, who has also stayed, tell her to lift Tove with me and take her away, drag her as far as we might. I do not know if it is my voice, but the ox turns, then gives a great shudder. Pushes towards the marsh, like its brother, and finds that there is a man in its way, a man who does not move swiftly enough, who falls backwards, lifting his eel-spear at the last as the beast bears down on him.

Then, a scream. An evil sound, high and keening and almost womanish in its suffering.

For a breath, we are all still. The ox takes another few, staggering steps and then falls to its knees, Sybba's spear pushing up through its neck and into its jaw. Its lifeblood falls from it in gouts, staining the earth, filling the ditch where it has fallen.

And a cough from Sybba. Soft, wet. On the earth, he is trembling and pale, trying to get up as if he is not already broken.

'I must stand,' he calls, weakly. 'Will nobody help me stand?'

Botwine and I run to him, our priest ahead of me. It is always so, soul first and then body. But I know already that I will be able to do nothing for Sybba and every step I take towards him makes it only the plainer. His chest has been crushed, ribs splintering out white through flesh. A hollow in him, where no hollow should be. There is the smell of shit, his bowels torn somewhere, or maybe he has voided himself in fear. He will not live through the day, perhaps not even the next few heartbeats.

Botwine presses his hand on Sybba's forehead, speaks low into his ear. The last rites. Sybba shakes his head, tries to stand once more. As if by belief, the world might be other than it is.

'Come now,' says Botwine, gently, as if he speaks to some child. 'Tell me of your sins, before it is too late.'

Mere

Sybba's skin is the colour of bone, his lips blue. He will begin to shake soon, and he will be lost to any confession then. Beside me, a few others approach. I see Eluned, vomit down her front, and Wulfrun, her own eyes wide. But I do not look at them. I press my hand into his, feel the last warmth in it.

I do not hear the sins that Sybba confesses. I hope that Eluned is among them, but I will never know, for as soon as his voice fades Botwine begins to speak, absolving him of his every trespass, promising him that he will rise again, body unbroken, soul shining, on the day of resurrection.

Sybba does not speak again. A few dragging breaths, each more painful than the last and then it is done.

His fingernails press against my cut hand. He is wearing a ring, a cross of gold with a single pearl in the centre. One finger is bent, from being broken an age ago. It was one of the first splints I did after the former infirmarian died, and though I would do it better now, it still healed well. I was proud of that, once.

My stomach turns, but I swallow down the bile. So quickly undone, all of it. I wonder if I can smell heartwort, somewhere.

Our priest takes his cloak, a fine thing now caked in mud, and lays it across Sybba's body so the raw wound of him cannot be seen. It will hide, too, the damp patch between his legs, at least until we can wash him ready for burial.

There is a silence, the emptiness that follows a great storm when none can think of anything but their next breath, their next step.

I stand, ready for the long work of preparing Sybba's body. But before Botwine or I can start to gather the others to carry him to the convent, Wulfrun speaks.

Danielle Giles

I lift no weapon, but kill more than the bravest warrior.

I turn at her voice, which sounds as if it comes from far away. Another scop's trick, I think, and yet her dark eyes flicker, her head lifted so that her throat is bared with prophecy. I can see each holy word as it trembles through her.

I live on women's tongues and in men's minds. I am a spilt pot, a razed city.

A few sisters reach for her, pull at her sleeves. But she stands firm and unmoving, showing them no heed.

I am light as air, heavy as stone. No leechbook has cures for me, nor heroes swords against me.

The riddle complete, she sways and blinks. Slowly returns to us, to the dead man in the mud and the hungry women. There is sweat on her brow and her eyes are clouded and weary. And yet, I think I see a flicker of deep cunning there.

'No,' I say, for I think I know the answer and I do not want any to speak it. 'No, do not—'

But it is too late. 'A curse,' says Botwine. His hands are bloody still with Sybba's wounds. 'You see a curse set upon us.'

Chapter 5

There is power in the speaking of curses. Wulfrun did not cast it herself, did nothing but tell us all what we would have whispered anyway, with oxen devil-taken midway through the Field-Remedy and now a man lifted to his burial, his cooling blood turning our priest's cloak heavy and sticky. His death adds to a growing tally of disaster: Eadwig's disappearance, the years of poor harvests, the relics and tapestries we have sold to no good end.

By the end of the day, half the convent is sure that we are all to perish, the other half looking about for a sin wicked enough to have brought with it such a heavy toll. Curses do not spring from nowhere, after all.

I hear it echo outwards, in chatter and hurried feet, to be told beneath eaves and through fresh-washed blankets, over smoking ovens and between whirling spindles. A whisper-tale, for whenever the abbess hears it she pales and orders penance for any talking of it. But she cannot stop it, for the sisters turn instead to the hand-language that we use in the refectory and all the other places where we are forbidden to talk. They make a sign well known to us all, lifting a fist as if they wish to strike and raising their two fingers. A scourge, it means, a scourge for us all.

I do not often agree with the abbess, but I share this hatred of hers. Every time they speak of Sybba, or make the scourge-sign, I cannot help but think of Eluned, vomit down her front. The heartwort I gave to calm Sybba's lusts, the way he clutched at his stomach the day of his death. If there was ever any curse, it is Eluned and I who have laid it.

The next day I find myself drawn to chapel, and I am not alone. Most of my fellow sisters are devout, either from true faith or duty or from both. But today, I see more of the ceorls attending. They usually only come on a Sunday, for few have the time for daily worship, but now they stand at the back of the chapel, ploughs and spindles left in their homes. Some attend every holy office, from the half-slumber of Matins through to Sext at midday and then a few hours later, None.

By the time I take my place at Vespers in the evening, the chapel is filled with at least a hundred souls. The stone, usually so cold, drips with the sudden warmth they bring, a hundred breathed pleas, a hundred rustling hopes.

I am well used to the smells of my fellow sisters: the smoke that seems as if it rises still from the dresses of the kitchen workers and the animal dampness about those who have been sorting and spinning wool, the soft child-scent of the oblates who join us as young as five and the cleaner smells of the novices, half-maids of fifteen or sixteen and beginning to show care for their bathing and their immortal soul both.

Mere

These familiar scents are joined now by those of the ceorls. The richest among them anoint themselves with herb oils that are forbidden to us: chervil, mint. Fair Alfred is one of them, his yellow hair glinting bright in the rushlight. He has taken more care than ever about his bathing and dress since Sybba's death, as if he might fend off misfortune with beauty alone. The other ceorls, the greater part, wear no oils and so always have a little of their labour about them.

All these fresh faithful wear their cross necklaces in new places of prominence. I cannot see the hammer charms hanging from cords, the carven boars on arm rings, but I know they will not have been forsaken entirely. They will be tucked within the collars of tunics and dresses or else placed in bags about their girdles.

The abbess and Botwine are busy with service, but these new signs of faith are marked instead by our portress, Ava, who stands at the front of the chapel so that she might watch the holy office and congregation both. She is an unbending woman but always turns, slightly, so that she faces our abbess, as moss grows on one side of a tree so as to taste more of the sun. I think she would be buried so, a dutiful slant to her even in death.

Sometimes I recall her otherwise. Younger, never full of ease but willing, at least, to share some joy with me. Her smallest finger reaching across to link in my own as we ate together in the refectory. Her laughter as I mimicked the former infirmarian's droning way of speaking.

But I have long learnt not to spend too much of my thoughts on Ava and so instead turn to my own devotions. I do not know what I pray for. It has been a long while since I have asked for anything, for my sake or for others, in this holy place.

There was a time when I was younger when I understood, at last, that I would never be leaving this convent and turned myself to holy devotion. I had already shown enough skill at healing that the infirmarian had appointed me as her apprentice, and thought I might master faith just as I had leechdoms, that it would take only long hours and patient study. I learnt every psalm and prayer by heart, but found that I could not cut away the sinning parts of me as I wished. A pilgrim's dark eyes or a piece of glistening eel left in the infirmary would undo any piety and I would confess and repent and tear at myself until there was little left and still I found no peace.

Now that I am older, my comfort comes instead from my fellow sisters. I sing with them not because I believe the words will be heard, but because when we do so, our faces all lift up heavenwards together. I lower my head and call out the responses not because I believe my devotion will be marked by my Lord but because I like the way that our voices ring together, firm and sure.

Today I am glad for this strength more than ever, for as soon as I leave with my fellow sisters, returning to the cold-whetted night, I hear Wulfrun again talking of Eadwig and this curse. It is all that she has spoken of since yesterday, more on her lips than any prayer.

I leave before I must hear more of it.

Wulfrun continues to flit about the convent over the next few days, telling and retelling her tale to all who would hear it. She urges her fellow sisters to join the search for Eadwig before he, too, is snared by this curse. Soon, there are parties of half a dozen at a time, venturing out with rushlights, Wulfrun at their head. She goes without food,

Mere

without sleep, the strength of her will greater than any other earthly concern. But even she cannot tempt the sisters too far from convent grounds. They linger at the edge, marking the boundary over and over, calling out Eadwig's name but never stepping too far into the marsh itself.

The abbess does not forbid this, in truth cannot, for Botwine is among those who search. But she offers no relief for any sisters who leave their duties to help Wulfrun. If bread is burnt, or laundry not washed, the punishments remain the same.

Still, the more Wulfrun speaks, the more join her. A dangerous skill, hers, and I wonder how the abbess feels with this cuckoo about. Wulfrun may be a member of this convent, but she has not yet made her holy vows. Most must wait at least a year first and I wonder if Wulfrun will be expelled before she might even have the chance to take them.

But I have interlopers of my own. One morning, a few days after Sybba's death, as Mildred and I are marking an inventory of the herbs, I turn to see a youth standing at my doorway. Alwin, Botwine's acolyte.

He is a little pale, for many of the men spent yesterday feasting at Martinmas, their hands bloody with the slaughter of swine and geese to keep us through the winter, their cups strong and plenty. Such a noise, I could not tell which were the bellows of men or the beasts that they slaughtered.

'Are there none here to greet me?' he calls out though he must be able to see Mildred and I both stood, both busy.

'Stay here,' I say to my helper, 'and continue to count. But come if I call you. I may need your help with this strutting cockerel of ours.'

She nods though I catch her casting a look to this

newcomer. She is not the only young sister who has been watching Alwin. I think half of the novices are ready to renounce their vows and marry him and the other half would not wait that long.

'Welcome,' I say, walking to greet him. 'What brings you here? Do you have some ailment?'

'What ailment would trouble me?' he asks.

'Well,' I say, lowering my voice, 'I know that young men might find themselves with boils in places that they might not wish to tell others.'

The meaning comes slow to him, then heavy. 'No,' he says, heat in his face and voice both, 'Infirmarian, it is I who am here to help you. Father Botwine has asked that I come and learn from you, for a week or so.'

So Botwine has bid him here to keep him from trouble, for our priest is busy and Alwin is a young man with idle hands. Botwine will act as if it is some great gift, a man in this trembling woman's room, picking at my methods like a crow at a carcass.

But I cannot refuse and so I say only, 'And is Botwine coming, also?'

'No,' says Alwin, 'he continues his search for Eadwig.'

'Ah,' I say, 'I have seen them out looking.'

'Eadwig was a fool for wandering,' says Alwin, still young enough to despise frailty. I envy the strength of his disdain.

'You knew him well?' I ask.

'Only from the journey from Gipeswic,' says Alwin. 'He was younger than me, a weakling. Sister Wulfrun will know more, for Eadwig was a servant in her household. Or he was, until her son ordered her to be banished.'

'Her own child sent her away?' I ask. I sound hungry and Alwin frowns. Too much like women's chatter. But I

Mere

understand more now. The boy is the last thread to Wulfrun's home left to her.

Yet Alwin watches me still with distrust and so I say, 'Tell me, then, what you have learnt of leechdom.'

'I have been taught of humours and how to plot the stars.'

I cannot tell him that these are rudiments, more dangerous than ignorance. 'You can read and write?' I ask.

'My Latin is fair,' he says. 'My Anglisc is better. I have the northman language, also. Why, do you have need of me in the infirmary? Some task I might do?'

'There is little to be done, today at least,' I say.

For the first time, Alwin allows himself fear. 'The others speak of a curse,' he says. 'You saw the oxen. Do you think there is something evil here?'

I think that evil has been with us a long time. Three years and each harvest worse than the last. The second church that the abbess began building is still but a single crumbling wall, for we had neither the stone nor the men to create the glory she planned.

Now, the abbess returning from her cousin without aid. We are rotting, slowly, and do not yet know it. Wulfrun named it a curse. I think it something deeper.

I only shake my head. 'Oxen are foolish beasts,' I say, 'and their keepers twice so. That is all.'

'But to break loose during Botwine's charm,' says Alwin. 'You know much of curses and their cures. Do you not think it an ill omen?'

I cast about for a reply that will not cause more fear and worry. There is none, but I see Mildred in the corner, her head bowed over the herbs, all sweetness and care. I raise my hand, summon her. She comes full of deference, her head lowered so far down that I worry she will walk into us.

'Mildred,' I say, as she approaches, 'I have other work to attend to. Will you show Alwin our infirmary, answer his questions? He is to help us.'

Her head raises a little. They are almost of a height, though she carries herself so much smaller than him. For a breath, they look at each other and then Mildred reddens and pulls me aside a few paces from Alwin.

'I do not know what to call him,' she says, quietly.

I can see Alwin, craning his head, watching us talk with a smirk. Not the first girl he has set blushing, I think.

'He is but a brother in Christ,' I say. Was I ever so wilting? A life in the convent does not encourage boldness, but I need Mildred to ignore her modesty. 'You must find your tongue and help me. If I am plagued with him further, he will end up in one of our sickbeds.'

'He is ill?' asks Mildred, concerned.

'No,' I say. 'I shall put him there myself.'

Mildred relents in the end. I promise her charge of the meals for a week, a position that allows her first choice of whatever scraps are scorned by our patients. I leave her with Alwin, her voice faltering at first but growing stronger as she moves from pleasantries to practicalities.

Then, I step out of the infirmary and into the open air. The paths between the buildings are quieter than before. Most sisters are at their duties, spinning, sewing, tending to gardens or sheep, watching pots or washing laundry. There is always much that needs doing even in a small convent such as ours.

In the distance I see the ceorls at their labour, goosegirls

Mere

with only wavering authority over their flocks, women turning raw fingers to mending clothes and the weaving of reeds. A few men sow the last of the wheat and barley in the fields, while others cut peat from the marsh in neat, square blocks, to be dried and then burnt over winter. Others gather bog iron at the edge of the fields, seeking out the red-brown water that marks the metal beneath the earth and stabbing the water with sticks until they find pieces the size of fists to take to the blacksmith for smelting.

It is still early, halfway between Lauds and Prime, the last of the martins and swallows and swifts marking the morning with song. The air is threaded with peat smoke, damp and rich. The smell of mere-rot, too, trembling, salty, like the wet between a woman's legs.

The last few days have been overcast and grey, but today in the brightness I can see miles in every direction, right to the edge of the farmland. It is the sort of day that strips the shadows and leaves us no nests, no holes.

And in this bare morning, there is nowhere for me to hide either.

'Hilda.'

I turn around. I did not think it would take her this long, but pride can keep us away, even in times of need. Wulfrun stands in the path, dressed for travel. She is wearing soft leather boots that reach her ankles and has a cloak pulled about her shoulders.

'I have need of you,' she says. We have not spoken since I crouched at Sybba's cooling body and heard her speak prophecy, though I have been waiting for her to find me.

'Is that so?' I ask. 'Was it that vision of yours? It can bring on head pain, I hear.'

'No,' says Wulfrun. 'They are holy and do not hurt me.'

So she says, but her voice has grown hoarser. Maybe the only woman in Christendom who speaks more in a convent than out of it.

The wind picks up, sets the reeds whistling.

'The abbess will be angry that you are away from your duties,' I say.

'She will not hear of it,' says Wulfrun. She looks at me and again I feel myself weighed. 'And where do you go so early?'

'To pick the last of the meadow saffron,' I say.

She casts about then points to a place a few feet away from the path, where soft purple spreads. The last bright blooming before winter. 'There,' she says, 'I have found it for you.'

I wonder if I might find another lie, but there seems little use in it. And I have been thinking on it for a while.

'Come, then,' I say, 'I will take you to the marsh.'

She gives a small smile. One of her teeth is of a different hue to the others, a different shape. A false tooth, taken or bought from the mouth of some other woman and placed in hers. Not even the abbess has the gold for such a thing.

'I thought I would have to talk you into it,' she says.

'Let us save all that time, then,' I say, 'and make the most of the daylight.'

'Why so willing now? Have you some thought of where he might be found?'

She is older than me by at least five winters, but hope makes her girlish, easily hurt.

'No,' I say, 'but you have not searched deeper in the marsh yet.'

Her face twists. 'The sisters will not go any further,' she says. 'Nor any of the ceorls I speak to.'

Mere

This is something I have marked, too. The ceorls are remaining closer to the convent than before. It is usual for them to venture out in twos or threes to forage and set traps and cut reeds, but now they do not dare even that.

'And,' I say, 'the sooner we find him, the sooner all this talk of curses will end.'

Wulfrun looks out at the sodden earth, the leaking roofs. The convent falling down about us even before Eadwig was lost.

'Perhaps,' she says and that is it.

Walking with her down to the marsh, I soon regret my offer. Wulfrun's stride is so long that I must run to keep alongside her and before long I am panting and damp. She does not slow at all. I guess she thinks I have earned at least some of it for taking so long to agree to come with her. She wanted to gather some more souls to take with us, but Botwine has already taken them out on a great search and so it will be only us two.

'You may doubt my vision,' she says, suddenly, 'but I have never spoken false.'

'Aye,' I say. 'Easy enough to do with a riddle, when each man has their own answer to please them.'

I have been thinking on it and I believe I understand Wulfrun's gift. She follows the currents and eddies in a crowd, understanding longings and hopes and letting them guide her to prophecy. It is a nothing but a scop's charm. I tell myself that this is why I dwell on thoughts of her.

'I do not recall what I say,' she says, 'when the holy spirit moves through me. But they tell me I spoke of cities falling.'

'And much else,' I say.

'Then this convent will fall if this curse is not undone,' she says, seriously.

She speaks as if such a thing were set, carved into stone and branded into flesh. Her dark eyes spark not with fear but with joyful certainty, the sort that catches alight in others and soon will have us all burning. It is beyond faith.

Her scar is bright today. It is reddened at the edges with juice from elderberry or blackberry, to make the marks of her pain clearer to all. Her lips too, just at their middle, perhaps from eating them after, or perhaps in one last vanity.

I thought Wulfrun a cuckoo, eager to topple the abbess as soon as she could. But the woman in front of me is something else, something more troubling.

And, despite my doubts, I cannot look away.

The way through to the marsh is not so much of a path, but a spine. There is a ridge that we can follow, earth piled higher every year against the water, which will lead us to an old yew. Here, we might follow a wooden causeway through to Gipeswic, or else take one of the three boats that are tied up there.

Wulfrun and I tread carefully along this bone-way. We pass a few of the ceorls out cutting reeds. They call blessings to us in the names of the saints: Edmund the Martyr who died by heathen arrow, Guthlac of Crowland who was afflicted by marsh-fever and demons both. A few other names are called to us, that of the Antler-God and the Earth-Mother. Wulfrun, hearing these, frowns.

'Are they not worried,' she asks, 'that they will be punished for idolatry?'

'No,' I say. 'For it would mean punishing all and we

Mere

would be left without any to serve the convent. They worship Christ above all and that is enough.'

I tell her how we learn from the marsh, how slow weight is better than sudden force. Year by year, the old ways are forgotten and Christ and all His saints are elevated further. Names are changed, revenants named as devils, charms as holy prayers. It is a slow path, too slow I think for the abbess, but it is the one that we must take.

'I see,' says Wulfrun. 'It is the same in the northern lands. Thegns do not like to be told how to worship by men who have never lifted a seax.'

We walk on, and soon there are no souls about to give us any kind of blessing. I thought the day would unfurl bright and warm, but cloud has blown in from the sea and the first fog with it. I have never travelled to the coast, have never seen the great spread of water to our east. Still, today I am able at least to taste its salt.

Beside me, Wulfrun stops and takes a breath. Even on this dull day, her cheeks are flushed, her eyes bright. She might be a maid out on a new spring's day.

She sees me looking and seems to remember herself.

'It tastes like Gipeswic,' she says, half shamed. I think she has grown used to not allowing herself even the smallest of pleasures.

'And what else does Gipeswic taste of?' I ask.

'There is no need to mock me,' she says.

'I am not.'

I see her turn her answer over in her head. Finding the words, no doubt. Wondering whether she should trust me with her joy. An elver wind blows between us both, thin and sinewy.

'Fish,' she mutters, at last. 'Spices.'

I nearly laugh. 'I have heard more poetry from the goose-girls.'

I wish I had not spoken so, for she only nods as if I am right, flushing a little. She has shown me something soft in her and I have answered with cruelty. I do not know how to talk to this woman.

'Well,' I say, quickly, 'I would not know, anyway. You must tell me more of your home, when you can.'

But I have sent her somewhere she does not wish to go. 'There is not much to tell,' she says, quietly. 'Damp straw, the smell of cooking meat, shit in the ditches around the hall. Half of my household wished to be elsewhere, in truth. When I told Eadwig he would be leaving to serve Botwine, he could not sleep for joy.' This boy, who has upended so much already, who I have never met.

We walk on and reach a pool where there are several raised mounds that act as a path. She goes to step onto the first of them but I put a hand out, stopping her. One has been crumpled by some past footfall and I think the rest of them just as unstable. We must go around instead.

'You are fond of him?' I ask, as we balance at the edge of the water. 'This child?'

'He is a sweet boy,' says Wulfrun, 'and he is of my household. It is my duty to care for him.'

'Is that why you asked Botwine to take him as a servant?'

'Yes,' she says, after some time, and it is not a lie but I am sure there is something she is not saying. 'A debt to his mother, too. She was my cook, one of my few allies in that place. The others, they would greet you with false smiles and shining words and then tell all that I had said to the thegn. But she never gave away my secrets, was never anything but truthful.'

Mere

She stops, a smile twisting the burn on her face. Again, I see that single dark tooth. 'Well, mostly.'

I wait for her to speak of it further, but she does not. We reach the other side of the pool and something crackles in the greenery near us, some ground-hugging blackbird out seeking one last meal before a long winter.

'It sounds a hard place,' I say. 'Are you not happy to be free of it?'

'I did not think I would ever long for Gipeswic,' she says. 'I have never been a good wife and not often a good mother. All that softness . . . I have never understood it. Even when he was a child, my son would sooner cry to the maids than his own mother. And as he became older, he only grew more like his father.'

'Is that why he banished you?' I ask. Her head twitches towards me.

'It seems you have been asking after me, as much as I have been asking after you,' she says, but it is not a rebuke. 'Yes, in part. He married a cunning little maid who ruled through him. We were not fond of each other, for I would not obey her orders. And so, she whispered in his ear about how I ate his food and drank his beer and did nothing but unsettle the household and the foolish boy was cunt-struck enough to agree. The first I knew of it was when Sigeburg came to my door.'

'A bad omen on any day,' I say, pulling a smile from her. 'Well, I wish nothing but misery on your son's wife. She will come to a bad end, I am sure of it.'

But Wulfrun only shrugs. 'I do not blame her,' she says. 'I would do the same, in her place. And I was no longer welcome in my own home.'

I think of her moving against the abbess from the first

day that she arrived here. I am not often grateful for having been kept here my whole life but today I am glad that the convent has allowed me to rise through my leech-art and little else. I do not think I have the cunning to survive many other places.

After that we are quiet, both of us only speaking to warn against a stone here, a branch there. We pass bowing reeds, a few lone midges. Where we wade through the mere-water, we set the silt blooming beneath us, reveal horseshoes of winter-sleeping leeches clotted together at the bottom. In the summer they rush towards any heavy-footed creature, sucking-jaws ready. But as the water cools, they grow sluggish, slumbering through their promise of spring.

The bells ring out for Prime, muffled through the fog. Wulfrun flinches, turns around.

'It has been so long, already?' she asks.

'It is hard to keep time here,' I say. 'Even if you know it well.'

'You have been at this place since you were a child?'

I laugh.

'What?' she asks.

'I am sure the sisters will have already told you how I came to be here.'

'I have heard snatches,' she says, 'but I prefer to hear a tale in full.'

I regret, still, talking of Gipeswic. Wulfrun is trusting me in a hundred ways today and I have not yet earned it. There is something, too, in her dark eyes. They open me up, unbind knots that I did not even know were there. And so, though I would be happy never to speak of my birth to another living soul, I take a deep breath and begin.

'Well,' I say. 'I myself do not know all of it. My father

Mere

is an Ealdorman, the abbess's cousin and founder of this place.'

Wulfrun tilts her head. 'Ealdorman Aethelwine? Of East Anglia?'

I nod. 'In his lusts, he took a slave here to bed. The abbess would not rest until their bastard was promised to the convent. And so here I am.'

'That was merciful of Sigeburg.'

'Some mercy,' I say. 'She squeezed a wyrm's hoard out of him for my upkeep, far more than I cost her. And until last week, she has used this sin against him, to draw more gifts and treasures from him when the convent has need of it.'

'Not only sin,' says Wulfrun. 'Ealdorman Aethelwine was betrothed once, to this abbess of ours.'

I stumble, the marsh beneath me suddenly new, strange. I thought I knew every secret of this place.

'What?' I ask. I cannot think of the abbess betrothed, though of course she was once young, once fair. And all rich women must marry, or else be sent here.

'All in Gipeswic know of it,' says Wulfrun. 'And I have spent enough time at the Ealdorman's table to hear him weeping into his cups about it. A cousin on his mother's side. They shared a great love, all told. The sort that scops sing of, the sort that tricks maids into marriage.'

'The abbess has never spoken of it,' I say. I have no claim to my father, I know. I have never cared much. But here I stand, made a fool of by Sigeburg and Wulfrun both. So much is kept from me. 'What happened?'

'Her side of the family fell out of favour, and in the end he could not have her.' There is a certain joy in Wulfrun's voice at this misfortune. 'He married a thegn's daughter from Mercia, an age ago, a pinched woman whom he loathes. But so it goes. He needed the alliance and I think the abbess never forgave him. For acquiescing to the marriage; later, for your mother. He gave her a convent and still it was not enough.'

Wulfrun looks over at me as if she has given me some great gift, then frowns. 'I am sorry,' she says. 'You said you were happy to speak of it.'

'I did not think you would know more of it than I,' I say, sharply.

'I do not,' says Wulfrun. 'I did not even know he was your father, until you spoke of him. I thought it would help you to know.'

'It has not,' I say, aware of how I sound. Ungrateful, bitter.

Wulfrun slows her steps and we are closer now. I hear the huff of her breath, smell her sweat even through her perfumed oils. I want to make peace, to tell her that talk of my birth always unsettles me and it is not her fault. But I cannot find the words and in the end it is she who offers peace first.

'Men know less than half of what they should and I have had my fill talking of them,' she says, firmly. 'What of your mother?'

'A scrap of land, her freedom and a lifetime called a whore for it,' I say. 'Or worse.'

Wulfrun takes another few of her long steps.

'My mother was taken once,' she says. 'With my aunt. Bandits caught them both but my father found them before they were taken across the sea. They asked a great price, knowing of his wealth, and so he paid only for my mother to be returned. He had never held love for my aunt. She had married into his household, also, but he always thought she laughed too loudly. So, she was taken across as a slave and we never saw her again.'

She spits in the water. 'No Christian soul should be in bonds.'

I do not know if Sweet would stand up to be counted among Christian souls at all. And she is free enough to walk the edge-lands, even if it is under the abbess's watchful eye. Even that loses its power with each passing day, for there are now so many ceorls that rely on Sweet that the abbess would find it hard to truly move against her without causing trouble.

Wulfrun takes my silence for something else. Shame, perhaps.

'I have known many bastards in my life,' says Wulfrun. 'They often overcome the fault of their births.'

She means it as a kindness, which is worse. I begin to answer her but this dies in my throat, as I see the old yew tree ahead of us.

I have known this tree longer than many of my sisters. It marks where the convent ends and the marsh begins. A north star, in a place where we sometimes cannot see the sky spread out above us, it is a place of resting and planning, meeting and plotting. Wives have lingered here away from husbands and more than one suffering oblate or novice has wept here, safe from prying fellow sisters.

The tree itself is large enough to embrace us all. It is the height of five or six men, bark twisted and knotted as if some giant has reached down and braided it. The green leaves shine even in the dimness, the last of the red berries hanging within arm's reach.

On the other side of this tree is a post, driven into the

ground, and a pool of water which leads outwards through rivers and lakes to the mere. A man might leave the marsh in a few days, rather than the two weeks or so it would take by foot, by rowing down its tributaries and dragging his keel overland where the water grows too shallow. There are three boats there, slim crafts with room for half a dozen at most.

All three of them have been sunk.

'We should return,' I whisper. In all my time out here, where every far-off howl might be a wolf and each close-treaded step might be a bandit, I have never felt a fear like I do now. I can see, through a handspan of water, the way that these have been hacked. Small holes, everywhere, as if from a knife.

Wulfrun leans closer. 'It is not that they have been neglected?'

'No,' I say. 'And it has not been long since whoever did this was here, else others who came out here would have seen it.'

'Who would destroy them?' asks Wulfrun. She does not understand, yet, why she should fear.

'I do not know,' I say. 'They are the largest boats we own, though there are a few that will hold a single man and his traps. But with these three sunk, it is harder for us to travel to Gipeswic, to send a message.'

'I came by cart and horse,' says Wulfrun.

'Aye, but the two that pulled you here were our finest. The rest are old, and slow. And in the winter, when the water rises, a boat is better.'

A few feet away, something rustles in the reeds. A bird, but I hear no wingbeats. A rat, but the sound was heavy. We look at each other.

Mere

'Let us make haste, then,' says Wulfrun. Her voice is calm but her hand is at her knife. Mine, too, though I do not remember moving it.

We do not run. We know enough of the hunt, how a bolting hare is snapped in the fox's jaws, and so we walk careful and slow. But we retrace our steps, back past the yew tree and towards the convent. It feels as if it takes an age, our progress silent and wary. Only the sound of our panting and the suck and gasp of wet mud as we lift our feet. I am sure that each breath will be our last, that I will turn and see Wulfrun snatched away, or else be caught myself. But nothing shows itself.

And then we are back between tilled fields and cut ditches, the convent above us. 'We must tell them of the boats,' I say, dully.

'The curse,' says Wulfrun. 'It is strengthening about us.'

'It is no curse,' I say. 'Only a few holes made by some spiteful hand.'

'Do you believe that?' she asks.

I do not answer, but instead turn, kicking the mud from my boots and beginning the walk back up to the convent. Wulfrun follows, matching my stride. She, too, is quiet, her thoughts filled with splintered wood and sunken escape.

We are both so absorbed that we do not see the kitchen sisters until we are almost upon them. Three of them on the path, each burdened. One has a basket of eggs beneath her arm and the other two hold a large wicker basket between them. There will be eels inside, given as tithes.

The woman holding the eggs is our cellarer, Leogifu. A small, loud woman feared by many, she came to visit me in the depths of winter, with evil dreams so strong that she would awake screaming and weeping and be wary of closing her eyes even in prayer. I gave her a charm to speak before sleeping and betony to place underneath her head and ever since she has been an ally to me, of sorts.

'Fair day, sisters,' she says, nodding to me and then, in turn, Wulfrun. She is not shy around our newcomer, as many sisters are.

'Fair day,' I say. I draw myself up, hoping she will not see how drained I feel. 'You have much food with you, then? We eat well tonight?'

Leogifu shakes her head. 'A poor catch and a worse meal. The ceorls say the eels are like smoke nowadays. I think they keep some behind to fill their own bellies. That Sybba was the worst of them, sitting back and telling me that he had nothing even as there was the smell of roasted meat in the air.'

'God rest his soul,' I say, quickly, my stomach turning.

'God rest his soul,' repeats Leogifu. 'But the sisters tell me that I cannot go and raid his home, not until his brothers finish their squabbles over who gets the land and the slaves.'

She gives a lion's smile, fierce and hungry.

'I think that is for the best,' I say. 'Portress Ava would not like you to be searching through his dwelling, and the abbess even less.'

'Portress Ava has not come upon a beast or man that she did not dislike,' says Leogifu. She leans in to Wulfrun, her voice low. 'We cannot stop for long, but I only wish to say that in the kitchen, we are sorry to hear of this Eadwig of yours. His mother was a cook at your household, I hear?'

'Near her whole life,' says Wulfrun. 'I knew her from girlhood.'

'A shame,' says Leogifu. 'We pray for him.'

The kitchen sisters are from lower families, are almost

Mere

servants themselves. At every turn, the abbess shuns them, brushes them off as dirt from the hem of her habit. They hold no great love for her.

But Wulfrun reaches over, holds Leogifu firm by the shoulder. Alike in their sorrow, rank and wealth gone. 'Thank you,' she says, her voice thick, 'for your kindness.'

There are tears in Wulfrun's eyes. I wonder if her gratitude and grief are the same as her scar, the pain true enough but strengthened by other means.

'How goes your search?' asks Leogifu. 'I would join you, but the abbess has told me if I burn a single loaf I shall fast for a year.'

'Not well,' says Wulfrun. 'And today, we found the three boats by the yew tree, sunk.'

Leogifu pales. 'It is this curse,' she says. 'It spreads to the fields, too. Perhaps the ceorls speak truly and they hunger just as we do.'

This bodes ill. I have known Leogifu half a lifetime and have never heard her speak even the smallest kindness about the ceorls, each of whom she believes hides in their eaves stores of food, kept from her and her kitchen. If she thinks them starving, then she thinks far worse will come for us.

'All this talk of curses,' I say, 'you will only strengthen it.'

They both give me warning looks, but it is true. I have seen my share of curses in the infirmary, know how they may ail a man and drive him to ruin. But all this chatter and plotting only make it worse. Best to think of the cure, not the cause.

Then, Wulfrun gasps and stands rigid, staring past me and towards the marsh. We all turn, follow her gaze. At first, I do not understand what it is that she has seen. There is only the marsh and its mists. A few bare alders, some bursts of sedge.

Then, a shiver. Not a tree but a figure, small and thin, stumbling towards us. A boy not fully grown, dark-haired and pale, and I have not seen this child before but I know who it must be even before Wulfrun cries out his name.

Eadwig.

Chapter 6

We take Eadwig to the infirmary. He came as far as Wulfrun's arms and then fell into her, unmoving, silent, and he has remained that way ever since. The boy is filthy, mud and damp covering his tunic and hose up to his neck. Even his face is smeared with dirt, two white eyes staring out, seeing nothing.

I dress him with a clean tunic and wash him as best as I can. Our infirmary has no private room but the storeroom, and so I must place him among the patients, at the far end closest to the hearth. It is not how I would wish it, him in open view of any who care to see, but in the convent we must share all things, even suffering.

His ribs are stark ridges and furrows, the bones in his face far clearer than they should be for a boy his age. The work of more than a few days of hunger. Though he is thin, I cannot risk that he has been poisoned and so I purge him with a spewdrink of betony, henbane and garlic. I find nothing in the vomit. There is only a little greenness at his lips and teeth, as if he has been chewing on some wort. I wash it away.

Wulfrun has run to fetch Botwine, who is still out searching, though Vespers is soon and we will need him. While I wait I perform every magic that I can think of. Lacunas and prayers, salves and the nine-herb charm. Even a taste of the stronger cures: poppy seed and mandrakes. Poor Mildred is aching and sweating from grinding and heating and mixing them all, but she does not raise her voice in complaint even once. Alwin, too, is sent to replenish every herb we have and goes with only a single sigh to his evening spent searching for plants in the rain. I think he is half-glad to be out of the infirmary, for seeing a boy around his age so unwell unsettles him.

But none of my leechdoms have an effect, fair or ill. None stir Eadwig from his half-dream.

I even leave him alone, go to the door and look out to the marsh. I do not know what I wait for. But I was born to fog and moss and Sweet has taught me every mere-way that she knows. I wonder if I can feel it, out there. A hollow. A hole.

Nothing comes, nothing makes itself clear and so I only return to Eadwig's bedside, crouching down and holding his hand in mine. It is warm, at least. Calluses and scars already from work, but still childish softness at the folds and the very ends of his fingers. Wulfrun told me that he was thirteen winters, but he looks younger, a pale face beneath dark hair. Not enslaved, for there are no marks of a collar around his neck or shackles about his wrists, but a hard life in service from when he could first walk.

I am at his side when Wulfrun returns at last, alone.

'Is Botwine not with you?' I ask.

Mere

'No,' she says. 'I found him, returning from the marsh. He will be here soon.'

I do not understand why he is staying away, when he has been so eager in his search for Eadwig. But our priest often works in hidden ways, his thoughts shrouded, his feelings deep.

'Well, I am glad you are back,' I say. 'Do you know what month Eadwig was born in? I think if I might read his stars, we might unlock him.'

'August, I think,' she says, slowly, 'the weed month.'

I reach for the charts, then stop. There is something in her manner since returning.

'None of your magic has worked,' she says. Not a question, but I answer anyway.

'No,' I say, 'not yet.'

'I know what will wake him,' she says.

'Is that so?' I ask. 'I did not know you trained in leechdoms. Between you and Alwin, I might as well pass all my duties over.'

'And I did not know that you understood all in heaven and earth,' says Wulfrun.

We watch each other. One day, I think, she will truly know defeat. Will find him sneaking beneath the eaves, knife in hand, or else breaking down her door with an axe. And having denied him so long, she will not know how to meet him.

But that is not this day and so I only wave my hand and say, 'What is it you wish to do?'

Wulfrun steps forward, eager, certain. She walks as if all the kingdom is stone underfoot and built just for her.

'When I was a child I was taken north, to Dane lands still half-heathen. We stayed in the hall of my great-uncle.

His wife was pregnant and he wished to know if it would be a boy or a girl. He called in seers, heathen and Christian both. If they guessed correct, they would have the child's weight in hacksilver. If they failed, of course, they would be sold into slavery.'

She laughs at this, fondly. A maid in a house of brutality.

'None would dare, until a priest stood. He had come from Dubh Linn, an exile for the Lord. He raised his eyes to the heavens and prayed on a piece of the true cross. He gave us a riddle. *Not a boy or a girl*, he said, *but both in one.* He was not believed, of course, but when the child came they were neither man nor woman, having both parts at once.'

'I have never heard of such a thing,' I say.

'Nor I,' says Wulfrun, 'but he was right and there was not a single heathen there who did not convert. I had him teach me his spell.'

'And the child?' I ask.

'The child trains now to be a warrior, do great deeds,' she says, without much feeling. That is not the tale she wishes to tell for it does not shine its brilliance on her. 'I think Eadwig has been snared by this curse I foretold and I would unbind his tongue. We might then find the source of it and cure him.'

'You have a relic with you?' I ask. I would have thought she would wear it about her, if so. A piece of bone or a fingernail, kept in the bag hanging from her girdle.

'There is no need,' says Wulfrun, 'when Botwine has agreed to let me use your holy heart.'

I stare at her. The convent's most-prized relic has been locked away in its reliquary for years. The abbess was once free with it, tempting in pilgrims from as far away as Lundun

Mere

and Jorvik. But as the convent has grown poorer she has grown more covetous of our most precious treasure. The last time it was taken from its reliquary was at Easter earlier this year and even then Botwine shielded us from seeing it, holding himself between us and its holiness.

'And the abbess is willing to let it be used for Eadwig?' I ask. For a servant, no less.

Wulfrun shrugs. 'I asked Botwine,' she says. 'I do not need to ask Sigeburg.'

I should refuse her. Yet, with Eadwig's hand still in mine, I cannot. There is something of the miracle about her today and if she can cure him I would see it. Still, I wonder. I think she would stride into the lion's den for Eadwig, but I do not know whether she would wash him and tend to him, all the small mercies that seem like defeat.

'What will you do,' I ask, 'if you fail in this?'

'I will care for him, the best I can,' she says, evenly. No saint, nor seer, but a woman again. And then she smiles and my breath catches.

'But you need not worry,' she continues, 'because I will not fail.'

When Botwine arrives, carrying the reliquary, he brings also some of his old cheer with him. His step is a little lighter, his greeting a little kinder.

The reliquary gleams in his embrace. Each side is inlaid with gold decorations. On one panel is the crucifixion, Christ serene even speared and broken. Another shows Him resurrected, though He looks more wearied than peaceful as if the harrowing of hell is but another duty of many.

Within it, a holy heart. Mary Magdalene's, I have been told, dried and salted. It is our convent's greatest treasure, but I watch as Botwine places it roughly beside Eadwig's bed and bends over the child like a fussing nursemaid, takes his hand and presses his palm to Eadwig's brow.

I do not know how I did not see it before. Perhaps because Eadwig is so small where Botwine is so large. But they are together now, their hair of different shades but with the same thick curl, their eyes the same soft brown. Eadwig's build after his mother, maybe, but the lines of his face from his father.

I glance at Wulfrun and I am sure. She does not seem shamed that Botwine would dote so openly on the boy. It should be a stain on her piety, for one of her own servants to tempt a priest, even a decade or more ago. But she spoke earlier of the woman as one of the few allies in that uncertain place. Sin might break some friendships, but in others it forges them into something stronger.

Something else, perhaps. Wulfrun would not be the first lady to find herself tangled with those who served her. Though, maybe I think this only because I wish it to be so.

As I watch them both, I understand that I would never have been able to turn them from this. Too many threads of guilt and duty and love, too tight together.

Botwine is as I have never seen him before. He is murmuring to the child. 'We shall get you resting,' he says, 'and return to Gipeswic for Easter. I might see if we can find honeycakes. You have not tasted wine yet, have you?'

No answer. The boy lies staring.

Beside him, there is the heavy sound of the inlaid wood being lifted. Carefully, Wulfrun holds the relic between her two hands, cradling it to her body as if it is her own heart finally returned to her.

'Let us begin,' she says.

Mere

Silence falls and the other patients start to mouth prayers. There is a wave rising, lifting us all, and Wulfrun steps around Botwine to the other side of the bed, drops to her knees and places the relic on Eadwig's chest. She presses it downwards gently and begins to pray. It is not a sort of prayer I have heard before, her voice low and strong, the words passing quick, falling like rain on a lake, a patter that redoubles so that she speaks not with one voice but a multitude. She does not look up, she does not doubt and a miracle, a miracle perhaps, because Eadwig's eyelids begin to flutter, his breath begins to quicken and she, seeing this, only begins to speak faster. Beside him, Botwine moans in relief.

Mildred pulls my sleeve, whispers, 'Is this not witchcraft?'

'None more than our own charms,' I say. 'Do not worry, child, she learnt it from a priest. If it is done in Christ to help another, if it does not upset the natural order, then it is permitted.'

And yet, I know why she asks, for this is like no magic I have seen before.

Wulfrun rocks back and forth and when she breathes in Eadwig breathes out. It is as if they have become one creature, the relic held between them.

'Speak,' she says, 'awaken. Speak, awaken.'

No prayer now, but a plea and Botwine follows her, repeating the two words and soon the whole infirmary pleads with her, a dozen voices calling for Eadwig all at once.

Eadwig's fingers shiver. Wulfrun's eyes grow wide and her mouth opens ready to shout with joy, for this it is, she has awoken the sleeping child but there is something here, a draught somewhere in the infirmary, cold and damp and winding around my ankles and

his hand reaching for hers
about her wrist

not a touch but a shackle and as soon as he touches her she falls as heavy as sin itself, landing on her arm, bruising it I am sure, scraping it against the splintered floor and her eyes are fluttering but Eadwig has not released her and Botwine roars and pushes forward, lifts Eadwig's hand and then he too is on the floor, trembling, heaving as if he is on a storm-caught ship and Wulfrun is still touching the boy, writhing, sobbing and there are words in her sobs.

'It hurts,' she says. 'A burning, in my head. Too much, too much, unending.'

I step towards them all and I do not know what I think I might be able to do, where both Wulfrun and Botwine have failed, but I place my hand on Eadwig's arm, hoping to pull him off and

his heart in my ears and above martins flying in fear from the eaves and fleas leaping from straw in search of warmth and food and spiders laying traps in dark corners and

I pull away gasping. On the other side of the bed Wulfrun has weakened and crouches, limp and keening, still snared by the child she hoped to cure. Botwine pulls, still, at his arms, but even his strength begins to fail him.

Eadwig turns to look at me, still holding Wulfrun tight his eyes shrewd and old and other

'*I end,*' he says, '*and then I end.*'

I cannot move. As a child, newly come to the convent, I would sneak to the marsh and gaze into the dark mere-pools, seeking some magic beneath. Others might plant a stick in it, tell you that the water would go only to your waist. But I could see, even then, that they were wrong. It was the kind of water that would drown you and leave not

Mere

even bones to be found. It is this depth that swallows me now.

'Eadwig,' says Botwine. He pulls himself to his feet. In his hand is the relic, which fell into the rushes. 'Take this. It will help you.'

Such a little thing, salted meat and nothing more. Eadwig watches the heart for a breath, then releases Wulfrun. She falls away, all brightness gone, scraped skin on her palms where she struck the floor.

Botwine grows eager. 'Good,' he says, still on his knees. 'Come back to me, little one. You wish for this relic, yes?'

I hear, as if from far away, a crowd arriving. Called here by the screams. Mildred is already lifting Wulfrun away and to a bed of her own. There are dark hairs on Botwine's hands, slicked with sweat. He will be making the relic damp, but I do not think he cares, if it will bring his son back to him.

Slowly, Eadwig reaches for the heart. Takes it in both of his hands and lifts it to the light. Then, he shakes his head.

'No,' he says and tosses it to the fire beside him. It catches quickly, burning before any can quench the fire or even reach into the flames, for the holy heart is worth more than our own hands. The other sisters moan, cross themselves and no, he cannot, his cure and our relic now gone, gone as if it never was of worth in the first place.

I look back to Eadwig, but he is lying down. He curls himself into the straw, breath soft, eyes open and empty once more. I reach out and touch his forehead, bracing myself for the devil-sickness to pass through me. But there is nothing. Whatever filled him, he is empty now, leaving behind only the smell of meat and a few handfuls of holy ashes.

Chapter 7

The abbess sends men as soon as she hears. Eadwig will be taken to the storeroom in the morning, at the very edge of our convent's bounds. I think Sigeburg would have ordered him excommunicated then and there for his sins, had Botwine not spoken for the child. As it is, Eadwig will be kept apart from us for the next three days and whipped on Sunday, at midday.

He is not the only one who Botwine defends. It was Wulfrun who used the relic and spoke the spell to wake Eadwig and it was I who let her do it. We share the blame for the heart's destruction and the abbess would have us sharing the punishment also.

I am not there to see Botwine speak for us and hear it only later from Wulfrun. He stood, I hear, the whole time, not moving. His voice was low and gentle and yet he would not be moved until the abbess relented and agreed that, instead of being whipped, Wulfrun would fast and I would sing psalms in place of sleep. He was an oak, Wulfrun told me, lashed by a storm and still unyielding. But when I see

Mere

Botwine later, directing servants to help him prepare the storeroom for Eadwig, I do not see strength or stoutness but only weariness.

If Eadwig understands his fate, he shows none of it. I wish he would cry out, or weep, or beg. The men are gentle enough, giving him warning when they heft him between them, telling him that he must be careful of his head as they go. I know a few among them: Edwin, who was sold into slavery by his own father to pay off debts, and Oswy, who came to me with his belly complaint just a few days ago.

I am glad that it is kind men who come to take Eadwig away.

Neither Wulfrun nor Botwine come to carry him. Botwine is at the storeroom and Wulfrun, too, is elsewhere. Though she has been saved from the whip, the abbess has given her an impossible list of duties, for she must work washing the blankets, herding the cows and sheep, churning the milk, weaving the thread, mending the tunics, tilling the soil and cooking the meals. Any duty the convent offers, she must learn it.

It is meant as punishment but she has already used her time well. The abbess's rule may be absolute, but each of us has our vote. The lowliest sister in the kitchen might stand as high as the portress, on that day. So, as she did with Leogifu, she begins to turn the sisters of our convent, slowly, over to her. It does not harm her that she is bruised and pale still from her fall, that she winces as she bends her head to her duties. How the abbess punishes this already hurting soul, they say. How well she bears it.

She speaks to all, it seems, but me, for she has not come even for a salve for her wounds.

*

The silence after Eadwig's departure unsettles me. I am used to a soft, friendly quiet, the burps and murmurs and small sounds of half a dozen women resting together. But now it is the quiet of the chapel, all stone and fear and prayer.

I cannot stand it for more than a day, and so the next morning I leave the infirmary in Mildred's keeping and walk over to a building closer to the church, a small hut where half a dozen sisters spin and weave, their bodies curved around distaffs or bent over wheels. Most are outside to use the best of the light. It is a cold day but their industry warms them. All have their sleeves pulled up and their skirts lifted, the smell of sweat and damp wool and fresh wood thick in the air.

I see Tove, letting out the hem of a tunic that has grown too short for a novice, her hands trembling but her stitches strong and neat. Novices and oblates work here, too, their small fingers picking insects and knots from the wool before it can be spun.

And at the centre of them all, Wulfrun, spinning thread and much else. She tells, again, the tale of Eadwig holding her tight. The devil-sickness that passed through his grip, the vision she received.

'The pain was like burning,' she is saying. 'I think it a warning for I have had such visions before.'

She keeps spinning, but her mind is not on her hands. There is a searching in her, a pressing of those around her that allows her to know what her listeners wish to hear before they themselves do. A little like with Eadwig, her breath in his, the borders between them softened.

'Are you sure that we should be talking of it so?' asks a sister. Ethel, who helps Portress Ava and skitters around

Mere

the convent like a blackbird. 'If he is too often on our tongues, the Devil will think we are calling him.'

An echo of Oswy's fear. It is true that the naming of a thing has power. How often have I talked of the boar and the bear, when willing strength into an ailing patient? How often will Sweet spit of snakes and worms, if she is cursing a man?

Wulfrun waits a while before she answers. Allows the cowardice of Ethel's question to spread. I think she even turns her head to the sunlight, to make her burn appear all the redder.

'I am not afraid,' she says.

A hush falls. If I let it last too long, they will be marking her for a seer then and there and so I step towards the women, make my greetings.

Tove is the first to lift her head and see me.

'It is not time for me to return already?' she asks. 'I have been here half a heartbeat and this poor novice will have half their habit trailing behind them if I do not mend it.'

'Not yet.'

'Then what brings you here?' she asks. 'You cannot need more thread already. We gave you enough last time to wrap twice around the church and still have spare.'

'I wanted to talk with Wulfrun.'

Wulfrun lifts a spindle, begins to spin flax, twisting the thread between her fingers into strength and good use. Her eyes on mine, she lifts the flax to her mouth, wraps her tongue around the thread, wets it between her lips.

'I am working,' she says. 'The abbess has told me not to be slothful.'

'I will be quick,' I say, 'I only wished to hear more of Eadwig. To help in his cure. You have not been to see him, have you?'

She frowns. There are many listening ears now and first among them is Tove.

'I will come with you,' says Wulfrun at last. 'But not for long.'

She puts down her tools, asks that Tove watch over it. We walk away from the circle, away from eager ears and searching gazes. From where we stand I can see the marsh unfolding behind her, silvery water below and silvery sky above. The spit of land between them seems like a mistake, a smudge made by a careless hand and we just as careless for building our lives atop it.

'So,' says Wulfrun, 'what do you wish to ask me, since it cannot be of Eadwig?'

Now that I am close, now that she is not speaking of her vision to the crowd, there is a dullness about her. She is as a summer flower, spreading out to greet the sun when it is there and turning inwards when it is not.

'I brought you a salve,' I say, taking it from my basket and holding it out to her. 'For your injury. Since you will not come to see me.'

She has her sleeve pulled back, where there is a bruise with the colours of both dawn and dusk the length of her arm. She is fortunate that the fall did not break any bones.

'It is swollen. Surely the pain keeps you awake at night.'

'I have slept through worse,' says Wulfrun.

I do not know what to say. She wanders around the infirmary, telling all who will listen of her suffering and yet she will not take even the smallest kindness from me.

'It is not pity, if you are worried,' I say. 'Only part of my duty.'

'Then I do not want that either.'

She goes to turn. I see, then, why she has been keeping

Mere

her hands filled with thread and spindle. There is a tremble in them, steady and unceasing.

'Wait,' I say. I reach out, go to touch her fingers but she flinches, twists her body away just as she did from Eadwig and pulls her hand back.

Our voices startle a hare from the grass. It bounds away, so fleet it looks almost as if it flies. Both Wulfrun and I watch it, our breaths slowing in our chest. Laughter drifts across from the spinning women. I sense that whatever I say next will set the path for us for the rest of our years.

'I have a riddle,' I say and I have her. She tilts her head, waits for me to continue.

'What do we share,' I say, *'that no others do?'*

'Well, we are in the same convent. There is nothing we do not share, nothing we do not lack together.' This, with bitterness. She wears her veil still, but fewer of her rings on her fingers. Piece by piece, this place takes her riches from her.

'No,' I say, 'something else. *A gift that is not, a burden that is empty.*'

'Learning?' she says, then stops. 'No,' she says. 'That cannot be it.'

I wait. The tremble in her hand has slowed. Above, a single gull spins. I hear the lowing of our few cattle.

'A debt,' she says, at last.

'I thought you would have it faster,' I say.

She smiles. I see again that single dark tooth, taken from the mouth of another woman.

'I can only answer as well as the riddle is spun,' she says.

'I have not your quick tongue.' But it was enough for her, I think. She remembers that I have my own wit and learning, too.

'This debt,' she says. 'You speak of Botwine?'

'We owe him much,' I say. 'If you were not bound to him before, you are now. The abbess looked as if she wished to have him whipped, too.'

'I would like to see her try that,' says Wulfrun. 'You would need ten men.'

'If you believe the abbess, there will be twenty coming with her cousin by Christmas.'

Wulfrun's face grows serious. 'She talks of that, still?'

'Yes,' I say. 'Why?' I do not often hear much of the outside world. But Wulfrun was married to a thegn, ate at high tables, sewed with well-born daughters.

Wulfrun sighs. 'The king has been disbanding holy houses since the Bishop of Wintancaester died. Her cousin is close to the king, but it means that he must spend more and more of his time away from East Anglia, advising him. He forgets this place.' She gives me a sidelong look. 'And kings are not known for their loyalty. The Ealdorman may find himself as cast aside as the rest of us, one day.'

I feel a chill. I knew that the abbess did not return from Gipeswic laden with wealth, but I did not think that the convent itself would be threatened. If this place was disbanded, I would have nowhere to go. We would have to walk to Gipeswic, a journey of at least a week, now that we are without our boats. Many of the patients in my infirmary would not survive such a hardship.

'Why did you not talk of this before?' I ask.

'Because I have been thinking of Eadwig and Eadwig alone,' says Wulfrun. 'And I knew this place was a ruin before I even came.'

'I would not know,' I say, 'I have known no other home.'

She blinks at me and I think the weight of it hits her.

Mere

She has lived across seas and in the company of kings. I have never seen more than two hundred souls gathered in one place at one time.

'When I was first burnt, there were many who flinched from me. As if it were catching, as if I might curse them just by looking at them. But Eadwig's mother was a good woman, mostly. We grew up together and I brought her across to my new household with me when I married.'

There is a seed of something there. I have grown practised at listening for it over the years, the tales of confidences and trusts between girls that are weightier than they ought to be.

'His mother,' I say. 'You and she were close?'

'Of course,' says Wulfrun.

'More than . . .' I stop. There is no way to say it without it sounding like an accusation, or worse, a confession. But I am sure of it, in the glancing way that Wulfrun speaks of her. And I am right, for Wulfrun lowers her head and murmurs, 'As girls, only. When I married I did nothing that might bring shame on either of us.'

It would still be enough to go to the abbess with, if I wished. She has placed a small faith in me and I feel myself glow with it. Perhaps Wulfrun sees this, because she lets her gaze rest on me a long while before continuing.

'As I have said, his mother and I were close. She told Eadwig to bring me my food in bed while I recovered from my burns. Always a helpful boy, even through his fear. Though, he dropped most of it half the time or else let the hounds steal some of it, or else the older boys knocked it from his hands. They were so cruel to him.'

Her fingers tighten around her habit. 'I cannot do all that you do, but I fight for him all the same. If I was not here, talking with the others, they would be already calling for his blood, you understand?'

Her hand is trembling still. And, little as I like to hear it of my sisters, she is right. Hunger and fear make us all cruel. My first winter as apprentice in the infirmary, a rot came into our wheat and spread a terrible sickness. There was a woman, a known adulterer, who had long been chided for her ways, but in the freezing night the men decided that they must punish her as the law allowed and cut off her nose. I only heard of it when they brought her in to be treated and I remember still the terrible ruin of that wound.

'I will try and speak to the abbess,' I say. 'I think she knows about whatever has caught Eadwig. And, if not, perhaps I might talk to her. Have her show him mercy.'

Wulfrun laughs. 'Mercy,' she says. 'I called for that when my husband held me to the flames. It is not as easily found as you might think.'

'And yet,' I say, 'I ask for it.'

Wulfrun releases her hands from her habit. They have stilled a little. 'I know I have been distant with you,' she says. 'I am not used to others pitying me.'

'Nor I,' I say. 'Something else we share.'

She smiles, apology and welcome all at once. She looks down at the gift I have brought her, still held in my hands.

'Tell me,' says Wulfrun, 'would you go so far for any other sister? Bringing salves down to them and such?'

A question beneath a question. Her lips are parted, her dark eyes keen. I might ruin myself here. The abbess has punished enough sisters in the past for breaking their vows of chastity, for taking lovers.

There are a dozen reasons not to trust her. But there

Mere

would be no gain in betraying me to the abbess, and though I have not known her long, still we have already been through much together. She has told me of matters that I am sure she has not revealed to others.

'There have been others,' I say, quickly so that I will not lose my courage, 'men and women, in the past. But today, it is my gift to you and you alone.'

I have known she was fair from the first. Until today, she has been away, apart. First consumed by her search for Eadwig and then spelling magic that I had no knowledge of. I think of what she would feel like against me. The animal smell of her, her lavender oil. Kissing the berry juice from her lips. Heat rises in my belly, twists between my thighs.

She sees it, too. Another riddle of sorts, though a little simpler to solve.

Still, she is unsure. So few true friends in her old household. So few here. I ask her to risk everything, for so little in return. I am not in the abbess's favour, cannot tell her all of this place's secrets as Portress Ava can. I have my infirmary and my patients and little else and I know she should refuse me and still my chest grows tight with the thought of it.

'The path ahead will not be easy,' says Wulfrun. 'For any of us.'

It is as if she thinks herself the only one able to see what is plain to all: we are falling to ruin. 'Another holy vision?'

'I am speaking in earnest.'

'And I,' I say. I hold the salve out once more and wait. Far off, I hear the piping of lapwings. A single crane lifts itself from the reeds and into the frosted sky. The abbess hunted them once, with a falcon that is long since dead, lost one day, its bones sinking into the mere along with so much else.

'Take it,' I say. 'I would not see you in more pain than you must be.'

Her eyes flicker. Slowly, as if all before her is dark and she cannot see, Wulfrun reaches out and takes the salve in her hand. Her fingers brush against mine, stay there. The cold morning air sends our breath up in plumes, raises the hairs on our hands and the back of the neck. We are signals, now, bold as any fire set.

Speaking with Wulfrun gives me some courage and I spend the next day and night seeking the abbess, hoping that she might tell me more of what she and Sweet fear in the marsh and that by it I might find a way to help Eadwig. But she avoids me, always finding another sister to speak to or another duty to take her away from my questions. The most skilled hunters do not pursue their prey, clumsy and slow. Instead, they lie in wait for it. So, as the abbess finds other work to be done I walk the paths of the convent, taking laundry to the stream, digging for roots and mushrooms, cutting peat, finding little acts of service while I wait. Twice I go to where Eadwig is kept and twice Botwine has met me at the door and shown me the child sleeping still. Not better, but not worse either.

The whole time, I am sure that I taste something on the air, some bitterness that was not there before, some iron in my mouth. I thought the marsh a refuge, a home. A place where I walked bright through secret ways. But it is changing, reaching out grasping fingers, grinding impatient teeth.

*

Mere

Two days after Eadwig was first locked away, and this darkness is still on my mind as I walk to the stream. The bells for Sext are not yet rung and I have a basketful of laundry with me, tunics from the week that I have been leaving to wash for it is always a cold duty in winter. The infirmary and church are already far behind me, when I come upon the abbess walking the other way. Strange, for there are only the hives and the marsh down there and I do not think she would have gone to see Sweet. Nor have I seen her so far from the convent in a long time. Even in happier times her age means she cannot walk far by herself.

'Mother Superior,' I say, dropping my basket and stepping towards her. 'Will you wait a while? I must talk to you of Eadwig.'

'There is little to say,' says the abbess. In the daylight, the ruby she wears on her brow looks almost soft, a pale flesh colour that I cannot turn my gaze from. 'I have made my decision. Even Father Botwine stands by it. And you are fortunate that it is only the child being whipped.'

She steps ahead and I follow her, blocking her path. It is insolent, but I will not be able to speak alone with her like this for a long time.

'Please,' I say. 'I only wish to cure him.'

'Sister Hilda, I shall not ask you to stand aside,' says the abbess, calmly. 'I shall not ask this of you, for it is not something that I should have to ask of any sister.'

'You know, he would give scraps to the beggars at Wulfrun's home,' I say. 'When he was not at his work. He would pray with any heathens he found to try and turn their souls to God.'

It is a lie. But I think of what Wulfrun told me of his childhood. Each meal he brought her its own little prayer.

'Botwine has told me he could not wait to grow to manhood and find a wife of his own,' I say. 'And that he would send his daughters here and not Ely.'

It is too far, I am sure. Yet the abbess nods along as if it is a tale she already knows the end to.

'They are wicked over there in Ely, I have heard,' she says. 'Grown rich and fat.'

Neither of those are a danger for any in this convent but I only agree and say, 'Please, tell me why you and Sweet feared us searching for him. Or else, all his pain will have you at its root.'

The abbess watches me, thoughtfully. 'You care for him,' she says. 'And all tell me he was a pious, gentle boy once.'

It is in her breast, her throat. A tale not long in the telling but still hard to speak. Now, more than ever, I must be bold, else I will lose her.

'Please,' I continue. 'For the sake of the convent.'

She glances, briefly, towards the marsh, as if she fears that her voice will carry, as if the mere's dark pools will drown even words.

Then, footsteps. We both turn to see Portress Ava, walking towards us from the convent gates. There is a slate in her hand, with which she has been marking the tithes. She takes small, precise steps, as if always waiting for her path to unfold in front of her. She was ever so. I found pleasure once in this delicacy of movement, though that was long ago.

Her dark eyes show wariness as she recognizes me. She greets us both, bowing.

'I have been speaking to the ceorls,' she says. 'Sister Leogifu has been visiting them and collecting eels even though she knows that this is my duty. They fear they have been tithed double what they ought to.'

Mere

'She only goes because she cannot wait for you,' I say. 'We would all starve, if every rule was followed just to your liking.'

'But how am I to know that Leogifu took the right amount?' replies Ava, sharply. 'These laws of ours are not simply plucked from the air, Hilda. And when they are not followed, there is disorder, there is disaster. Something you might have learnt these past few days.'

'If you speak of the relic—'

'Hush, sisters,' says the abbess. 'You are both filled with a love of your duties, that is clear.'

She speaks to both of us, but it is Ava's arm she links in hers, Ava who is pulled close to her. I believed myself beyond caring but the sight of such closeness stirs something small and envious in me.

'I also wished to know,' I say, 'did the Ealdorman have that book I asked after? *On the Properties of Plants*?'

I do not know what drives me to speak of this, for all know that the abbess's journey to her cousin was not fruitful.

But I have not yet heard the abbess speak of her failure.

At my question, the abbess stills. Her limbs, her back, even her face might be of wood or stone, and fear worms through me, for the abbess is only quiet like this when she has made a choice. Such choices are rarely kind.

'He has the book,' says the abbess, 'but he could not spare it. I have asked him to bring it, when he comes later this year.'

'Besides, matters of the convent are not your worry,' adds Ava. 'You must only keep that infirmary of yours.'

How Ava loves it, telling me over and again that I must care for the part while she rules the whole. But the abbess is not finished.

'While we speak of the infirmary,' she says, 'Alwin will be staying with you a while longer. To ensure that all the proper rules are being followed, as well as to learn.'

I can do nothing but nod. A spy, then. I would rather not have that strutting cockerel about but at least he is already half-blinded by pride.

The abbess does not smile. There is no pleasure in this for her, I know, and yet I wish she would show some anger or hatred. She only reaches up to her circlet, tightens the knot in the gold thread that holds the symbol of her office in place.

Then, the abbess turns and, together with Ava, they continue their walk away from the convent. I watch them pass, wondering what it would be like to be held in such trust again. There was a time when I was a girl when the abbess would keep me in every confidence and it was only once I became infirmarian that this ended. Now, I understand that she kept me close as a cowherd might his favourite heifer, telling me all in the belief that I would never find a use for it. A love without shadows or echoes.

Perhaps the abbess tells Ava of her worries, of her plans for the convent. Perhaps Ava already knows the nature of the curse that has snared Eadwig but, loyal as ever, will not tell another soul. Or perhaps she is kept as ignorant as I am.

But there is nothing else to be done and so I walk my solitary path back to the infirmary and all its knots and tangles.

Chapter 8

That evening, I go to the storeroom where Eadwig is being kept. A large wooden building, towards the edge of the convent, as far from the infirmary as any building could be. I pass the kitchen on the way, give my greeting to Cellarer Leogifu and fill my basket with what she can spare.

There is a single guard standing at the door, keys at her waist. Eluned, leaning against the wood, eyes softened by weariness. When she sees me, she lifts herself up. They have given her a single blanket against the cold, but when she presses her hands against mine in greeting they are as cold as the dead's.

'This is your duty now?' I ask her. There was not a guard the last two times I have come.

'The abbess ordered it and none of the men would do it,' she whispers. 'And Sybba's brothers argue about his estate still, so while they fight they have offered me in service to the convent.'

'It is a dangerous duty for you,' I say.

'There are worse,' she says. Around the wood in the doorframe, she has been carving. Holy crosses and knots in the Wealh style, chipped out over careful hours. Blessings to protect and cure, to contain and cleanse.

Eluned gives a quick smile. I think of Sweet's belief that the best way for her would be Sybba's death. She is right, I think, for even with her fate uncertain, she has grown stronger and bolder by the day.

'I saw you at the mass for Sybba,' I say. It had been a small, bare day. Sybba had put aside gold and silver for a grand event but he had not told a soul where he had buried the hoard, not even Eluned. I see his brothers sometimes, shovels in their hands, digging holes all about his land.

'You wept greatly,' I say.

She shifts her weight. 'It was a brutal end,' she says. 'But I am glad that Father Botwine gave him the last rites.'

She speaks lightly, but I do not believe it. 'And the heart-wort?' I ask. 'Is there any left?'

'Heartwort?' she asks. 'What would I need heartwort for?'

I do not answer. I cannot. After some time, she shakes her head as if I am a fool and takes my hands in her own. In a low voice, she says, 'I have confessed already to Father Botwine. He gave me penitence for the trick, but it was the curse that killed Sybba, not us.'

'You told Botwine?' I feel fear, then, not for my own soul and sins but that Botwine will think the less of me. A child's worry.

'He came down here earlier. He spoke to me about it, though quickly for Eadwig was calling out to him. The child has been talking strangeness.'

'How so?' I ask.

Mere

She looks at the basket that I have brought with me, at the loaves and fish within. I am not attending our evening meal and hoped to eat while I spoke with Eadwig, but a few missed mouthfuls will not harm me.

'I have spare,' I say, reaching for the food. 'Tell me, what should I know?'

Afterwards, still picking fish bones from her teeth, Eluned unlocks the door to the storeroom. The darkness settles around me, coarse and heavy. I thought speaking to Eluned would prepare me but it has only stoked my fears.

The storeroom smells rich. Dried meat and fish, onions, apples, peaches, beer, hard cheeses, vinegar, dried grain in earthenware jars, bales of hay for the beasts, all of this to bear us through winter. Though every year the stores grow smaller and the harvests poorer, to enter the storeroom is to enter our future. Some of it is the donation that paid for Wulfrun's admission, her son's betrayal now sustaining all of us.

Much of the food is kept in the undercroft. It is built into the hill itself, so there are no steps as I walk downwards but only a long, steady slope. Even in the dim light, I can see the trail of a body dragged in the dirt.

I wish I had brought a rushlight or two with me, for with every footstep down the light grows weaker, the path harder to see. But I would not dare a flame here, where a single spark could catch the straw, then the stores, then condemn us all to famine. A few months ago, a kitchen sister lost her firesteel in this place and though she searched for a week and a day, could not find it and had to report so to the portress. She was whipped as if she had strode up during the holy hours and spat on the cross and most about said it was still not hard enough a punishment.

Step by step, my sight grows used to the gloom and I see him. At the very end of the undercroft, stakes driven into the earth and shackles about his neck and wrist. It is as if the abbess hopes that the earth will swallow him, chains and all, and save her the worry of excommunicating him. There is a bucket close by, one that I am glad to see has been emptied recently. Even so, there is a faint smell of piss in the damp air.

Botwine is sat beside him. He has no cloak, though he must be cold. An oak to Eadwig's sapling, same in his features if not his size. Our priest is speaking in a low voice. I think, for a heartbeat, that he is reading the bible but of course he cannot, not in this darkness. He recites it instead, from memory.

I stand at the edge, waiting. I knew Botwine was a scholar, but I never knew he had such a skill within him. He is the sort of man to be shamed by his own brilliance.

He is speaking of miracles. Of Christ exorcising the demon at Gerasene, of our Lord turning that devil-sickness into a herd of swine, who ran at once into the water and drowned themselves. Two thousand all at once, Botwine is saying, what a sight that must have been.

Botwine looks up at my footsteps.

'I came to see Eadwig,' I say. 'I have some food for him.'

Eadwig has not spoken this whole time, but at the sound of my voice he stirs.

'And do you have it? My cure?'

His voice is hoarse, tired, but it is a boy's. Whatever spoke before is gone, or has at least ebbed away for now.

'Only willow bark and poppy seed,' I say, placing the basket down. 'To lessen the pain.'

'Father Botwine says that he has no cure either. But he is the priest. I thought he ruled this place. Maybe he could ask Wulfrun to come down again?'

'Serve,' says Botwine, quickly. 'I serve the sisters here. The abbess rules.'

Still, Eadwig is not wrong, for Botwine might overturn this if he wished. He fought for Eadwig, but not as hard as he might, for there is a part of him that I think is relieved to have Eadwig away. He fears his own son.

'We believe it best you stay here,' I say. 'While we cure this devil-sickness.'

'They say I am to be whipped,' he says, 'and if that does not cure me, excommunicated.'

'I work to cure you before that,' I say.

'But I do not want to leave the convent,' says Eadwig, 'I do not want to be alone, to be with them all in my head. It is too much and I—'

'Hush,' I say. 'We will not let harm come to you, I promise.'

An oath I do not know if I can keep, but the fear of a beating is often heavier than the punishment itself. Excommunication, even worse. Eadwig, a child, sent away from God's grace for ever. The abbess will not send him out to the marsh, for that would mean only death or slavery, but he will remain outside of our bounds in some ceorl's home, if any will take him. Always in reach, never to join us.

'But come, Eadwig, you are already improved. I have half a mind to fetch the abbess back.'

'No,' says Botwine. He glances at the child. 'Not yet.'

There is something he is not saying and so I only hold out the loaf. Eadwig is eager as he takes it from me, but eats with care.

'I have been taking his confession,' says Botwine. 'Maybe there is some small sin that has let this in and might drive it out again.'

'I have thought of more sins,' says Eadwig. His words are growing quicker, as if soon he will run out of them. 'I looked at a fair maid in the fields and defiled myself later that night. I did not give alms to a beggar. I laughed in Vespers when Botwine stumbled his words.'

'So did I,' I say. 'I do not think that is why you suffer.'

Botwine grasps Eadwig's shoulder. 'She does not need to hear them, child, only I. She cannot give you absolution.'

Not true, for I take confession on my sisters' deathbeds in the months of the year that Botwine is not with us. But our priest does not like to think of us without him. And while he is talking of wrongdoings, I have a question.

'Was it you,' I ask, 'who sunk our boats? I will not be angry, I swear, for I know you are not yourself. But you may tell me.'

Eadwig stares up at me. 'No,' he says. 'I passed them, saw the yew tree and knew it for safety.' He shivers. 'But it matters not, for I have destroyed our relic. I did not understand . . . I do not know why I did that. It was not the answer.'

I frown. 'The answer?'

Botwine shifts his weight, slowly. No longer a doting father. This is what he did not tell me. Eadwig holds the bread now as if it were something new to him, as if all the earthly wants of the world were for other people.

'It is too much,' he mutters. 'Too much. Beetles in the

wood, snakes in the grass. Newts in the water, gulls in the air, a snail spreading itself across damp stone. I am sorry. I was trapped and waited for a week, two weeks, but nobody came for me and I was hungry and I was thirsty and I am no coward, there was but one choice for me, one choice.'

'Two weeks?' I ask. 'You were gone but a handful of days.'

He bows his head and I reach out for him, but Botwine catches my hand and shakes his head.

'I would not touch him as he is,' he says. 'It rises and falls, as with the tides.'

Botwine is stiff, his hand reaching out for something he has kept beside him on the earth. A cudgel. My stomach twists.

'My skull,' moans Eadwig, clutching at his head. 'A ring about my skull, growing tighter, growing tighter. Lice in your hair,' he says. 'Lice about your cunt, breeding, growing, bleeding.'

Botwine flinches but says nothing. He has heard the like before, it seems. And there is nothing that has not been spat at me in my long time serving this convent.

'What has caught you, Eadwig?' I ask.

He turns to me. In the darkness, I cannot see his eyes at all.

'*I end and then I end and then I end,*' he says. '*Forge me in heat, knot me in thread.*'

Then, as before, he collapses back, the bread falling from his hand and into the dirt. Botwine is ready for him, softens the fall with his great arms. He lifts Eadwig easily, lays him back. Moves the shackles so that they will chafe him the less.

A breath shivers through Eadwig, a whisper so quiet that I must lean in to hear it.

'I destroyed the relic,' he says. 'What if I hurt someone?'

'You will not,' I say. 'You do not have harm in you.' But I am thinking of Wulfrun's fall, the strangeness Eadwig passes through us with a touch. Done without any thought or understanding, but full of danger all the same.

'I do,' he says. 'I have it in me. I can feel it, about my skull. There is too much, too much, mouseling, trembler . . .'

He trails off.

'Take heart,' I say. 'Pray and all will be well.'

But the words feel empty even as I speak them.

Botwine does not return to the convent with me. He does not like leaving Eadwig alone. He walks me, instead, back to the doorway, talking the whole time about Eadwig's life in Wulfrun's home. His love of beasts, how he wished always to be in the stables or with the hounds. How Botwine will find a place for him in the household of some thegn, once he has learnt how to serve a bit better.

'He is but a child,' says Botwine. 'I do not know what sin he can have committed that would bring this upon him.'

'I have read,' I say, 'that sometimes a soul might be punished for another's sin.'

'That is what the abbess believes,' says Botwine, 'and she does not have to say whose.'

The sin hangs between us. He does not have to tell me, of course, of the lot of bastards.

Then, he shakes his head. 'It was the only time I stepped off the path. I have repented and prayed and supplicated myself and thought it done.'

He sighs. 'I have not seen demoniacs treated so anywhere else. In Gipeswic they are cared for, given food and drink

Mere

and prayer, even when in their frenzy they have tried to kill their own family with an axe. I do not know why the abbess would punish a boy so? Why any would punish Eadwig like this?'

He looks at me then, desperate, wanting. I know now how he must feel in confession, all those wracked souls begging him for something he cannot truly give them. I have no answer and so we only continue walking on until we are at the threshold, with Eluned guarding it beyond. Reaching it, Botwine frowns, as if he has just remembered my own sins. Sybba, the splintered man.

'I would have you come to me,' he says, 'to confess as Eluned did.'

'I will,' I say, 'when Eadwig is well and you can leave his side once more.'

'Yes,' says Botwine and I cannot bear the hope in his voice. 'Yes, I am sure that will not be long.'

The infirmary is still uneasy when I return, Eadwig's blasphemy heavy in the air. Even Tove has been talking less than usual and I find her at prayer, glass beads clinking between her fingers. They catch the last of the evening light, sending greens and reds and blues sparkling all over the old sister as if she is some precious object herself. Like Wulfrun, she seems as if she came from a jewelled place.

'I have never seen you pray outside of chapel before,' I say.

'It has never been needed before,' she replies. She does not stop her prayer, lips moving silently asking holy mother, holy father, take pity, take pity. The colours shimmer.

'You pray for Eadwig?'

'All of us,' she says. Reticent, where I have never known her so before.

I watch the beads turn in their devotions.

'Have you eaten yet?' I ask.

She places the Pater Noster cord down with a rattle. 'Ask what you want, then leave me to it, Hilda, for I cannot stand your breathing in my ear.'

'How do you know that I did not come only to talk?'

Tove tilts her head. 'You have as many duties as there are stars in the sky. I know you do not have idle hours to talk with me, as you once did. I am no fool.'

Here, she stops. 'At least, not in most matters.'

I laugh. I cannot help it. 'I cannot think of a time when you have not been cunning,' I say. 'Is something worrying you?'

'A soul may be the most cunning in Christendom and still foolish,' she says. 'More often, for they think that wit alone is a shield against ever acting.'

She takes a breath. I see her watching her Pater Noster cord.

'Am I a good sister, Hilda?' she asks.

'Of course you are,' I say. 'You speak to any who come to you, you help me around the infirmary. You are loved in this place, you know that.'

Tove smiles. 'You are kind to say such a thing,' she says, 'but it is a lie. I do not serve any more. Worse, I have grown content. I have let the abbess become something she was not. The Sigeburg that first arrived here would never have sent a child out to freeze in our storeroom.'

I watch her. She has been here the longest, saw Sigeburg in nearly all of her ages. 'You alone cannot turn the tide of the whole convent,' I say.

Mere

'True enough,' says Tove, 'but I had Sigeburg's ear once. I saw her grow fearful and grasping, did nothing for I thought it would only cause strife.'

'It is not too late,' I say. I place my hand on hers, feel the thinness of her skin and the bones beneath. I had never truly feared Tove growing old, for she showed so little fear of it herself. But today she looks emptied, her dark skin dull.

'You may help me,' I say. 'I seek Sweet, for I wish to talk to her about Eadwig. You hear plenty that I do not. Where is she hiding?'

'I do not know for sure,' says Tove, 'but I hear she has been going to her hives at night, rather than during the day. You might find her then.'

'Thank you,' I say, clasping her hands. 'You help me greatly.'

'I am not so sure,' she says. She lifts the beads again, begins her steady prayers. Their clacking sound follows me through the infirmary as I go to speak to Mildred and make my preparations to steal away.

But it is Alwin that I find first. He comes up to me, hand on the knife in his belt, full of eagerness. His dark, curled tonsure is freshly shaved, his clothes clean and neat. The image of the willing pupil and still I cannot like him.

'Sister Hilda,' he says, 'you are back. The abbess says I am to help you a while longer.'

'I heard,' I say.

'You must be glad,' he says. 'It will be good, to have a man about. Yourself and Mildred are skilled but there is much here you cannot do alone.'

We have been managing this infirmary fine until now, just the two of us, but Alwin looks around as if this is some midden.

I see Mildred behind him, hurrying away, her head down. She has been avoiding the boy as much as she can, and if I do not catch her, she will slip away for an hour at least.

'Now that you speak of it,' I say, 'we need to draw some more water from the stream. Would you go for me?'

'That is woman's work,' he says.

'It is,' I say. I lift my arms as if they are heavy from all that I have done today. 'But seeing Eadwig has wearied me. You have not been down to the storeroom yet, have you?'

Fear in his face, then guilt. He will never be a good healer, for he is drawn always towards victory, towards glory. But my duty is one of defeats, some slow, others sudden. I do not know whether he has avoided the storeroom because he cannot bear to see the child sick or because he fears the curse. Either way, he has left Eadwig alone.

'I will go to the stream,' he says. I watch him shrug on his cloak and hurry out, so quick that he leaves the pail in the doorway. A few breaths later, he trips back inside, red-faced, then hurries back out again, holding it in his hands now.

When I am sure he is gone, I walk over to Mildred. Where Alwin came to me clean and neat, she is unkempt, stains down her front and tufts of dark hair peeking out of her wimple. While I have been out with Eadwig and Alwin has been underfoot, her duties have doubled and doubled again.

'Good evening, Mildred,' I say.

'It is evening already?' she says, looking about as if woken from a dream. 'I have not yet made those salves you wished, nor washed the sheets.'

'Do not worry,' I say, 'I will take those both on for you,

Mere

later this evening.' Another sleepless night for me, but they are becoming common enough.

'You will?' Her eyes narrow. 'So what will I be doing?'

'You will be with Alwin tonight,' I say. 'Making sure he does not spy on me while I go about my work.'

Mildred stiffens. 'I will not tempt him,' she says, 'not even to aid Eadwig.'

I might almost laugh. Mildred is not ugly, but she is far from the fairest of the novices. If Alwin wished to find himself tempted, he would have half a dozen other girls to choose from, many of them who do not have stains all down their dress.

I place my hand on Mildred's. 'I do not ask that,' I say, soothing. 'Only that you teach him some complex potion, some long charm.' I tilt my head. 'Or should I ask Tove to do this, if you are not able? I'm sure she could find two score and one duties for him.'

She bristles at that. 'No,' she says, 'I can do it.'

'Good,' I say. 'I will be back as soon as I can.'

I turn to leave, but Mildred grips my hand. 'Please do,' she says. 'It is not safe out there, once the light is gone.'

I stare at her. The girl I have known since she was but seven or eight winters, speaking as if she were the mistress and I the foolish apprentice. I see, all at once, her future spreading out ahead of her. I will live, God-willing, another decade or two and then find my duties too hard to perform alone. She will take them from me softly, as I did to the old infirmarian, and when I die she will ease me from this world with all the skill I have taught her. I do not know if this comforts me or not.

'You worry like an old woman,' I say and she laughs.

*

Danielle Giles

Alwin and Mildred will go and use the moonlight to find mandrake in the fields, a dog with them. If they find any of the shimmering leaves, they will tie rope around the hound's neck and the other end about the mandrake and let the poor creature bear the weight of the plant's scream so that neither of them will hear it. Mildred does not like this, for she is a gentle soul, but she understands the use of even a coin's worth of mandrake root in our remedies. This single hound's death might save half a dozen sisters.

Alwin insists that he must bring a spear, to defend them both against whatever threats might come, but we have few weapons and so he must carry only a sharpened stick and a cudgel. It does not look enough, even with his strong hands and broad chest, but Mildred says there is nothing to be feared of, even as she loosens the knife in her belt so that it will be quicker to hand.

I wait until their rushlight is most-swallowed by the dusk, then pull on my own cloak and pick my way down, once more, to see Sweet.

The hives are quiet, most of them asleep in readiness for the winter. There are half a dozen of them set out, each of them built from grass and then rubbed with cow dung and ash. Sweet walks between them in the half-darkness, checking to see if any have begun to show signs of mould, leaving pounded barleycakes mixed in oil and wine to sustain each little kingdom. Her face and hands are covered with ash and mallow juice but the scars of past stings still mark her.

At the sound of my footfalls her head lifts. No shock that I have come, no anger either. She simply finishes laying out the food and then walks over to me, steady and slow.

Mere

Against the ash, the grey strands of hair across her face look pale and thin as spider silk.

'So, you have found me,' she says. 'At my convent duty of all places.'

'Well, I know how you love to serve.'

She laughs, though there is not much heat in it. Then, brushing some of the ash from her hands, she says, 'A poor fate for Sybba, eh?' There is not much feeling in her voice.

'It was an evil death,' I say.

'Do you think so?' asks Sweet, watching me. 'Truly? You know what he did to Eluned. What he would do to any, given the power for it.'

'We might have found a way,' I say, but even I do not believe it. 'A manumission, perhaps.'

'Maybe,' says Sweet. 'But he would only have bought another and the abbess would have urged him to it. The convent holds no slaves but it is happy enough to take the tithes of those that do.'

I have no answer to that, for it is true. It is why Sweet has never changed her name though she has been baptized.

'I wish to ask you something,' I say.

'Aye,' she says, 'it is always so.' She bends down, lifts a jug and pours the water within it, washing her face and hands. 'So, how may I help the infirmarian with her work?'

I flush. It is she who has been avoiding me, she who should feel shame.

'Eadwig,' I say. 'Do you know what devil or elf has him? He spoke something, a riddle of some sort.'

She wavers. Not long, but I know her well.

'It is this riddle?' I ask. 'That and the curse are bound together?'

Sweet does not nod, but nor does she deny it. Instead,

she asks, 'And what will you do, once you have solved it? Go out and defeat this mere-devil? Outwit and outpray him, like some great hero?'

'Whatever will help Eadwig.'

She looks at me with pity.

'I do not agree with the abbess on much,' she says. 'But we are of a mind on this. It will only bring misery. Let this rest.'

'Let the boy die, you mean?'

'Of course not,' she says.

'Nothing else will help him,' I say. 'He is to be whipped, and if that does not work, excommunicated. We cannot let that happen.'

'I wonder,' she says, 'if you speak for yourself or this Wulfrun.'

'Does it matter?' I ask.

A small smile. 'I thought that you would have learnt after Ava. The abbess hates sodomy in all its forms. It was fortunate with her that neither of you were caught and whipped.'

I will not be drawn by her. If she wishes to shame me, it will take more than that. I know many women who lay with men on holy days, or else let them spill their seed onto the ground, or else in their arses or mouths. Some of them ceorls, but some of them sisters of the convent. All sodomy, all danger. My time with Ava was no different.

'I am not here to talk of that,' I say. 'Why do you fear the marsh? Why now?'

Sweet looks up at the darkening sky. 'It is not a tale I like to tell.'

There are still smudges of ash about her face, at the edges, at the hollows. They make her seem even gaunter than usual. Both of us, thin-boned, narrow-faced. More needles than women.

Mere

'Please,' I say.

'Some souls are beyond saving,' says Sweet. 'It would spare you much pain, if you learnt that.' She sighs and then looks about. She beckons me closer, so that there is a handspan or two between us. Then, bidding me stay in place, she collects an armful of sticks and lays it about us both so that it forms a circle. I have seen her do so before, when a mother is losing her lifeblood or there is a rot in the fields. It is not so different from the Field-Remedy that Botwine performed. The securing of a boundary and then a blessing.

Once she is sure that there are no breaks in the circle, she steps inside.

'I thought you would not fear speaking of the curse, as the others do,' I say. 'I thought you too cunning.'

'I am wise enough to know when I must fear,' says Sweet. Even though we both stand tight within the bounds, she still looks about. 'I would not call disaster upon us both by speaking of it more than I must.'

Sweet is a talented storyteller. I have seen her weave giants and heroes from the air, tell of King Arthur sleeping beneath his mountain or sailors landing on little isles, only to find themselves on the belly of a whale. But her voice now is flat, empty.

'The abbess was given this land four decades ago. Until then, not many had ventured so far. No wealth, or great settlements, or rich farmland. Only water. When she came, it was as if Christendom came with her. She saw the old ways and hated them.'

'As she hates them still,' I say.

'She was right to,' says Sweet. 'Not all of them were good.'

I stare at her. I did not think she had any praise of the abbess in her and in this of all things.

Sweet takes a breath and I think that she has lost her courage. But then she says, 'Your Lord I think weak, but at least merciful. These old ways were sometimes hard. There was one ritual above all that the abbess wished to move against, but none would dare speak of it, to her or others. And so, one night, when I was ten winters or so, I slipped away and offered myself as witness.'

This is not all of it, I am sure. Sweet has always acted when a wrong is done in front of her, but I cannot think that she would ally with the abbess, even as a child.

'What was this ritual?' I ask, but Sweet is not listening.

'I spoke of it to the abbess and it ended. We waited for disaster, all of us, not daring to venture beyond the boundary. But nothing came. We understood that we must not speak of it. That we must not walk the marsh alone. We obeyed these ways and nothing awoke and we remained safe. Even the abbess warned every sister against it, though she did not tell them why. It is not as if many of you walk much further than that hill of yours anyway, and any pilgrims would always come in a great party for fear of losing the path and drowning.'

'But Eadwig was not warned,' I say. 'He strayed. So what is this riddle he speaks?'

There is a hole in her tale, a place where it has snagged and torn and she has not gone back to mend it. I have never known Sweet to flinch from anything, yet she flinches from this.

But before she can answer there is a shout, far off in the distance. We both turn, stare. Torches, a great number of torches flaring all at once, in the direction of the marsh.

Mere

Not our paltry rushlights, but something hotter and brighter. A procession, of some sort, or a raid.

No, not torches. A fire, a signal lighting up against the black. It is only when Sweet swears and begins running towards it that I understand.

The storeroom is aflame.

Chapter 9

*S*weet and I stumble over ditches and through water, legs heavy, legs slow, and the storeroom is still so far away and the only sign that we are closer is the smoke that begins to fill the air and choke us. Soon, I cannot see her for it and still I continue on, groping forward slow and useless.

I have seen hell before on tapestries. They show sinners impaled and boiling, split apart and squealing. But this must be closer to what awaits. Knowing that there is disaster and ruin ahead and finding yourself weak against it. My throat burns and my eyes sting and

Eadwig is in there

Botwine is in there and

so slow I am I cannot

Then, Sweet pushes out of the smoke like some revenant and grips me by my wrist, hard enough to hurt. She says something but I cannot hear and I do not care. She is warm and strong and, step by step, she pulls me along with her.

As we grow closer, I see that there are dark shapes against

Mere

the flames, souls who reached the blaze before us and pass buckets filled with mere-water between them. But I do not think there is any way this fire might be stopped, even if the entire marsh had been emptied of all it contained. I feel the heat, even from a hundred feet away, see the wood in the walls crackling and sun-bright. The roof is already gone, quickly fallen in.

Beside me, Sweet loosens her grip. I know why. She smells, as I do, what is on the air. Cooked meat and flour, stewed apples. The smell of a kitchen, spreading out all around us. Our winter stores, turned to ashes.

We continue on and the shadows begin to slow in their efforts. They have been shovelling dirt in a large circle around the flames and so it has not spread to the grass or caught any other buildings. They have saved what they could. Some have wrapped cloths about their faces and there are a few barrels lying on their sides away from the building. But the water cannot douse the flames and there is nothing to do now but to watch the rest of it burn.

I cannot see Eadwig.

Botwine is here, though. Four women around him, three holding him back. The fourth holding his face in her hands, talking to him in a low voice. There are burns running up his arms, his hair and eyebrows singed and his face blackened. He strains still, pushing to be free, to run back inside.

I stumble closer. Not a woman with Botwine but a girl. Mildred, pressing her forehead against Botwine's. He is moaning and swaying like some great ox and he is a large man, our priest, at least twice Mildred's height and twice her width again. She shows no fear, suffering his raging like a willow bending in a storm. After tonight, none can call her Littlevoice again.

I call out her name and she turns. Her own face is dark with smoke, her eyes red. Some burns of her own, about her right hand.

Slowly, she shakes her head.

The flames begin to sputter with dawn. Cruel that they should retreat only against the light, when we still have splinters in our hands from the dousing buckets, when our breath comes dragging still through scoured lungs.

I stay, wrap what wounds I can with poultices and cloth that Sweet brings for me, send Mildred back to the infirmary with the worst of them. Eluned is among those who need the most help. She was the first to smell burning, the first to run in with a bucket to douse what she thought was a small flame, but was instead already a roar. The smoke was enough to bring her to her knees and she is fortunate that she had the strength to drag herself out into the clean air. Still, her every breath crackles and she cannot speak more than a word at a time.

Botwine should go, too, but a few hours ago he fell to his knees, his stomach and head pressed to the ground, his palms clasped upwards, heavenward. He has not stirred since. Alwin came to coax him, Mildred whispered to him, but he would not be moved, our penitent of stone.

Throughout the night, sisters from the convent make pilgrimages to the site, stumbling away ten years aged and weeping as they return to their duties. Some mourn for Eadwig, I am sure, but I think most weep for themselves. I feel it, too. A scrabbling fear claws at my throat and wrist. Famine, with its dry breath in our bellies. Eadwig will only be the first.

They whisper, too, of Wulfrun's vision. Only she was

Mere

bold enough to speak of this curse. I cannot see her about at all. She must be still in the convent, where the abbess stays, watching smoke on the horizon.

Towards morning, when the bells for Lauds ring, Ava comes with her helper, Ethel. The two of them take a few steps towards Botwine and then retreat and come to me instead.

'I must make a tally,' says Ava.

I almost laugh. There might be northmen at our door and Ava would call out to them, asking how many of us they intended to rape and enslave. She would count the devils in hell itself and think it a comfort.

'You must wait,' I say.

'Some of the barrels in the undercroft might not have caught,' says Ava. I wish she had not told me that, for in her hope for the supplies I feel a hope for Eadwig. The earth damp around him, a shield against flames.

'The wood is still hot,' I say. 'You would be buried in sparks and ash. That is what we have saved.'

I point towards the small pile of supplies rolled out, the pitiful three or four barrels of apples and grain.

Ava stares at it for a long time. Tallying an absence greater than she could ever manage. Counting, perhaps, the lives that we will lose now. She is a spear of a woman, slicing through the days and years here and never wavering. But the storm's wind might take even the best spear off-course and for a heartbeat she is silent.

'Why are you not at the infirmary?' she asks at last. 'There are wounded.'

'I am needed here,' I say. 'Why, should I have stayed in the infirmary and let the building burn?'

'No,' she says, quickly. 'It has been a bitter night for us all.'

She rubs her face. Her eyes are red, not from smoke but weariness. I cannot remember who came down to help douse the flames and who did not. Perhaps she was here helping. I must believe that all my sisters did, that they came and breathed smoke and fought screaming flames not only for the stores, but for the sake of a single devil-sick boy.

When the sun is finally high, as the bells ring for Prime, Botwine rises and begins to dig in the ruins. Sparks burn through his habit, rise into his eyes, but he shows no pain or fear. Sweet lifts herself to help him first and then there are others. Oswy and Edwin, who went most with him into the marsh in his search for the boy, who came to take Eadwig to the storeroom in the first place. Ava, who stuns me by staying at the storeroom ruins, her lips moving in silent prayer, and Alwin who stumbled out through the smoke, having been shoring up the trenches. Soon there is a great host of us, overturning earth as if some treasure lies beneath it.

When we find Eadwig, he is curled in on himself, sheltered from the worst of the flames by the collapse of the undercroft. Small burns, about his wrist and hands. He looks as if he is only waiting for a little water and sunlight and he will unfurl for another day. Botwine gives a cry and pushes forward, dropping his spade and lifting the boy up.

Our priest raises his eyes to me. Waits for me to tell him that I can revive the child, that the smoke and earth did not choke him, that he did not die gasping out for help. I have told a hundred lies in my time, when sisters have gripped blankets and cursed me for a whore, when men have locked their jaws and shat themselves in fear. Yes, she

Mere

called out only for Christ. Yes, he was brave till his last breath.

But Botwine knows, already, the truth of it and so I say nothing.

I do not say that there is a firesteel, glinting nearby. I do not say that Eadwig's fist is bloody, as if he used it over and over again until, at last, something caught alight. I cannot say any of it, for my chest is tight, my breath not coming. I am drowning in silt and mud and mere-water and yet I still stand over this child's body and look for words of comfort and find none.

We wrap Eadwig in a shroud and carry him up to the convent. Whatever rules bound him in life from entering, Botwine must think they are undone by death, for he strides past the chapel and into the small hut beside it we use for washing and preparing the bodies before burial. A large man, a heavy man, the force of the door as he opens it sends house martins chirping from the eaves and mice weaving away in panic as if from a storm.

Above us, the sky is darkening once more. It is nearly Vespers and this day has passed in a heartbeat and it has passed in an age. I cannot believe that only last night I was with Sweet at the hives.

'I went only to draw water,' says Botwine, as he lays Eadwig down on the table. 'I did not leave him alone long.'

Yet, it was all Eadwig needed. The firesteel, left long ago by a careless sister who had no hope of finding it again in the dark. He must have set alight to the straw around him first, waited for it to spread. Thirteen winters and he felt as if the only path left to him was this.

I cannot rouse myself to sorrow or anger. I only watch

as, gently, Botwine unpicks Eadwig's clothes from him and places them to the side. Whatever scraps can be saved will be used as rags. He dips his own sleeve into a bucket, begins to clean Eadwig's face of the dirt and soot. Sometimes he smudges it across Eadwig's skin and tuts and tells Eadwig he is sorry to mar him so. He warns Eadwig before lifting his arms and legs, tells him when he is about to clean the soles of his feet in case it is ticklish for him. Whenever he finds some burnt skin, he sighs as if it is no worse than a scraped knee and reaches his hand out to me and I pass him a bandage to wrap around it.

'I will have to tell his mother,' says Botwine, dully, 'when we next return to Gipeswic.'

'You can tell her he died of illness only,' I say. 'You could tell her that and it would be the truth.'

Botwine raises his eyebrows. 'She is the shrewdest woman you could meet. Has no knowledge of any letters but knows if a man is lying after a word.'

His face warms with this memory. Then, he presses his forehead against Eadwig's and closes his eyes. He is telling him something, I think, something that is half a song, but I cannot hear it and I do not try to.

Botwine is still there when the abbess arrives. She stops at the doorway, horror and pity on her face. Both are quickly stifled. I thought she would fear this dead place, but her steps are sure and unwavering. Behind her are half a dozen sisters, Ava and Wulfrun among them. I cannot feel cheer at seeing Wulfrun, but her calm, watchful face is at least steadying on this day where all else is upended.

The abbess goes to Botwine, takes his hands in hers. She

Mere

has taken off her rings and wears none of her finery except the single ruby about her head.

She whispers into his ear, grief-words, the comfort of old friends. Of all the souls in this convent, Father Botwine stands alone as her equal. Whatever strife they have, mostly they only have each other.

And then, something else. The softest of words, but Botwine rears back like a spooked horse, shaking his head.

'I will not allow it,' says Botwine. 'He needs a Christian burial. He died a Christian death. He was even shriven. I saw to it myself.'

The abbess glances about. There are a dozen or so people watching. Not the time or place for a battle. 'Shall we go elsewhere to talk of this, Father?'

'I stay here,' says Botwine. 'At his side.'

'It is only that I worry for your senses—'

Botwine reddens. He has always been a man of great kindness, great indulgence. Always a merciful penance over a hard one, always laughter over outrage. But the higher the height, the deeper the fall, and so it goes with him. His fists clench, his arms tremble and I think he could hold himself against a charging bull in this mood.

'My senses?' he says. 'My senses?'

The abbess lifts her chin, the gold of her circlet flashing. She will not give, not an inch. 'Eadwig has murdered himself. If we bury him in the graveyard, he will poison the earth, his soul will come back and inflict torments upon us over and over again. We will bury him at the crossroads, a stake through his heart and his hands bound. We will forget this sorry business and this curse shall be lifted on us all.'

'I will never let you take him from this place,' says

Botwine. 'Sigeburg, you forget your position. You forget yourself.'

'No, Father,' says the abbess. 'You do. Your feelings for the child, for your—'

She stops herself. If there was any doubt in the convent, it is gone now.

'If I may speak?' says Wulfrun. Quiet all this time, it makes her words fall all the heavier.

'This does not concern you,' says the abbess.

'He was born in my household,' says Wulfrun, 'came of age there, too. I have duties to him, to his mother.'

At this, she falters. Not much, not for long, but it must tear at her. Eadwig's mother loved her, entrusted her son to her. And now we stand in the cold of the chapel and argue over his stilled body.

'All I wished to say was that I have seen deaths such as this before and these souls were given Christian burials.'

'Yes,' says Botwine, slowly. 'Yes, I have seen it before. What was his name? I forget.'

'Alfred Halfhead,' says Wulfrun. She straightens as she moves into the tale. 'A horse kicked him in the head as a child and let the demons in.'

She watches the small crowd. It is the same skill she shows during her visions. A reading of people, a scrying of the now to weave a story of back then that they wish to hear. 'He hanged himself in a frenzy, under their influence. Not self-murder.'

'The act of an ill man,' finishes Botwine. 'Eadwig was driven to this and should be buried in consecrated ground.'

The lie is plain to the abbess, I am sure. But she cannot openly accuse our priest of falsehood. And, most importantly, it is a lie that we all wish to believe. It is in the eyes

Mere

of the other sisters, the longing for something kind, for something good. The abbess offers punishment but Wulfrun shows them salvation.

Then, Ava steps forward. Ava, who I have not heard speak an ill word about the abbess in nearly a decade. Her face is dirtied from the smoke and ash, and when she speaks her voice is charred.

'I have also seen this,' she says, steadily. 'When I was younger, in Kent. A woman grew devil-sick and drowned herself and her child.'

The portress and the priest, speaking with one voice against the abbess. I would never have thought to see it in my lifetime. I stare at Ava, trying to understand whether this is simple mercy or something else, but she does not look at me. She speaks her disobedience to the abbess and the abbess alone.

Yet, the abbess does not seem angered by it. She is silent in the way she often is with choices ahead of her.

'Eadwig was shrived?' she asks, after a while.

'Yes,' says Botwine. 'I did it in the storeroom.'

'Alone?' asks the abbess.

'You doubt my word?' asks Botwine.

'I saw it,' I say, quickly, before the battle begins again. 'He had just finished when I went to see them both.'

I keep my eyes lowered, on the cuts on Eadwig's hands. We shall have to bandage those as well, cloth for wounds that have already stopped their bleeding.

'Very well,' says the abbess. 'Then, we will wash him and bury him in the orchard.' She raises her voice. 'Remember, this is what our priest has ordered. And we have no choice but to obey.'

If Botwine hears her bitterness, it makes little difference

to him. For as soon as the abbess agrees, all his anger fades and he returns to Eadwig. I think he will always be doing so, from today onwards, a long pilgrimage with nothing but sorrow at its end.

She glances at Botwine, his bent back and tender care. 'If you wish, I can ask one of the sisters to finish washing him for you.'

Her meaning is plain. It is woman's work, preparing the bodies. And if our priest acts as a woman, what of the flock that he tends?

'No,' says Botwine. 'I will do it.'

The abbess leaves, all the others with her. They do not wish to linger, I think. Only Ava stays. She beckons me away from Botwine, into the cold stone of the church. The last of the evening light shines through the single stained-glass window, above the altar. Christ on the cross, His blood made thick and dark by the sunset, pooling out over us.

'What now?' I ask her. 'Are you to tally up the cost of it all? Or would you like Eadwig's clothes off his back?'

'That will come later,' she says. 'I know people say I am unfeeling, but that is not true.'

'Well then, say what you must and be gone. We have work to do.'

'The abbess thinks of all of us,' she says. 'Without favour. You know this.'

'She will be glad for such a stout defender,' I say. 'But you know pets are forbidden in convents. If you keep barking, all will know how well she keeps you.'

It is unfair, I know, to chide her for this. I hope, sometimes, that cruelty will draw something from her. But she remains as steady as ever.

Mere

'I spoke for Eadwig,' she says, calmly, 'when you and I both know he was not shriven.'

'Do you doubt our priest?' I ask.

'No,' says Ava, without much feeling. She has always been so, as if by thinking herself apart from us all she will not be touched by our pain. 'I only wish for this house of ours to remain orderly, that is all. And if the abbess and the priest argue, that brings chaos. You have not seen it, Hilda, what men might do to each other.'

Here, her voice snags. She rarely speaks of her life before coming here, but I have heard snatches of it, in nightmares and sleeptalk. Her parents were merchants from far south across the sea, in Aragon. They travelled here, but a raid at some Kent port left only her and her uncle, stranded and desperate. Ava was always a cunning child and her uncle bartered her a place in a convent. So she has stayed here all the while, grateful for every day of safety and stability.

'Is that all?' I ask.

'Think upon it,' she says. 'Not all is battle, Hilda.'

She bows to me and then departs, her slate tally spinning as it hangs from her girdle.

I offer to help Botwine, but he waves me away. He would be alone and I would let him be so. A darkness is beginning to settle on him and I know that nothing I might do for now will help.

As I walk to the infirmary, I pass the orchard. We will all lie beneath the apple trees, in the end. Some of the graves have small wooden crosses marking them, others are left unmarked. Above, the knotted branches are bare. Only a few months until the buds and then the quickening and then the fruit and yet looking up at them I cannot think that such riches will ever come to us again. We were thankful for every mouthful and still we were not thankful enough.

A figure moves between each tree, waiting a while and then walking on. Wulfrun, still in her gleaming veil, her head bowed to the earth. I watch her, wondering what she can be searching for. I would not disturb her, for this is the first time that I have seen her without a crowd. She is different when she thinks none are watching her. Taller, somehow, as if she no longer has to force herself into the moulds that others make of her.

She only looks up a few footsteps away from me, her face bleak. I wait for her to shift, as I have seen her do so often, to become a seer or saint or even proud thegn's wife. But when she speaks, her voice is hopeless.

'Can you tell me,' she asks, 'which of these trees would grow best with Eadwig under it?'

We crouch together on the ruins of a tree felled by lightning a few years ago and she leans against me. I point at the trees that do not have plots yet, pick out some of the youngest ones, for I think Eadwig should be near something full of life. She listens carefully to my advice and does not weep.

'I thought we would save him,' she says. 'Do you think that is why? Was I too proud?'

I shake my head. 'He chose his fate, I think. He was scared of hurting others. That, and the devils in his thoughts. A pain about his head, he said. Too much all at once. I should have listened.'

'And done what?' asks Wulfrun.

'Sweet was telling me something,' I say. 'Before the fire

Mere

came. I should have pressed her harder and earlier. Or the abbess.'

'And the abbess should never have locked him away in the first place,' says Wulfrun, with venom. 'Cruel old sow. And to have Botwine beg for his boy's soul like that, she did it to shame him, I am sure. She has always hated that sin of his and now she is rid of it.'

'Ava told me that there was no cruelty in it,' I say.

'The portress?' asks Wulfrun. She frowns at me. 'I did not know you were friends.'

'We are not,' I say. With every day that passes, that girlhood foolishness seems further away and I will soon speak of Ava as I would a stranger. 'She is a little serpent who thinks I do not mark her poison.'

We are both silent. Above, a rook takes flight with heavy wings, searching for carrion in the grasses.

'You are hurt,' says Wulfrun, reaching over and taking my hand.

'It is nothing,' I say. 'Some burns about the fingers, that is all.'

She bows down and brushes her lips against every finger and then turns my hand so that she can trace my palm, with all its calluses and scars. It feels an age since I brought her that salve and I wonder if she still feels as she did.

As if in answer, Wulfrun leans towards me. I taste her breath against my own, the sour sweetness of her. The kiss is quick as a wingbeat and then we are apart.

'It is good,' she says, 'to know I have a friend here.'

The word is too small and yet it fills everything and, all of a sudden, it is too much. I pull my hands away from her.

'I am sorry,' says Wulfrun. 'I thought—'

'No,' I say. 'It is only—'

I do not know what to say. How to tell her that I cannot bear to see the bruises blooming on her wrist, the scar that is bright, still, on her face, that for all her strength and holy visions, she is still too easily broken.

Wulfrun's breath blooms in front of her. It is growing dark again, the cold winding about our fingers.

'I went to the fire early on,' she says. 'Helped with the buckets and the earth, until I could help no more. I knew it was over long before the others. I know flames, you see. And so I ran up to see the abbess to tell her that Eadwig was dead. Do you know what she did? She wept.'

There is real hatred in Wulfrun's voice. 'She wept, as if it were some terrible blow of fate and not one dealt by her own hand. I do not think this curse is finished with us yet, Hilda, and this abbess would see us all dead and then she would weep about it.'

'What must be done?' I ask. I know already, but I would hear her speak it.

'She must go,' says Wulfrun. 'And I will need friends to help me with it.'

She lifts her chin. It is less than two weeks since she first came knocking on Sweet's door, yet so much has changed already. Gone are any scraps of her old life in Gipeswic. But she still has that surety about her, that belief beyond faith. She will overturn this whole place, if needed.

'Tell me,' I say, heart quick. 'Were you not scared of the flames at the storeroom? With your burn?'

She shakes her head. 'They have done what they can to me,' she says. 'What remains of me cannot be touched.'

She is wrong in that, I think, but I believe it anyway and when I kiss her again I taste berry juice on her lips, salt on her neck.

Chapter 10

The first of our sisters flees, early the next morning. Leogifu, who takes with her a loaf of bread and a knife and our swiftest horse. Her flight is discovered by a kitchen girl no more than ten who weeps so much that she cannot get the words out.

Eadwig is buried beneath the apple trees. Many come to bid him farewell but still not as many as I had hoped. The abbess is not there, though Portress Ava attends. Father Botwine performs the mass and carries Eadwig, shrouded, and then when he is finished praying he walks past all of us and returns to his room in the pilgrims' house and does not leave unless we come to fetch him.

For a few days, the sky is bright and clear. A last gasp of summer, or spring coming early, it does not matter for it sets the marsh in confusion. Buds bloom that should have remained sheltered inwards, bees awaken that should have remained asleep. An early quickening and though some of the sisters praise it as a sign that the curse has been lifted with Eadwig's death, I know otherwise. A woman who gives birth too early loses the child and so it is with our winter, for the frost that comes down after those warm few days is all the heavier for being held at bay. Buds wither, bees fall in curls to the hard ground and all understand, then, that it is not over.

Common disasters follow.

Ava tallies what stores we have left, what has been kept in kitchens and spare corners, what is within our own infirmary and even what the abbess keeps in her own dwelling. She finishes her count on Saint Cecilia's day, that long-ago Roman martyr, she of song and sword-sheared necks. It is the same day that Wulfrun takes her vows to become a full sister of this place. She takes them far earlier than is usual, but such things are not unheard of, especially when a new sister comes with large donations as Wulfrun did.

The cantor has only just finished leading us in song, holy echoes ringing in our ears, when Ava stands and tells us solemnly that it will keep us through the winter, just. We will have to fish more and collect more herbs from the marsh around us and will be able to eat but once a day.

When half the geese perish of a flux over the next few days, she tallies that and tells us we still will eat through the winter, just, though we must begin to eat the roots from the reeds and whatever nettles have not yet died down to the ground.

When the swine do not return from their foraging in the marsh the next morning, she tallies that, too, and tells us we will eat through the winter, but must be without meals for some days.

When the goats' milk sours in their teats, the first day of advent, she marks it down on her slate. She talks no

Mere

longer of the winter and spends more time with the abbess, arguing for her to send a party out to walk to Gipeswic and ask for aid from her cousin, for he could not refuse fifty starving holy women. But the abbess tells us she cannot spare any souls though several are willing.

The abbess fears something deep in the mere, I know. But if Ava cannot get it out of her, I will not be able to. Nor will Sweet say anything, for when I catch her at the hives she only shakes her head and tells me that it is over now.

'It is not,' I say, gesturing about, at fields that grow emptier by the day. The overwintering wheat should be coming up in horse-haired heads and spreading green, but the few I can see are so pale they look grey and I do not think they will last the month. 'What was this ritual that was bound up with the curse? That the abbess stopped?'

'I have spoken of it once,' says Sweet, 'and our stores burnt, along with that poor boy.'

'There was no meaning in that,' I say. 'It was not you who caused it.'

Sweet does not answer, instead picking up pounded barley and mixing it in a bowl. She is using water now and a little honey. No oil and wine to feed the bees when it must go on our tables instead.

'You have grown thinner,' she says.

'We all have.'

'Not Wulfrun,' says Sweet, shades of both praise and envy in her voice. 'Still hearty in soul and body, that one.'

It is true, for Wulfrun came in broad and has stayed so. Another proof of her holiness that her face is still plump even as she starves with the rest of us.

'Here,' says Sweet, holding up one of the bee-cakes she

has been making. 'Not fit for a convent table, but it will fill your belly at least.'

'I am meant to be fasting,' I say. All of us in the three weeks till Christmas. Even so, I take it from her, hold it carefully so that it does not crumble in my fingers before I can eat it. If she thinks to bribe me to stop asking my questions of her, she is wrong.

'You would truly help me,' I say, 'if you told me more.'

'No,' says Sweet. Her face is bleak. 'It could help no one.'

'I have met seers before, of course,' I hear Tove say later that day in the infirmary. She has a crowd around her, young oblates who should be at their studies, patients who should be resting in bed. Together, they have been stringing the infirmary in holly and ivy, man and woman, the prick and the cling. Mistletoe, too, hung over doorways across the convent's holding. Blood-red berries, shielding us against evil. I even saw ceorls dragging up the yule log but this morning, a great trunk fed slowly into the fire in the refectory to smoulder every day until the year is new again.

'I saw it in Jorvik,' continues Tove. 'A holy woman who could tell your fate just by looking at you.'

It is Sext, around midday, and though the sun is high it is still cold enough in the convent that our breaths billow before us. With Leogifu gone, the kitchen has fallen into clatter-handed disorder. The bread was burnt from bottom to top and the meals for our patients grow ever more paltry, shrunken turnips and sour meat.

There have been lean years before. I have lived through my fair share of them, of days where even lifting myself out of bed left me dizzy and empty. Another week or so and we will be close to this.

Mere

'The thegn took her on as his seer,' says Tove. 'Promised to convert if she spoke true. But she failed to see a storm and he had her eyes put out.'

Tove looks up at me as she eats. 'What think you of this? Does Wulfrun speak true, do you think?'

If I did not know Tove well, I would suspect her of malice. But she has always been so. Testing and probing all about her, finding those few who she thinks worthy. She is too old to spend time with the meek. And if she asks so many questions of Wulfrun, it means she is considering her as an ally.

'You should talk to her yourself,' I say. 'Ask her for a vision.'

'My future contains but one thing,' says Tove.

'Even so,' I say. 'I will ask if she wishes to visit. Sit with you in prayer. For your ailing health and your soul.'

Tove turns to the children. 'And won't that be something to see, little ones? If she can save my soul, then she will truly be a saint.'

There is a sudden quiet. The word saint glimmers in the air and now there are none who will not be thinking of it. Wulfrun, cast in iron. Wulfrun, in shards of coloured glass and as a gilded icon. The scribes will use cinnabar for her lips, goldleaf for her brow.

Tove knows this. It is no slip of the tongue. Not long ago, her beads clacked as she prayed for Eadwig and herself, full of guilt for not restraining the abbess more. Today, I think she has found an answer.

I leave Tove to her audience, seek out Mildred. We are shorthanded and my helper is nearly as busy as me. But I find her at the doorway to the infirmary. She is smiling.

Danielle Giles

I approach with care. There has not been enough joy in Mildred's life, only duty, and it is good to see her laugh. Then, I see who she is talking to.

Alwin marks me first. He has not stepped foot in our infirmary since Eadwig was buried. Botwine is still not well enough to act as our priest and remains shut away in the pilgrims' house that beds him and his acolyte and so Alwin has taken on his duties and begins to be called Father. That he is still half a boy, that he could not tell you Matthew from Mark, matters not. He is the most learned man left to us.

At least this has meant, also, that his work as the abbess's spy has ended, for he is too burdened to listen under eaves or cast watchful eyes towards us. Though the reasons for it are evil, I do not think this new role is as poor for him as I would have thought. There is less of the hunt about him, his mind turning more often to what he might give as to what he might take.

Mildred has something in her hand, clutched to her breast. She tries to hide it but I am too quick and see the blue petals between her fingers. I do not know how long they have been talking, but a dozen souls might have already seen them.

'Alwin was asking,' says Mildred, gathering her lie together for me. 'Alwin was asking after the infirmary. He learnt much with us and wondered if we need help.'

'A sister has loose bowels and we must change her blankets,' I say.

Alwin nods. 'If that is what is needed,' he says, 'I can only serve.'

He grows more cunning, or perhaps simply more kind. Either way, he turns me into the sort of infirmarian who must make the priest help her wash the linens.

Mere

I wave my hand. 'Do not bother yourself, I will do it later. But surely, Brother Alwin, there is somewhere else you must be?'

'No,' he says, standing a little firmer. 'I came here to offer comfort to the ill. If I have your leave?'

How sure he is. He has no need to fear me, now that he acts as our priest.

'Of course,' I say. 'As you comforted Eadwig?'

'I was needed here,' says Alwin, 'as you know, for you sent Mildred out with me.'

There is a seed of shame there, somewhere, though I think that Alwin would rather die than admit fault. But he stayed away when Eadwig might have needed a friend, when Botwine, too, could have used his help.

'I am here now,' he says.

Mildred lowers her voice. 'He speaks truly,' she says. How softly she looks at him, how tangled they both are already. 'He prays for Eadwig whenever he can, I know.'

I think his prayers are not for the dead alone. But I only say, 'Small relief, that. Brother Alwin, you may tread wherever you will, as long as there is a need for you.'

I look again at Mildred's closed fist. A wilting cornflower, surely the last of the season left. He must have found it in some sun-warmed spot. 'And next time you come, don't forget to bring me a gift as well.'

Alwin does as he promises, flitting through the infirmary, offering prayer here and consolation there. If he feels any shame, it does not show on his face. At least Mildred has the good sense to hurry to some corner and hide the cornflower before any others see it. None would question her for owning it, for we soak cornflower in water and use it for fresh wounds. What betrays her is the care she shows. We are not used to seeing flowers kept whole.

I need air, a quiet place to think.

So, my feet heavy, I go to Eadwig's grave in the orchard, the earth marked by a wooden cross. There is a chill in the wind, winding up my sleeve and through the holes in my habit, as cunning as a snake. Perhaps this cold reaches further, perhaps it blows in Gipeswic, the wind permitted passage through the mere where we are not. Though, I think it is bound here and only here. Just as we now are.

I fall to my knees in front of the grave, clasp my hands together. A passer-by would see a sister at prayer, but my thoughts are empty. I simply watch as the grass and clover shivers.

'Sister Hilda?'

It is a man's voice. Father Botwine, come visiting. His face is pale and he is thinner than when I saw him last. But something burns in him. Alwin has taken most of his duties for now and none know what he does with his time in the pilgrims' house. I have heard talk that he pores over what books are left in the convent, searching for something.

I stand and brush the dirt from my habit. 'No,' he says, 'do not stop your prayers for me.'

'I have come to the end of them,' I say.

'I see,' he says. We stand a while, both in silence. I wait for him to speak, but his thoughts have drifted elsewhere and so I say, 'Have you found what you are looking for? In your books?'

'No,' he says, vaguely. 'Not yet.'

'If you tell me what it is you search for,' I say, 'I might be able to help.'

Perhaps, together, we might convince the abbess. Or even

Mere

Sweet; she holds priests no different from any others but I think her fond of Botwine. But our priest does not answer, instead takes out a knife and points to the small wooden post that marks Eadwig's grave.

'You might tell me what I might carve into that. Eadwig is a princely name, but I thought a crown would not be fit.'

'A name of riches and war,' I say. 'Perhaps an arm ring?'

'A gift won after a long battle,' he says. 'Yes, that is good.'

He sits down and begins to cut into the wood, shavings falling quick and pale as snow. He is a skilled craftsman, making his marks deliberately and with ease. Yet his breathing is heavy, and when he is finished his hand shakes.

'Fine work,' I say.

Botwine inspects it, not content. His hay-coloured hair is becoming unruly, but he has not cut it.

'I do not know,' he says, 'I do not know if he would like it. Do you think he would like it?'

'He was not familiar to me,' I say. 'I do not know what he liked.'

'I think he would like it,' says Father Botwine. 'He always did have love of gold and jewels, though they were far beyond his reach. Left him dazzled, his mother told me. When he was but four winters old, I showed him my bible. He thought the sun was shining from the page itself. I thought I would leave my duties then and there. Find some place, far away from any who knew us, raise him into a man. But I could not. I had already given myself to God.'

Botwine stops. A gull cries. It scythes through the clouds, leaving behind a harvest of nothing but empty air.

'You have not confessed since I arrived, child,' he says,

suddenly. 'You said you could go, after we found Eadwig. Well, we have found him. You must go to Alwin, make penitence.'

I would rather cut out my own tongue than seek Alwin's forgiveness. But I only say, 'I have been busy. I shall come when I am next able.'

'It is important that we repent while we can,' he says. 'For we do not always know when the choice might be taken from us.'

He is speaking not only of Eadwig, but of Sybba. The terrible crush of him, his last gasps of penitence.

'I know you spoke with Eluned,' I say, carefully. 'That you took her confession.'

'I did,' he says, eyes still on Eadwig's grave-marker. 'I cannot tell you of it, though.'

'I know,' I say. 'She believes it was the curse that took Sybba.'

'Yes,' says Botwine. 'A kindness, to tell her that. Sybba was not a good master, it seems. If she had come to me, I would have helped her.'

A small rebuke, but it is enough. I have always enjoyed Botwine's visits, his gentle wisdom. I remember running to him as a child, asking him for tales of distant lands and cruel kings and brave Christian martyrs. But he is wary of me now.

'I know,' I say. 'I did not think, I did not think it would truly harm Sybba.'

'Then you are a fool,' says Botwine, coldly. 'You are not some mere novice, with no power. You hold lives and deaths, Hilda, as much as I do, and if you treat them lightly, you invite only ruin.'

'I know,' I say. 'It is only—'

Mere

I do not know what to say, for I do not think Eluned wrong in defending herself, or myself wrong in aiding her.

'I am tired,' Botwine says, rubbing his face. 'I would be alone.'

I nod and stand. Our priest remains bent, intent on finishing his carving of Eadwig's arm ring.

'I keep Eadwig in my prayers,' I say, but I do not think he hears me.

The next week passes in quiet, if not ease. Our twice-halved meals begin to take more flesh from the sisters and there are more coughs and shivers than I would like. More souls come to me with vague ailments that they are sure will be cured by warm meat and soft beds. I share what I can but with every day I have less to give. When I sleep at last, I dream only of a great maw, full of mere-rot and teeth.

Wulfrun is dutiful in every task she is given, no matter how dull or foul-smelling or shameful. Her arm heals well, another trace of Eadwig that is fading along with the rest of him, but she keeps a bandage on it anyway, so that none will forget her pain, or his fate. The lower the abbess casts her, the more take note of her humility and grace.

Even so, it is a test for her. She comes to my storeroom late one evening after Compline, as all the sisters prepare to go to their beds, dirt beneath her fingernails and wrath on her tongue. I myself am already beneath the blanket in the small bed we keep there, but sit up as she enters, pulling my blankets around me. I am in nothing but my shift, my head bare. The first time Wulfrun has seen me like this, though she shows no sign of it.

'I can bear it no longer,' she says. 'She has me herding the goats.'

'So I can smell,' I say.

Even so, I am glad to see her, glad that she comes to me with her little rages, which she shows to no other. Ever since our kiss in the orchard, she finds some reason or another to visit me. Until today, though, it has always been in daylight.

'Do you have anything that might help?' asks Wulfrun, sitting down beside me on the straw. She removes her wimple, so that now we have both of our heads uncovered. Her hair is dark, freshly cropped when she came here.

'With goat-stench?' I say. 'It is not in my leechbooks.'

'No,' says Wulfrun, tartly. 'Because there is no cure for it.'

'It is not so bad,' I say. 'You must only change your shift, I am sure.' I mean it elsewhere, but she watches me and then, slowly, lifts it over her head, taking care to tilt her injured arm. Meets my gaze again, daring as any I have seen. As if she was born to this, as if it was as set as saints in stone.

I cannot move with the wonder of it and in this she reads shame and in it she reads sin. Her arms cross over her bare breasts, her chin tilting downwards.

I lean forward, first kiss the fine hairs at the nape of her neck and then the hard bones of her shoulders and the gentle flesh of her belly. Her breath snares, her body held tense. We are unsure, this first time, afraid that we will be seen, or heard, as if this sin could echo across the miles like a pealing bell. But when I slide my face between her thighs and taste her sour-sweet cunt, I feel as if I would not care if they heard us all the way in Gipeswic.

After that she visits more at night and each time bolder. Presses her own tongue between my legs, wipes her chin, her mouth and then slides her fingers deep inside me. I show her, wrapped in a cloth and hidden behind a box of dried lavender in the storeroom, a member stitched from leather that a passing pilgrim once taught me how to make, for he had come to be cured of his lusts by our relics and knew that he would be shrived of the sin the next day. Sodomy, that I even own such a thing, and I find myself flushing as I unwrap it. I tell her that we do not have to use it, that it is only a passing lust.

'A shame,' she says. 'For I would think you a fine husband with it. And I an even better one.'

So we spend our evenings together, in heat and slickness. There is a new boldness between us that is without limits, a loosed arrow when neither of us is yet certain of our target.

We wake each morning wrapped about the other and each morning the abbess continues to tell us that we must only remain and hold the faith and each morning Botwine does not come to take the holy office but stays, instead, in his rooms.

We are at Vespers, two weeks before Christmas, when the abbess tells us all how we will be saved. The winter has crossed our threshold now, set its feet on the table and demanded ale and beautiful maids. Many of us have cloaks, even in church, and the youngest and oldest and most ill among us wear two pairs of hose beneath their habits, so that when they walk it is thickly. Our cheeks are pink, our bellies empty, our prayers either dull or too shrill. But Botwine is here to lead the service, the first time he has done so since Eadwig's death, and this sets us all glancing at each other. The abbess must have asked him to come, though we do not know why.

It is only at the end of the service that she calls out, asks us to wait a while. She wears as many of her jewels as she can today, and about her head, as always, is the ruby circlet. I would tear it from her head and grind it into the ground if I could.

'Will all sisters of high positions step forward?'

One by one, we obey. So few of us left, so few. Portress Ava is the first, proud and precise. Then myself and the new cellarer, who is still but a girl. The cantor, a quiet woman who wishes to be left to her hymns and scriptures and has no desire for anything beyond that. The novice mistress, last, who in truth has grown too old for her duties, but cannot find another able or willing to take on the position. We are too small for an almoner or sacrist and while we once had a guest mistress, to allow for the hospitality for pilgrims, she died several years ago and we have not had enough pilgrims coming to appoint another in her place.

And behind us Wulfrun, who does not make herself known. She has no position yet.

So it is us five, facing the abbess and Alwin. Together we are the heave and the drop, the seed and the harvest, the prayer and its answer. I feel fondness for them all, even Ava. We have spent a lifetime in service of this convent, writ in our lined faces and greyed hairs and roughened hands. The abbess cannot mean to sweep us aside, for without us the convent would not hold a week.

'So few,' says the abbess. Her face shifts and I see in it a sudden abyss. Such emptiness she sees in us. So little in our futures. How it must pluck at her in her bed, in her waking thoughts. How she must hate the task of leading us through it all. Then, she blinks and the void is gone.

Mere

'I speak to you five as paragons of this convent. Those below you follow your example, just as you look to me for guidance in turn.'

She bows her head. If Wulfrun believed herself the only one able to command the sisters, she was wrong. The abbess has us wrapped tight as yarn on a spindle. 'I have failed you all,' she says.

Quiet. I want to look back to Wulfrun, to see her fear or calm or joy. But instead I must watch the abbess. She is a harpist at the beginning of her song, seeing where the first notes settle before continuing.

'I have not been the shepherd to you all. I have been lax and there has been sin. I know you feel it. This convent was sliding to ruin before this curse was laid upon us.'

A few sisters turn back, to the half-finished second church, the foundations built in hope and abandoned a year later. We can see it, always, from the doorway, a ruined shadow, three-score stones that tell us that we were never fated for glory.

The abbess continues on. 'So how might we make this right?' she asks. 'Is it through flight, through abandoning our holy mission? Is it through fighting among us, scraping for power?'

She shakes her head. 'No,' she says. 'It is through repentance, through the rejection of the Devil and his works. If we are strong and pious, we will survive this winter and defeat this demon that afflicts us all.'

Beside her, Alwin nods. He is not the only one. I hear murmurs of approval, rustling sleeves as the sisters sign skittish agreement to each other, the hand-language we use at refectory and church.

'There are wolves stalking us, my children. Wolves that

cause us fear, make us doubt the true way. They talk of burning houses, but do not give us water. I encourage you, sisters, to ignore these words and focus only on obedience of our Lord.'

It is a strange thing for fifty gazes to collect all at once. It turns the floors uneven, the walls slant. It pulls in the roof close so that there is only one sister beneath it and that sister is Wulfrun.

There is fury in her face.

'And so,' says the abbess, 'from tomorrow, myself and Brother Alwin will be inspecting each part of this convent to ensure that we are all following the path. Do not worry, for many of you will have nothing to fear. I mean only to discover the source of the sin that has brought this curse down upon us and free us all.'

It is nothing but it is enough. Hope, knotting through us all. Even I think, briefly, how wonderful it would be if she was right. If we must only continue on as we are and wait to be saved. A vision, of a sort. Our past will be our future and all will be well.

I wonder that Alwin allies with her, even as he seeks out Mildred in my infirmary to give her cornflowers. But if he is at the abbess's side, perhaps he hopes to avoid scrutiny himself. The abbess for her part watches this new ally of hers as a farmer does a bull. Glad for the strength, but wary of the horns.

Then, almost as an afterthought, she says, 'And we shall be reburying Eadwig by the crossroads, a stake in his heart, so that we know he will not rise again. Then, tomorrow, we shall feast to mark this new age.'

A great cheer comes up. Botwine stands, shouts, his voice deep and strong and full of outrage and none heed him

Mere

and I understand now the mistake Botwine has made. He fought for Eadwig, fought for Eadwig so hard, and he has fought for none of us.

Botwine looks around, hopelessly. But he has no friends here, not any more.

'Take him, then,' he says. 'Rebury him and be damned.'

Chapter 11

The next day is cold, rain falling grey and steady. Poor weather for grave-digging, but the work is done quickly and Eadwig carried to his new place at the crossroads. I watch from the infirmary eaves, see Alwin crossing from the orchard with the grave-marker in his hand. I think he means to throw it on some midden but instead he takes it to the pilgrims' house where he and Botwine are staying. He does not fully belong to the abbess yet, then.

The day is a silent one. There is not a sound that we have not placed here, from the dulled fall of the axe to the simmer of charcoal beneath peat, the songs of women spinning thread and the jokes of men setting eel traps and digging ditches. But there is nothing beyond that. An emptiness that we cannot fill, not even with the loudest industry.

I stare beyond the crossroads, past the dwellings, the trees and scrub and fields, to the marsh. I think of mossed rocks laid out like slumbering dreamers, springs so deep there is no end to them. Sometimes, I feel as if I can taste an answer.

*

Mere

The next week passes in quiet. We hear no more of the abbess's inspection, though Ava and Alwin talk in dark corners and share heavy looks during the holy offices. And so it is but less than a week until Christmas when I return to the infirmary and find Wulfrun there, sitting at Tove's bedside with a basket of bread in her hand. She is breaking it out and giving it to whomever puts out their hand: fellow sisters, women, children. White bread, too, the finest that the bakery has to offer. To be served at the high table, not handed out to any who ask for it. The rest of the convent eat only brown rye.

They thank her as if she has baked the bread herself. And, in turn, she whispers in their ear. I know already what it will be. Talk that the abbess has lost her sense, that we should flee to Gipeswic now before we grow too weak. No grand vision but full bellies make open ears.

She stands between the two pallets on which Tove and Eluned rest. All three greet me as I enter. Eluned has recovered quickly from her burns the night of the storeroom fire and might return to light labour if she wished, but she has lingered here instead and I am happy to let her. She has already made friends among the patients and if Sybba's brothers come to argue, they will find it hard to drag her away before she is completely well. Mildred, for one, would cling to her like a weed, for my helper sees in Eluned the shadow of the half-dozen older sisters she left behind to come to this convent.

'I am not hungry,' I say, as Wulfrun lifts a crust in offering. Ever since Eadwig was reburied, I have felt a sourness in my guts that does not allow me more than a few mouthfuls at a time.

Eluned snorts and holds out her own hands. 'I will have

it, then,' she says, in a half-whisper for her throat still pains her and she coughs up black and grey every day still. 'I did not know the convent sisters had full enough bellies to refuse food.'

'She speaks true,' adds Tove, as Wulfrun passes Eluned the bread. 'You should have some.'

I watch Eluned eat it steadily, for even softened in beer it is dry enough to pain her throat. Tove is right. None of us are in the position to refuse food.

Tove has her blankets wrapped around her against the weak fire. Over the years she and others have embroidered them, sewed patches of colour onto whatever space they can find in the material. In winter, she hides herself in their folds like a treasure in a reliquary.

I envy Tove this scrap of beauty. Even as we all starve and scrimp, she finds a way to make herself gleam.

'Where has this come from?' I say, turning from Tove to the bread that Wulfrun holds in her hand.

'I was in the bakery,' she says, 'and saw that they were keeping white flour over, for Christmas and Easter. For the high table only. And I said, take a portion of that, whatever would be my provision, and I shall have rye until next Christmas.'

'A bet,' I say. 'How many loaves did they give you?'

'Three,' she says. 'Three, for the year.'

A good trade for her, if she dies soon or we are relieved by our abbess's cousin. A shrewd trade for the bakers, if Wulfrun survives the year.

'I have said I shall make the same trade,' says Tove, 'next week.'

They are both glowing with the light of their own charity. Bringing glad tidings, filling hungry mouths. It will not

Mere

last, but people will remember their goodness when the abbess reduces our meals further.

They have also bet against themselves, against long lives. Tove, who I have known my whole life. And Wulfrun, who called me friend and yet offers herself up so easily.

'I must go,' I say, pulling away. 'Thank you for your charity.'

Tove pushes herself upwards, to follow me though she knows she will not be able to catch me. But Wulfrun places a hand on her shoulder, whispers something.

And so it is she who follows me across the infirmary, to our storeroom. I push the hanging cloth aside and press myself in. To comfort, to safety. A room where I have sorted everything into its rightful place, including myself. I can see the mattress stuffed with straw and bog-cotton in the corner, where only this morning Wulfrun and I woke together. She has been coming less, since the abbess's announcement, but still we find our time together where we can.

I lean down to the bottom shelf. Where we keep all the bitterest herbs, the remedies that turn sour in the mouth. I hear Wulfrun enter behind me, basket of bread still in her hand.

'Thank you for coming to speak with me,' I say, 'but I am well.'

'I thought you wished to be friends?' she says.

'Not wished,' I say. 'That is what we are.'

'Then, eat. You should be strong.'

She reaches into her basket, pulls out a rough-hewn slice of bread and presses it into my hand. And though I do not like where it has come from, it is good to bite into something that has not been left by another. I have lived on scraps for so long.

'And you?' I ask between mouthfuls. 'What will you give away next? At this rate, you will starve before any of us.'

'I am not worried,' she says. 'I will be abbess long before I grow hungry.'

I laugh. She asks for the impossible and I think she will be given it. Wulfrun frowns at me.

'Do you doubt me?' she asks.

'No,' I say, 'you are only unlike any I have known before. I feel as if I am speaking with a king.'

'If I were king,' she says, lifting my hand to hers, 'you would be my thegn, my warrior. Always at my side.'

I kiss her then, fierce and strong. There is only the warmth of her against me, her breath in my ear, the glorious flesh and folds of her belly. Her hand on my waist, pushing up my skirts. Her fingers between my legs and I cling as flame to wood, and she smirks, pinches the flesh of my stomach, digs her nails into my hips. A little pain and I might faint with the joy of it.

Then, there are footsteps outside. Half a dozen of them, arriving all at once. Low-talking, serious and holy.

Wulfrun bites her lip as she watches me pull my skirts back down. I am as wet as I have ever been and I feel the deep ache of pleasure denied.

'Our inspection,' I say. 'It begins.'

'The abbess does always know when she might catch me at my worst.' There is a smile on her face, despite it all, and I smile also.

We both stand. Just as I go to pull the cloth aside, Wulfrun leans over, kisses me. Foolish, when we are so close to danger, but I soften into her.

'Strength,' she murmurs, 'for both of us.'

Mere

And we part and walk out to meet the abbess. I feel as if I could topple an oak.

The crowd is much as I had expected. The abbess, Ava and Alwin beside her. Five or six others. Some will be there out of loyalty but others, I think, follow the abbess only out of habit. As a sheep chooses the same path day after day, so they choose her.

'Welcome,' I say. 'Are we to be inspected? As you can see, the infirmary is crowded.'

The abbess surveys all of us. Half with white bread in hand, with full bellies and smiling faces. The warmest room in the convent, not because of the fire but because of the people. In the light, the gold of her circlet looks instead like hay, thin and brittle, the ruby itself nothing more than the hue of soft poppies.

'That I see,' she says. 'Do these women not have other places to be? In the fields? Cooking, spinning?'

It is an order. One that would normally be obeyed without hesitation. But today, only half of the women and children leave and even then they do so slowly.

Wulfrun stands, her shoulders firm, her face turned upwards, and she looks half a saint already, surrounded by illness and hunger, and shining still.

She lifts her basket to the abbess. 'Greetings, Mother Superior,' she says. 'Would you like some bread?'

Ava pales at the insult, but the abbess only shakes her head.

'I am not hungry, thank you,' she says. 'But it is good to see such charity.'

'Inspired by your example, of course,' says Wulfrun. 'In welcoming me so warmly.'

'And I am sure that you did not know how it takes them

all from their rightful work,' adds Ava. She has her tally with her today.

Wulfrun glances at Ava, briefly. She does not let herself linger or consider Ava's words in depth. She treats Ava as if she was a servant of her household, not the second highest-placed woman in this convent.

'I am glad that you consider such things for us all,' she says.

'When none other seem to,' says Ava, 'I must. But I am glad to serve my sisters so.'

'Enough,' says Alwin. He has been itching this time, as if he has trained his bow on a doe but must wait to loose the arrow. 'We are here to talk about your visions, Sister Wulfrun. Their source.'

The abbess's face shows anger, but only briefly. Alwin is too blunt a tool for today. She needs a needle but has only an axe.

'I am always free to talk of matters of God,' says Wulfrun.

'It is not of God that we speak,' says Alwin, darkly. He feigns that he is touched by none of it: not Eadwig's fate, nor Botwine's abandonment. But it is clear to any that there is a storm within him.

'Do you deny, sister, that the curse came upon him after your arrival?'

'We arrived in a party of nearly a dozen,' says Wulfrun, smoothly. 'I am sure you remember, for both you and the abbess were with us.'

Alwin reddens. He has practised these questions, I think. A call and response, in which he would always be righteous and Wulfrun would beg. But now there are nearly thirty souls watching this.

'We are talking only of you,' he says. 'And do you

deny that you claim visions, the source of which is unknown?'

'My visions are holy,' says Wulfrun.

'But you do not know their source?'

'You have eaten goose before, yes? Before you took holy orders?'

Alwin frowns. 'Of course.'

'And how did you know it was gooseflesh and not, say, crow? Did you see the goose slaughtered yourself? Butchered and plucked and cooked?'

'No,' says Alwin. 'But I know the taste.'

'As you know the taste of gooseflesh,' she says, 'so I know the touch of the divine.'

Wulfrun looks about her, watches each of the women. Then, when she is sure of their smiles, she says, 'Though, the cook in my old house was a talented woman. Perhaps all this time I have been feasting on crow.'

Gentle laughter. An escape. If Alwin wants, he could leave now. He looks to be considering it.

And then, the abbess speaks.

'Do you deny,' she says, softly, 'that you cast a charm on Eadwig? That this charm awoke a beast inside him and injured yourself and Father Botwine? That as a result, he burnt our winter supplies and murdered himself?'

I expect another cunning answer, a deft-woven joke. But Wulfrun is silent. We are all waiting for her but she will not speak a word in her own defence.

The abbess's face is calm. She thinks she has won. She has believed it from the beginning and I feel the anger returning. I will not let Wulfrun be blamed for only trying to help.

'It was you who ordered him to the storeroom, Mother

Superior,' I say. 'It was you who threatened to excommunicate him, drove him to his death.'

'I am not talking to you, Infirmarian,' she replies.

'No,' I say. 'Of course not. You call on me when you need me and leave me by the side when you are done. Well, the Ealdorman has stopped his payments for me now. Perhaps he has found that he is done with you as well.'

I have gone too far, but if I meant to hurt the abbess, it has worked. Instead of her fury there is that sudden empty look.

So it is Ava who takes her arm, who turns to me and says, 'Speak carefully, Hilda.'

'Or she will punish me?' I say. 'Will she shackle me like Eadwig? Bury me at the crossroads with a stake in my heart and deny me heaven?'

Ava shakes her head. 'This is not you, Sister Hilda. What evil drives you to speak so?'

'Not evil,' I say. Wulfrun stands so close to me. I might almost reach out and touch her. Grasp her fingers in mine, twine ourselves so we would never be untangled again. It is potent, this courage, addles me as nothing else has done before.

'Spare me all this clucking,' says Alwin, raising his voice. 'We have not yet finished questioning Sister Wulfrun. Have you an answer for the abbess?'

'I do,' says Wulfrun, quietly.

'And?'

I wait for it. The answer to absolve her, to turn the abbess's question against her. My glorious, shining Wulfrun, victorious once more.

Mere

'I cast the charm,' says Wulfrun. 'A Christian charm, one performed elsewhere by priests that I have seen. It did not work and I will be punished for it.'

This time, the room is filled with a quiet I have never heard before. Even though we live in silence, there is always noise. The rustling of habits, a cough or a sigh. The sounds of life.

But at Wulfrun's confession, nobody moves. Nobody breathes.

The abbess, still pale, still quiet, gives a quick nod. 'You admit it,' she says, weakly.

'I do,' says Wulfrun. 'I know the penance, too. Two dozen blows, is that not right?'

'The penitential speaks of a dozen,' begins Alwin, but the abbess shakes her head.

'Two dozen, on Christmas Eve,' she says. 'It is agreed.'

We are less than a week from Christmas now, when the year turns and the nights are at their darkest. She wishes to end Wulfrun before the start of this new year. All the bravery, all the strength I felt before is gone. I look around. Surely Tove or Mildred will speak out, surely someone will come to Wulfrun's aid, but they too are silent, as if struck dumb by a blow and it is me who is standing beside her, me who must stop her.

'You cannot,' I say, stumbling forward. 'It will break her.'

'Ah, Sister Hilda,' says the abbess. 'Now that you have found this voice of yours, how quickly you raise it.'

'She will die,' I say, looking at Wulfrun. How does she not understand? We are all weak enough as it is, living as we do in cold rooms with shrinking meals. However strong she believes herself, it will not be enough.

'And,' says the abbess, turning to Ava, 'three blows for Sister Hilda for her loose tongue.'

But I cannot care too much. I can only see Wulfrun. Her face, so beautiful and so strange and full of joy, as if she has won.

Chapter 12

'Before dawn tomorrow,' I say, 'drink this.'

Wulfrun looks at the potion I have prepared for her. A clay jar of poppy seed and willow bark brew, made with the strongest wine I could find.

I have taken her aside, beneath the infirmary eaves at the back of the building so that we will not be seen. I did not wish to speak, even in the storeroom, for even there we would be found by one sister or another. A few days have passed since the abbess's judgement and the entire time Wulfrun has been pressed on all sides. Some souls come in outrage, others in fear. Still more come to see her, I think, to touch her on the hand before she is gone. They think her already a martyr. A dead woman who still yet lives, if only for a day.

And she speaks to each of them. She gives a little part of herself away and she does not care what will be left for her. For me.

Now, at least, we are alone. The morning fog has settled, clotted. It trails behind us in wisps, turns the familiar strange. A shape in the mists might be a tree or an elf or a man. I cannot even see the boundary of the marsh any more but I know it to be there. The wanting mere-water, a thousand different damp mouths and, somewhere deeper than I have ever gone, the sharpness of teeth.

Today is cold. A chill hand on the back of our necks, a chill rope around our ankles and wrists that sets us both shivering.

'What will it do?' she asks.

'Dull the senses,' I say. 'Take the pain. If fate favours you, it will help you survive.'

'I do not need it,' she says. 'I must feel every blow.'

'You do not know what it is like. After three, we plead to be released. You must be taken out of your senses or else they will betray you. Do you wish to beg in front of the abbess?'

'That is her game, I think,' says Wulfrun. 'She wishes me to beg. Only then will she show mercy.'

'So take this,' I say. 'You will feel the blows but it will be as if it hurts another person.'

She looks at my offering.

'And where is yours?' she asks.

'Mine is the lesser punishment,' I say. 'I can take it. And we do not have much poppy seed left.'

'So you might live through it and I will not?' asks Wulfrun.

'Please,' I say. 'For my sake.'

She reaches out and takes the bottle. 'We will share it. I will take the greater part, but you will drink also. I do not want its full power, anyway, for I must look alert.'

'Have you ever been whipped before?'

'Not whipped,' she says, slowly. 'But my husband was not a kind man. A gentle thegn will not live long.'

Mere

The scar on her face is proof enough but I would have guessed even without it. The widows who come here, the cast-aside women, they tell me of this. Of heavy fists and bruised skin and night after night of lying in bed, hoping that it would hurt less this time.

'I know the other sisters say that it was because of my pride,' says Wulfrun. 'But it is not so. My husband was too loose with his men.' She speaks coldly, as of another. 'A girl or two might be taken, such things must be borne. But every month there was a new father coming asking for gold for another daughter ruined or murdered. It wearied me and so I asked him to punish the worst of them. He refused and so I took a knife to his best horse.'

She smiles, then. A bitter, beautiful thing. 'I was punished, of course. And it was as I lay in bed, burns across my face and half-dead, that all was revealed. The first of my visions. So, the first day I was able to walk again, I went in front of him and all his warriors to beg for his forgiveness. And as he held out his ring for me to kiss it, I gave him his vision.'

'What did you see?' I ask.

'I think you will answer it quicker than he did,' says Wulfrun. 'For he was not a cunning man and I do not think he had read that gilded bible of his even once. *I cannot lift even a sword, yet I have the strength of God in my fist. I sleep beside a lion-slayer and yet he is now the weaker. My knife cuts through hair and holy vows both.*'

'Delilah,' I say and she nods.

'A woman might undo even the strongest of men. I meant it as a warning, but the first fit took him the next day. He lived for a few years after that. But the fits, they grew stronger and stronger. He lost the use of his arm first, then his leg, until he could not leave his bed and called out to me, so piteous, so sweet.' She shakes her head. 'My son had no trust in me, after that. He always thought I had put a curse on his father, whom he loved greatly.'

I have not often heard her speak of her son. Whenever she does, her words slow, as if she must pick them very carefully.

'So,' she says. 'I know what I can bear. You do not have to worry for me.'

'No,' I say. 'It sounds as if it is the others I should worry for.'

She laughs and it is as if there is a candle between us, a shared light and warmth, and I am pressed up against her, for if we are to be punished tomorrow I might as well sin today.

Then, a shout. A woman's voice, in full throat. Scolding some man, loud and heedless. Him starting his words but finding them cut off each time. They are coming around the corner and we pull apart, flushed and ruffled, our wimples askew, our lips reddened with each other.

The voices grow louder. They are almost in sight now and Wulfrun and I bend to our knees, feign to be searching the ground for herbs.

'For all my hatred of my husband,' she whispers, half in praise, 'I think I never scolded him so. What a shrew she is. And him, not yet a word.'

'The most loving maids are the worst scolds,' I say. 'Anger is not the opposite of love.'

'Well, I shall have to look out for your tongue, then,' she says.

'If we grow old enough,' I say, 'I shall lash you with it every day. You may count upon that.'

Mere

She smiles, but unsure. It is because I have spoken of the future.

The two turn the corner. I thought it would be some ceorl and his wife, but it is Mildred who comes walking up, Alwin trailing behind her. He has a look of suffering that the most tortured martyr would admire.

Neither of them sees us, hidden in the shadows beneath the eaves. Like many a youth and maid in love, their world is but an armspan long, the breadth of the distance between them.

'As I have told you over and again,' he says. 'With Botwine shut away I must obey the abbess. Or else she will start asking questions of me and of you. You understand this, surely?'

'I understand that you would sacrifice Infirmarian Hilda and Sister Wulfrun for our safety,' says Mildred, hotly. I have never seen her so stirred. It seems a quarrel that they have had more than once already in the week since Abbess Sigeburg's visit to the infirmary. I wonder that they have found quiet corners and dark eaves enough for such battles.

'You cannot deny that Hilda has been baiting the abbess lately,' says Alwin. 'She walks around proud as a king's wife. And,' he draws his hand about her waist, 'if she is abed after the whipping, might you not take her place?'

My heart is fast. I watch Mildred think on it.

Then, she shakes her head. 'I am skilled enough,' she says, 'but Hilda would haunt me once in life and twice in death. If you think her scolding is bad now, it would be doubly worse if I betrayed her. She'd pull open the gates of hell and claw me down with her, I am sure. I would not pay that price.'

It is a foul thing to say, but there is a spark of pride

within me. Beside me, I hear Wulfrun holding in her laughter.

Then, Mildred pulls free of Alwin. 'And what of Wulfrun? The kitchen sisters told me I might bet on her surviving. Said she would give me good odds. They all think she will die and they delight in it. You seem as if you do, too.'

'She is a strange woman,' says Alwin. 'I do not know what she has invited in.'

I look at Wulfrun. She has her head down and I cannot see her face.

I cough.

Few creatures, man or beast, move as quickly as Mildred does when she realizes that she has been overheard. She startles, pushing free of Alwin and pulling her wimple close.

'I did not see you,' she stammers. 'How long—'

'I do not know,' I say. 'Would you place a bet on it?'

Alwin looks to us both. We have tales of shapeshifters, of beastmen who are a wolf one moment and a ceorl the next. I think Alwin moves between two states of man instead. With Mildred, he is a youth in love, a fool and a hero all at once. Now, I watch him change his skin, lift his shoulders and grow serious again. He is our priest and not to be argued with.

I know which of these men feels most joy.

'What are you doing out here?' he asks, as if it is us caught in wrongdoing and not him.

'Collecting what we can,' I say. 'Seeking weeds, those that will grow. It flavours the pottage.'

'And are the both of you needed?' he asks.

He looks between us, understanding at last. Perhaps the last in the infirmary to know, saving maybe the abbess. I see the rebuke readying on his lips. There is scripture enough to damn us, I am sure. Though, there is scripture enough to damn anything.'

'Wulfrun thought the air might help her,' I say. 'Prepare her for her trial tomorrow. You would not deny her this, surely, Father?'

'And we see you have been taking the air also,' adds Wulfrun, slyly.

The priest fades and he is a youth again, turning to Mildred, as if she might have the answer for them both.

'I must go,' he says. 'I have been detained here long enough and I have my duties.'

'Yes,' says Wulfrun, 'I am sure the abbess misses you at her heel.'

Alwin narrows his eyes. 'She still wishes to hear of wrongdoing, of any kind.'

My heart quickens. Wulfrun thinks herself beyond harm, but I do not.

'Go,' says Wulfrun, 'tell the abbess if you wish. We would not stop you.'

'The punishment—' he begins. Then Mildred places her hand on his arm, shakes her head.

'Tomorrow is enough,' she says. 'I do not have the stomach for more whippings.'

Alwin sighs. 'You are lucky,' he says to us, 'that you have an ally in Mildred.'

'I have always believed so,' I say.

Mildred smiles at me, shyly. A woman now, with all a woman's ways.

And if she is caught, she will suffer a woman's punishment. That adulterer, all those years ago, her nose taken from her face and a great wound left in its place. And she was only a ceorl. How much worse for the two standing before me, who are both under vows of chastity. They will rip her apart as hounds would a doe.

'I know that my guidance is as wind against stone to you,' I say. 'But I would have you follow me in this. Neither of you must let the abbess know that you are lovers.'

'We were but speaking—' begins Alwin, but I raise my hand.

'The sisters here will not see that and you know this. I say only, whatever sin you commit, do it quietly. Or else, we will all suffer, you understand?'

Alwin looks as if he has tasted sourness in his beer.

'And you have much knowledge of this sinning, then, Infirmarian, to give orders as you do?'

'No,' I say. 'But I have known the abbess my entire life. She will not spare you. No matter your birth, no matter any previous service you have done her.'

I think of tomorrow. Of pain, given and shared as bread at our table. Of the abbess's hand, placed on my back as a child, guiding me from my mother to the promised safety and riches on the convent's shining hill.

'No matter any love she once bore for you,' I say.

When Alwin is gone, I pull Mildred to me. Wulfrun, understanding, gives a quick nod and returns to the infirmary, to the throngs of sisters who wish to see her. Mildred, for her part, stands straight-backed and tight-shouldered. The shadows beneath the eaves give her face more hollows and edges, the last maidly softness gone. Her hands go to her girdle, her wimple, anything she can clasp at.

'It was you bade me help him,' she says, a defiance I have never known stirring in her.

Mere

'In the infirmary only,' I say. 'You do not spend other time together? Outside of your duties.'

Mildred's face is empty of any guilt and so I say, 'At night, perhaps?'

Her jaw twitches.

'No,' she says. 'No, I would not, I do not . . .'

'Don't worry,' I say, 'I will not report anything to the abbess. I would not see you hurt, for one thing. And for another, you are far too skilled.'

Even amidst her unruliness, she smiles at that. 'Too skilled?' she says. 'You truly think that?'

'But skill or not,' I say, 'I will not be able to protect you if you are discovered.'

'I do not know what would be discovered,' she says, quickly.

'Well,' I say. 'If I were to warn you, I would say that we women might stir lusts in men by our very temperament. You do not need me to tell you the consequences of such a sin. I would say bide your time and do not act, no matter how honeyed the words.'

Mildred nods. 'I understand,' she says. 'But I promise you, sister, that neither of us has committed any sin.' Her brown eyes are large and imploring. How young she is.

'Then,' I say, 'in that case, all is well.'

We begin to walk back to the infirmary, side by side, keeping close to the walls for warmth. The wind has grown stronger, blown in from the coast. We are half-flayed by gusts from a sea that neither of us has ever seen.

'I would say,' I say, beneath the wind, 'that if any girl were foolish enough to let herself get with child, she might come to me for aid. The child would die in the belly and if it is buried quietly and quickly enough, none might ever learn of it.'

'It is good,' says Mildred, 'that none of the sisters I know are so foolish.'

'Well,' I say, 'that is because they probably know of how a man may spill his seed onto the floor, or onto a belly, so that he does not get a child on a woman.' I do not tell her that I know this from my own maidhood, from worldly pilgrims who came and taught me much.

'Of course,' I say, 'this is a sin and would be sodomy. Truly, a wicked deed, worthy of at least seven years' penance.'

Mildred is a deep red now. 'I have heard all this already,' she says, 'I do not need you to tell me.

'Good,' I say.

We continue to walk ahead. I have a dozen questions for her, half of which I cannot ask, and so before we grow too close to the infirmary, I say, 'But truly – Alwin? He does not seem stout of heart, despite all his barking. He did not even go to offer Eadwig comfort in his misery.'

'I know,' says Mildred, softly. 'He did not know what he would do there to be of use. And he feared that place, more than he feared anything. He spent much of his time in the stables, as Eadwig once did, and I think he hoped for a friend in him. I know he repents for it now.'

'I have not seen it,' I say.

She lifts her chin. 'And why must he show you, over any others? He has nobody to counsel him and he worries that the other sisters do not trust him as their priest. Botwine barely speaks to him to guide him. I know you dislike him because he is young and proud and because he is sometimes a fool. But he wishes good for us all, I know it.'

'That is why he follows at the abbess's heel, then?' I ask. 'Has us all whipped?'

Mere

'Would Botwine himself take any other path?' she asks.

I do not answer. He has been here when the abbess whipped others and done nothing. I always thought him a shackle against the worst of her wrath, but perhaps he has been less than that.

'He would counsel her against it,' I say.

'As Alwin has,' says Mildred, calmly. 'He has been speaking for us when he can. And before the abbess comes, he has been sending word to the sisters so that they might hide the worst of their sins.'

'Not for the infirmary.'

'No,' says Mildred. 'But the abbess began with us and I do not think she was to be turned from whipping Wulfrun.'

'No,' I say. 'We must only hope that fate favours us, for once.'

Cellarer Leogifu's body washes up at the edge of the mere later that day. She has lost her wimple, her bright, unruly hair loose. Fortunate, in some way, for otherwise I would not know her. Some beast or bird has eaten her eyes and her body is strange, limbs that were once thick withered down to nothing, cheeks gaunt and empty. She looks as if she has been starving for a year now, not gone for less than a month.

She will join all the other souls in the orchard earth.

Chapter 13

The prayers over Leogifu's body that evening come fierce and hoarse. Many linger for as long as they can. They wish to see with their own eyes, I think, her death. So impossible, so strange. So terrible, for it means that even fleeing this place might not mean escape. Though the church is always cold, the heat of our piety soon grows stifling, stealing breath from my lungs, strength from my limbs. It is the warmth of rot, of the slow, unstoppable crumbling of it all. And I cannot take my eyes from Leogifu's sunken, shrouded face.

When it grows too much, I stumble outside to the cold twilight, take a few, deep breaths. I do not look up at the farmland, at the marsh. False spring and the sudden winter that followed has left the mere and fields empty and I do not want to sink into such dark thoughts the night before I am to be whipped.

So I walk, as always, back to the infirmary and the comfort of duty. On the path from the church, I pass by the abbess's dwelling. She came to pray over Leogifu, but only quickly

Mere

and then returned to the sanctuary of her bed. She is the last soul I wished to see this evening and I was glad to see her go.

Her refuge is a small hut, wooden-walled, set on the same slope as the dormitory and church, but a little apart. She meant, in the long-ago past, to build her second church next to it, so that she would have holiness not more than a step away, but now all that remains of that are the stone foundations, worn down over the years like old teeth.

I glance up as I walk and see three women stooping at the threshold. Two are members of the convent, dressed in the browns and greys that make us all dun sparrows, all alike. The other in faded green. I know one woman with such a dress, but I cannot believe she would go willingly to the abbess. I step off the path and begin to climb the hill towards them both. As I grow closer, I see those beads of antler and pearl, that pale hair that always comes loose from its covering.

It is Sweet. Her head is bowed as she speaks with the abbess and Ava. I cannot hear their voices but their shoulders are high, faces pale. Whatever they speak of weighs on them all.

I cannot understand it. She would not speak of the curse to me, would claim that to do so would bring disaster, and yet she talks of it with Ava of all the souls here. They cannot keep it from me. They cannot keep it from us all.

Ava is the first to see me coming. She flinches upwards so quickly she knocks her head against the doorframe, then she is holding her hands up, pressing me away.

'Not now,' she says, more than anger in her voice.

'Why not?' I ask. 'I would talk to you all.'

'But not all might wish to talk to you,' says Ava. She

turns back to look at Sweet, who nods. She has her eyes cast down. The abbess has shrunk back into the darkness of her home. The place is closed up, the windows shut and covered so that I cannot even see through the gaps in their wooden slats. Only the door remains open and if the abbess closes that there is no way she will emerge again until I am gone.

'But why call Sweet?' I say. 'The abbess does not need any leechdoms, surely, or else she would have asked for me.'

Sweet swallows, keeps her head down. Ava braces herself. Others might not see it, but I have spent a lifetime with them both. I know when I have hit a mark.

'The abbess is ill?' I ask, my words coming out trembling. I do not know why, for I always knew that this day would come.

Neither of them responds. And that is worse, for if it were some small ailment, easily cured, then neither would fear to speak of it. Past them, I see the abbess still waiting on her threshold. She is very still.

'Return to the infirmary,' says Ava. 'You must rest before tomorrow.'

'Kind of you to think of me,' I say. 'But it is my duty to help every soul in this place. Including our abbess.'

I stand and wait. If I am to be whipped tomorrow, I would have this one last disobedience.

'Very well,' says the abbess. She steps, finally, into the light. She is not wearing her wimple, nor her crown. The bones of her skull are stark beneath the thin, pale crop of hair. Without her marks of office, she looks far older. I have not seen so before, her authority over me both shield and shroud.

Mere

'Infirmarian, I would speak with you.' She lifts a hand in Sweet's direction. 'And you may return to that mere of yours.'

I wish that Sweet would say something, even as I know that she is not free to. She only nods and lifts her wicker basket for the long walk home. As she passes, she reaches out, grips my hand briefly in hers. A small kindness, a small defiance.

Ava does not leave, but nor does she accompany me inside. She waits, instead, at the doorway, a guard as fierce as any Cerberus. As I pass, she says in a low voice, 'Tread carefully, Hilda.'

I do not respond, but instead take a deep breath and step inside. It has been a great many years since I last entered the abbess's dwelling, not since the previous infirmarian passed and I was appointed. I was but a girl then. I know Ava comes here most Sundays, the convent's most dutiful and favoured daughter.

The abbess is sitting on her bed, hands clasped between her in half a prayer.

'So,' she says, 'you obey me in this, at least.'

I do not answer, but instead look about. The abbess does not have her fire lit but the warmth from last night is in the room, the smoke lingers in the walls and the furs that lie on the bed and floor. There are rich, foreign spices in the air: cloves and cinnamon.

The plastered walls are damp and flaking, each painted scene cracking: Saint Catherine's wheel has been broken before she might even be lashed to it, Saint Daniel finds that the lions in his den are without teeth, that their entire fierce faces have been worn away. Underneath these frustrated martyrs lies a goosefeather mattress and an empty box beside it.

She sees me looking and smiles. 'Honeyed dates once,' she says. 'Given all away to Ava's tender care now.'

My belly aches at even the thought of such sweetness. No doubt it will come to us in slivers and scraps.

'You have removed tumours before, I hear?' she asks, sharp and sudden.

'Once or twice,' I say. 'The operation is not always successful. It places the patient in almost as much danger as if they were to be left to die.'

A sister, shaking as her lifeblood leaves her. Another drinking too deeply of the poppy and slipping into death swift as a springtime rill. For all my dislike of the abbess, I would not have her die that way.

'If you have a growth,' I say to the abbess, 'you must show me. I know you have not come to my infirmary often but it is good to be bled once in a while.'

'I speak only of the theory,' she says. 'The removal of a part, to save the whole. I would have you know that I feel no joy in tomorrow.'

I believe her, but it brings me no comfort. And she is talking round and round of anything other than what ails her. There is only one thing that would fill Ava with such worry, that would have her call on Sweet instead of me.

'Are you dying?' I ask. It comes out clumsy, full of need. A child's question, not an infirmarian's.

Her jaw twitches. Almost a smile, almost a grimace. The abbess keeps her feelings so closely bound that I think even she cannot tell between them any more.

'We must all prepare for death,' she says. 'But yes, for me I think it will be soon.'

She says it so calmly, as if she speaks only of yet another matter of the convent and not her own end. She

Mere

is wrong. She cannot be dying. She would not allow it, for one thing.

The abbess closes her eyes and lifts her habit to her stomach. 'Press,' she says.

Her belly is very pale, the bare flesh marked by wrinkles and spots. I do as she says, pushing my fingers into her skin, burrowing deep until I find the masses. They are many and well spread.

'Oh,' I say, and that is the end of my words.

The abbess drops her habit and I stand back. I wonder if they are paining her, the fleshworms, the wolf that devours all. If they do, she shows no sign of it. But I have seen the illness progress, how it blossoms outwards in sores and ulcers and whimpers.

'Sometimes,' I say, 'a cancer might be caused by an excess of black bile. A change to your diet might help.'

'It will be like trying to keep water in your hands,' says the abbess. 'And I have spoken with Sweet already. It is in my sight, my taste. There is no part of me that it has not already touched. Save your ministrations, Infirmarian, for those who might benefit from them.'

I cannot believe she lives with this, holding her own death within her precious as a relic. I hate her, then, for her weakness. For how easily she wishes to slip away from all this. My eyes sting.

'Ava bid me call someone, for she thinks I can be saved somehow,' says the abbess. 'She wanted you, but I told her to fetch Sweet. At least she knows how to keep a secret.' She sighs. 'But you have seen us and for all your sins, you are no dullard.'

It is perhaps the kindest thing she has ever said of me. I almost laugh.

'So,' says the abbess, 'the other sisters cannot know of my illness. It would unsettle them.'

'I will say nothing,' I say. Not to keep order in the convent, but because I would do the same for any other soul in this place.

'And you would treat me?' asks the abbess, tilting her head. 'Even after I have beaten you and those you love? You would bend your knee to me, wash my sores and salve my bruises?'

I meet her gaze. I will not be as she is, trading lives as if they mean nothing.

'Yes,' I say. 'I would do so for any that came to me. No matter if they were abbess or some poor servant child.'

For a moment I think the abbess will speak. Talk, perhaps, of Eadwig or even Leogifu. But she only reaches out her hand, a dismissal. I bend and kiss it, feel the softness of her skin and, beneath that, the knuckles that are beginning to stiffen.

I meet Ava outside. She flinches when I open the door, moves away from the door so it does not look as if she has been listening to us.

'Well?' she asks. 'Sweet told me, but she has been wrong before.'

She does not even try to hide the hope in her eyes.

'She is not well,' I say. 'She will need much care over the next few weeks.'

'But might she recover?' asks Ava. 'If she was given that care?'

The abbess was right. Ava, so wise and careful in all that she does, is made a fool by her worry. She knows my answer.

Mere

I tighten my cloak about me, ready to leave. But Ava takes my arm.

'Tomorrow,' she says. 'Have faith.'

I stare at her. Perhaps she means to help but it is shallow comfort when she and the abbess might release us all from the punishment with a single word.

'If she worsens, you must call Sweet again, not me,' I say. 'From tomorrow, I may not be able to stand, let alone treat her.'

I return to a feast. There is no other name for it, women sitting about in a circle around Tove's mattress, laughing and drinking. She and Wulfrun are at the centre of it, arranged about them Eluned, Mildred and half a dozen other patients.

I stand in the doorway, watching a while. Their feast has none of the flavour of a day like Easter, full of new life and with richness ahead of us. No, this feels as it does on Shrove Tuesday, the gluttony before the fast. The laughter is high and a little wild, the talk of anything else but what tomorrow morning will bring.

It is Mildred who sees me first and starts. One by one, the others turn to me.

'Why,' says Tove, 'it is Hilda the Wise, come to join us!'

The corners of my mouth twitch but I still linger at the door and so Mildred stands and weaves her way over to me.

'It was just Tove and Wulfrun at first,' says Mildred. 'They told me I should join them in this. They called it a last supper.'

She puts her hand to her own mouth at the unintended blasphemy. She is drunk, maybe for the first time in her life.

I open my mouth for some harsh words, more out of long custom than from real feeling, and then Wulfrun is in front of me and shooing Mildred away.

'I know we should have waited,' says Wulfrun, smiling at me. She is flushed, too, about her cheeks and her burn. Her wimple has slipped so a few wisps of dark hair trail about her ear. 'We wanted to, but you were so long away.'

She stops, waiting for me to tell her what has happened. But I only look past her, at the beer.

'It is not yours,' says Wulfrun, quickly. 'Tove traded a ring with some of the sisters in the kitchen and they gave her some of what they have been brewing secretly. I cannot speak for its taste, but it is strong enough. Come, join us.'

'I should sleep,' I say. The abbess's illness weighs on me still, and I do not want to be beer-sick tomorrow.

'As if you will sleep,' says Wulfrun, 'when there are so many of us sinners, so loud and close by. Just a while and then you may go to your rest.'

She grasps my hand and pulls me towards her. It is so sudden, so open a movement that I stumble. I look around, fearful, but Wulfrun only laughs.

'They all know already,' she says, 'one way or another.'

I stare at her. She risks far too much. But still, there is the warmth of her hand in mine when we sit, side by side. I have never been able to do this with any lover and after I have taken my first sip of the beer, which is sour and foul and strong, I rest my head against her shoulder. One by one, each sister tells some tale or joke. Eluned tells many I have not heard before, of warriors falling in love with the daughters of giants, of enchantresses who brewed potions of wisdom and poetry.

They begin to lull me and I close my eyes. It has been

Mere

a long while since I have been able to rest. I can hear Wulfrun's heartbeat, the soft workings of her muscles and the rushing of her belly. A whole kingdom, inside of her. When she begins to speak, it is a tremble through her and a tremble through me and I do not hear what she is truly saying until the end.

'So,' she finishes, 'the maid takes a look at him and says that such a knife might be admired in Lundun, but here in Gipeswic, the men heft spears.'

There are a few small coughs, a murmur. But she has been hoping for more, for she sits upwards, knocking me from her shoulder and back into wakefulness.

'You see,' she says, 'I am not talking of knives and spears, truly, but of—'

'Yes, yes,' says Mildred. 'It is only, we have heard it before.'

I am not so lulled to sleep that I miss that.

'And who has told you it?' I say.

'I am fifteen winters now,' says Mildred. 'Old enough to know it.'

'You may think yourself a woman, but you are not too old to be set to wash the dirty blankets for a week.'

She blushes, but does not bow her head as she might once have done. Some of Alwin's boldness has passed to her, I think.

'If you wish, I would do it for a month. Anything to serve my sisters,' she says and beside her Tove laughs until there are tears in her eyes. It is far more than Wulfrun's tale was given and Wulfrun speaks again, telling us that maybe we did not hear the start of the tale for it is not easy to follow.

'Do not worry,' whispers Eluned, patting Wulfrun on the arm. 'Maybe the next one.'

Wulfrun shakes her head, baffled, and I see her as she

might have been. Had her husband not been cruel, had the visions not come to her. Had her life been easy and without any duty. She would have been sweet, sometimes a little foolish.

But she is not that woman. Now, she is so used to counting the weight of each word that she cannot speak with any lightness unless she is turning it to some purpose, cannot speak as herself but must always be a seer, a worker of miracles.

And then the circle looks to me and it is my turn. And I find, like Wulfrun, I cannot think of anything with any truth, something that they will not already have heard. I lift my hand to say so and then catch movement at the door. A sister, quickly hidden.

We all grow quiet as I lift myself up to greet this visitor. We have been loud, but not enough to rouse any sisters in the dormitory, I think, and so it must be someone come to see me with some sudden illness.

But it is Ava. She stands in the shadows beneath the eaves, back as straight as the beams above us.

'I came to thank you, for earlier,' she says, 'for seeing the abbess. I know what she asked of you.' She stops, looks past me to the feast. 'But I see that this is not the time.'

I have not seen her like this since we were both girls. Even as lovers we were not a good pair and it was this feeling that I remember the most, that we both stood, always, at the edge of some cliff. We were never certain of each other.

'You might join us,' I say, 'if you wish?'

She purses her lips, though it is not a refusal. I have never seen her take an excess of anything. But tonight, with so much ahead of us tomorrow morning, she might drink with us all. I do not know how I feel about it.

Mere

Then, Wulfrun is at my side.

'Can we help, Portress?' she asks.

She gives no explanation for the feast or why she is here and not in the dormitory, or why even now her arm is rested against mine, lightly. Ava's eyes flicker to it, this space where Wulfrun and I press against each other.

'No,' she says, shortly. 'I came only to advise that you rest. Tomorrow will be hard for you both.'

'We thank you for your care,' says Wulfrun, laughter in her voice, and it catches me, too, for as soon as Ava is far enough away we giggle without end, as if we were maids of fourteen.

But when we return, even Ava's shadow is enough. The feast is already beginning to slow, the women remembering all that weighs on them. Mildred is the first to make an excuse, going to prepare salves for tomorrow. Then Tove says that we all cluck like hens and with the same amount of sense and she must get some sleep. All the others fade away until it is Wulfrun and I, holding a cup of beer each. We walk outside, sitting under the eaves once more with the sky spread above us.

It is very cold, but we have brought blankets and cloaks and wrapped them about us. Wulfrun is broader than me and heavier and so she pulls me onto her lap and between her legs, so that my back is to her. We sit like this, curving into each other. I point out the constellations to her, tell her how we are in Capricorn season, and so it is a good time to treat the knees, as well as nerves and sinew and skin. A season of turning, of threads and links.

'And did you tell Ava all this?' asks Wulfrun.

'I didn't,' I say. 'But it was so long ago that I did not know it, back then. I would now, were we to become lovers again.'

I lift her fingers and kiss each of them. 'Why?' I ask. 'Did you think me innocent of all this, just because I have never left? I can tell you of all the others, if you wish.'

She does not answer and so I say, 'Ava was the first, of course, but she and I parted when she grew fearful of the abbess finding us. Then there was a pilgrim called Olaf, who used to be a scop in some thegn's house. He told me stories of a great king across the water called Atilla and a song sung by the Christ-rood itself. He came with his wife, who was twice as lustful as her husband but only half as fair. Once, with Fair Alfred. He was not a good lover.'

I glance around at Wulfrun, who stares down at me, wondering. She is not used to finding herself wrong in her judgements of others and I feel a small pleasure that I have been, in some way, larger than she first thought me.

'I do not know how you have found the time,' she says, and though there is delight in her voice, there is a little envy there also.

'There were many pilgrims here once,' I say. 'It was easy enough to slip away and I was often walking the convent collecting herbs. What of you?'

'Only my husband,' she says, 'and Eadwig's mother, for a short time. Though I think she loved Botwine far more than she ever did me. I never . . . Truly, Fair Alfred?'

I shrug. 'You have seen him. It was a long while ago and I was careful.'

'Poor Mildred,' says Wulfrun, 'you have chided her so.'

'She is not as careful as I was at her age,' I say.

'Ah, so speaks Hilda the Wise,' says Wulfrun, smiling. I see again that single false tooth in her mouth. I turn so that I face her and run my hand down her belly, her thighs. She says that we should return to the storeroom, that we

Mere

should be quiet, but I shake my head and say, 'Be still, love,' and then slide my fingers inside of her.

She is still for as long as she can be but I feel it in her, a great knotting and unknotting and then all at once a shiver and I hear her give a low laugh.

'You mean to live, tomorrow?' I ask, afterwards, in her arms. I have not said it all this while, but she feasted tonight as if it was Christmas. As if she did not think to live to see that day itself, but two days from now.

'Of course I do,' says Wulfrun. She presses her lips against my neck. 'I will be with you.'

Chapter 14

The next morning, we each take our share of the potion. I am glad for it, for my stomach roils and my head aches, beer-sick.

I feel the leechdom as we walk to Lauds and set our knees down onto the cold stone floor. The world slows, my cheeks flush and I feel a great thirst. We all mumble our way through prayers. A few among us, those with the whip in their future, find their voices high and desperate, full less of praise and more of pleading. Theirs are petty sins. None of them more than two or three blows each, their beatings a candle to Wulfrun's pyre.

The church is the only one of our buildings with glass and since I was a child I have spent hours watching the light spread through the stained picture of Christ, bathing us all in the glory of His sacrifice. This morning, though, I watch Wulfrun. She turns her face to the window and I see Him reflected in her eyes, brighter than anything else in this dark winter of ours.

When the bell rings, she rises eager and ready.

*

Mere

Our path down from the church to the bridge is a slow one. Most of the souls in the convent must come with us, save those who are too sick or tired to walk.

The dawn is edged and cold, the sun sheared above by heavy clouds into nothing but brief slivers. With every step we grow closer to the marsh. Sweet showed me the trick once of holding a handful of moss to my ear, listening to the slow seep of water through it. A gift from the mere, she called it, but I did not hear anything then. Now I wonder if it has reached me at last. A calling-song.

My sisters press against me, whispering words of reassurance and strength. Tove is first among them, the others moving aside to allow her to pass.

'The abbess would see you on your knees,' she says. 'Do not let her.'

'There will be posts,' I say. The brew is curdling in my belly and I giggle. 'So you must not worry.'

Tove inspects my face. Then, she nods. 'You have your cure already, it seems. Well, strength, sister.'

Mildred is next, her face pale and worried.

'I do not wish to be infirmarian,' she says, 'so you must not let too much harm come to you.'

'I will do what I can,' I say and again it is such a strange thing to say that I laugh. I can make no promises to Mildred. 'Besides,' I say to her, 'you would be a fine infirmarian. Sharp wits and a sharper tongue.'

She frowns but the crowd bears her away before she has her answer. There are others that follow her but they bleed into each other. The brew is at full power now and my words come slow and slurred. I watch my feet instead. The hardness of the frozen earth through my thin leather boots. I will pass down this road and leave not even a footprint.

Then, we stop. The crowd pulls back and it is five sisters left standing in the centre of this circle. Four posts have been freshly driven into the soil. We have never needed to punish more than one sister at a time before. I wonder if they thought five at once too much.

I look around. How cunning the abbess has been in her selection. There, a sister from the kitchen and the cantor. And another, Ethel, Portress Ava's helper. I do not yet know her sin.

No seeming favour in this selection, no malice. Only justice.

I look above. There is a single crow among the clouds, a black smear on the hunt for carrion. I wonder if it waits for us. My heart beats very quick.

Then, Alwin and the abbess step forward. Botwine has not come today to witness our punishment. Still locked away in his room, seeking our salvation even as the life is half beaten from us.

I have not felt much fear this morning, the brew taking it from me. But I see the switches that have been cut for us today. Not too thick, not too cruel. Birch for a clean edge, a narrow tip.

My knees fall out from under me. Weakness beyond weakness but I cannot help it. There is a gasp as I drop to the mud, murmurs from the crowd. My arms ache from the fall, bruised before the punishment has even begun.

Beside me, the other sisters chosen for today pull away as if they will catch my frailty. Only Wulfrun comes to my aid. She offers her arm, lifts me up.

'I am with you,' she whispers. 'All is well.'

I lean against her, stumbling as she leads me down to the bridge that spans the ditch separating the convent from

Mere

the land about it. The posts are placed here so that as many sisters and ceorls might gather to watch as possible. We will be pressed against each of them and fastened with ropes for the whipping, wood keeping us standing upright when our own weak flesh fails.

I watch as, one by one, the sisters are turned around, their habits and shifts pulled down to bare their backs so that their clothes will not be damaged by the blows. A waste of good cloth otherwise.

It reveals their breasts also. We see plenty of each other, in the dormitories and infirmary. Some in the kitchen even pull off their habits themselves, in the summer when the oven seems to bake the very air.

But this is different. A shame upon shame, a stripping of any modesty. Ethel begins to weep, her thin shoulders shaking with humiliation. Cruelties pass through the crowd, talk of the ugliness of the sisters, of their ill forms reflecting their ill souls. Some of the ceorl men, saying it is a good thing that these women are already given to Christ for no man would have them otherwise.

Even Wulfrun, they say. A widow's body, the marks of childbirth stretching across her belly. She is no seer, no martyr. Only a woman who was once a wife. I want to wade into the crowd, rip their tongues from their mouths. They would dare, some of them the very same who came to her yesterday to touch her one last time. They would dare.

I am the last to be stripped. I wait, willing strength into myself so that I will not fall once again, so that I will be able to stand by Wulfrun's side in this.

But there is nothing. I hear behind me a slow tread. Then, a hand on my shoulder that makes me start. Not rough fingers but a gentle guidance.

'Infirmarian Hilda,' says the abbess, turning me around. The gold of her circlet makes me flinch back. Too bright, too much.

'I have thought upon your punishment and think it harsh. You will show penance by abstaining from wine and mead for ninety days and by wearing a hair shirt for three days.'

This mercy comes upon me as a sudden plunge into icy water. The abbess's face is as serene as ever. I do not think I have hated her before, not truly. My feelings have always been blunted by pity, by the understanding that she does all this because she believes it will save us.

Now I could scratch her eyes out, bite her wrists and neck and all the soft, exposed parts of her, bear her to the ground and tear out whatever goodness is left in her. I would leave her for the crows and even if she cried out to end her suffering, I would not help her.

Portress Ava sees my anger, steps towards me.

'The abbess shows mercy,' she says, 'the sort that begets further mercy.'

This is her doing, then. She has convinced the abbess to spare me, so that I might treat her. I cannot even suffer without first thinking of my duty to the convent.

I open my mouth to reject this gift. I am no coward. But at my side, Wulfrun gives the smallest shake of her head.

'Do not refuse,' she says. 'You will be needed, after this.'

I cannot look at Wulfrun. I cannot look at any of my sisters.

And the brew is strong within me. Not protecting me any more but giving me visions of skin split and flesh unknotted. The wound souring spreading dark fingers of poison from my back to my heart a shaking death in my very own infirmary and then a shallow grave next to every

Mere

other sister I have failed to save and I do not wish to join them I do not want to die I do not want the abbess to kill me and I am sparrow-weak lamb-meek a kicked cur called to heel and I do not want them to hurt me.

'Please,' says Wulfrun, leaning her head in. 'For me, if no other.'

I barely feel my legs as I stumble from the centre of the circle to its edge. I wish I saw bitterness in Wulfrun's eyes as she watches me leave. But there is only a gladness that makes me sick. I have not earned this, no more than she has earned her punishment. It is cruel, this mercy.

Mildred comes to fetch me to help her with the salves. She has gathered what she can on an old tree stump, brushed away the moss and leaf-fall and laid down a cloth so that it resembles the table in our infirmary. It is a fine trick, one that will bring relief much earlier to each poor suffering soul. My cunning, loving apprentice.

'I am glad you are here,' whispers Mildred, passing me a pot. She has made it far too thick for spreading, but has with her a jug of water taken from the stream. I pour a little into the pot, but I cannot turn my mind to this slow grind of herbs and cures, not when Wulfrun stands there, so proud and alone.

It is not the abbess that reads out the sins, but Ava. Wulfrun's are well known: conducting magic that brought out the devil-sickness in Eadwig and gave rise to the destruction of our relic. A kitchen sister has been slothful in her duties. Our cantor, in all her silence, has been stealing from her sisters, taking their shoes and habits for her own even though there is no difference between them. Then there is Ethel, who helps Ava in her work as the portress. Here, Ava's voice grows hoarse.

'It was discovered,' she says, 'that she has been drawing figures of men in the margins of our tallies.'

Ava wishes to end the charge there.

'And?' asks the abbess.

'And,' continues Ava, 'these men were sometimes not clothed as they should be. Their manhood for all to see.'

The abbess waves at her to carry on. Ava closes her eyes, swallows. There is a deep blush in her face now.

'And such figures resembled our priests, Alwin and Botwine, strongly.'

Laughter, then, shocked and cruel. Ethel's face is turned away from us, her back bared, but I am sure I hear the sound of her weeping.

A small punishment for Ava as well, then, and a warning. For she cannot have missed these tiny priests revelling beside her own careful numbers. And, as we all do, until today she has not minded it. The younger sisters are hotter in their curiosities, but they rarely stray to any sin that would harm them. Only a lingering on the men as they work in the fields, only a flush when the priests speak to them.

Aside, of course, from my own apprentice. Mildred has stopped her preparations, her hands stilled, her gaze on Alwin and Alwin alone. Foolish child, her guilt is plain as any. She is fortunate that none look to her, for the birches are being handed out to any who will take them.

I keep my head lowered, but I know what will come next. So, when the abbess approaches, stick in hand, I feign that I have not seen her.

'Infirmarian Hilda,' she says, 'take this. You will deal the first blow for Sister Wulfrun.'

I shake my head. 'I am needed here,' I mumble.

Mere

She comes closer. 'You have trained Mildred well, she will manage. You can spare just one moment.'

'I have not the strength for it,' I say.

'You do not need strength, daughter. Only courage and righteousness. Take it.'

Again, she holds out the birch. Fine lines seam the wood like a woman's unbound hair. Soft, too. The blood will stain it quickly.

'Enough,' says another voice, taking the wicked thing out of the abbess's hands. 'You play with her as a cat does a mouse. I am the oldest here and have the right of this.'

'I did not ask—' begins the abbess.

'No, Sigeburg, but I am answering anyway,' says Tove. 'Come, let us get on with this before we all freeze to death.'

And so, we start.

As always, the switches are held out to any who might want them. As always, each sister is permitted a blow before she must pass it on to another. We share all things, including cruelty.

I do not look at the shivering figures, my poor fellow souls. No, instead I turn my gaze to the faces of my sisters.

All my life, I have studied man. His humours, what might give one man a fiery temper that spurs him to duels and another a melancholia that tempts him to drown himself. There is a balance, I believed, to every one of my sisters. With care and time, we might all be turned to goodness.

Now I see only strangers. A sister I once thought to be meek, her face twisted with hatred that I have never known from her. Another who bloodrot brought close to death last year after a beating, lifting her own hand to continue this cycle. Another who wept to see a convent cat kicked, watching hard-eyed.

Tove, who I have never seen shirk from any task, who spins tales of blood and glory, looks as if she has swallowed something foul when she lifts her arm for the blow. Her arm falls gentle, more of a brush than a blow, and I thank her for it.

I turn away from my fellow sisters, look only at my hands and their work of pressing salves. Still, though, I must hear it. The snap and the cry, the raking breaths and the wetness of flesh. I can pick out Wulfrun's own sudden gasps as if each pain is new to her. The others have been sentenced to only a handful of blows. Their sobs come quickly and quietly and then they are untied and led away from the posts and to me and suddenly there is no turning away, there is no hiding, there are three women with wounds on their backs that I must treat.

An age ago, Sweet taught me a spell. A charm, a trick, a prayer. There are certain pains that are larger than one infirmarian, than one woman, can take in. You might as well pour the sea into a cup, she would say.

And so, in such times, she thought only of the waves. Allowed them to pull her, a little, to whom she might help the most. For some nights there would be a woman in birth, quiet and soft-boned as her lifeblood coursed from her, and there would be another running to seek aid for her fevered only son and another who had but an excess of phlegm but was of a high position and so could not be ignored.

Now there are three in front of me, Wulfrun soon to join them. I cast my gaze across each of their wounds. Split skin, cuts that are the length of a man's arm. Though Ethel's are the fewest, they are the deepest and so it is her I turn to first, for she is not a stout soul at the best of times.

Mere

'Wash the wounds,' I instruct Mildred, 'honey and wine and garlic. Then a poultice, pack it with bog-cotton and then bandage it.'

She nods and I begin my work on Ethel. I feel, still, my shame and guilt at leaving Wulfrun. But it is buried for a while until my duties are done. It will have been a poor bargain if I do not help those who need it.

I give Ethel the same poppy seed brew that I took earlier. I feel its effects still but my fingers are well used to healing and so I do not hesitate. It is as if I tend to her in a dream, as if all about has been swallowed by the mere and we float, half-drowned.

The potion quietens Ethel a little but she is a small, timid thing and so I speak to her kindly, telling her what I will do as if I speak to a child. She is not much younger than Mildred, but I think Ava's tutelage has kept her innocent.

'I shall wash this, sister. You may feel a burn but that is usual. Then, I shall sew some of the deeper wounds and pack them with a poultice. You can see Mildred doing that already, can't you?'

'Yes,' she says, drowsily.

'I have heard,' I say, 'that you come not from East Anglia, but were born in Wessex. Is that true?'

She begins to speak of a childhood, of wheatfields and apples. Summer, safety. And as she talks, I begin my work. There is one wound that worries me above all, a deep slice across her ridged spine that will open every time she bends her back. I expect her to flinch as I thread the needle, knitting the wound closed, but she is too busy telling me of the cats that she used to save scraps for, how they would come to sit on her lap and bring her dead mice as gifts.

'Well,' I say, 'you must talk to the kitchen sisters, for they keep cats to catch mice. Though, they sound far rougher than those in your childhood.'

'I have asked,' she replies. 'The portress says that would be idleness.'

'You shall be abed a while with this,' I say. 'I shall see if we can tempt one in for you.'

'Yes,' she says, slowly. 'I would like that.'

I catch Mildred's eye. She has done well with the other two, but her face is pale and tired. She worries about Wulfrun. Our next patient, the one in greatest danger.

'Take these two to the infirmary,' I say. 'Have the other sisters help you, if needed.'

'I should stay—' she begins, but I shake my head.

'Go, keep the fire warm and fetch the water. We will have need of both.'

Only when she goes, the cantor staggering behind her and another sister leading Ethel as a ewe does a lamb, do I finally stop my fingers.

Still, I do not look up. I cannot see what they have done to her. What I have done to her, in my cowardice. There is a count of blows now, and we are at twenty. Four more and it will be over.

But the day has soured. Before, my sisters were filled with righteousness, their pain and anger ready to be shared. They have had their punishment, stripped their flesh, and found that it has not helped. And Wulfrun prays in between her sighs. She prays for the souls of those who stand to take the birch and she prays for them by name so that none will forget who did this to her. She sings, too, little songs of hope and light and she has not screamed yet, not once.

Mere

I hear the last few blows, soft and quick. The women keen for this to be over.

'Two dozen,' says the abbess. Even she, I think, regrets the severity of today. 'Untie her, bear her to the infirmary.'

Only then do I look up. What I see turns my stomach and I forget my fury at the abbess and my every sense and start to run to her because

her back

the skin, the flesh open

they have killed her surely with this and if she does not die today it will be tomorrow and no saint ever suffered as she suffers and they have untied her wrists and hold her by her shoulders one woman on each side bearing her back to me and I must help her I must cure her if I do nothing else in my life.

Her head is bowed and she seems near senseless. Her lips move still in prayer but it is too faint to be heard.

'Wulfrun?' I say, running to her. 'Meadowsweet?'

The other sisters look at me, I know, but I care not. I would have love on my tongue, on this day of all days.

Then, a miracle. She looks up at me, sharpening.

'I am well,' she says and shrugs off the women who bear her to the convent, stands with a strength I do not know how she finds.

A hush falls. We are still now, all of us, and the only sound is Wulfrun's footfalls as she begins to walk to the abbess. A stagger, really, but they will not remember her weakness, they will remember only what she is saying, her voice rising louder and louder over their heads.

'I will pray for you,' she says. 'I will pray for you, sisters.'

I watch as she reaches the abbess. Wulfrun lifts her head, smiles as if she is greeting dawn for the first time.

Danielle Giles

'I will pray for you, Sister Sigeburg,' she says. She reaches her hand out to the stunned abbess, presses it against the abbess's breast. Her heart, in Wulfrun's grip.

And it is not Wulfrun, broken, who collapses, but the abbess. She falls, light as a leaf, and there is a roar about me in the wind and in my ears and from the throats of my sisters and it is a roar that will not be silenced again.

Chapter 15

I worried for Wulfrun, but it is Ethel who falls into danger in the end. Three days after Christmas, four days after the whipping, bloodrot comes. The eternal enemy.

The others' wounds show the beginnings of scabbing, of knitting, of life. Even Wulfrun, who has been in bed the whole time recovering, shows good healing. A relief, for I do not have to trace the ruin of Wulfrun's back, nor swallow my guilt and shame.

I go to her bedside only when she is asleep and then I hold her hand and brush her brow and whisper everything I cannot say in daylight. How I should never have left her. How I barely feel the hair shirt that I wear at the abbess's order and that I should be in that bed next to her. If Wulfrun wakes, turns to ask me some small question or give me some small comfort, I say that I must go to Ethel and that I will speak with her later.

But today I can see, before I even begin to remove Ethel's bandages, the slow seep of blood, the green and yellow pus leaking into the pale cloth. It is so foul that I must cover my mouth. The girl, wan, marks this.

'Is all well?' she asks, twisting to see my face though it pulls and tugs at her wound.

'Nothing that can't be healed,' I say and it is a truth of sorts. But there is swelling, too, and small sores around the wound. Though the infirmary has only one fire lit, still Ethel sweats, her face flushed and feverish.

Mildred, walking past with a knife and bleeding-bowl, halts in her step. There is so much she has seen in her short life already. She knows death as I do and all the forms it might take and there is little that scares her. But as she looks down at Ethel, a tremble begins, in her hands, in her chest. She knows what she sees and opens her mouth to say something, but I shake my head.

'I must go fetch some water to wash this,' I say. 'Wait here a while with Ethel, will you?'

Grass and clover crunch, brittle with cold, as I walk down to the stream. I hear songs from the church and remember that today is the Feast of the Holy Innocents. All those babes, put to the sword in long-ago Bethlehem.

I think of foxes and mice. How there is no deadlier time for both than the silence before the leap. The mouse might escape and condemn the fox to starve. Or, the fox might be the victor and crunch sharp bones in sharper teeth. But for the span of a held breath, none know their fate. So it feels today.

I bend to the stream. Ice forms at the edges of the water and when I fill the bucket the cold closes about my fingers, eeljaw-keen. Soon, we will have to break the ice each time. Soon, our water will freeze unless it is kept next to a fire.

Mere

I do not think Ethel will live to see this. Bloodrot takes kings and slaves alike and it takes them quickly.

When the bucket is filled I wait a while, on my haunches. My eyes sting. Another one, lost, for nothing more than a few errant lines of ink.

A sound breaks my mourning, makes me look up. It is Sweet, with a bucket of her own. Her dress is thin and worn, her leather shoes with a hole at their toe and I see red on her bare wrists. Her headdress falls strangely, as if she has put it on in a hurry.

She hails me, then crouches to the river to draw water.

'How fares our saint, then?' she asks.

'She grows stronger by the day,' I say.

Sweet grunts, lifts the bucket back to the bank. Her thin arms strain under the weight and I think, not for the first time, how alone she is.

'And the others?' she asks. 'The child Ethel took it hard. Her first beating, I think.'

I swallow, look down.

'Oh,' says Sweet. 'I am sorry.'

She reaches out to touch my shoulder, then thinks better of it and pulls away. She rests both hands in her girdle, as if unsure what to do with them.

'I did not see you in the crowd that day,' I say.

'No,' says Sweet, softly. 'I stayed long enough to see you pardoned, then left. I did not wish to see the beating. But I have heard nothing but the tale of Wulfrun's miracle since.'

'Do you think me a coward?' I ask. 'For accepting the abbess's mercy?'

She tilts her head, watches me. 'I have always wondered, even as a child, how you all court pain. The gods I knew were strong, would never let their enemies defeat them. I am baptized now and a lot older, but I still do not understand.'

I think of Wulfrun, standing even as the abbess fell to her knees. 'I do not understand either,' I say, 'but there is magic in it.'

'Aye,' says Sweet, 'and we must use what we are given.'

She stops. 'You should know,' she says, 'that Wulfrun has charged me with a task. I am to spy for her among the ceorls, along with Eluned.'

It is not strange that Wulfrun has such a plan, only that Sweet has agreed to it. She is not fond of masters. As for Eluned, she resides still in the infirmary, for Sybba's brothers continue battling over his will. He promised her to one brother in speech and another in writing and until the matter is decided neither are willing to let Eluned into the other's household. So, she continues to serve the convent, sweeping and carrying and finding ways to make herself useful. I wonder what will happen, when her masters come to fetch her at last.

'And what has she promised you, then?'

'More,' says Sweet. She meets my gaze and her pale eyes might be my own. With each passing year our kinship grows clearer. 'But highborn women do not always keep their oaths.'

'She is no oath-breaker,' I say.

'No?' asks Sweet. 'That is good to hear. We shall see. The abbess promised me freedom and land in return for . . .'

She looks up at me, then away.

'Remember,' says Sweet, 'they care for us only when they are forced to.'

Mere

As with so much, there will be no convincing her. She has spent her whole life in battle and will not lay down her weapons easily.

'Would you tell me more of the curse?' I say. 'You can see the pain it brings us all. It is already woken, I think. What further disaster could come if you spoke of it?'

'No,' says Sweet. 'There are two paths for us: we stay or we flee. The abbess wishes to stay. Others, later, may flee. But if we flee, we must do it together. I think that will be the only way, else end up as poor Leogifu.' The cloud breaks above. For a breath, pale winter light falls on us all, picking out the hairs on Sweet's bare arms, the cracks on my cold, worn hands. It is as if we live in a different realm, brighter and clearer. Then, the sun slides from view and leaves us to the chill and the quiet.

'Remember,' says Sweet, 'you are no coward. Even had you called on the Devil himself to come and sweep you out of there. It is not wrong to wish not to suffer.'

She glances at me sidelong again. 'And find some meat, when you can. You grow thinner by the day.'

I return to the infirmary, my hands shaking. I am glad, for once, of the cold. It masks my fear for Ethel.

And there is Ava. She, who thinks that if she avoids the infirmary she will never have to use it. She, of careful ledgers and long memory. There is a scrap of cloth between her hands.

'We have enough rags,' I say, 'but thank you for your gift.'

She reddens and opens her hands. Not a rag but a poorly embroidered patch. I cannot see what it is meant to be at first, must narrow my eyes and tilt my head. She cannot have stitched a devil, surely, but that is how it seems. Russet and black and full of wrath.

'A cat,' says Ava, 'it is the cat in the bakery.'

For all her nimble mind, she was never skilled at embroidery. There are tiny wounds on her fingertips, pricks that are still bleeding onto the very gift she wishes to give to Ethel.

I look at her face. Hopeful, penitent. She does not know yet, then. It might almost make me laugh, if the day was not already so damned. Ava, hunched over her embroidery like the most thick-fingered novice.

'It is best that you wait a while,' I say. 'There are cuts on your hand, let me attend to them.'

She looks down, frowning.

'I did not feel them,' she says. 'They will wait.'

'Sit down,' I say. She stuns me by obeying.

I bid her pull her sleeves up, check the cuts. None are deep, thankfully, and so I put over them only a light poultice of garlic and rosemary.

'There is something you are not telling me,' says Ava. 'It is always clear with you. You always hide in your duties.'

'How long and well you know me,' I say.

'You turn bitter when you are scared,' she says. 'That I know, too.'

Her voice begins to shake. I let her sleeves fall down. I see how she has unravelled, already. Her wimple is not tight enough and her thick, grey curls are pushing loose where she has not shorn her hair back. Her habit is dirty at the hem and there are tears in it that she has not mended.

'I know, also,' she says, 'that you are angry at me. But Wulfrun has been courting this a long while. You cannot blame me for her punishment.'

Mere

'Were you glad to be able to report Ethel for her little drawings?' I ask. 'Glad that no search would come to you?'

Ava's jaw tightens. 'I did not report her,' she says. 'It was found, as the abbess searched for sin.'

'But you stood back,' I say. 'You let it happen. You did not advise her to burn the pages or blot them out.'

'Do you know,' asks Ava, 'how long it takes for vellum to burn? To watch over it as it shrivels and puckers in the flames? Alwin came to me with warning, but my ledgers have the same worth as a ceorl's cottage and that is before we talk of what records they contain. Now that we are without our relic, our tapestries, they are among the most precious things left in the convent.'

I laugh. 'Ever you think of the cost of things, over all else.'

'I say this,' says Ava, calm, 'because we cut out and burnt half a dozen pages, the night before the abbess came. Our robes stunk of burning pig. But we missed one.'

She sits back, watches me.

'I did not know—' I begin.

'No,' she says. 'You think that if a soul is not your sworn ally, they are an enemy. Not sisters, as we should be. And while you berate me for my cowardice, what of yours? You cleaved easily enough to the abbess when it would save you from a whipping.'

I do not answer this.

'Now,' she says, 'is that enough? Am I worthy enough to see my own apprentice, pray for her? Or have you more questions?'

'No,' I say. 'But you must know, she has the bloodrot.'

Ava's face does not change. Slowly, she reaches down and presses her bleeding fingers into the embroidered cat. Red spreads across the cloth.

'Somebody must fetch Alwin,' she says, in the same tone she uses when talking of the convent's stores, of its riches. Thinking of what must be done, first. 'She will need last rites.'

I nod. 'I have not yet told her.'

'I will go,' says Ava. 'She will hear it from me, at least.'

She stands and walks, stiffly, to Ethel. There is murmured conversation and then a sudden sound of disbelief. The huff of a doe as it is felled by the arrow. Then, Ava's voice as I have not heard for over a decade. Soft, soothing. A deep tenderness limning its edges.

I go to find a priest.

Chapter 16

*A*lwin is not in the convent. I tell my fellow sisters that we must find a priest as soon as we can, but none have seen Alwin. A poor flock indeed, to not know the whereabouts of their shepherd.

It is Tove who tells me.

'He is gone down to Botwine, last I heard,' says Tove. She is sitting in bed, mending her embroidered blanket today, pulling some fresh-woven thread through her hands, testing it for strength. The last few days have taken much from her and ever since Wulfrun's whipping she is found more and more by herself. The more she places herself back into convent life, the more precious her time alone.

I thank her, but she only shakes her head.

'Do not thank me. I hear our Father Botwine grows worse by the day.'

She fumbles at her side for a needle, then glances up at me. 'Wulfrun wishes to speak with you,' she says.

'I know,' I say.

'They are all calling it a miracle,' says Tove, 'that she could stand, that the abbess fell in her place.'

'Do you think it a miracle?'

'There are times, aren't there, when you must throw the dice?' asks Tove. 'When a sister is ill and the leechdom you give her will either cure or kill?'

'Not often,' I say, 'but yes. It cannot stay the same, either way.'

'You begin to sound wise,' says Tove. 'That is when I know our fates grow truly evil.'

'Not evil,' I say, 'only different. Wulfrun will be abbess, I am sure of it.'

'I thought there would be another path. That I would not have to choose a stranger over a woman I have known for half of my life. Seeing her fall like that, so weak . . .'

'What would you do?' I ask. 'Let the abbess continue as she is? Whipping us until there are enough dead that the stores will stretch again?'

'No,' says Tove. 'But if I had acted earlier, when we first sold the tapestries, maybe. Or when she first wished to build that foolish second church. I have abandoned my duties to this place too long and in taking them up again find them suddenly heavy.'

She finds, finally, the needle and leans into the light so that she can begin to thread it.

'But you do not have to stay and listen to an old woman's regrets,' she says, eyes still on her thread. 'Go, fetch Alwin, help that poor girl.'

When I go to the men's dormitory, Alwin is not there. I find only Botwine asleep in his cell, one great arm spread across the table, a bible beneath the other hand. His face is slack, so deep in his slumber that he does not hear me open the door to the men's dormitory, nor the sound of me drawing aside the cloth that separates his room from the others. Here was once the pilgrims' house, but we have few pilgrims any more, nor relics left to pray over.

There are no fires lit. I do not see Alwin, and Botwine has left his own hearth empty. There are not even ashes in it, no sign of warmth for a long time. We are all sparing our firewood but the cold here is different. Botwine's lips are blue. He will freeze himself, before long. Self-murder, in all but name.

The smell of him is strong. We only bathe once a month, less if it is cold, and so most sisters have some stink about them: sweat, moon-bleeding. Mostly, we wash our face, hands and underarms with cold water and this keeps the worst of it away. But it seems as if Botwine has not even been doing that. His hair is growing long from his tonsure, stubble at the centre of his head like cropped early wheat. He has always worn a beard, but it hangs straggly and dirty.

I walk over to stir him. He should be in the infirmary: a bleeding and a warm fire would heal at least some of what is wrong with our priest. There is a quill close to his hand, its tip dried, its feathers ragged with use. Botwine has been writing in the margins of his bible.

I lean in to read it. Difficult to make out in the gloom, Botwine's hand overlapping with the far more careful letters of some long-ago scribe. It is open on Genesis, the story of the Binding of Isaac. Devout Abraham, knife in hand and his son before him as an offering to our hungry God and only when he lifted the blade ready to let it fall did an angel come and release him from his charge. I have never liked the tale. It has too much of the trick about it.

Beside the passage where a ram is sent in Isaac's place to be sacrificed, Botwine has written 'Eadwig'. This is the neatest of all the words and he has embellished it outwards and outwards and outwards, as if not willing to let it come to an end.

I reach forward, shake our priest's shoulder. Botwine is an unwilling pilgrim back to wakefulness, his eyes red-webbed.

'We need a priest,' I say, 'for the last rites. The abbess's punishment was a harsh one.'

Botwine frowns. 'Punishment?'

'The whipping,' I say. 'One of the sisters will die from it.'

'Ah,' says Botwine heavily, 'a shame. Alwin went to check the eel traps. When he is back, he might give the rites.'

The last time I saw Botwine, it was more than two weeks ago, pitted against the abbess, arguing to keep Eadwig's body from being reburied. He has not been there for the abbess's inspection, for her beatings. All this time, he has locked himself away on his solitary quest and now he does not even ask after his flock. We might all starve to death and he would still remain here, poring over his books.

Melancholia is selfish, I know. It takes the light from you and leaves nothing in return. But Botwine is not the only soul in this convent that grieves.

Our priest waves at me. 'Sit,' he says. There is nowhere else but the mattress on which he sleeps and so I fold myself down onto it, feeling like a child. Botwine has not ordered his rushes changed for a long time. They are wet underfoot, beginning to rot. This whole room might collapse around Botwine and he would barely mark it.

'I am close,' he says, leaning in. His eyes are bright. 'I

have been thinking. This demon in the marsh, it took Eadwig? Why?'

'I do not think—'

'It took him as sacrifice,' says Botwine. 'It knew that we were kin. And I did not stop it.'

I wait. In the wooden walls, I hear skittering. Mice, rats maybe. Or sparrows, shivering back from the frozen sky into the warmth of thatch and nests. A strange comfort, to think that we are never as alone as we believe ourselves to be.

'I was in the Archbishop's home,' says Botwine, 'a long time ago. I was a favourite, you see, served him as a clerk. Not of high birth, but quick of wit and a strong man, also. They put me on a yoke once, to see how I would fare. I nearly beat the ox himself. The glory of God, reflected in man.'

He gives a little smile. 'Well, that is past vanity. When the Archbishop lived still and the king was Edgar, God rest his soul, I saw riches I have never seen before or since. Silk from the east, a spice called pepper that conjured heat on your tongue . . .'

'It sounds a marvel,' I say. In truth, I cannot imagine it. A long way from this chill place, at least.

For the first time, Botwine truly looks at me. Remembers who he speaks to.

'You have never left,' he says.

'No,' I say. 'And never will.'

Something of his old kindness comes into Botwine's eyes. It is almost worse seeing it there, knowing that he might be gentle again if truly he so desired. I had thought him unchanging. Our winter visitor, solid as the oak. Telling we oblates stories of revenants and giants and laughing when we shrieked.

Then he remembers what has passed. The heartwort I gave to Eluned, Sybba's death. The kindness slips away and he is a priest once more, his duty to provide guidance to even the worst of his sinners.

'Let me continue, then. In the Archbishop's home, he kept animals also. A wolf, a bear. And a pelican. You know of this last beast?'

I nod. 'If food is scarce, they pierce their breast with their own beak. Feed their own blood to their chicks.'

'The Christ-bird,' says Botwine. 'A fair hunter of demons, so they say as well. I think about that often. What would drive a mother to that?'

I think of Sweet. A hand, guiding me behind the walls and away from her. Seeing my face near every day but speaking to me in snatches, in shadows.

'They would think it was the least evil of all the paths, I think,' I say. 'The only choice left to them.'

'Well, when I heard of the pelican, I ran to see it. Shameful, and the Archbishop laughed at me for it but I did not care. I would meet this creature. And when I got there, what did I see?'

'It was dead?' I ask.

'No,' says Botwine. 'Worse, in a way. She lived still. But so sadly. Her feathers fallen and bare, her eye clouded. Her chicks had been taken from her, you see, once they had hatched and she had no mate to make any others.'

'A pity,' I say. I do not know if I mean it in truth or not.

Botwine watches me. 'It was,' he says. 'Tell me, Hilda, do you think that the Christ-bird would still pierce herself, if those lost chicks returned to her? If they were in need? Do you think they love any less?'

Mere

He slams his fist down on the table, so hard and heavy that I flinch back.

'No,' says Botwine. 'She would do whatever she had to. I will not leave Eadwig at the crossroads. I must ride out, with as many men who would come with me. Together we will fell this demon and the curse will be lifted. The abbess will bury him back in the orchard where he belongs.'

I stare at him. He will not freeze to death, for the marsh will kill him first.

'The abbess will not allow it,' I say. 'Priests should not bear weapons. And more than that, you must stay here. For her. She cannot lead this place without you.'

Botwine reaches over and pats my hand as if I am an oblate that has forgotten her scripture.

'But you will not be without me long. I will win and return and these evil days will end.'

'But Leogifu—'

'Leogifu did not have the faith that I do,' says Botwine. He lifts his arm. 'Nor the strength. I am not as young as I once was, but I have battle in me yet.'

I look at the hollowed man before me. His dirty hands, his fevered eyes. He believes he will win, as strongly as if he has already claimed victory.

And he will meet the same end as the rest of them, washed up and bloated on our shores.

I do not stay long after that. There is no talking him away from it and so I ask him only to wait. To bide a while longer, for Wulfrun has her own plans. He agrees but not without complaint.

'I am not to be ordered by the abbess, nor Wulfrun,' he says.

'Not an order,' I say. 'A plea, from an old friend. She recovers from her wounds and would welcome your visit.'

Botwine stops. 'No,' he mutters. 'I must stay here. There is much to read, prayers and spells and exorcisms. I must be both pure and strong. Out there, they will tell me of sins, pollute me. I cannot leave this place, do you understand?'

He fears not our pollution but our judgement. In his cell, he might still save Eadwig. But past the threshold, there is every reminder that his son is gone, that nothing he can do or defeat will bring Eadwig back to life.

But I only nod and stand to leave. He turns from me quickly, back to his scribblings and tales.

'Whatever happens,' I say, 'the convent will need you. And we would not see you unhappy.'

Botwine grunts, waves me away. He has still not asked which sister is dying.

I find Alwin returning from the eel traps empty-handed and bring him to the infirmary with haste. When we arrive there, red-faced and panting both, Ethel is worse. She is beyond seeing us now and she reaches out for Alwin, calls him uncle.

'Go to it, then,' I say. But Alwin is pale, his jaw clenched.

'I have not,' he says, 'I have never . . .'

I stare at him. Botwine leaves his own acolyte to these bitter tasks, with none of the knowledge needed to face them.

'All will be well,' I say, 'I know the rites and am with you. You must only say so and I will step in.'

Alwin gives a quick, tight nod. 'Thank you,' he says. I wait for the next thoughtless word, the proud, easy

Mere

disdain that carries him through life. But his face shows only gratitude.

He gives the rites poorly and I have to remind him when he forgets a word. Ethel is too far gone to confess all but the most remote of sins and so he forgives her for stealing a bronze ring as a child and for dreaming of Christ taking her as His wife. But, at last, it is done and she reaches out her hand and asks if he will go to the orchard with her.

'I will,' says Alwin, 'tomorrow. We will go and pick the apples you speak of.'

He looks about fiercely, cheeks red, to see if any will challenge this falsehood of his. But I have been at enough deathbeds to know that truth is sometimes an unwelcome visitor. A lesson that Alwin is learning, too.

Ava does not leave Ethel's side, though she is called away by the abbess, by Alwin, by all her sisters begging her for aid. She stays there praying until she loses her voice and even then she begs for Ethel's health, for her soul.

Even so, it is a wretched death for Ethel lives another two days. First, her skin pales, cold and clammy to the touch. She vomits and what she does not vomit she then voids. Her heartbeat quickens, then slows.

Even at the end when her body is taken away to be cleaned and shrouded, Ava goes with it. The portress has not eaten these past days and has barely taken a sip of wine or water. She was not a large woman to start with, but the hollows of her cheeks are as deep now as they have ever been and I worry for her. We cannot lose them both.

'Thank you,' she says at the doorway, after Ethel is taken away.

I wait for the sting, the warning. Surely there will be something. But she only clasps my hands in hers.

'You were never my foe,' she says, 'and I would not be yours.'

'So you tell me,' I say. 'But the abbess hurts us all.'

Ava is not easily moved from her ways, but when she does crack it will be with the violence of a decade's dutiful obedience. It will release something in her and I do not think she knows yet what.

Perhaps that is why I see fear in her eyes. Perhaps that is why she shakes her head, says, 'If we elect Wulfrun, we invite disorder. We invite chaos.'

I look around me. Three wounded sisters, one dead. Another half a dozen ill with the sorts of sicknesses that come after long hunger and long cold. The abbess in her bed hiding her disease and our priest muttering alone in a freezing room.

'What is this,' I ask, 'if not chaos?'

It is a cruel question and she knows it. But Ava is loyal, Ava is certain, and so she offers no argument. She only gives me a bow and leaves to follow Ethel's body to the chapel.

Chapter 17

*E*ven after such a death, there is much to do. It is always so. Together, Mildred and I pull the blankets from Ethel's mattress and put them in the pile for washing later by the stream. It is past time to change the rushes and so we gather them up, wet and stinking, to be used for feed for the goats. New ones are strewn on the floor, scattered with whatever dried flowers I can spare: lavender, sage. Our peat for the fire grows low and so I go and fetch a great pile of dried-out blocks.

My hands ache, but this is not the end of it. My infirmary is prepared, but the patients are still in need of me. Three sisters come in to have their blood let. Another cannot eat but for vomiting, cannot sleep but for nightmares. I think it a malady of the mind and so give her betony to ease her days. Tove's toenails begin to cut into her flesh and so I soften them in hot water, cut what I can, though it is a battle that I fight every few weeks or so. While I am there, I massage her knees and back. And there are still others who come, who wish only to talk. From them I hear only one name: Wulfrun. Her miracle, her visions, her strength, her kindness. How the abbess has not left her bed since that day. The same sisters who lifted a switch to Wulfrun but a few days ago now speak as if she were already sainted.

I listen and smile and nod, but every time they say her name I remember how I have failed her.

And then when they are gone and there are at last no more duties for the day, I go to speak to Wulfrun.

She is sitting on her bed, a book of psalms open on her lap. A gift loaned from some admirer, for there have been plenty enough of them visiting, praying with her, laughing even. Upon the page is a psalm of David, calling for the Lord to shatter the teeth of his enemies.

She is mercifully alone. Her visitors are away at Compline but we both are spared attending tonight.

I step in and she looks up. She wants to say something to me, but I go quickly to her back and begin to look at the dressings on her wounds.

'I do not need to change them yet,' I say. 'You heal well.'

I hate undressing the bandages, reapplying the poultices and pressing in wads of bog-cotton, for every time I see the split skin and bruises so deep that they must go to the bone. How strange, that she with two dozen blows might live and Ethel with three might die.

She nods at the bed.

'Sit with me.'

'I have much—'

'Not long,' she says.

I do as she says, lowering myself to the mattress. I can smell her, the sweet berries which surely are no longer fresh. The heady stench of the poultices on her back, rich and life-giving. The sweat of her, that animal smell that belongs to her and no other.

Just before ice cracks, it creaks. Warnings, signals of weakness. I feel it in my whole body, the urge to clasp her hands in mine, beg her forgiveness. Tell her that I would never leave her again, even at the cost of every other soul in this convent. But I have not earned even that.

'You have been hiding from me,' she says.

'If it has seemed that way, I—'

'No,' she says, fiercely, 'do not lie to me. You choose Mildred, always, to attend to me, even when you might do it yourself. You soften your tread when you pass me, hoping that I will not wake and call to you. You act like a thief, though you have committed no crime.'

She reaches out her hand, but I do not take it. I cannot, not yet.

'They are telling me it is a miracle,' I say. 'That you took so much pain and stood yet. That the abbess was the one who fell to her knees and not you. I am sure you have heard that she has remained abed since. Not dead, but not well either.'

Her eyes flicker. She knows this, but it interests her still. If the abbess died, it would make her ascension much smoother. Not that any would dare say so.

'I think I know what happened. The brew helped, in part. Mercy, also. Your blows are far lighter than poor Ethel's, though I am sure they do not feel so. Many sisters stayed their hand for you, it seems. Maybe out of kindness, maybe out of fear. So it is a miracle we have made, together.

'And you have healed well,' I continue. 'No bloodrot, no shaking. You are fated to live, it seems.'

'So all is well,' she says, softly. 'Do not blame yourself. I asked you to leave me and you did.'

Anger comes sudden and fierce. Tightens my throat, hurries my words. 'You should never have asked that of me.'

Wulfrun gives a small laugh. 'I should not wish to protect you?'

'It is not your place,' I say. 'You do not think I care for you, as you care for me? That it does not still nearly fell me to see you hurt as you are? You lived but it might have gone otherwise. I have seen an illness burn a sister from the inside out and spare another. Plenty of my sisters tell me it is a sign of God's favour, but I have seen the most devout among us die in agony, while the ordinary sinners live.'

'You speak of Ethel,' says Wulfrun.

'And the rest,' I say. 'Leogifu, Eadwig. You might be as any of them, in a cold grave.' I take a long, shaking breath. The confession comes in a tumble of words. 'All my life, I have been put aside. Sent here by Sweet for my own good. Ava and I parting for our own protection. But I would never have chosen these things. And then, to do the same to you, to betray you. And this time, by choice.'

'It is different,' says Wulfrun. 'You have not given me up.'

'It does not feel that way,' I say.

Wulfrun takes a deep breath and then kisses me. In full view of the infirmary, of any who would care to look at us and she kisses me still, as if we were husband and wife.

'I will not ask it of you again. You have my word,' she says.

'Good,' I say, 'for I would only refuse.'

Mere

'I have no doubt of that,' she says. There is that light in her again, the sort that shines golden from chapel stained-glass windows. 'Now, speak with me a while. There is much for us to do, while we both still live.'

Our meeting of allies is held the next morning. It is Saint Sylvester's day, he who turned the heathen Roman emperor Christ-wards. A day for the new month, a day of empires turning.

We meet in the infirmary. Not a secret place, but we are beyond secrecy. Besides, Wulfrun is still not strong enough to leave her bed. I wait with her, cleaning and changing her wounds and then talking with her in a low voice. The air is thick with the weight of what is about to fall and we both find we must move, laugh, do anything but dwell on what is to come. I thread my fingers through hers and mark, only now, that her first finger is a little longer than the others.

'My mother said it was because I was a shrew,' says Wulfrun. 'Always pointing, always ordering. She said it grew long with over-use.'

'It will be as long as your arm, if we win this. A whole convent to order.'

Her face twists. 'I hope not,' she says.

Our allies join us carefully. Tove is first, calling Mildred to help her over for her limbs are particularly stiff today. She sits calmly, her hands clasped, like some carven saint.

Next is the new cellarer. The cantor and the novice mistress, too, though neither have far to walk as they are both in my infirmary, the former for her whipping and the latter for an issue with her belly that I cannot cure but that, praise God, has not worsened. A half a dozen others who have no title but our convent cannot do without: porters, weavers, laundresses, dairy maids, goatherds.

Then Sweet, who ignores the stares of the other sisters and walks towards us all, sitting on the other side of Wulfrun's mattress as if she were born to it. Eluned is at her side and Mildred goes to greet her, holds her hands with both of her own as if she were an older sister about to be wed away.

Botwine does not come. I had asked him, knowing he would not, but even so I cannot stop my dismay. If he were by our side, we might call the election right now.

Wulfrun looks about her, counting. 'Two score of us,' she says. 'A good number. A strong number. You know why I call you. The abbess is leading us to ruin. I will speak truly: I would be in her place. To lead you from this curse and towards the light. You have seen already what power is in me. She no longer has God's favour.'

I thought there would be argument at this. Some question, some doubt. But Wulfrun's miracles are in their ears, on their tongues, in their dreams. So most of them nod, murmur.

Then, Tove speaks.

'You speak of the curse,' she says. 'How would you lift it?'

'The abbess has cowered behind our walls. She thinks that prayer alone will save us. I would flee. As the Trojans fled and founded Rome, so we will build anew in another place. Sweet has agreed to guide us through the marsh.'

Here, I look at Sweet. Think of what she has told me and what she has not. She stands at the edge of us, her arms crossed, her head twitching at every sound outside. She has not grown as thin as the rest of us, for she has

Mere

been living with hunger half her life, knows every trick a soul might learn to keep themselves alive. Still, I see the strain elsewhere, in the bags beneath her eyes, in her fingers growing stiff.

'You think we would live through such a journey?' I ask.

'It is the best path we have,' says Sweet, heavily. I know she is telling the truth and I know, too, that she does not think we will live to see Gipeswic.

The others sisters look between us and begin to understand, their faces growing ever more fearful as if the mere might seep in beneath the door, rising until it is about our throats, our gasping mouths.

Then, Wulfrun claps her hands and we all flinch. She is not smiling, but if she feels any dread she shows none of it. Her back is straight though it must pain her greatly. 'It is decided, then,' she says, 'and in time, we will return and rebuild.'

It is not quite enough, but the strength in her voice takes the edges from our fear. Wulfrun understands that hope is like a rushlight, that she must always be watching for its dwindle, ready to replace it with fresh flame or else send us all into darkness.

'No easy thing, to build a convent,' says Tove. 'I have met only one woman who has done it in my life and it took much from her.'

'As long as we live, we might come back to restore this place,' says Wulfrun.

I am used to Tove's wit, her words that sting but never wound. Now she regards us all seriously. Tove has more of a claim to be abbess of this place than any. All eyes are on Wulfrun, but it is Tove who is the oldest, the richest, the most respected.

'And how, sister, would I flee? I cannot walk very far even when I am well. The journey would kill me.'

'The stronger men and women would carry you on their backs,' says Wulfrun.

'And when the demon comes for them? When they panic, drop me and leave me to my death?'

'We would leave none behind.'

'So you say, but I have known of loving husbands who left their wives to slavery. Mothers who watched as their children were killed by northmen and did not cry out even once so that they themselves might remain hidden. Fear makes cowards of us.'

Wulfrun leans forward, wincing for the first time since she called this meeting. 'I give you my word, then. That I will not leave you behind.'

Tove smiles, but it is not a full-hearted thing. She thinks of Sigeburg still, of the further pain this betrayal will cause her.

'I must trust you, it seems. So, sister, what must we do to make you abbess?'

We set our plans, how the most senior sisters will talk to those beneath them, strengthen the currents that are already turning away from the abbess. Most leave quickly afterwards, hurrying back to duties that they will be missed at. But Sweet and Eluned stay, draw Wulfrun away, bowing their heads and speaking together. I see Sweet hold up her hand, counting something.

'They ask a greater price each time I speak to them,' says Wulfrun, shaking her head when they have gone. 'I should have brought them both to the market with me in Gipeswic. I would have come away richer than I arrived.'

Mere

'What have you promised them?' I say.

'Sweet has been petitioning for Eluned's freedom, or if I do not become abbess, the gold to buy it anyway. But now she wishes Eluned to have land also, a plot of her own.'

This is the more that Sweet spoke of. Not for herself, but for another.

'The land will be harder, but it is worth it,' says Wulfrun, her thoughts full not of mercy but only of good sense. 'They tell me that my miracle is believed, among most of the large households anyway. They would accept me as abbess. I have charged them to spin a few tales, where they can.'

'In praise of you?'

'In awe,' says Wulfrun, then smiles at me. 'Come, I do not have to believe it myself. But they must think me powerful at least.'

I imagine them both, whispering across hearths, heads together as they fetch water. A cunning plan, for between them Sweet and Eluned will come across most of the women who are not in the convent and most of the women in turn will then pass the tales of Wulfrun's holiness to the men.

All this talk of her divinity has brightened Wulfrun. 'Let us call the election,' she says. 'Tomorrow, at the latest.'

'You heal still,' I say. 'Wait until you can walk without opening the wounds and then begin the votes.'

'By then half the convent may have perished.'

'So you will need fewer votes to win.'

She frowns.

'I did not mean that,' I say. 'But you must wait. Tove worried about the journey, but you might not survive it either. You will be no use as an abbess if you serve a day and then collapse and die.'

Wulfrun picks up a tuft of bog-cotton from her mattress, winds it about her finger. She does this more and more, slowly unpicking everything about her.

'Very well,' she says. 'But as soon as I can travel, we will go.'

There is a noise at the doorway. We both turn, see a man standing there. I do not recognize him at first, for he has pulled up his cloak to cover his head. But I know that broad frame, and beckon him over.

'It is Botwine,' I whisper to Wulfrun.

Wulfrun gives a bitter laugh. 'He comes too late. For my whipping, for my council. All of it.'

'Even so,' I say, 'he is friend to both of us.'

Her eyes shine. I understand, too late, that she has felt Botwine's absence even deeper than I. She has risked so much to save Eadwig, out of love for his mother maybe, but also for Botwine's own sake. Yet he brushed it aside like old rushes.

'He was once,' she says. 'No longer.'

Then, she raises her voice, loud enough to carry across the infirmary.

'He is only a coward now.'

At the doorway, Botwine stops. I see the battle in him and for a breath I think he will tell Wulfrun that she is wrong and that he is sorry for abandoning her. The last link to her old home, her own life.

But he only turns and leaves, the doorway empty behind him. A revenant, gone as swiftly as he came.

'That was not wise,' I say.

'No,' says Wulfrun. 'But it was true.'

*

Mere

The rest of my day passes unsettled, my mind half on Botwine the whole time. Wulfrun sees it in me, I think, but does not apologize.

That evening, she beckons me to her bed, winds her arm around mine so that we sit side by side, leaning on each other as great old trees do over time. Her head rests on my shoulder. She has her cloak on her lap, has been mending the embroidery where she can. There is no spun gold left and so she uses wool. The stags and saints shine a little less bright, despite her efforts.

The fire crackles. There is laughter from the corner of the room, Mildred talking with Tove. If we were not so hungry, if we did not have the winter ahead of us, if we did not have this mere-devil haunting us, trapping us, I might almost feel content.

'I shall go speak to Botwine,' I say, after a while. 'His melancholy worries me.'

'Do what you will,' says Wulfrun. 'But do not apologize for me.'

'Never,' I say. 'Once I started, I might never stop.'

She smiles at that, but it is quickly gone.

'I know him,' she says, 'of old. I know I may have seemed hard when I spoke earlier—'

'Hard,' I say. 'Cruel.'

'Well, it may be all of those things,' she says, 'but Botwine needs a firm hand sometimes. This will pull him from his melancholia, spur him on. I give you my word on this.'

'I hope so,' I say, 'for I have not seen him like this before.'

I am not even halfway down the path to Botwine's dwelling the next morning when a cry rises up. From the old pilgrims' quarters, from a handful of dwellings about the marsh.

Shouts, wails and everywhere men and women with clubs and axes.

I recognize the cellarer hurrying past me, lifting her skirts.

'What is wrong?' I ask, pulling her aside.

'Father Botwine is gone,' she says. 'And he has taken two men with him.'

Chapter 18

The day after Botwine's departure is strange. The tale comes out slowly, from unwilling tongues. He went round the houses, it seems, after Wulfrun's words in the infirmary. Spoke with the men only, asked them if they would fight a battle with him, the only battle. Four agreed and he told them to take whatever weapons and supplies they had and meet him before Vespers. Two baulked, remained by their hearths, but Oswy and Edwin went. The bravest of us all, perhaps.

We cannot know whether the three men won and carried on to Gipeswic or whether they must now be lying dead somewhere in the marsh. The abbess does not speak of it at the holy offices. It is as if Botwine is still shut in his quarters. And we continue our lives unbalanced, disaster thick about us even as the abbess tells us we must only live through the winter.

We go out more often to the land, to hunt and trap what we might. But the rivers are bare, the pools and ponds empty. Birds no longer sing in the trees and there are not even crows to circle us. Our meals consist of small triumphs: bitter roots and tough herbs and bark cut from the tree and boiled into pottage or ground into flour. Ava complains that the tenants keep stores back for themselves but it cannot be much for they are as pinched as we.

After two years of weak harvests, feeble animals and paltry gifts from the Ealdorman, this latest tightening is dangerous. The children and the old will be the first to go and I watch over Tove with greater care than I ever have before.

Wulfrun is quiet. She thinks on Botwine's fate. It worries at me, too. How we might have talked him from such danger, how we might have kept him with us. She tells me none of this, though, and I wish she would. She is slipping away somewhere, I think, and leaving me behind.

'It matters not,' says Wulfrun, dully, when I speak to her about it. It is Epiphany today. The day marking the three kings from the east, bearing gifts for the newborn Christ-child in His stable. And still we wait for our own pilgrims, though I think the stars too clouded for any to find us now.

Wulfrun is dressing for the cold, thick hose and two cloaks. Today is the first day she is returned to light duties. The abbess has ordered her to the dairy. A humiliating duty for one so highborn, but Wulfrun does not care. She will sit and spin her tales to the maids and if any come to check if she is working, she will fall to her knees, appearing to all a poor sister doing nothing but humbling herself. I do not think she has even learnt to churn butter, all this time.

'You cannot mean that,' I say.

'I think it the truth,' she says. 'Look about you. The curse has not been lifted; we suffer still. We gave him a fool's death.'

There is a melancholy about her since Botwine left. One by one, every thread tying her to her home is cut and I think it is a greater blow than she would ever say.

'You do not pity him?'

'Of course I do,' she says, curtly. 'And I have wept for him and prayed for him. I hope, still, that he will come back to us. You forget, Hilda, that he came to my home as often as yours. Many times for longer, for our dinners were far grander and the hunting was good. He was a friend.'

'Is he no longer?' I ask.

Wulfrun does not answer, only pulls the sleeve of her habit down, unsnags it from some bandage. She winces.

That evening I go to confession. We would usually go but once or twice a year, whenever Botwine came to visit, but now the abbess orders it as much as we can spare the time for. Another duty for Alwin. He has taken to wearing Botwine's old spare robes, hastily hemmed. They sag in strange places, so that when he talks to us of being our rock his gestures are soft and shifting as sand.

His penitence, too, leaves the sisters with little comfort. He is too easy on those who must be chastened and too severe with those who have already endured much hardship. I kneel as he stands above me and tell him that I have been wrathful with Mildred, spoken to her unkindly. My helper has been making many mistakes of late, when she is usually so steadfast, and I think it half Alwin's fault. If Ethel died for nothing more than a few drawings, she is in far greater danger.

'There is nothing else?' he asks when I am done.

'That is what I am here to confess,' I say. If Alwin thinks he might guilt me into speaking of any other sins, he is wrong. I will not be shamed by an adulterer.

Alwin stops, tells me to pray as I wait, and I hear him turning the pages of the penitential, seeking out the prayers and fasting that I must perform.

'For sins of this degree,' I say, 'Father Botwine would usually tell me to abstain from fish for a month.'

'Well,' says Alwin, 'Father Botwine has left us all and there is no fish left on any of our plates. A hair shirt for another three days.'

A harder penance than usual. It was little more than a few moments' anger and I did not even strike the maid.

'I wonder,' I say, as I leave, 'if I had chided at any other sister, whether that penitential of yours might be a little kinder.'

'It is without favour,' says Alwin, quickly. 'I will show you the book if you wish.'

'There is no need,' I say. I do not wish to pore over the writings of far-away priests.

Waiting outside at the head of the queue is Ava. She returns for confession over and again, seeking always the answer that will absolve her. But no matter the prayers, the hair shirts, the abstentions and penances, I think she will never be cleansed of Ethel.

'What did you speak of?' asks Ava, as I leave.

'That is for his ears and his alone,' I say. 'Or do we break sacraments today?'

'Was the penance fair?' she asks.

'It was,' I say. 'He follows the penitential to its every word.'

I ought to return to the infirmary but I instead stay.

Mere

There is something about today that unsettles me. Ever since the whipping, we have left our wounds open. They linger, phlegm in the throat, rot in the gut, ready to spread and claim us all.

I lean into Ava. 'The abbess is not here,' I say. 'No sins staining her soul, then?'

'She will come,' she says, 'in time.'

Ava sweeps past me into the chapel and still I wait. After a short time, there comes a cry of anger and Ava spills out, Alwin behind her. Alwin's face is red and he holds tight in his hand a ragged copy of the penitential.

'I will not have your questioning,' he says, to Ava, to us all. 'All of you, needling me, digging the ground out from beneath me!' He lifts the book as if it is a weapon.

'What has happened?' I ask.

'I only said,' says Ava, fiercely, 'that Father Botwine had a different punishment. One more suitable for the severity of my sins.'

'I am weary,' moans Alwin. 'This is her third time visiting me today.'

He is nothing more than a child and I am not without fellow-feeling. I know what it is to be asked to right every small and petty ill. I know what it is to find yourself not enough for it. And Botwine has left him little of use. Only old words and a memory of kindness.

Wulfrun should be here, quick-wit, bright-tongue. Or even Mildred, to calm the boy, steer him away from this fight. But there is only me.

'I am sure she does—'

'I can speak for myself, Hilda,' snaps Ava. She looks between us all, at the gathering crowd. She is used to her quiet tallies, to standing always at the abbess's side and never stepping forward. So many gazes on her and I see her shrink with their force.

'There was only one sin,' she says, quietly. 'A fellow servant of Christ that I failed.'

It is hard to see her like this, cowed, full of grief. There is so little that bends in her and I know that she will be just as unbending towards herself. And while there is much that I might blame her for, I do not think she could have helped Ethel any more than she did.

I reach out a hand to her shoulder, but she shrugs it off.

'The abbess will have need of me,' she says. 'I do not have the time to argue with you all.'

She turns and leaves, her body stiff. No doubt to return to her duties, to lose herself in her tallies and counts. Alwin does not even stay to watch her go, walking back into the church and calling out for the next soul to enter and be cleansed.

'The year has turned,' says Tove, when I return to the infirmary. She has not been to confession and I think not even the abbess would dare to force her to it. 'When will your Wulfrun call this election of hers?'

'She is not mine,' I say, but my face glows at the words.

'So you say,' replies Tove. 'In my youth, I knew plenty of men who were not mine either. And when will this woman who is not yours call her election?'

'She waits,' I say, 'a little longer. Botwine's departure has unsettled things.'

'Aye,' she says. 'I knew him when he was new to the priesthood. Only a few years older than this Alwin of yours, but a life behind him. A youth spent in wars ages a man differently.'

Mere

'He never spoke of it,' I say. I had heard of Father Botwine's past only in snatches, in gossip and long tales that did not seem true. 'Perhaps he will be strong enough for it, after all?'

Tove looks at me, not with pity in her eyes but something like censure. I should not be tempted by such hopes, no matter how fair-seeming.

'I think he would have returned by now,' she says, 'if he had won this battle of his. He was a fool to think he might win.'

'Not a fool,' I say. 'The only path left to him, I think.'

Tove lifts up a spoon of the pottage and lets it drip back down. 'You are right, I think. Even so, if I could walk as far and fast as our old priest, perhaps I would be joining him before long.'

'Do not say that,' I say. 'Even in jest.'

'It is not in jest,' says Tove. 'Wulfrun must call this election sooner rather than later, or else I will not be able to travel, even with six men there lifting me.'

I go to the water that evening, to wash my face and my moon-rags. My bleeding started yesterday and has seemed to end today, a halting, strange reminder of how much time has passed. With the hunger of these last few weeks, soon enough I will not bleed at all.

The day is cold once more and the banks of the stream slick with last night's rain. There are few others at the river, most saving their washing for warmer days. Some not here washing at all. One, a woman who works now in our kitchen, sits by the water, holding her hand as deep as it will go. Her jaw is tight, her skin red as fever up to her wrist. I try to sign to her, to offer some salve or bandage, but she does not want me or my care. She offers pain, perhaps even to our God, and would not have me lessen her gift.

Another, who I know as one of Sybba's brothers, has in his hand a wooden token. Seeking protection from this curse of ours, perhaps, or maybe he wishes only to find his brother's hoard at last. He cups the token in his hand, breathes some hope into it and then flings it to the water. A woman's shape, thick-hipped and with unbound hair.

Such worship is not for me to see. I turn my face from them, towards the river. Something has snagged in the reeds. At first I think it another token, another gift given as Sybba's brother gives a gift. But it is a ring caught in the weeds, set with opal that gleams bright as teeth.

I know this ring. Botwine wore it almost every day, cast wide for his thick fingers.

Before I can reach to pull it out, the water shudders and the ring untangles itself, is borne along downstream, out into the marshes. I follow its gleam and then stop. In the distance, two shapes sprawled and thin-limbed, unmoving.

Chapter 19

*M*en come to take Oswy and Edwin to be washed and then into the chapel. There are no signs of wounds on the bodies and their axes and knives are still in their belts. Their lips are cracked and dry and their cheeks are pinched. It is as if they perished on a long journey, of thirst or hunger or cold. But they had been away less than a week.

Oswy had no family yet living, but Edwin's wife comes when I am washing him, with her three children. I have seen her a few times; she is one of the ceorls who is closest to Sweet and comes often for cures and spells. She stares at his body a long while. I am tense, waiting for a wail of mourning, a rending of her clothes. But she only crosses herself and then turns to me with hard eyes.

'Father Botwine was not with them?' she asks.

I shake my head.

She reaches over, brushes Edwin's forehead, lingers on the features of his face. His thinning, pale hair. The freckles about his cheeks, a disjointing of the nose where it had been broken.

'I told him not to go,' she says. 'But he would defend the faith.'

'Perhaps he did,' I say. 'Maybe it was not in vain.'

'Far better that he had stayed,' she says, 'save what remains.'

I return to the infirmary bone-tired. It is well into the night already, and I am to sleep here until dawn, watching over the patients. There are half a dozen pressing around me, calling to me, asking me to tell them what I found. Asking if it is true that Botwine has failed, that we are doomed. I have no answers for their questions, no hope against their despair.

Circled by their questions, I sit down on a stool and clutch my head.

'We are not doomed,' comes a voice from out of sight. 'As long as we do not lose heart.'

I do not look up. I sometimes wonder if they do not hear it, how she smooths the edges of her speeches here, whets them there. She speaks as if we are in a poem and tells any who listen that they are the hero.

'Have you seen something?' asks one of the patients, eager. 'A vision?'

'Please, let Infirmarian Hilda be,' says Wulfrun. I feel her hand on my shoulder. 'Can you not see she is half-ill herself? Your questions can wait until tomorrow, at least?'

Murmurs of assent, though some are more eager than others. They are beginning to learn her tricks. That she would rather not answer than speak wrongly, that she weaves and feints and never admits that she does not know.

Even so, they remember the whipping. How she stood, after so much suffering, and walked across to the abbess.

Mere

The glow of her grace that day might be fading, but it is not yet fully gone and so at her words they return to their own beds and leave me my peace.

When she is sure that they have all gone and that she cannot be seen, Wulfrun slumps down to the ground. Her legs and hands are trembling and blood is seeping through her bandages on her back.

'Would you take me to my bed?' she asks, weakly.

'I can do my best,' I say, 'but I am not full of strength myself.'

'Between us,' she says, 'I think we might do it.'

It is an ungainly walk, made worse by the fact that whenever Wulfrun feels a patient watching her she straightens, lengthens her stride, unbalancing me as she does so.

'If you do that again I shall drop you,' I say, after the third time, 'wound or no wound.'

'Truly your suffering knows no end,' says Wulfrun, between grimaces.

I rest my gaze on her back, looking for the tell-tale shadow of bloodrot. She cannot die like Ethel did. I will not let her.

We reach her bed and I lower her down to the mattress. She pulls off her habit slowly and I frown when I see the shift beneath.

'You should have called me,' I say, dropping to my knees and peering at the bandages. I will not be able to do much in the darkness, but they will need changing tomorrow.

'You had much else to do,' she says. She removes her wimple and her dark hair springs in tufts about her ears. She must cut it soon, have it shorn down as we all do, but for now I lift a curl between my fingers. What a glory it must have been when she was a wife, half a mane.

'I might be able to brew something to help, if it pains you badly,' I say.

'Will you stay a while? It will help more than any leech-doms.' She gives me a smile. 'You might even add it to one of those books of cures of yours.'

'And what would I call such a cure?' I say, knotting my fingers in hers.

'Hild-brew,' says Wulfrun, 'Hild-remedy.'

So much is dark about us and still I laugh. 'You have been abed too long, to spend time thinking on those.'

A blush on her face but she nods all the same. I find myself glad that she has allowed herself some foolishness even if she shares it only with me.

I lower myself to the bed so that I lie in her arms, her breath against my neck. I feel the jump of her lifeblood in her wrists, the slow rise and fall of her chest. I match my breath to hers. She will take in all this air and I will breathe it out. One loop, stretched across two souls.

'You have been in a dark mood since Botwine left,' I say. 'Will you talk of it?'

'I have not,' says Wulfrun. 'I have only been in prayer and in thought.'

'I see,' I say, but I do not. It might not be plain to the others yet, but it is plain to me. Botwine's fate lies heavy on her.

And so I wait there in her arms and feel her begin to shake beside me, the shake of a soul weeping who does not want to be heard and I hold her all the tighter, feeling the bones of her knuckles against my own, until at last she whispers, 'There is a great fear in me, Hilda.'

'It is not wrong to feel fear,' I say, though it is, for her. She must be beyond such weakness. 'You are not alone in this. Half the convent cannot sleep.'

Mere

She thinks on this a while. Her weeping stops, but when she speaks it is low and dull.

'The book talks of an apocalypse,' she says, 'full of trumpets and fury. But I think it comes in parts. Eadwig's death, Botwine's loss. The birds and eels and fish who have all fled. It will all slip away and when Revelation comes it will be gentle and all the more total for it. If we banish this demon, another will take its place. Or else there will be war. Or plague. We build on sand, Hilda.'

I have never seen her like this. Gone is her courage. There is a hollowness about her, the kind of empty air that fills churches and crypts.

'No,' I say. 'No, we build on bog. On water, ready to come sweep us away. It is far harder. But I have been here a lifetime. All the sisters here, all the ceorls, raising children and crops and beasts.'

'I will die here, Hilda.'

A chill runs through my body. 'You have seen this?' I ask, dreading the answer.

'No,' she says. 'No, but I know it. I feel it. Eadwig's riddle hangs on me still. *I end and then I end and then I end.* It can only mean disaster, for us all.'

'It was devil-sickness speaking,' I say, but I do not fully believe it.

In the darkness, I trace the knuckles of our hands. If I could, I would never let go of her again. Despite the dark, I can pick out the smallest movements of her eyes. How they flicker, looking for signs of falseness.

'What you said, last time,' she says, 'that you would stand by me. You mean to keep this oath?'

'With all of me,' I say.

'My husband,' she begins, halting. 'He did not protect

239

me. I was but a girl when I married him, dreaming of girdles and gold and handsome warriors. My son, too, turned from me. Sent me away, for no reason other than his wife did not trust me. And then I came here, a place I thought to hate, and I have found so much more than I ever thought I might.'

Her eyes stop their flickering. Most of the time she plans even as she speaks, her thoughts never singular but as a swarm of bees, searching and buzzing and working, always working. Now, I can almost hear the hum of it all, turned upon me.

'I have a gift for you,' she says. She reaches down beneath the mattress and pulls out a length of rope. It glimmers, even in the dim light.

The girdle she wore when she first arrived, gold thread spun through. One of the finest objects in the convent not belonging to the abbess. She should have given it to the convent when she first arrived, but in the chaos it must have been forgotten.

It is also the gift a husband would give his wife, the night of their wedding. A gift for someone precious, for a lifetime together. I would have her always about my waist and always in my mind and every time I looked down to fetch my knife or some flint my heart would skip with the thought of her.

'I cannot,' I say, my voice thick. 'With that hanging about my waist, even the slowest pig-herder would know of us.'

The hurt in Wulfrun's face is so absolute that my breath catches. She would not fall to her knees even after a whipping, but now she sits back, as if knocked by a blow.

'I see,' she says, softly, winding it about her wrist.

'But,' I say, reaching out, catching the end, 'that does not mean I do not want it. That I cannot wear it.'

Mere

She frowns, but lets the girdle loose. I roll up my sleeve and wrap it around my upper arm several times, tying it as secure as I can in a knot.

'There,' I say, 'a girdle and an arm ring all at once.'

'You look like a king's wife,' she says.

'I have always thought so,' I say. She pulls me back to her and we lie there a while. Her fingers trace the new knots beneath my sleeve, a treasure that only we will ever know of.

'I have nothing to give you in return,' I say.

'You have given me plenty,' she says, pressing her lips to my ears. I feel the warmth of her breath on my neck.

I think of her talk of apocalypse. Of the hollowness, the melancholy that she only dares show me.

'I do have a gift,' I say, slowly. 'Not of equal value, but it is the best that I own.'

I stand and go and fetch a cup from the stores. A little spiced wine, a pinch of dried fly agaric. We are low on honey and so it will be a bitter drink, but I do not think Wulfrun will mind.

'Here,' I say, handing it to her. 'Redcap brew. You have had it before?'

I like her when she is unsure, for it happens so rarely. It makes her both girlish and somehow flat, as if she is already shown in glass or vellum.

'I have,' she says, 'yes, once or twice. In my youth. It relaxes the body, cleanses the mind. And beckons visions.'

'I do not think there is enough here to bring a vision,' I say, 'but drink slowly, just in case. It helps with melancholy.'

'I am not melancholic,' she says, quickly, as if she is afraid someone will hear.

'Then, it protects against it. If you were to ever feel it creeping over you,' I say.

'I suppose I am bound to follow my infirmarian's orders,' she says and takes a sip. The rest she holds to me and I swallow it myself, my mouth pursing, for the wine is already beginning to sour. Then, we lie down together and stare at the roof.

The infirmary shudders. I know sisters who have taken this, have seen elves with their wicked arrows nocked in bows, have seen giants pushing through the clouds in the far horizon. Others have only felt themselves slowed, their worries and cares falling from them. Others have not been able to stop laughing for the strangeness of it all.

'You are well,' says Wulfrun, behind me, 'you are safe.'

I do not know if she is speaking to herself or to me. But she is right. We are oak and ivy, bound and never to be separated.

'There is no use,' I say, 'in an abbess who believes herself marked for death.'

She does not reply. She has gone somewhere and I can pull her back only with great effort.

'No use at all,' I say. There is something stirring in me. Anger, that she surrenders so easily. Resolve, to be strong where she is not. If she fears the dark, then I will be the nightingale and carry us both through.

'And so what, if it all turns to ruin? What other choice do we have left to us? To lie down, to let all crumble about us?'

'The abbess would say that is correct,' says Wulfrun, 'that we would be submitting to God's plan for us.'

'If this is His plan, then He is a fool,' I say. Only a whisper, but Wulfrun's eyes grow wide. 'Or worse, cruel.

Mere

He is not here, shitting His guts out into the rushes. He does not bury yet another child. Whatever sin has been committed, it cannot be worth this.'

'You would be whipped for that,' says Wulfrun. 'Excommunicated, killed.'

'Come, Wulfrun,' I say. 'You have been through flame and now is the time of water. I do not know what will be forged at the end of it, but it will be bright and wondrous.'

Wulfrun's hand goes to her burn. Traces a past life. For a heartbeat I see the flames there, flickering still, singeing the ends of her hair.

'Yes,' she says and there are flames in her throat also, burning away all doubt. 'We cannot turn back.'

The rest of the evening passes gently. Wulfrun tells me stories of her youth, of the finery and riches she saw as she travelled north to south with her Norse father and Wealh mother. I am sure she mocks me, talking of creatures with necks the length of two men, of snakes so poisonous they could kill with a single look. But I listen anyway, lulled towards sleep with a brilliant menagerie flashing before my eyes.

Then, just as I am nearly asleep, she lowers her voice.

'Please,' she murmurs into my neck, 'do not tell the others of my melancholy. My fear. They would begin to doubt me.'

'I heard nothing,' I say.

I awake the next morning, Wulfrun's arms still about me. It must be dawn, for the bell is ringing, but it is a sickly light, the colour of dirty water. I feel, first, the tightness of the girdle around my arm. Then, slowly, I see there is a figure standing at the end of the bed, shadowed in the early morning gloom.

I start upwards, fumbling for the knife at the side of the bed. The figure steps into the light. It is Mildred. She is often worried, my apprentice, but I have never seen her as she is this morning. She looks like the hare when it has scented the hounds.

'The fields have flooded,' she says. 'The water came up sudden just before dawn, drowned everything, when many were asleep.'

I scramble to my feet, pulling my wimple into place.

'What else?' I ask. Flooding is terrible, but it would not frighten Mildred like this.

'Botwine is back,' she says, her voice hoarse with fear.

Chapter 20

The convent is turned over, a warren when the ferret enters. Any souls who were out in their dwellings woke to water and fled to take shelter in the chapel, bringing their households and tools with them. Some had the chance to carry provisions also, but others have nothing but the clothes they were wearing.

A throng of a hundred souls or so at the chapel and more, still, making slow ways up the hill from the flood. I find Sweet on this path, her and Eluned helping those who were left behind as too old or weak to climb the slope. She has many of her supplies with her, was among those who felt the danger keenly and moved swiftly. She lifts her hand in greeting, but she is busy herself.

And so we continue on, Mildred, Wulfrun and I the only three souls who are walking towards the mere instead of away from it.

From the crest of the hill, I can see down to where the fields once were. No longer. All around is brown water, slow, steady, hungry. The stream where but yesterday we found the bodies of Oswy and Edwin is no stream but a river, grasping out at tree boughs, at homes, splintering what it can and seeping into what it cannot.

There are rats, scurrying around our feet. More fleet than the sheep and oxen that now float drowned and bloated in our fields.

The ruin of it all stops me in place. Trees that I thought would outlive me lie toppled. Dwellings built with care over the course of years reduced to posts and cut wood once more. Crops that would only barely carry us through winter drowned.

'Gone,' I breathe. 'So quickly.'

Wulfrun and Mildred at my side, saying nothing. They, too, struck by it all.

Then, Wulfrun shifts her weight. 'Come,' she says, gently. She reaches across, presses her head into my shoulder, briefly. I smell her berry scent, feel the warmth of her, and it will never return what has been lost, but it is enough.

We walk down to where a knot of people has gathered. Wulfrun still cannot move quickly with her injuries and so Mildred must support her. It is raining hard, heavy drops sliding down the back of my neck.

Ava stands at the bridge. Or, where the bridge once stood, for I can see no sign of it any longer, save for a few planks that float in the ditch. This is already nearly filled with the flood, though it is as deep as most of us are tall. It has swallowed the fields and now the water comes for us. I can see already a few men digging, trying to redirect water through new paths in the hillside. It is slow work, the soil heavy with dampness, the rain only growing stronger, falling on us all.

I look about for our priest, but cannot see him.

Mere

'What has happened?' I ask Ava.

'The flood came of a sudden,' she says, shortly. 'There was the rain and then upriver a great swell.'

Upriver. We are used to our floods here, but they tend to come on slow, sending gentle warning over a couple of days, so that we might move what we need to higher ground. Welcomed, even, for after the fields are flooded in winter any crops planted only grow all the better in the summer.

Not today. The swell came from the marsh, sudden as a storm and violent as any northman raid.

'A few souls were swept away. Both of Sybba's brothers, lost trying to lead their cattle to higher ground. The rest are wet and cold. You will have them in your infirmary, so that they can be warmed again.'

No question there, only an order.

'I heard Father Botwine—'

'Do not speak his name,' hisses Ava, but it is too late. I see movement, across the ditch, what I thought some fallen lumber twitching to life. The water on the other side of the bridge is up to his belly but he shows no sign of cold, no unsteadiness of his feet. It is as if he has emerged from the depths themselves.

Botwine.

At his movement, all those around me lift up their tools, holding them outward like spears. Those without tools reach for knives in their belts. It is at least a man's height across the ditch, maybe more, but they look at Botwine as if he might leap it at any moment.

'He has been trying to cross,' whispers Ava. 'He came after the flood. We cut away the bridge but he has lingered here.'

'Sister Hilda,' calls Botwine, 'I am glad you are here.

None of the others talk sense, none will let me in. They say that I have been away a week.'

His robes are so covered in mud that they are almost brown and his fingernails are long and dirty. Nebuchadnezzar, his feet clawed, his back feathered.

'How long,' I ask, 'how long do you say that you have been away?'

'It has been but a day,' says Botwine. 'I returned from the marsh and saw this flooding, knew that you would all be in dire need of me.'

I look to Ava, who places a finger on her lips.

I do not reply and Botwine raises his voice. 'I am sorry,' he says, 'we failed. I wandered through the marsh all day, Oswy and Edwin by my side. But first Oswy grew lost and we could not find him though we searched half a day and then Edwin, too, fell away. I found myself alone.'

He frowns. His speech is like a skipping stone, surface only. But there is something deeper that he is avoiding saying. 'I said I would save you all.'

The men hesitate at the ditch. I see Fair Alfred among them, his face marred by fear. Slowly, Ava shakes her head at them and they lift their weapons once more.

'Save us,' says Botwine, to himself. 'Save us, release us. Undo us, reknot us. Man and wife and wife and man and a million little children in every breath. Heaven and earth, great and terrible and unending and I cannot bear it, it is tight, do you not see, around my skull, poor Eadwig—'

His voice falls so that he is muttering now, in loops and spirals for which only he has the meaning. He seems to have forgotten us.

'The Devil has him,' breathes Ava. 'It has driven him mad.'

Mere

I watch our priest, lost to himself. He who strode out so bravely.

Wulfrun steps forward. Even in this morning's chaos, she brings a hush with her, bowed heads and sidelong gazes. Though the wounds on her back must pain her, she shows none of it. She makes herself invulnerable for them.

Ava's jaw tightens. 'We have no need of you here, sister,' she says. 'Go, rest.'

'I would be here,' says Wulfrun.

'Is that Wulfrun?' calls Botwine. 'I know that voice.'

Wulfrun lifts her chin, looks past Ava. 'I am here,' she says.

He begins to walk towards us, hopeful. 'Would you help me? It hurts, you see, it is too much all at once.'

'He is devil-sick, as Eadwig was,' says Ava. She stands in front of the ruined bridge, as if to bar it herself. 'We should have never let the boy return, never let this disaster in. The abbess is ill and she has appointed me in her place in this and I order that not a single soul is to pass into the convent, no matter what they plead.'

'You truly believe this will save us?' I ask.

'It is the abbess's orders,' says Ava. 'If we do not obey, what are we?'

Botwine stumbles in his progress, falls to the water. He gives a low moan, calling for aid, calling for relief. A medicine, a shriving, a confession. Anything that would release him from his agonies.

'I went,' he calls, 'I went, bravely. Under water over earth and through the mere that is both and neither. I waited but I was hungry, so hungry, there was nothing else, you understand, and ah how my head aches, oh poor Eadwig, my child, I did not know it was so, a skull and a circle.'

His voice takes on a little of the song.
'I end and then I end and then I end.
Forge me in heat, knot me in thread.
I do not belong to one soul alone.'
Wulfrun has paled. Eadwig's riddle, grown longer.

'The worms beneath,' he says. 'A chick, frozen in its nest and taken in a fox's jaws. The fleas in your hair, the fleas about your ankle.'

I take a step towards him, despite myself. 'You can feel them?' I ask.

'All of them,' says Botwine. 'A kingdom quickening and it is too much, it is too much.'

He looks directly at me.

'You know this, of course,' he says. 'You have felt it, too.'

Eadwig's grip on me as he raged and that sudden swoop and Botwine is smiling as if he has found an old friend.

I stumble backwards, towards Wulfrun, towards certainty. Botwine laughs, an odd, untethered thing. Dread fills me. He reminds me of men on their deathbeds, their thoughts flitting like a sparrow and never alighting too long.

'I am hungry, I starve,' he says. 'My throat aches and I cannot drink from the flood. But I was away only a day and so much has changed.'

He begins to sob like a small child. As Eadwig once sobbed.

Ava takes a long, shaking breath. 'You spoke with this devil?' she asks.

For a heartbeat, Botwine's agonies stop. He stares at Ava with strange eyes. 'No devil out there, nor angel. Only the old choice. A single mouthful.'

Ava's fist clenches so tight that her fingernails draw blood but she does not see this. I do not think she sees anything

Mere

but Botwine in front of her. One by one, our pillars are taken from us.

'Now,' he says, 'please, in the name of the Father, let me in. I will die otherwise.'

'The name of the Father . . .' whispers Ava.

'Portress Ava,' says Botwine, 'you must understand. I went to help, I went to—'

'Do not admit him entry,' says Ava to the men about her, as if Botwine were not there. 'And if he tries to cross the ditch, drive him away.'

Wulfrun presses forward. 'I cannot allow this,' she says, 'I will not let you harm our priest.'

'He is our priest no longer,' says Ava. 'He is something else. And it is not for you to allow or not allow, Wulfrun. You are not abbess.'

'Nor are you,' says Wulfrun. 'And where is our Mother Superior hiding?'

'She recovers,' says Ava. 'From you and your works.'

I think Wulfrun will call the election then and there. Then, comes a man's voice. Alwin, hurrying down, Mildred behind him. I did not even see her go to fetch him. He looks young in the dawn light, wrinkles and cares taken from him. A boy, rushing to meet a father after a battle.

'He is back?' shouts Alwin. 'He is safe!'

But as he draws closer, his joy fades. He turns to each of us, frowning. 'Why do you not help him across?'

'He is devil-sick,' I say, softly. 'As Eadwig was.'

'But we might save him,' says Alwin, continuing on to the broken bridge. 'Perhaps there is a way, through prayer, through leechdoms. Come, help me pull him up.'

'Brother Alwin—' begins Ava. For all of her dislike of

251

Alwin, I hear pity in her voice. She, too, cared for Botwine. She, too, grieves for him.

'Father Alwin,' he says. 'It is Father Alwin and I order you all to allow him entry!'

The men do not obey. There is a new hardness to them, the sort that comes on a man when he must kill an ailing horse or whip a beloved dog. And all the while Alwin stands in front of them, proud, but powerless.

'Sorry, Father,' says Fair Alfred, after a while. 'I've two sons and a few daughters here with me. I'd not let that devil in for my weight in gold.'

'Alfred, I am your priest and this—'

Then, there is a burst from the other side of the ditch. Botwine rising, water falling from him in sheets and it is a great leap, a heroic leap, and for a heartbeat I think he will land with us, he will cross our boundaries and be with us once again.

And then a stumble. He lands not on the other side of the ruined bridge, but on the ditch's slope, an armspan or two away from us all. Falls into the soft mud and what was strong and glory-filled becomes a scrabbling, desperate churn as he fights his way up the slipping-wall of the ditch. If it were any other man, I would know he would not be able to climb it, this wall that is a man's height and half again. But Botwine is strong and Botwine is fast and soon he is almost there, at the very edge of the ditch, and he reaches out and grasps at the closest thing within reach and it is Alwin's ankle that he grips.

And then Alwin is falling himself, more like a swoon than a trip, and I see his face grow empty for a moment, think of Eadwig's hands about my wrist and the strangeness he passed through me. I hear Mildred crying out that Botwine is devil-sick, that the very touch of his fingers is poison. Then, Botwine's grip shifts so that he is holding only the hem of Alwin's habit. The youth reaches out for safety, throws his arms around one of the posts driven into the ground for our whipping not two weeks ago.

'Please,' Botwine calls out, 'I must be allowed to cross. My skull so tight, so small it—'

Alwin struggles, each twist and kick dislodging the whipping-post more and more from the earth. Botwine does not let the boy loose. He is close now, might lift himself up once, twice, and he will be on the convent land with us. Or else, the post will pull free and he will drag Alwin down with him.

'He cannot,' whispers Ava, as if merely saying the words will make it so. She fumbles for her knife. I can see Mildred, running towards Alwin, heedless of the danger or how many will see her. He is reaching for something that has been left on the ground, some weapon to defend himself.

My mouth is dry and we are unbound, writhing and crying out like a beast in a trap and we must be careful, so careful, because I can taste it in the air. The same hunger as when Wulfrun was whipped. For quick ends and clean blood.

'Alwin,' says Botwine, roughly, 'come. You are a merciful soul and—'

The spear catches Botwine in his belly. Not more than a sharpened stick but it strikes true all the same. A blow quickly made, and then the weapon withdrawn once more. Skill born of long practice with old warriors.

I see the pink and yellow of him, the darkness of his blood and all I can think is that I must go down there, smell the wound to make sure it has not caught his guts and then begin the work of stitching it together and I should go to him and as we children once ran to him waiting for

tales of distant lands

cruel kings

brave Christian martyrs

the children they ran to him and I ran to him, once, my legs not taking me fast enough back then in my eagerness and not fast enough to Eadwig's storeroom and I am still so slow.

There is a hush. Botwine releases Alwin, frowns, presses his hand to his middle.

'Oh Lord,' he breathes, then falls backwards into the dark water. We watch, waiting for him to emerge, but he does not. There is only the flood, the lurch of swollen currents.

And Alwin scrambles up, spear in hand, eyes red and wild.

I do not weave much, but I know the feeling of a thread ready to break. Because it has been pulled too tight, because of a weakness in the spinning. It does not matter in the end, only that it breaks.

A great cheer rises. The men throng around Alwin, clapping him on the back, declaring him Beowulf himself. The women call out praise, for he has slain the demon and saved us all. Alwin does not move, nor release the spear. He is as still as a tapestry figure, more from a saga than this blighted place.

Above, the sky is empty. No crows, not even rooks or gulls. No carrion-birds to pick us clean. The winter wind cuts colder for their absence, shears through my cloak and habit and rests deep in my bones. It is not even midday yet.

Chapter 21

Alwin's deed was heroic, but it did not send the floodwaters rushing back. And so, almost as soon as she is back up the hill, Ava orders that the men be sent to join Alwin in the pilgrims' house and the women and children are to be with me in the infirmary.

'They will be in even greater danger,' I say to Ava as she tells me of this. We stand outside the kitchen, where Ava has been counting what we have left. A dismal, diminishing number, but she returns day after day, as if by careful tally she might discover some new salted eel, another barrel of apples.

'Pestilence will spread quickly,' I say.

'And you would have them in the dormitory?' she asks.

'There are spare cots there,' I say. So many of our sisters have died and have left their beds empty and cold.

'You would have some wife and her seven children running about all hours? Disturbing our prayer with their squalling?'

'Even with all that,' I say, 'I would let them in. There

are not many with children left and if you put them in the infirmary, there will be even fewer.'

'There are those among them who do not follow godly ways,' says Ava, 'who use strange blessings. Who treat the Lord as if He is but a visitor, passing through, quickly gone and even quicker forgotten. The Devil will not have to force his way through: they will invite him in.'

She speaks of many women, but I think of Sweet first. Her old tales, her little magics.

'I know these women,' I say. 'They wish to live, only. They are in our house and they will follow our ways.'

'The abbess has made her decision,' says Ava.

'The abbess has her own dwelling,' I say. 'And is beyond the fear of pestilence now, anyway... You have not forgotten Ethel so quickly?'

She sighs. Above us, cold drops fall from the eaves. The paltry thatch of the kitchen roof is wearing through and offers no protection from the cold. We were to patch it in the summer but there were no spare hands and the abbess told us to wait. Next year, she said, next year when my cousin sends us more.

I peer out to the smudged marsh. Sweet once told me of secret realms out there, portals and gateways that led through water and earth to kingdoms of riches, where none were ever hungry or sick or beaten by cruel masters.

I think of Botwine, his confusion when we told him he had been away from us an entire week. Eadwig, too, thought he had been away only a few moments. Wherever they go, it is beyond our earthly paths.

'Very well,' says Ava, pulling me back. 'I will see what can be done.'

*

Mere

In the end, Ava sets aside beds for maids and any of the girls old enough to sleep away from their mothers. The married women and their children will remain with me.

My infirmary changes. At night, there is a press of bodies, the smell of the fifty or so women and children who take shelter. Their sweat and farts and monthly bleedings fill the small room. They are not unkind, their gratitude to be behind wooden walls making them keen to help. But I have not trained them, and more often than not they are underfoot and in the way.

Sweet is among them, but I do not often see her. She keeps to the walls and shadows, slipping from one conversation to the other, always in praise of Wulfrun and her works. I try to speak to her a few times but it is like skimming stones across water, our talk shallow and quickly gone.

Sometimes I will hear a half-song, or a dirty joke and remember the end of it before it is finished. Memories from a childhood that was as a dream to me. Hunger, carrying water and scaring crows from the fields. Until I grew large enough that a stranger might look at my face and see in it the likeness of our Ealdorman, quick with his guilt and lingering in love and regrets both.

But I am kept too busy to be lost in the past for long. A hundred ailments and illnesses that were previously outside the walls are now our guests. I have always provided relief to any who ask, but there are many who have not come to me before now, out of pride or fear or the strictness of their masters. Men come with sores on their legs that have been weeping for months. Mothers bring fevered children and beg for aid.

There are deaths, too. As if they have just been waiting for a soft bed and a warm fire, seven souls pass in two weeks. One, Fair Alfred's youngest babe, mewls and will not take the breast: the little girl wastes to nothing over a couple of days. A novice comes complaining of her stomach: that morning, hunger driving her, she left her duties to forage for what she could in the marsh. Yew berries, and no matter how I try to purge it from her, she dies with her throat closed, her skin a blue-purple. Another, an old man who has lived as a slave in this place his whole life, simply lies down to nap and dies in his sleep. Each is shrouded and taken in turn to the chapel, cries of mourning in their wake and with each of their deaths our convent grows a little emptier.

It is nearly three weeks into the new year when Wulfrun beckons Tove and me at last and tells us she will call the election. It is late in the day, after Vespers, and in the infirmary many holy sisters and others are quiet at prayer, for tomorrow is Saint Sebastian's day and if holy Sebastian survived a plague of arrows and lived still, then maybe his strength might pass to us. My stomach aches with hunger and when I stand to walk over to Wulfrun's bedside, a blackness eats away at the corners of my eyes that saps the strength from me.

'Two days hence,' she says. 'I will call it on Saint Agnes' day.'

A cunning choice, the day of virgins and children and all those raped and bruised. Between them, most of the women in this place will find some fellow-feeling.

'And you are not worried that the abbess is once again beloved by all?' asks Tove. 'I cannot move for hearing how much mercy she has shown, letting all these souls shelter with us.'

Mere

'She has no choice,' says Wulfrun, an edge to her voice. 'She does what any in her position would.'

'Even so,' says Tove. She enjoys pricking at Wulfrun, forcing her to show her faults. 'I would begin to doubt myself if I were you.'

'Well, you are not,' says Wulfrun. 'I have their love also. And I promise them a future.'

'A future away from this place,' says Tove. 'There are many who would not want that.'

I am only half listening to this old argument. I can hear something, far in the distance. The sound of a dozen people or so, all talking at once.

'Something is happening,' I say, standing. 'Do you not hear that?'

'Yes,' says Tove, 'I heard some of the other sisters earlier. It is the men. They drink and sing, as if they were in a thegn's hall and not a holy place. Times past I might have joined them as Alwin has.'

I think, suddenly, of Mildred. I sent her to bed but it is an easy enough thing to slip out of the dormitory, especially with so many new souls about.

She cannot be there with them. It would be foolishness on top of foolishness.

'I would see this,' I say, 'with my own eyes.'

Wulfrun raises an eyebrow. 'You will not find much of use.' She and Tove both laugh and I feel, suddenly, my every year I have spent in this isolated place. They have seen enough of men's feasting in their time and so they will stay, talk of the election and the plan to flee this place.

So I walk down, through the darkness. The pilgrims' house is the brightest building in the convent this evening, the small flicker of the rushlights gathered by the score.

Other dark shapes flit from the convent, wives and lovers of the men, perhaps even some sisters. We walk at a distance from each other, heads bowed. Far easier to forget a face that you have not seen much of.

Even so, I keep watch for Mildred. I would know her from her stride alone.

I approach the door, keeping to the shadows and peering in from the threshold. I can feel the warmth even from here of a few dozen bodies. There is the smell of roasting meat, so thick in the air that I could almost take a bite from it and it would be the best meal I had eaten in a month.

Nearly every man is awake, old and young, free and enslaved. They press together in song, arms linked, singing full-throated. A fire is set and the heat is enough that several have taken off their hose, as they do in summer, their white legs bare beneath tunics. In the corner closest to the door there is a heavy smack of flesh on flesh, a great roar and two men stagger backwards, one with a bloodied nose. A fight, then, and I hear calls, see pieces of silver and bone tossed in bets. There are women among them, sitting on floors, on laps. Most are not sisters of the convent, but I see a few faces among them that I know, two of whom are speaking to Fair Alfred.

Alwin sits at the head of it all. They have given him Botwine's old chair, raised it on a few planks of wood. There is a cup of mead in one hand, dice in the other. On his lap is the sharpened stick which served as a spear, the wood a deep brown at its end where it has not been cleaned. His face is red, his eyes looking at nothing and he is laughing.

I watch him a while. Alwin does not stop moving, does not stop talking. But for all his celebration, I see no real joy in him.

Mere

'Sin upon sin,' says a voice at my ear. I start, turn around to see Ava. I do not know how long she has been here for.

'Come, Portress,' I say. 'I am sure if you ask, they would welcome you in.'

Ava narrows her eyes, then spits on the ground. 'He is not fit to be our priest. They have raided our stores, butchered one of the horses, made us all hungrier and poorer. I would have them all whipped for it.'

'Then you would whip nearly every man in the convent and some of the women,' I say. 'Besides, Alwin is a hero, did you not see?'

'I see well enough,' says Ava. 'How he parades about that weapon like some northman raider. A priest who bears arms, who drinks and gambles and eats meat. The only sin he has not committed is whoring, but I am sure that will happen in time.'

I remain silent, for fear of betraying Mildred. Almost in answer, a great roar comes from the feast. I flinch, look about to the two men fighting, sure that one of them has broken some nose or cracked some skull, but they, too, have stopped their battle. They turn as one to the head of the table, to Alwin's seat of honour.

There comes a cry. I think it a woman's at first, or a child, but as the men gather I see, through the crowd, that they have brought a goat, a rope tied about its neck. We have but half a dozen left to us and this the fattest of the ones that lived through the flood, the youngest, the one that gives us the sweetest milk. About her head, they have placed a crown of woven reeds and ivy.

I turn to Ava, thinking that she will hiss some more of sins and wrongdoings. But she is only watching, quietly.

The ceorls gather about Alwin, whisper into his ear.

Fair Alfred is among them, his yellow hair less bright now that he can no longer wash it in lye every week. At their words, Alwin pales, places one hand on the spear in his lap. He looks about for another, for Botwine perhaps, to guide his answer. And then he gives a slow nod and stands.

The din grows louder. Men and women shouting, wailing, trembling. There is the taste of devil-sickness in it, I think, and also of Wulfrun's visions. Selfhood lost, and in its place a great emptiness ready to be filled. It is something like holiness.

Usually placid, the goat strains against the rope, but is held fast. Her crown shifts on her horns, grows loose. Alwin is laughing, perhaps. He is smiling, or baring his teeth. He is standing on the table and lifting his spear and taking a great leap, forward and down and it is a clumsy blow, one that misses the goat's head and neck and hits instead her back and belly. The roar quietens. There is only a wet sound, a half-huff through pierced lungs, a scrabble of still-living hooves against earth.

Beside me, I hear Ava let out her breath, slowly.

'I thought you would stop this,' I say. 'Is it not idolatry?'

I cannot look at the goat, the shuddering hooves. The crown of ivy, half-lost in the dark-soaked rushes. I think of Sweet, telling me that not all of the old ways were good. I have seen beasts slaughtered before, have killed many myself. But there is something in this that I do not like. Death for death's sake, sacrifice as escape.

'How would I stop two-score men?' she asks. Even as she speaks, the goat stills. One of the men reaches to the wound, dips in a finger and then smears it across Alwin's lips, and then his own. One by one, each of the crowd does the same, so that soon every soul among them has lifeblood on their lips.

'They mock our very mass,' says Ava.

'No,' I say, softly. 'It feels something else.'

Ava's head turns but I will not be censured by her, not when in front of me our very own priest lifts the spear once more and shouts his victory.

'I do not think he understands,' I say, 'what he is doing, truly. He is too drunk, too foolish. Too scared. He will not see it for what it is.'

Even I am unsure. Sweet is not among the feasting. I do not think this can be the ritual she spoke of, but I am sure there is a reason that she stays away.

'They love Alwin now,' says Ava. 'But they will hate him tomorrow, when they wake to empty stores and sore heads.'

She echoes my own thoughts. Botwine knew many of us from our childhood and still he was driven off with a spear-wound in his gut. Alwin has only this single glory to his name and it will fade soon enough.

When Ava speaks there is regret in her voice. 'Better no priest than a wicked one.'

I leave shortly afterwards, for I cannot see Mildred among the great throng. On my way back, I stop in the dormitory. It is far more crowded than usual, but I can still pick out Mildred's bony elbows in the far corner of the room. She is asleep, surrounded by women, all of whom she could not walk across without waking. Safe, chaste.

'You are not often up here with us,' comes a voice. Eluned, sat in the shadows beside her mattress. She is closest to the doorway, closest to the cold and all that the cold brings with it. She has a ragged blanket wrapped about her and her voice crackles still from the night of the storeroom fire, from the lungfuls of smoke she breathed that night.

I crouch on my haunches. For a heartbeat I think of that evening, nearly two months ago, when I crouched so in Sweet's home, pressing my hand up against Eluned's stomach and knowing I could help her only a little.

'My infirmary is warmer,' I whisper, though that is growing less true by the day.

'The dormitory is the place for maids, is it not?' Eluned tilts her head upwards. Though all knew of Sybba's lusts, she never bore him a child, was never married. She might be a virgin, if she lived in a different household, and if asked to check her that is what I will say.

'Of course,' I say, 'you must stay where you can.' Shivering, at the border of it all, and still she would fight for such a place. 'If the cold keeps you awake, I might find some more blankets.'

Eluned gives a small laugh. 'I have felt this cold before. I am not a soft-heart, like the rest of them.'

She keeps her voice low, though, so that none of those soft-hearts will hear her. There is a longing there, for something she was never given.

'You were not asked to join the men at their feast?'

'I was asked,' she says. 'I would not go even with a blade to my throat. They drink and with it comes quicker lusts and quicker tempers.'

We are both silent. There is a rustle of blankets from the other sisters, a cough. Some are sleeping two to a bed, to share the warmth.

'I have been thinking,' says Eluned, 'I cannot stop. Of Sybba, or his two brothers. They are both gone and their next kin does not want to take me on, for they do not have enough to feed or clothe me. I think I am free, in all but name.'

'They met ill fates,' I say. 'But by it, they have made yours brighter.'

'That is it,' says Eluned and she looks up at me with her large, maid's eyes. For all of it, she cannot be more than eighteen winters. 'I should be joyful, that I am without them. I should grieve and repent for my own part in it. But all that is within me is . . . there is nothing, Hilda.'

I reach over, pat her hand. Palms calloused though the flesh of her arms still soft. 'We do not always feel as we should,' I say.

'I never thought to have a future,' says Eluned. 'I thought it would end giving birth to some bastard I never wanted, got on me by a master I hated. But now, there are so many paths and I do not know how I might choose them.'

She wraps her arms around herself, this freedom of hers making her tremble as cold and hardship never have.

'Sweet will care for you,' I say. 'She knows what you face.'

Eluned buries her head on her knees. 'She has given me so much already,' she murmurs. 'A debt I can never repay.'

'That is true for both of us,' I say, 'and half of the convent, for all the aid she has given. We must only live long enough to repay her.'

Eluned nods, wipes her eyes and then turns her face up to me. 'I will make sure of it,' she says, fiercely. 'Do not worry over me.'

Alwin arrives the next day, bleary-eyed and pale with drink. He is not the first to come that morning, but one of a dozen or so men who have made the journey here seeking a cure for an illness they have brought upon themselves. Their visits set the women and children laughing, calling out insults and kindnesses. A few wives jostle their husbands, set them retching in buckets.

Mildred sees Alwin at the door, coaxes him in as if he is an unwilling colt. She has enough sense to beckon me over to the storeroom. There is, at least, a cloth that might shield us from prying fellow sisters.

I think of turning him away, or else giving him some useless salve. It is clear that it is drink that has brought him so low, not anything else.

'My sleep,' he says, 'I need something to sleep.'

'I would have thought you slept well enough last night,' I say.

'No,' he says, absently. 'No. Only half-sleep.'

'Well, drink does not always help a man to his rest,' I say. 'I would stop that first and then return here.'

He flushes and Mildred steps to his side. 'You have given sisters sleeping draughts for less,' she says, 'I know it.'

'But he is our priest,' I say. 'I would not have Father Alwin out of his senses if he must give the last rites.' I look around at the crowded room, at the coughs and shivers. 'Which he will have to do more of before long, I think.'

Alwin's face grows redder. 'It is useless,' he mumbles, turning away to leave. 'I am being punished, Mildred, do you not understand that?'

She hurries to him, whispers something in his ear. Reluctantly, he turns back.

'I dream,' he says.

'Of what?'

His shoulders tighten. For all his high rank, for all that he is a man and a priest and I am a woman and a healer,

Mere

I am reminded of confession. He wishes for a penance, for guilt lifted. But with Botwine gone, there is nobody left to tell.

I sit down on a stool, guide him to the other. He follows easily. I lift his hand to the light. A wound there, one I did not see before. Mildred has done a fair job in bandaging it, as well as my own. I will not be able to call her apprentice much longer.

'You have hurt your hand,' I say.

'Yes,' he says. 'The spear.'

'For Botwine?' I ask. 'Or that she-goat?'

I wait for him to answer, but he does not speak. Morning often clears the comforting fog of drink and I think he begins to understand that last night's feast was not a simple evening of fellowship, passed in mead and song.

'I can make you something for the wound at least,' I say. 'Vervain in butter. How is that?'

He nods mutely, remains sitting as between us Mildred and I gather the ingredients. Mildred goes to fetch the butter and I fetch the dried plant and begin to grind it down. The only sound is the crackle of stone against stone.

'He hates me,' says Alwin, suddenly. 'He comes to me in dreams, a revenant. An angry ghost.'

'Father Botwine may not be dead,' I say.

It is a foolish thing to say and even Alwin knows it. 'No, he may only be dying, slowly.'

'Many think you a hero,' I say. 'A shepherd must protect his flock, as well as guide them.'

'Mildred does not think me a hero,' says Alwin. 'She is kind, but I am smaller to her now. I do not know why I drank with those men last night. I thought if there was some noise, some good cheer, it might help.'

I do not reply. Botwine was always so quiet in confession, always leaving the silence to be filled. I thought it wisdom, but perhaps he only felt as I do: lost.

'I was not meant for the priesthood, for my older brother was often ill and we did not think he would live beyond fifteen winters or so. But the years passed and he was heartier by the day, as well at twenty as any other man. So one day my father brings Father Botwine in and tells me I am to be a priest. Me, who read as slowly as the seasons themselves, who could not get through the scriptures without my head hurting!'

Alwin shakes his head.

'I thought he would be like all the other teachers. That he would whip me, beat me. But he never lifted his hand to me. Not once, in all our time together.'

'A gentle soul,' I say. It is odd to hear of Father Botwine in another place, in another household. But it seems he was constant wherever his path took him.

'In my dreams,' says Alwin, 'he does not hurt me. He only comes and stands, his stomach bleeding. He is shouting something. A warning, I think. But I cannot hear him.'

Alwin reaches up, rubs his eyes of tears.

'I am sorry,' he says, weakly, 'I know not what I do here.'

I embrace him then. A strange thing to do, but I pull his head down to my shoulder and feel him shudder against me. His weeping is silent, done through gritted teeth and tight muscles, and still he presses himself against me and I tilt my head to his curls, whisper that he is well, that he is good, that there is nothing to fear.

Mildred returns. She stops when she sees that Alwin and I embrace, for I have not hidden my dislike of the

Mere

boy, but she pulls the cloth back across quickly behind her and continues the work of preparing the salve while Alwin gasps his sorrow.

After a while, he pulls away. His face is red again.

'I am tired,' he says. Then, he turns to the side and retches into a bleeding-bowl. I rest my hand on his back.

'You are beer-sick, too,' I say. 'And you came for help with it,' I say. 'It is as simple as that. And that is what I will tell others, if they ask.'

He nods, grateful. Out in the infirmary, somebody coughs. Mildred pours the draught into a cup, hands it to Alwin, who swallows it quickly.

'He has something else he wishes to tell you,' she says, gently, when Alwin is finished.

'Yes,' says Alwin. He is flushed, shamed. A boy coming with a toy he has broken. 'I know before I may have seemed as if I stood by the abbess alone. I thought she would protect me, protect others.'

It is painful, watching him search for the words. But I let him stumble on anyway. Some pains must be endured. 'What I mean,' he says, 'is that I stand by whoever is best for the convent. For its flock. And if that changes . . .'

He gives me a last, desperate look.

'I understand,' I say. 'Wulfrun will be happy to hear it.'

For the first time in a long while, I see cheer in him. I have never understood why Mildred loves him so, why she would risk so much for a careless boy who does not fight for anything beyond his own gain. But his joy is so open, so unbound by worry, that it passes to Mildred as well. She smiles and together we watch him gather his robes and depart, returning to his world of men.

'You are still meeting him at night?' I ask after he is gone.

'No,' says Mildred, shortly. 'He does not sleep alone any longer, with all those men in the pilgrims' house.'

'But you meet him at other times?'

She gives me a sidelong look. It is all I need.

'Use caution,' I say. 'We have lost one priest. We cannot lose another.'

'They would not harm him, surely?' says Mildred. 'He has done nothing that might not be forgiven in time. Even the feast last night was no great evil.'

'You were not there,' I say. 'You did not see him.'

'He killed a goat,' says Mildred, calmly. 'He has told me already. He regrets it, for he did not understand that the others saw a greater meaning behind it.'

A child's reasoning, in many ways, full of trust and goodwill. But I am tired already of taking hope from Mildred's life and do not wish to argue with her.

'Well,' I say, 'even if they stay their hand for him, they may not show the same mercy to others.'

Her jaw tightens. 'Abbess Sigeburg would not,' she says. 'Nor Portress Ava. But if somebody else was in post, perhaps it might be different.'

'Yes,' I say. I glance over to Wulfrun's bed, where Sweet has now joined Tove in low conversation.

I think again of spun thread pulled too tight. Alwin was the one who dealt the blow, but it might have been any of us.

I do not think that hunger has left us and I do not think Wulfrun will sate it easily.

'Let us see what dawn will bring,' I say, for it is Saint Agnes' day tomorrow. A day for wounded girls, the day when we go to call the election.

*

Mere

I cannot sleep that night. I spend my time in the darkness, sitting at Wulfrun's bedside, pacing the infirmary. I turn back every so often and I cannot believe that she is still there, that she sleeps so peacefully, her head thrown back. I mark the stretch of her neck, the hollow where I see the pulse of her lifeblood. Her wrists, so bare. Her cheekbone, her eyes. Unmarked for now.

A woman of flesh, for all her efforts otherwise. I cannot bear how easily she might be broken, how quickly she might be taken. There is cruelty in every love and bravery also. To see how it will hurt and to love all the same. I thought I might fight it, but as I reach over and brush a stray strand of hair from her forehead, I know there is little to be done. I was lost from the very start.

'A battle-dawn,' Wulfrun says as soon as she wakes, and though there is a smile on her lips, she cannot hide the fear in her voice.

She will call for the election after we have finished our morning devotions at Lauds. I stay close to her the whole walk to the chapel, my legs unsteady, my heart so loud that surely others must hear it. Wulfrun herself walks as if half dreaming, but I see the pulse jumping in her throat, know that she is as scared as I. I thought to see Mildred in the infirmary, but she has not come to help and I wonder if, at last, she has slept through the call to her duties. I would not blame her.

The morning is as wet as the one before it. Several sisters slip in the mud, bruising arms and backs. The smell of rot hangs in the air as, beyond the walls, beasts and crops are broken down by the water. As we gather together to meet the dawn, the flies, too, seek each other out in this new day, hanging in great angry clouds. They alight on our lips, our eyelids, too impatient even to wait for us to finish our worship.

We take our places in the chapel, heads bowed. Then, as we look to the altar, whispers shiver through us. Alwin is not in his place. He is gone and we are without a priest. Portress Ava, too, has not joined us in worship. Ava, who is never late.

Wulfrun turns to me, eyes wide, and this is wrong, our voided church our rotten land our fled priest and where is Mildred, where is Alwin, they might be dead devil-sick taken and there is a sound from the church door the abbess walking weakly but determined her crown pulled tight about her head the ruby shining darkly and behind her Ava and behind them Mildred bound beaten and Alwin behind her not bound not beaten but face furious and the fear is a bloody flux creeping through my lungs catching my breath and as the abbess speaks I know what she will say even before she opens her mouth to speak the words.

'We have found the source of our troubles,' she says, each word a dropped stone.

Chapter 22

*M*ildred stumbles in her bonds and Alwin moves towards her, steadies her at the elbow, then looks about, defiant. His chin is tilted high. It is as if Botwine is still with us, protecting his acolyte. Alwin does not believe, yet, that he might ever come to harm. He is dressed as if for mass: the white alb tunic and chasuble cloak bright against the dark silk of his stole.

This strange procession walks through the church, up to the altar. Ava keeps her gaze distant, elsewhere. There is a slight tremble in her hand, one that she is not thinking to hide.

The abbess seems restored. She walks as if she is ten years younger, as if she is the brave maid who first came to raise this place out of the mere. Who brought with her a crown and all the power it contained. But this return cannot hide the stiffness of her walk, the thinness of her frame. Even in her triumph, she is sicker today than she has ever been.

At the back of the church a crowd forms: Sweet, Eluned,

Fair Alfred among them. All the souls in the convent that can walk are here. Drawn by curiosity perhaps, or maybe the abbess has called them.

'What is this?' I ask, stepping forward.

'This,' says the abbess, pulling Mildred in front of the entire gathering, 'is the convent's whore.'

Mildred falls to her knees. Her wimple has slipped, revealing curls of brown hair. She has let it grow too long, like many of us.

She does not look at me, does not look at anybody. I wish she would. It would remind them that she has been at the infirmary for six winters and that there is not a soul in this convent that she has not tended to. Now, they will see only a maid, ruined.

I hurry to lift Mildred up. She trembles against me.

'Mildred is no whore,' I say. 'She is my helper and to speak such lies—'

The abbess shakes her head. 'Two sisters found her with Alwin, in the stables.' She turns, first to Alwin and then Mildred. 'Do either of you deny it?'

I will the lies to their mouths. But Mildred is dazed and Alwin haunted and so they only nod.

'I am sorry,' says Mildred. I do not know who she is speaking to. 'I am sorry.'

'The stables?' I ask her.

'There was no other place,' she whispers. 'The men in the dormitory, the women in the infirmary. We lingered, did not know they would be looking for Alwin so soon.'

Anger in the crowd. There has been sin among them the whole time. All of the punishments have been for nothing. There are wounds that are still open, bellies that ache from

Mere

fasting and all this penitence might be undone by a foolish maid and our wicked priest. Snakes in the grass.

I wrap my arms around Mildred. There is a sourness in my mouth. I remember Ethel, her sin so much smaller, her death so bitter. We tread a dangerous path and a single slip might mire us all.

They want an answer, only. A reason for this suffering, an end to it all. I think of Botwine and Eadwig, their reaching hands, their pleading words. There was something they wished to tell us, I am sure.

'I think there is another way.' My voice comes out small. I am not Wulfrun or the abbess, used to swaying great crowds. I feel, for a heartbeat, the eyes of all my fellow sisters on me. I do not know how Wulfrun stands the weight, for I feel it crushing me even as I raise my voice again, louder this time, speaking as I might if I were born to another life, to a life of gold and stone, not fog and mere.

'Botwine and Eadwig spoke of a riddle. *I end and then I end and then I end. Forge me in heat, knot me in thread. I do not belong to one soul alone.* I have heard tell of a gift, given once. I think we must only answer this riddle and be saved.'

I see it sway them. Who among us has not spent a lifetime listening to tales of heroes, outwitting devils and beasts with their cunning as much as their strength or faith? I do not know if I believe what I speak, but it matters not. I must only save Mildred and the hope I see in the crowd might be enough.

'Nothing but the ravings of the devil-sick,' says the abbess. She does not even put much feeling into it. 'All know that devils must be driven out by faith. Look to King Ecgfrith, whose wife was possessed by a demon until he stopped his wicked imprisonment of good Saint Wilfrid.

Look to Saint Guthlac, who did not speak with demons, even as they roared about him in his hermitage. We must take both of them as example, remain steadfast even as we seek out the sin that has led to this curse.'

We have all heard the tale of Saint Guthlac, who lived three centuries ago in Mercia. Who drank only dirt-water, wore only animal skins, battled every day against the bellowing demons who came to his hermitage. Who died holy and fevered, speaking with the angels, nectar pouring from his mouth.

She speaks firmly enough, with much knowledge and learning, and I see my sisters harden once more. But the doubt I have seeded does not go away, not fully. Not all of us wish to die as tormented saints. A few thoughtful faces, a few defiant ones. A little more and we might turn them back to us.

Then, Tove stands and calls out. 'There is no doubt that Mildred has done great wrong,' she says. Her voice is warm, as if she speaks to a close friend. 'But she is young and foolish. Who among us was not so, as a girl? I know myself that the convent was the only place for me, for where else would I be able to repent enough for all of my sins?'

Some laughter, even on this hungry morning. Tove might charm the hoard from a wyrm itself when she chooses to.

She lowers her voice, moves closer to the abbess. She whispers something in the other woman's ear and I see the abbess's face soften, briefly. A reminder of old friendship, perhaps, or an appeal to mercy. The two of them who have been here the longest.

Then, Alwin speaks.

'I do not deny my sin,' he says. He does not look at Mildred. 'But I deny your authority, Abbess Sigeburg. This

Mere

is a matter that I must bring to the bishop, when we are able to travel.'

Tove is shaking her head at him but Alwin pays her no heed. The abbess looks as if she has been struck. In past times, she would have measured her words before speaking. But she must be clouded by pain, for she bites back, 'And how will you go to the bishop? Walk through the marsh all the way to Gipeswic?'

There is silence. We have never heard the abbess admit the desperation of these past weeks.

Alwin flushes. 'It would be a better fate than starving here, when there is not enough food to go around.'

We have all known that we would not all of us live, that we might soon have to draw lots for our one meal a day. But there had been a comfort in the abbess's faith. Now, I see that even the abbess does not believe it any more. She looks like a woman who has come to the end of a path and all spread out before her is wild and untrodden. Ava hurries to her side, whispers something in her ear, but the abbess waves her away.

'You ignorant child,' she says to Alwin. 'No thought for your words, for your actions. A boy, promoted beyond your ability.'

'Boy?' Alwin's voice rings loud in the church. This stone was built for his sermons, his service. 'I am your priest, Sigeburg.'

Ava begins to speak some calming words, soothing us into uneven peace. Wulfrun, too, tries to say something. But it is in the air: cockerels with their spurs, dogs in the pit. Whoever loses between the abbess and Alwin will end up bloodied, I am sure, and my heart beats as if I watch a real baiting.

'If you are our priest, then what were you doing with Mildred? Prayer? Confession? You have destroyed the sanctity of our convent, you have sinned over and over again. I heard of your feast, child, the killing of that goat. Yet, still you stand in front of us and tell us that we need your penances.'

'I—' begins Alwin, but his voice shakes. A boy, dressed in robes that have been hastily hemmed, a boy who must still flick through his book of penance at confession, for the worst of man's heart is not yet familiar to him. He glances to Mildred as if she might answer for him, desperately, sweetly, and it is this gentleness that undoes us all. Whatever love he shows her is love stolen from the rest of us.

'You speak to me,' says the abbess, 'not that whore.' She reaches out, pulls him by the arm.

He shrugs her back. Some old habit, from when he was a child in boyhood scrapes, from when he trained with the seax and the spear. The very quickness that made him a hero in driving Botwine away. But the abbess is no warrior. Only a small, frail woman, who stumbles back, tripping over the edge of her habit and onto the stone floor. There is a crack and a gasp and she touches the side of her head, comes away with blood on her palm. Her circlet has been knocked askew but the ruby still remains about her brow, a bright, clean red beside the smudged wound.

'Blood,' says somebody. 'He has spilt blood in the church.'

Holy ground polluted, sacrosanct house destroyed, no more mass, no more confession, the abbess her eyes clouded and oh Lord he might have killed her with this.

I hear about me whore, sodomite, apostate, devils leaping

Mere

from tongues, echoing through the air and hands on the abbess pulling her to her feet and hands on Alwin dragging him away even as he shouts against their treachery and they are pulling at Mildred as well and I reach for her but there is nowhere to hide her, nowhere she might run. We are rats, fierce, cornered, hopeless.

Mildred twists against me. My apprentice, calmest and sweetest of all, is keening, a strange, animal sound. As Alwin is pulled from sight, towards the doorway of the chapel, she howls his name.

I see Wulfrun, rising above it. So tall, her hands raised, calling peace, for pity's sake but they are beyond even her power now and I can no longer tell who tugs at me to help and who is reaching for me to rend, my sisters are gone and there is only panic and fear and screams of pain and we are too many all pushing forward and pulling back at the same time

breath knocked from lungs and

bones snapping and

I cannot breathe it is too

I fall my vision loosens the back of my head pulses the flagstones on the floor are pools shimmering and deep it is the mere pushing up through our foundations come to claim

Wulfrun still stood tall high shining

it is her it was always

The word in my mouth, on my tongue and I call out and none heed me but Ava who has her arms around me, protecting me maybe, and it is she who turns at my words to watch Wulfrun no this is my knowledge alone the answer to the riddle the gift that must be given

about her head forged and knotted, golden, shining,

Danielle Giles

ending and ending and ending and it is too much for a soul alone to bear and still she longs for it
   a crown
   I close my eyes and sink.

Chapter 23

The infirmary roof has a hole in it where the thatch is wearing through. I had not seen it before in all the busyness.

Through it I can see the sky. Pale blue, heartless blue, a beautiful day.

Tove calls my name and grips my hand and my body aches, shin to fingertip, rib to throat. I want to tell her of the sky and its beauty but the words
slither away
eel-swift
It is hard to wake.

When I see the roof again, the sky is dark. I raise myself to my elbows and look about. The others sleep. The infirmary is still crowded, still full of sweat and farts and snores.

I am not wearing a wimple and the sudden cold about my bare neck is something I have felt only rarely. It makes me feel as if something is about to pounce on me. My stomach lurches and I retch, but bring nothing up.

I let my fingertips brush the wound at the back of my head. The hair there is matted with blood, but the cut is already healing over. I do not press hard, for there is a hot swelling there, the kind that can bloom across a sister until she has no speech, no legs, no spirit. I have seen plenty die from injuries such as this.

The abbess. Her own wound bright in that crowded place, Alwin's shouts, Mildred's screams. And then Wulfrun. That moment after the blow to the head, where I saw her crowned, at last. The unending circle, forged and woven both.

It is the answer to the riddle. The gift we must give the mere, to end all this suffering. The goat that Alwin killed a poor mockery, not of the consecrated blood but of something else. The giving of a crown, a leader.

And though the abbess still wears her ruby, I think she will never give herself up. She has not even let herself be polluted by speaking to any of the devil-sick, let alone bargained with them. Which leaves only Wulfrun. My stomach turns to think of it.

Standing, I look about me for Mildred, for Tove, but I cannot see them. A blackness comes to the edge of my sight, from hunger, from pain, from it all, and I must stand, breathing slowly until I can move again. The infirmary is filled with the quiet, but it is not the solemn silence of the church, or the contemplation of a sister at work. It is a pressed, millstone quiet.

My feet bare, my tread soft, I walk towards the door. It is a slow step, the rushes on the floor barely whispering beneath me.

'Next time you tell me to rest in bed, I shall remind you of this. Walking about before dawn as if your head is not half-split.'

Mere

I start, turn to see Tove at my side. She speaks in a whisper, glancing about her to see if the other women and children have awoken.

'How long have I slept for?' I ask.

'Two days,' says Tove. 'And a fine two days it has been. I wish you had never taught me a single one of your leechdoms, for I am infirmarian in your stead and I cannot stand it.'

'What happened?' I press my hand again to the wound. 'Did somebody strike me?'

Tove shakes her head. 'I do not think so,' she says. 'You fell, in all the chaos, and knocked your head. You have not been sleeping all this time either. You babbled about the sky, the mere. You remember none of it?'

'Only a little,' I say. I do not want to speak of my vision of Wulfrun, of the crown that would answer it all and take everything from me.

Tove shakes her head. 'Here you are with your senses half knocked from you and the abbess was standing up and giving orders almost as soon as she fell. I do not understand any of it.'

'Where are the others? Wulfrun? Mildred? Alwin?'

Tove puts a finger to her lips and gestures me to follow her. She leads me back to my bed, her slow, deliberate steps still much faster than my own. Walking through the infirmary, for the first time I understand how frayed it has become: rushes that have not been changed because we cannot go to the marsh to collect them; blankets and bandages that remain dirty because we cannot go to the stream for the water for washing; thin arms that have grown thinner because there is no food to be had. There are also far more sisters in here than before, ones once healthy who now have splints on arms or bandages on heads.

'Was Mildred hurt?' I ask. 'Does she live still?'

'Mildred is safe.'

'Safe, but not in the infirmary? Where is she?'

We reach the mattress. 'You should sit,' says Tove. My legs are so weak that I have no choice but to do as she asks, but I say again, 'Where is Mildred?'

'The abbess ordered her to be imprisoned in the stables, the site of her sinning,' says Tove. 'To be punished later.'

'She will freeze there,' I say. She is too far, as far from me as Eadwig was from us all, cold and shackled and scared, and I cannot leave her there.

Tove sighs. 'When you were struck, Wulfrun petitioned for her safety, told all that we would be doomed without her knowledge and you were senseless by then. She saved Mildred's life.'

Saved Mildred, only to let the abbess bind her to that dark place.

'The names I have heard them call Mildred these past days,' says Tove, 'as if they themselves never had a tumble in the reeds, or a kiss from a passing pilgrim. It makes me glad that I have stayed in the infirmary these past years, missed all their poison and bile.'

'And Wulfrun?'

'She is safe also,' says Tove. 'She has been at your bed most hours, but she goes now to speak with Ava.'

'Ava?' I ask. 'What business has she with the portress?'

'It was them that calmed the storm when nothing else would. When that fool Alwin—' She stops, swallows her anger back. 'He is gone. We are without a priest.'

'He is dead?' I ask. So strong, so hale. But a few days

ago I held him in my arms as he sobbed his dreams to me.

'By now, yes, I would say so,' says Tove.

'Tell me,' I say, 'all that has happened.'

There is something about the scop in Tove and the tale is long in the telling. She did not see much, in truth, for others pulled her away before she might have been hurt. But she has learnt enough in the time since.

Alwin spilt blood in the church, a wicked sin. They tried to take him, to ready him for punishment, a whipping or an amputation of his hand, but he fought. As a stream might flood and wash away even a house of stone, so the smallest of blows grew, suddenly, into a war. A rush of souls running in to fight, another rush calling for peace and another rush fleeing the violence. Snapped arms, trampled fingers.

'You saw the illustrated copy we had of *Psychomachia*, before it was sold?' asks Tove.

'Only once,' I say. Still, I remember it well. A poem of good and evil, with sin and virtue each presented in the bodies of battling women. The strong fingers of Good Works as she throttles the life from Greed. Faith lifting her sword and shattering the skull of Worship-of-the-Old-Gods Idolatry.

'Well, I think old Prudentius must have spent some time in a convent before he wrote it, for it was as bloody a scene as I have seen for a long while. It is no wonder Alwin fled.'

She tells me how he ran for the ditch, crossing the broken bridge in one brilliant leap, his young body bearing him across where Botwine's had failed him. Then through the flooded land, making for the cover of the marsh.

'He left Mildred?'

'They would have hung him by then,' says Tove. 'And she was screaming for him to go. He called out, told her he would be back.'

Tove reaches, pulls the blanket over me. A gesture I have done for her more times than I can count. It is strange to find ourselves swapped like this.

'The abbess is in bed still,' says Tove. I wonder if I hear reproach in her voice, for I have not asked any more of our Mother Superior. 'Ava is with her now, guards her door like the gates of heaven itself. I have helped with her wound, but without you, without Mildred, it has been hard.'

'I would go to Mildred,' I say.

Tove shakes her head. 'The abbess has ordered it,' she says. 'Visitors are forbidden.'

'But you have been, to treat her, to check on her health?'

'I have,' says Tove.

'Then I shall do that also.'

Tove purses her lips. 'If you had not been struck about the head, you would be in that stable with her. They say that you have let sin bloom here. If they see you awake, they will wish to ask you questions. I do not think a visit would be wise.'

'And still, I go.'

Tove looks upwards. I do not see her pray in earnestness often, for she says that she has already told God all that she might and the rest is just waiting. But I think she prays now.

'You will have my silence,' she says at last. 'If you tell me one thing. What was that you spoke of, in the church?' she asks. 'Of this riddle? I have heard whispers of it everywhere.

Mere

You have seeded something in the other sisters, but I do not know what.'

'Nothing,' I lie. 'I do not even remember what I spoke of.'

Mildred is kept differently from Eadwig. No chains for her, for they know that a barred door is enough. She sits among hay and blankets, her knees held to her chest, her head bowed. If I did not know she was here, I would think her but another shadow. The stench of shit comes from a bucket in the corner.

'Hilda?' Mildred pulls herself to her feet and embraces me. 'You live, still.'

'So it seems,' I say. My apprentice is thin, all hollows and bone. But there is strength in her arms and this gladdens me. 'You, too.'

'I thought they would, I feared . . .' She trails off. A girl, who cannot find the words for the horror of it. She knows each and every sister, bone and blood, maid and widow. And yet they were calling to hang Alwin, to murder her.

'I did not think it would cause such harm,' she says at last.

I want to slap her. 'I warned you,' I say and hate myself for sounding so small. It does not matter now that I was right. The only difference between us is that I have been careful where she has not. Or, maybe not even that. It is only that she did not have the sense to love somebody powerful enough to protect her.

Her jaw tightens. 'I thought we would not be caught,' she says. 'And, if we were, Alwin is a priest. Do they not respect him? Love him?'

'It is because they love him,' I say. 'They say an ordinary

man might beat his wife if she commits adultery, but a loving husband will kill her and be done with it.'

'Well,' she says, 'he is safe in the marsh.'

I stare at her. She knows, surely, what Alwin's flight will end in.

'Have you word?' she continues. 'Has he returned, or been seen? Or else, do you think he is in Gipeswic?'

How bright she is, how brittle. I think the truth will kill her. My eyes are growing used to the gloom of the stables and I see the wounds and bruises starkly. Browns and purples and golds, deep and rich as any tapestry. She has fashioned a splint for a finger that is swollen and looks to be broken. One eye is red, the pupil large and unseeing. I see, too, that she has a limp that she did not have before, favours her right leg over the left.

'Here,' I say, 'let me help with those.'

I take her by the arm, lead her to the entrance of the stables where the light is best.

We find a stool from some corner and Mildred sits on it. She has her face raised to the sky, her eyes searching for fading constellations in the dawn.

'We are but a week from Candlemas,' she says, 'is that right?'

'So they tell me,' I say. 'I have been asleep a long while.'

'We are in Aquarius, then,' she says. 'A good season for weddings, but not for any long travel. I wish I had told him that, before he left. Did he have his cloak with him do you know?'

She twists herself to face the marsh. 'The nights have been very cold,' she says forlornly.

'I will try and find it,' I say, 'bring it to you.'

Mere

'It is not I who needs it,' she says, but there is blue on her lips and stiffness in her fingers.

I lift the hem of her habit to inspect her ankle. It is three times the size it should be, clumsily bandaged.

'This will need a salve,' I say, 'and rest, in a proper bed in the infirmary.'

'It is Aquarius,' she says. 'I should not receive long treatment, for it brings ill-fortune. And the infirmary will not have me. The abbess's orders.'

'Abbess Sigeburg?' I ask.

'Yes,' she says. 'We have no other.'

'Not yet,' I say. 'And what brings more ill-fortune is a broken bone that goes untreated. And here I was thinking my apprentice had learnt something these last few years with me.'

'Apprentice?' she asks, her voice thick. 'Still? After all I have done?'

'Always,' I say. 'You would have to travel to Rome and murder the Pope himself for me to disown you.'

She nods, then turns her head to the stars again. Her throat tightens, her jaw shakes, but she does not cry.

'And,' I say, 'there is another question I must ask. If you have been late in your bleeding.'

She swallows. 'Sometimes,' she says, 'Alwin and I, we would feign to be other than we were. Me a maid, daughter of a merchant. Him a thegn, ruling his father's house. No vows binding us, other than what we chose ourselves. We would have five sons, each braver than the last. A magic number, a holy number.'

She gives me a sidelong look. 'I know that is foolish.'

'No,' I say, 'we are not fools to dream that our lives might have been other than what they are.'

She fiddles with her hands. One last secret, the one that none other has uncovered from her yet.

'Not a dream,' she says. 'Not any more. I missed my bleeding last month. I was going to tell you.'

'But you thought to wait until Wulfrun was appointed abbess,' I say. 'She might forgive you a child.'

'And if she did not, you might make her,' says Mildred.

Out in the marsh, there comes a scream. A boar, maybe, or a fox. Some creature in pain, in death-throes. Mildred stiffens beside me, for she knows as well as I that a man might scream like a pig, in his last moments. Like Sybba, the first of us to perish.

'It is but an unlucky hare,' I say, quickly. 'Do not worry.'

She continues to frown and so I ask, 'Your child, have you any other signs? Vomiting, or weakness?'

'No,' replies Mildred, 'I do not know how far he is grown. New, I think.'

'I will mix a potion, bring it back to you with a blanket,' I say, then stop. 'If that is what you want?'

Her shoulders are high, her small face resolute. 'No,' she says. 'Alwin will return soon, I am sure, and maybe Wulfrun will be abbess then and might release us? We are wed, in all but name. He vowed to be at my side and me at his. But I would be a full wife and he a full husband.'

I am glad it is dark, that my face will be hidden. This is a fool's choice, but I cannot deny it to her.

'If that is what you choose,' I say, 'then I can only obey.'

I push myself upwards, groaning with the effort of it. 'I might bring you to the infirmary,' I say. 'We at least have a fire there.'

'No,' says Mildred, weakly, though I can see how it tempts her. 'They will only beat me again, or worse.'

Mere

'We shall see,' I say. 'Perhaps Wulfrun will have a vision of your redemption.'

'She has been to see me, you know,' says Mildred. 'Last night, though it would place her in great danger if the abbess or other sisters found out. I spoke of Alwin, she spoke of you.'

'And what did she say?'

Mildred smiles, glad to have a secret once again. 'Small virtues,' she says, 'large sins.'

I help her to her feet, lead her back into the stables. I empty her bucket for her, throwing it in a nearby ditch, and gather what spare hay and rushes we have into a thicker mattress. I wish I had bog-cotton to stuff but we do not have any to spare now, for we must dress wounds instead of easing sleep. The chores are small but I am hobbled by my aches and bruises.

'You know,' she says, watching, 'you are half-dead yourself.'

'I live,' I say, shortly.

'You have slept for two days,' she says. 'If you were my patient, I would be calling for the last rites.'

I kiss her forehead. 'I will not be felled by a little scratch and neither will you.'

I am walking back from the stables, paltry dawn seeping through the sky and the bell ringing for Lauds, when I see Wulfrun, coming out to look for me. It has only been two days, but she seems far older. The lines in her face are deeper, the shadows beneath her eyes darker. A woman of earthly concerns, not heavenly ones.

And there is much to worry her. Now that it is lighter, I can see the flood again, the mere-veins spreading out already into the water, brown and silty and rotting. Where crops once grew will now be salt, where men built walls we will find clenched, brown bodies.

And then Wulfrun's arms are around me, pulling all of me towards her, strong enough to knock the breath from my lungs.

'You are back,' she says. There are tears on her cheek and she looks at me as if I were some precious, delicate psalter, one she thought long gone.

'Walking the earth once more,' I say, as much life in my voice as I can manage. 'Lazarus himself.'

'I am glad you are well,' she says. 'You fell so hard.'

'And you?' I ask. 'You were not hurt?'

She shakes her head. 'Heaven be praised,' she says. 'Though I am sure there were many who might have wished harm on me. Who still do.'

She stops. There is something strange in her manner.

'I wished to ask you of something,' she says. 'You spoke of the riddle, back in the church. Before you fell. You told us that you thought it might save us all.'

'We must flee through the marsh,' I say. 'You have said so.'

'So you do not think there is another way?' she asks. A chill falls on me as I understand what I hear in her voice. Hope. She does not want to travel through the marsh, does not think we will all live through such a journey. But it is the best way left to us.

I think of her, crowned, the answer to all this made flesh.

'No,' I say, 'I spoke only to turn the anger from Mildred.'

'I see,' says Wulfrun, softly. We walk on another few steps before she speaks again.

'We have been holding mass in the chapter house. The church must be consecrated again and none wish to step inside it for a while, anyway.'

Mere

'Who gives the mass?' I ask.

'Tove, myself and Ava,' says Wulfrun. 'When each of us can be spared.'

'A triumvirate, then?' I say. 'How Roman. The abbess allows you to do so?'

I cannot imagine it. Women are forbidden to speak on behalf of the Lord, to intercede with Him. Yet there are now three of them. Wulfrun shifts her weight. 'She does not know of it. The other sisters, they were so afraid that we would be without worship. We had no choice. It was Tove who first spoke of it, of all of us, said she had seen you shriving souls when Botwine was not here. When she speaks, the others follow.'

I wonder if I hear fear in her voice. As some herbs will grow into the space they are given, so Tove is spreading outwards through the convent. Though, I do not think she would ever covet the abbess's position.

'And confession?' I ask. 'Who is taking that?'

'We have not offered that yet,' says Wulfrun. 'That remains in Sigeburg's power.'

I tighten my grip on Wulfrun's arm so that she will not see my hands shake. 'They have not confessed, then? Those that near killed Mildred and drove Alwin away? No penance, no punishment?'

'They would not listen,' says Wulfrun. 'I have tried, over and again, to have her freed. But none will heed me.' She gives a bitter smile. 'Not even those I thought allies.'

'I thought you were a saint, a seer? Surely you can see some way through this, turn the crowd gentle again?'

'I have not the power you think I have, Hilda,' says Wulfrun, urgently. 'Give me some time, at least. Men's hearts do not change overnight.'

'Then what purpose do you serve?' I ask. 'A toothless bitch, who howls in the night but cannot bite even if she wishes?'

The insult lands harder than I thought. Wulfrun runs her hands across her face, brushing some of the fatigue from it.

'The abbess knew what she did, in exposing Alwin and Mildred so. I wonder if she knew of their sins from the start. And now she has run to her bed and still none will listen to me. Always, I cannot help. Eadwig, Botwine. Now Mildred.'

I stare at her. There are tears in her eyes, as if this battle was already ended. As if she might choose defeat. I look back towards the stables, that room without a single fire.

'Did you strike your head also?' I ask.

She blinks. 'No,' she says. 'As I told you, I was unharmed.'

There is an anger in me, deep and growing, and I will not sit by and wait while another of us dies needlessly.

'Well then, you have much left to do,' I say. 'You have already turned this place over once. You can do it again. Save all this mourning and despair for later, when we truly have lost.'

No rousing poetry, this, but it is what I have been telling myself over and over again, battling in the infirmary for every life. I think, not for the first time, that for all her pride and power, it is Wulfrun who is the weaker of us both.

'Where do you go?'

'I will petition the abbess,' I say. 'And will not leave until Mildred is freed.'

Wulfrun offers to go with me, but I do not want her. She will only speak my words for me, or worse dilute them. Better that she goes to give the mass that is overdue, that

Mere

she uses it to remind my sisters of the pity and mercy that they might show. And I think the abbess hates her enough to refuse her, even without listening to what I will say. I have my arguments ready. Mildred is needed in the infirmary; she must be kept in until the babe is born, for he may be an innocent; she has done no worse than any other; shutting her away has not lifted this terrible flood.

I am but a few paces from the abbess's room when Ava hurries out. She seems barely able to speak, fear clinging to her like weeds.

'You are awake,' she says and there is no gladness in her voice, though a little confusion. 'I was just going to send to see if Tove would come, but it seems you have heard.'

'Heard what?'

'I can't find Sweet,' says Ava, 'but the abbess, she needs help.'

Chapter 24

The abbess's room is hot, air thick and fragrant. The largest fire I have seen for months burns in the hearth and dried flowers have been scattered throughout the rushes. The very first breath that I take sets my head spinning, my stomach churning. If another sister ran about with the injuries that I have, I would scold her and send her to bed for a day or two of rest. But with Mildred locked away, there are none left to order me.

I approach the bed, where the abbess lies curled in on herself, pain turning her inwards and a long, hoarse keen coming, ceaselessly, from her throat.

A few days ago, she was well enough to walk out to the church and throw Mildred and Alwin to the lions. Now, she will not be able to walk again, much less lead our convent. She has taken off her wimple again, revealing her shorn head. At the side of her mattress is her circlet placed on folded cloth. The ruby at its centre has been chipped, I see, at one of its edges, revealing a deeper red beneath, the colour of dark wine and dying flames.

Mere

I have known this day was coming, ever since I first pressed into her flesh and found hardness. But I still cannot help the little gasp I give as I look into her face. Her eyes are dim with pain. It has taken all of her, every virtue and vice.

'This is Alwin's doing,' says Ava, fiercely. 'That dog.'

'No,' I say. The abbess's headwound is already beginning to mend, nearly as well as mine. Strange, how even a dying body will fight to heal itself. 'No, this is the wolf-disease.'

'You will help her,' says Ava, no question in her voice. She reaches over for the abbess's blanket, already preparing to pull it back so that I might see my patient more clearly.

I watch the abbess. She is in need and I would be wicked to refuse.

'No,' I say.

Ava stills, hands clasped around the blanket.

'You have treated men who have killed their wives,' she says, 'women who have drowned their babies. Far heavier sins for far lower folk.'

'Mildred,' I say. 'Go and fetch Mildred, release her. Then, I will ease the abbess's pain.'

Ava flushes. 'They would throw me in the stable with her,' she says. 'Or worse.'

'Go to Wulfrun, then. Both of you together might find some reason. You are both cunning enough.'

The abbess lets out a whimper, calls out for someone. Her voice is so soft that I do not hear the name.

'I might do it myself,' says Ava. 'Tove has been watching you closely, could tell me how to help her. Mildred might even give me a cure or two that might revive her. You have been holding back, I know. I know she might be revived from this sickness. She might lead us again.'

I stare at her.

'You understand, surely,' I say, 'that there is but one path for her? That I might only ease her pain or else bear her further along?'

Ava's voice is calm, but there is a panic in her eyes. 'Must it be now? Can it not wait, can you not let her tarry here a little longer?'

I glance at the bed, the abbess in her agonies. She looks like a soul in hell, naked and penitent.

'I think there is but one with that power,' I say, slowly. 'And He has not been answering us, lately.'

I think Ava ready to berate me for my blasphemy, but all of a sudden, the abbess's moan quietens. Both of us turn round, afraid that in our argument we have left her to die alone. But her eyes are open, her breathing steady. That wakefulness that comes upon the dying and falls from them as waves on a shore.

'The Ealdorman will answer,' she says, as if she has heard our talk all this time, 'I know it. And it is harder to go out and bargain with that devil now that the boats are gone.'

She reaches out for me, looks full into my face. But whatever she sees there, it is not the infirmarian.

'I thought you would do it,' she says. 'I waited, but you did not. And so I went. I know you saw me sink those boats, out there in that midden of yours.'

I do not move. There is only one she would speak to so, only one in that edge-land, only one who shares so many secrets with the abbess and yet has none of her favour.

'Sweet,' she says, 'Sweet, you cannot tell them.'

Not Eadwig who sunk the boats, but the abbess. It must have taken all of her strength, to walk out alone to that distant place. I had never thought she would know the way,

Mere

but of course she built her convent on this land, she knows it as well as any of us.

At my side, Ava is shaking her head. 'No,' she says. 'No, she won't have.'

The abbess coughs, a long, wet thing. I lean towards her, lift her so that she is sitting. She is thin beneath her blankets and I feel the ridges of her spine against my palm. Her cough slows and she is slipping back into sleep, slipping away from me and Ava. I do not have long.

'Let us talk,' I say, 'of the ritual you forbade before.'

'No,' says the abbess, fretfully. 'No. I am done talking of this.'

I grasp her hand. 'I will keep it quiet,' I say.

The abbess frowns. 'But you know already,' she says, 'it was you chosen, after all.'

I am very still. At my side Ava, too, has stopped pulling me away.

'That mere-devil,' says the abbess and she is speaking in a great rush, as if in confession. 'All of them, they would gather and choose a soul, offer up some poor boy or girl. Once every two-score years and it was you who told me, since their grandfathers' time, and their grandfathers before it, all the way back to when giants ruled this land.'

She takes a breath. Ava and I might no longer be here, for all that she looks at us. She is gone, now, to her past, and I do not know if we will be able to fetch her back.

'You have not thanked me, for putting a stop to it. They would have put a string of flowers about your head, girl, and sent you out. But I thought it had ended, I thought we had starved him. Or that he slumbered, at the least.'

'But he was woken,' I say. Poor Eadwig, who strayed from the path just once.

She shakes her head. 'Cannot speak of it. Cannot tell any others.'

'But this devil took Eadwig,' I say. 'He took Botwine. Was he not content?'

'They are both dead,' says the abbess. 'Without use now. All those riddles he speaks, but we know, don't we? What the answer truly is?'

I have known for a while, I think, even before I struck my head. Something that does not end, but instead circles on itself. Something that might be forged, or threaded.

'A crown,' I breathe and the abbess nods. Beside her, her own circlet, the inset ruby knotted with thick golden thread.

I think of Wulfrun. How openly she has coveted the abbess's place and everything that comes with it. I cannot speak.

'So if we give whoever is crowned,' says Ava, slowly, 'the curse will lift.'

I turn to stare at her, for there is a tally in her voice. A weighing, of one soul against the total of us all. And I understand why the abbess and Sweet have said nothing of the curse, of the offering needed. For if Ava, most rule-bound of us all, is already thinking of it, then most of the convent would be looking among themselves for who would go.

Perhaps, if I did not think they would look to Wulfrun, I, too, would be making that same tally.

'You cannot!' says the abbess and she has been speaking so softly that her shout is like a rung bell, making Ava and I both flinch. 'No trade with the Devil, no worship of him. Just as Saint Guthlac understood the sibilant speech of the demons that tempted him and yet did not falter, so must we refuse all traffic with this beast.'

Mere

Guthlac again. But the abbess forgets that the saint spoke with kings, had his sister come to bury him. Even this long-dead hermit was not as friendless as us.

'You might have gone,' says Ava, to the abbess. 'You wear that circlet, you lead us all. At any time you might have gone, offered yourself.'

The abbess's face tightens. 'Please,' she says, 'please, I would have done anything, borne any pain, but that. I could not barter, could not give myself up to some demon. He would only grow the hungrier, I know it, and then he would come for you all. I could not lead you to the Devil. I will not.'

'Our souls,' says Ava. There is weariness in her voice, but something like pride also. Our abbess, unyielding to the end. 'You save our souls, not our bodies.'

'We women are such weak creatures,' says the abbess. 'So easily tempted to passion and sin. But that only means that our capacity for redemption is even the greater than for men. If we triumph here . . . if we outlast this devil, it will echo throughout Christendom.'

Ava takes a slow step back, presses herself against the wall and folds down, so that she sits among the rushes, her hands about her knees. I turn to the abbess, but she seems quietened for now and so I go to Ava instead, place my hand on her shoulder. 'There is sense in it,' she mutters. 'That goat we saw slaughtered, it had a crown, too. They remembered the crown, but not the meaning.'

My hands begin to shake. Such a web Wulfrun has caught herself in.

'Please, do not speak of this to any others,' I say.

The only sound is the abbess's strained breath. Even her dreams do not come easy to her any more.

Ava pushes herself upwards, so that she is standing again. 'I will go and see if I can release Mildred,' she says, dully. 'In return, you will help the abbess.'

'And the riddle?'

She sighs. 'There is no use speaking of it now,' she says. 'We both have our duties waiting for us.'

Chapter 25

I have her silence for now, at least, and so I hurry back to the infirmary and gather what I need. A potion of poppy seed and henbane, mixed roughly. Not much need for caution now.

When I return to the abbess's cell she lies exactly as we left her, curled in on herself as if she might trap the pain there. I try to place my hand on her bloated stomach, but at the smallest touch she gives a howl that sends me scrambling back, heart pounding.

'Sorry,' I say, 'Abbess, I am sorry, I—'

But as soon as I take my hand away, the cry ends. She does not care for my apology, no more than she cares for any other worldly thing right now.

'It is Hilda,' I say, gently, trying to stir her.

Her face twists, first with displeasure and then wryness.

'So you remember your duty to me at last,' she says. Then, with great effort, she opens her eyes. Through the clouds I see the same purpose that led her to pull the convent up from the marsh, that has kept it standing all these years. That kept this devil secret and might yet kill us all.

'Please,' she says, 'an end.'

We are called to see suffering as a gift. A long, slow disease as one of the greatest ways that a soul might repent. But it seems even the abbess cannot bear it any longer.

'You have had the last rites?' I ask.

'Yes,' she says, 'Ava shrived me.'

I watch her. If left alone, she would end raving and vague. Even now I see her hands claw at the straw mattress, scrabbling to hold onto life. Some go harder into death than others.

So, I hold my potion to her lips. She drinks it in small sips, dipping her head like a bird to water and it takes a long time for her to finish the draught. I feel no fear for the deed, for I have done it before, watched the previous infirmarian give this last comfort even as she talked of the wise woman who taught her of it, who learnt it from her own teacher. A chain of mercy, stretching back to the garden of Eden itself, and this the latest link, for one who has not earned it. But so few do.

And it is already beginning to take effect, for the abbess sighs, lies back and closes her eyes. Her fingers stop their deathly scratching, her cheeks flush, and when I place my hand on her wrist I feel her pulse, quick as rolling thunder. The poison taking hold.

'I wish,' she says and her words are already beginning to trip into each other. 'That I had never brought you in. A snake.'

I stare at her. There is no sign of a lie, or hatred. Only a final clarity.

My headwound aches. I feel as if I have spent a week on my feet, never stopping, never resting, and my voice comes

Mere

out as slow and slurred as the abbess's herself. 'I never wanted this.'

I stop. For I have, from nearly the beginning. Trees must be felled for new life to find root. We bleed and make the ground richer with our life. I wanted the abbess overthrown, but painlessly. A foolish dream. I tell others that I am worldly, that I know what it is I do. But I do not think I truly understood until now.

And so I am silent, watching the quick tremble of the abbess's chest. The poison is working quickly, spreading to every part of her. Slowly, she leaves us, and I find that I have no prayer for it, no holy words.

I begin to sing instead. A half-remembered song in British that was here before the abbess, that was here before the men across the sea came and took all about for their own. Sweet knows the words, would tell me if I asked, but I never have.

Her eyes close, her breath slows. I pull the blanket over her and sit back, waiting and watching.

'Aethelwine,' she says, weakly. It is the name of the Ealdorman. Her cousin, her betrothed. The one who raised her to abbess of this place and bound her to it all at once. I wait for her to speak further, but she only gives a small shiver. 'No,' she says, 'it matters not.'

Then, the door slams open and there is Ava, chest heaving and even her wimple gone, each of her grey hairs shining in the firelight. There is a dark stain on her front. I stumble upwards.

'An accident?' I ask, looking for signs of injury on her.

She shakes her head. 'Mildred,' she says, and that blood is not hers but it is Mildred who bleeds so much, so small a girl for so much blood.

Danielle Giles

 Ava is about to speak further, but then she sees the abbess behind me. 'What has—' she begins, but I do not have time for her questions now. I lift up my basket and push her aside. Day-bright, day-cold and the abbess dying at my hand but I cannot wait I must go to the stable where
 I run down the path, my throat full of strange wild cries I must
  should have been with her but
  couldn't have known only
  might have

Chapter 26

*M*ildred lies slumped in the hay of the stable, her head lowered. It is long past midday now, but with the doors barred little light reaches us both. She is kept in dark, in iron and pain that soaks into the rushes and pressed-earth floor.

I run to her, lift her wrists and feel in them the faintest hum of life. There is breath in her lungs, a slow gasp.

'Mildred,' I say, lifting her shift. A small mass there between her legs, the size of a knuckle. Such little flesh, to be heralded with such deluge of blood. I slide it away, hide it in some dark corner and then lift my own shift to wipe away her thighs. She has been bleeding a while and yet it has not stopped. It will drain the life from her if I cannot staunch it.

'Rags,' I call out, before I understand there are none coming to help. Ava is with the abbess, no doubt watching her die. Tove is at mass with Wulfrun, neither of them knowing what has happened, and I never know where I might find Sweet.

I take Mildred's cheek in my palm, turn her face to me.

Her eyes are without focus, rolling back towards her head. I pinch her, strike her lightly. If she slips away now, I will not be able to bring her back. My legs are warm with her blood, a stain that will rise up until my own stomach too is red and wet and I must be calm and I must save her but she is so pale so thin her lips growing blue and I have seen this before and we walk dangerous ways we walk where there is only one path and only one end.

My wimple is the cleanest piece of cloth about and so I take it off and knot it as thick as I can make it. I spread her thighs and push the bandage up into her belly. My hands come away slick but it staunches her, for now.

I take a breath, my first full one, it seems, since I entered the room. The smell in this place is so strong that I feel it on my shoulders and face, a second skin that I will never be able to shed.

'Mildred,' I say. 'Mildred, you must stay awake.'

She groans, blinks. 'Hilda?'

'Yes,' I say, 'yes, I am here. I am sorry that I was away.'

'I thought you might not come,' she takes a shuddering breath. 'Our son . . .'

I look down once more. The beginnings of a nose and eyes, webbed, tiny fingers. Something tears in me, then. An unknotting of thought from muscle, spirit from blood. Whatever animates me now is no soul.

'You must rest,' I say. 'Worry for yourself first, and then any child.'

'Are you angry?' she asks.

'Full of fury,' I say. 'You will have to work very hard the next few months to repent, do you understand?'

She smiles, nods. 'A fair punishment. But might I have time to dance for the abbess?'

Mere

I stare. She is in a half-dream. Loosing herself, already, from life.

'Alwin will return with a fine hunting hawk,' she says, 'Sweet will be our scop and we will go into the kingdom in the marsh together to rule.'

'A fine story,' I say, squeezing her hand. My cheeks are hot with tears but she does not see me any more.

'I will go to this kingdom, I shall have a bear for a mount and Alwin will have a horse with six legs and two heads and when we ride out all the realm shall marvel at us.'

'And is there a place for me in this kingdom?' I ask. 'You will need an infirmarian, maybe?'

'No,' she says, 'for nobody grows ill in that place. Only wounds may kill a man and even they must be grievous.'

'Maybe I might come anyway?' I say. 'Or else I shall grow lonely here, with half the convent away to serve you.'

'Yes,' she says. 'If you prove yourself, then you might come with me. Perhaps you might be a trader, or an envoy to distant lands.'

For a moment her gaze sharpens. 'You have always walked the boundaries,' she says, her voice strange. I flinch, hearing devil-sickness there. But my hand is tight around hers and I feel nothing passing through me that is not the thumping of my own blood.

Then, she sinks back, her breath slowing. There is no strength left in her at all. There are a hundred remedies for the loss of blood, but we have none of the herbs needed, and it is far too late now. The last of the woundwort used on my own head injuries, I think.

'Why did you not call for help earlier, sweetness?' I say. She smiles. 'Sweetness? Truly, I must be ill.'

'No,' I say, stroking her hair. 'No, it is only that I know

that I have not thanked you enough. That I have not told you how skilled you are, how kind.'

She does not reply. I look down to the rag between her legs, which is dark already. There are men wounded in the shield wall who would not bleed as much.

'You can begin, if you want,' says Mildred.

'Begin what?'

'The last rites,' she says. She speaks calmly, as if reminding me of some chore that I have forgotten. Always, always she surpasses me.

'Do not hurry me along,' I say. 'Let us get you to the infirmary, before we talk of that.'

'No,' she says, holding my arm with such force as I have never felt from her. She will leave bruises and they will last for days and weeks. 'I will not die unshriven, I will not be put at the crossroads with Eadwig, not be given to the marsh like Leogifu. Please, Hilda. I confess my sin, of sodomy with Alwin, of lust and pride, and you must give me forgiveness.'

I try to pull myself away from her, but I cannot. We have seen it in others before and now she patterns her death after all the sisters we have ever cared for. An able student, to her very end.

The words come quickly, as fast as I have ever spoken them. I am halfway through the prayer when her eyes roll backwards and her body shivers, as if God Himself is reaching down to shake her. Her fists and feet fly out her eyes open and staring but I do not let her go I hold and grip and speed my words and I will not lose this race though my hands are slick though my arms are slick and there is blood in my mouth perhaps hers perhaps mine and I press my forehead against hers clasp my hands about her cheeks

Mere

and she does not feel it and I tell her that it is done that her last rites are given.

She sighs, as if I have told her something that she dislikes. She does not take another breath and when I look at her it is flesh before me and nothing else. My helper is dead.

I come to, a hand shaking my shoulder. I am lying slumped on Mildred. On what was once Mildred. Eyes still opened and fingers cold and stiff and no holy light no bright smile all gone but the calluses on her hand from grinding herbs and a burn on her fingertip when she lifted a log she did not know was smouldering and how she shrieked and then put her finger into her mouth as a child might and told me it would heal in a few weeks not to worry not to

nine winters old when she first came to

twelve when she started making remedies without my

my habit is stained nearly to my neck with her

'You must stand,' comes a voice. Then, arms pull me up and I am on my feet, somehow.

I look up into the face of the visitor. Wulfrun. Her habit dirty now with me, with Mildred. She is still in her clothes from mass, a makeshift stole hanging from her neck. Alwin took the silk stole that was used for mass and so she wears one made of a hair shirt, cut into strips and sewn together. She has no alb tunic or chasuble cloak, but is in a white wool dress that has already stained a dark red at its hem.

'She's gone,' I say.

'I know,' says Wulfrun.

I feel my legs shake beneath me again and it is only Wulfrun who holds me up.

I should push her away. Take none of her kindness, take no kindness from any in the convent for they have all killed

Mildred. Me, worst of them all, for when Mildred trembled and bled, when she called for me, I was at the abbess's bedside, listening to her poisoned words, her talk of snake, snake. Perhaps she was right. Dripping disaster about me, letting evil bloom about me and I was not hard enough with Mildred I did not forbid her from Alwin and I let her keep his little love tokens and might she have been saved with a thousand choices that I did not make.

In the distance, the ringing of bells. Wulfrun stiffens, looks to me in fear. 'Botwine is back?' she asks, but I only shake my head.

'The abbess,' I say. 'She is dead.'

There is no urgency to the peals. Deep, slow, waiting for one note to die before the next is called. I press my face into Wulfrun's shoulder and howl until my throat is hoarse.

Chapter 27

We cannot use the church for our vigil and so the abbess has been taken to the chapter house, a much smaller building. Mourners jostle for entry, the press of so many bodies in the chapter house turning the air hot and sour.

Whenever I pass the doorway, I feel my sisters' gaze on me, hear their whispers of the riddle. Though I have denied it every time I have been asked, still I hear talk of it. They do not even understand what they hope for, but they hope all the same, even as they weep over the abbess's body.

In death, all has been stripped from her, save her wimple and the ruby circlet. That, too, should be returned, but Ava has not yet done it and I will never ask her to. Better that it be buried beneath the orchard than placed on Wulfrun's head.

Mildred is set on a lower bed of straw alongside the abbess. I thought Ava would argue it. But she is tired, a beast of burden that has been driven too far and too long.

I come to Mildred's side whenever I can. There is a cruelty

in my duties in the infirmary, for whenever I turn to ask for a salve to be ground or blood to be let, I find instead a stranger's face, a reminder that she is gone. Wulfrun has stirred as many as she can in the infirmary to help me, as well as offering her own aid, but it is not enough.

Mildred has fewer praying over her than the abbess, but they linger longer. Sweet brings a necklace of mistletoe, lays it about Mildred's breast, and mutters a prayer in a tongue I do not know. I have not seen her since these deaths and know I should ask her of the tale the abbess told me, but I cannot. It is too much to think of among our dead.

Eluned comes also, speaks prayers in Wealh and Latin. Her voice is grown stronger now, healing since she swallowed all that smoke in the storeroom fire, though I think it will always be a little hoarse. She unhooks her own wooden cross and places it around Mildred's neck.

'A safe journey,' she says, 'and may you find Alwin quickly.'

I think of Eluned and Mildred, giggling in the infirmary together. I wonder what they shared between them, what tales and riddles and laughter. A whole kingdom between them that I barely knew and that is gone now as well.

Tove is the last to come. She brings her embroidered blanket and lays it, gently, over my apprentice so that she is shrouded by saints and martyrs, their suffering brilliant against her bluish skin.

'It is not even half of what I owe her,' says Tove, tugging at a corner of the blanket so that it will lie neat. She sits beside the mattress, her head bowed. Her joints must ache, but she shows no sign of pain. Only a wince when, a few hours later, she stands back up and says, 'I am too old to see so many young maids die.'

Mere

She nods at Wulfrun, who is sitting on her knees in the corner. She is half-asleep having been awake most of the last day and night working in the infirmary for me. At the sound of Tove's voice, she starts awake.

'We must end this, Wulfrun,' says Tove. 'No matter the price.'

She talks of fleeing through the marsh, nothing more. She cannot know what I do, she cannot. But still, the words thread tight through me as I look between them.

'You have my word,' says Wulfrun, and I want to strike her.

'Good,' says Tove. She rubs her hands together to stir some warmth into them. 'Now, I must give my prayers for Sigeburg, for I think she will be in sore need of them.'

Both are buried the next day. I hear the abbess is honoured with stone at her head and a plot in the centre of the orchard, though I do not go to see her interred.

Mildred is placed beneath a young apple tree near a stone wall, where one day rosemary and fennel and chamomile will flower from her. I carve the post myself, a poor form of a girl with a babe in her hands and a husband at her side.

It is fortunate that Mildred and the abbess are buried then, for that evening a chill arrives and settles deep in the earth, turning pools to glass, earth to iron. Our breath blooms in front of us, our teeth chatter like penitent souls on the day of resurrection. The floodwaters, which we hoped would recede within days, are frozen in place, heavy and final as stone rolled across a tomb. There will be no hope of saving any of the winter herb now, the onions and parsnips and cabbage that would usually take us through the cold, lean months. They are gone and we have only our meagre stores left.

My headwound opens once more and I must fuss at it between duties, tying and retying bandages beneath my wimple. When I crawl into bed, but three days after Mildred's death, I am so tired that I fall asleep as soon as I rest my head. I wake to a small, rough hand on my arm.

'Do not sleep too long,' says Sweet, crouched beside me, 'or you will follow Mildred.'

I groan and turn away from the dawn light. A while longer, that is all. Away from thought and pain and duty.

Sweet pinches me.

'Up,' she says. 'Up.'

'You do not have to needle me so,' I say, sitting up.

'Good,' says Sweet, though she looks at me with concern. 'I have seen it before, you know. A blow to the head and three days later they went to sleep and did not wake.'

'Well, they did not have you at their side,' I say, lifting up my arm. Wulfrun's girdle is still wrapped tight about it. I wonder if Sweet felt it. 'You have a grip of iron, when you want to.'

'All the better for waking slothful girls,' says Sweet, though I have not been a girl for decades.

I look about my infirmary. Most are asleep still, waiting for the Lauds bell to rouse them. Mildred and I would usually wake the other before this, to start our day's work.

'Come,' says Sweet, 'help me draw some water.'

Sweet throws a stone down the well, breaks a hole that we might drop a bucket into. The water will only freeze again but we can melt it over a fire if needed.

We are the only two souls out at this hour, the sun in

Mere

the east straining up through heavy clouds. All the others are in their beds, grasping at sleep and warmth for as long as they can. We have begun to pull mattresses together, sharing blankets between any who are willing. It would usually be forbidden, but even Ava does not have the heart to punish this small sin.

There are a hundred things I need to ask Sweet, but I do not know what to start with. It is a relief, then, when she breathes into her hands and says, 'So, Eluned is to be freed. None can keep her, now that Sybba and all his brothers are dead, and so her manumission comes cheap.'

'It is done?' I ask. Eluned sitting by the dormitory door, her life laid out in front of her.

'Wulfrun has told Tove of the bargain,' says Sweet. 'And Tove has told some others. I would not trust each of them, alone, but together I think they will remember it. Just as long as we keep spinning these tales of ours. Have you heard, Hilda, of how Wulfrun was at a port and had a vision of clear sky, though all said a great storm was brewing? Only one boat listened and went out and returned with nets so heavy with fish that they could nearly not lift them to shore.'

'She has never told me of it,' I say, wondering, for it is the sort of thing that Wulfrun would boast about.

'That is because it did not happen,' says Sweet. 'But half the convent believes it and that is what is important.'

I reach for the bucket to hide my face. With every word, Wulfrun raises herself above us and brings herself into more danger. If there was any doubt before that she is chosen, it is gone. But the riddle spoke of a crown and if there are any among us that would earn such an honour, it would be her.

I cannot hide from it any longer.

'I spoke with the abbess,' I say, not looking at Sweet. 'Before she died.'

'And what did she say for herself?' asks Sweet.

'She called me a snake,' I say. 'Told me she wished I had never been brought into this place.'

Sweet puts down the bucket she has been holding. 'Well,' she says, after a while. 'We say many things when death approaches. I am sure she did not feel that way, truly.'

'She told me,' I say, 'about the mere-devil. How you were to be given once.'

There is nothing on Sweet's face to betray her, no fear or anger or guilt.

'I did not think the abbess would ever speak of it,' she says, at last.

'Why did you not tell me earlier?' I say. 'We might have found a way to save ourselves.'

'And how would you do that?' she says, fierce. 'Choose from among you? The poorest, the weakest? That was how it was done for me. I was enslaved and had nobody to speak for me and they dared say that I would be honoured with a crown. You do not understand what it is like, to be bartered away as if your life was of no value.'

She stops, glances up at me, but I do not reply. There is no use twisting all these regrets together now.

'Someone might have put themselves forward,' I say.

'That was how it was done, an age ago,' says Sweet. 'So the old tale went. Whoever was willing would take the crown and they would know that the call would come one day and they would answer it with joy in their hearts.'

She smiles, bitter. 'Then, one of them must have refused. Chose somebody else instead, to be taken and changed and

Mere

returned. They would be as Eadwig and Botwine were. Their touch a poison of sorts, for you never knew when it would take you away from yourself. I remember the last soul we crowned, an old man who lived half-wild, from the scraps we left for him at doorways, never greeting us, never speaking. But we kept him alive, told him he must be grateful for it. And it would only be the same now. They would trick some poor foolish girl into it and she would be told to smile even as she wept.'

'So many have died,' I say. 'A dozen, more soon. You would not weigh one willing soul against that?'

It is what I have been asking myself. Whether others die because I keep Wulfrun safe.

'I would not weigh them at all,' says Sweet. 'The abbess kept the secret because she did not want any to commune with this devil at the risk of their soul.'

'And because she would not give herself up though she herself was crowned,' I say, sour. 'She was scared.'

'No,' says Sweet, speaking to me as she did when she first taught me the ways through the marsh – patient, gentle. 'I bear no love for the abbess, but she was no coward. It would have been far easier for her to give herself up. To avoid the wolf-disease devouring her. But she would not do it herself and would not let any others in her care do so.'

I have no answer to that.

'For my part, I kept quiet because it is all the rest of you I fear. I would not have any feel like I did that night, when they told me I was to be crowned.'

'Alwin slaughtered a goat, not long before he and Mildred were caught,' I say. 'A wreath of green about her head.'

'The others remember the steps of a dance,' says Sweet,

'but not the music that must be played. They know that something must be given, but it has been so long since we have spoken of it that many do not know what. And it is not as before, where many were in great households, with girls and boys to spare. Now, we all starve together, on this scrap of dry land. Those who remember the old ways fear now that it will be their daughter, their son, their wife sent to the water. Or that by speaking of it they themselves will be marked to be given. Some even follow the abbess and do not wish to worship any god but the convent's. We will see how long all this lasts, when our days grow truly desperate.'

'So what are we to do?' I say. The words come out strange and desperate, a child's plea for an easy path, for all to be well and right again. 'We cannot stay and we cannot trade with this devil. We cannot flee, either, the abbess told me.'

Sweet gives a small, sad smile. She has never seemed young, but has a spirit about her that tricks others into thinking she is always firm. Not good cheer but a taut thread of tenacity woven through her every muscle and vein. Now, she looks as if that thread has been cut.

'If there is anybody to lead us through the marsh, it is Wulfrun,' she says. 'I will help as best I can, until I am no longer able. You should do the same, in that infirmary of yours.'

She speaks slowly, so that I will understand. She and the abbess both unyielding in their own ways, for their own ends. Twice she has bargained lives: first her own, and then mine. Now, she and the abbess have destroyed this convent and all who live within it.

'Do you regret it?' I ask. My throat is tight. 'Giving me up to this place?'

'No,' says Sweet, softly. 'Not once.'

Mere

The rain lightens, the clouds above parting. Winter sunlight spears through the mist and I feel, briefly, a warmth on the back of my neck. I smell damp earth, wet wool. Sweet's face is empty, some statue that has been polished and worn down so that they might be man or woman, saint or devil, ecstatic or melancholy.

'Are you not going to tell me I have grown thinner?' I say, thickly.

'No,' says Sweet. 'Only, I know Mildred was a sweet girl. I would be at your side, now.' She stops, suddenly full of doubt. 'If you wish it.'

'I wish it.'

I bow my head as she reaches her hand to my cheek and brushes it, her fingers strong and gentle.

The next few days pass somehow and before I know it Candlemas is upon us. There is strength in having Sweet beside me, for any time I look at Wulfrun and begin to doubt myself, she comes with some petty question or small duty and takes me away from my worry. Wulfrun, too, is busy, pressing children into chores or beds, judging disputes between sisters and others alike. Once in a while she will wince as the wounds on her back pull, but it is quickly hidden. And so we go whole days at a time without speaking much. It twists at me, deep within me, but my silence protects her more than my comfort ever could.

Tonight, Candlemas Eve, is different. When the bell rings for Compline, Wulfrun grows quiet. Since Mildred's death, she has spoken to me only of daily chores. She has not spoken of her plans to be abbess, though surely they are in her thoughts for we have been without one for a week. *An end and an end.*

Danielle Giles

Now I am close to her again and, for the first time, I see all that I have been missing. She has stopped putting berry juice on her burn to make it darker, no longer mends the tears in her embroidered wimple, nor remembers to put on all of her rings. All that is earthly, she begins to lose.

As we reach the doors of the chapter house, she halts. Half turns towards me, as if she wants to say something. I wait, but whatever it is it dies on her lips and we continue on instead.

Before the holy office even starts, she lifts up her head. I think for a heartbeat that it will be prophecy, but she is beyond that. She will not wait for Candlemas, as she promised.

'I call an election,' she says, her face tilted up, heavenwards, 'for the position of abbess.'

Chapter 28

All that plotting and worry, but in the end there is little battle in it. Ava counts the paltry tokens, lifts her voice up to announce that Wulfrun will be our new abbess. She has a softness in her face as she does so that I distrust. It looks too much like pity.

We celebrate with mass. After years of men's voices ringing through the church, it is strange to be in the chapter house instead, a woman's voice guiding us. It seems more lasting in some way. Alwin and Botwine's words glanced off our stone walls, but I think Wulfrun's sink into the wood, to be remembered until this place at last collapses. They are burning sage and lavender now, all our incense used up. The smoke is thicker, pulls us not heavenward but to the earth, to coming springs and promised harvests.

I try not to look at her in all her glory. My gaze is on my feet, on my other sisters, on the chapter house.

We have no wine left and so when Wulfrun holds up the cup to be consecrated, it shimmers cream and soft, and when I go to drink it leaves a sourness on my tongue.

Sheep's milk. A small heresy, but one we have no choice over. As I swallow, Wulfrun gives me the smallest of smiles and I smile back somehow.

Standing so long has made my head ache again, black patches appearing at my vision's edges. So it is with relief that I hear the mass come to an end and turn to go.

And then, beside Wulfrun, I see Ava. She has something in her hands. Something I thought buried and gone, though of course I did not see the abbess shrouded and placed into the cold earth, and it glints, gold and ruby, and she bows to Wulfrun and holds it out in her hands, an offering, a gift, and Wulfrun takes it from her as easily as if she were born to it and about her head

a crown

and there are whispers between pressed bodies, tales of visions and miracles that I know to be false, sobs, moans, painful sounds that come from deep within them.

I do not think many even know they call out, only that they say over and again, the answer is yes, yes, crown her, alleluia alleluia. I see Tove nodding, I see Ava with her lips pressed tight and in the faces of my sisters I see the same hunger that drove them to lay hands on Mildred and Alwin. They will devour her and she will let them.

Ava's eyes are fearful. Ava, who would keep herself steady against bears, against wolves, against the entire great heathen army. Only the two of us here understand, truly, what this means.

And then she speaks. 'You all must know,' she says, 'that I do this not out of hate, but because I think it to be good.'

All slows. I am watching the fall of the axe and there is nothing I can do about it. Wulfrun stands, unsure, exposed.

'You all know the riddle,' says Ava. 'Our own infirmarian,

Hilda, spoke of it but a few days ago though we did not listen at the time.' She has none of Wulfrun's skill in leading a crowd, none of Sigeburg's old authority. But that does not matter, for her sincerity carries her through.

'Well, sisters, the abbess told me with her dying breath of the answer. What we must give, to be freed from this curse.'

The air is thick as earth itself. She cannot, she would not.

'I end and then I end and then I end. Forge me in heat, knot me in thread. I do not belong to one soul alone.'

A few of my sisters look about, as if speaking the riddle in full will bring some new terror on us all. Beside Ava, Wulfrun repeats the words silently. Then, she pales, reaches to touch the ruby.

'No,' I call out, but it is weak, tired. 'No,' I try again and a few sisters look around but most do not, most keep their eyes ahead, blinkered as any horse. And she has learnt a few tricks, Ava, has seen how Wulfrun will have others answer for her and turns it now, against our new abbess.

'Have you any thoughts, Wulfrun?'

'A crown,' says Wulfrun. She has not let her fingers fall from the circlet. 'It wishes for a crown?'

But that is not right, that is too easy and Wulfrun knows it and Ava reaches out, holds Wulfrun's shoulder in fellowship and there are tears on the portress's cheek but she has always been able to do what is hard, what is needed.

'The crowned,' she says, softly.

There is no need for Ava to speak further because we all know. Only one of us is most precious, brightest. Only one of us is brave, truly.

Wulfrun nods, her face full of joy.

*

The chapter house is strangely quiet afterwards. They all press about Wulfrun, just as they did before her whipping. She receives each of them in turn with a nod, a smile of favour. I hate every one of them that comes to her, every one of them that goes away sure that this is what is meant to happen, that this sacrifice is beautiful and holy.

She wears the crown still.

The other sisters come to me, wanting to talk over the riddle. The answer so easy. I tell them no, no, I must be wrong, but my words are as knots in wool, combed out before they can cause trouble. I raise my voice, call out to Ava that the abbess would forbid her from this, that we should flee to Gipeswic instead. But it is hopeless. I offer them this half-defeat even as Ava shows them the path to victory.

And then, Tove stands up. She is slow to do so and I hear the crackling of her bones, but nobody raises their voice. They will wait as long as it takes for her to speak and in the silence I look up at Wulfrun. She looks away.

'When Wulfrun dies screaming,' says Tove, 'will you stand by this?'

'She will not die,' says Ava. 'By my understanding. She will only be . . . other. As Eadwig and Botwine were. We will not harm her, but nor will we give her entry to the convent.'

'A living death, then,' says Tove. 'All that devil-sickness in her head.'

'Yes,' says Ava, 'and if it is not successful, you may condemn me, then. Punish me how you see fit. But if Sister Wulfrun is willing, then I cannot stop her.'

And it is that which sways the convent. They have had their fill of violence, of driving Botwine away, of tearing at

Mere

Alwin. But if the soul is willing, they only clear a path for something that might be done anyway. The difference between bringing a rock down on somebody's head and simply allowing it to fall.

'And,' says Ava, 'if Sister Wulfrun triumphs, or otherwise saves us, well then, we shall have another miracle.'

Something in Wulfrun falters. A twitch of her mouth and a tremble of her fingers. She understands now that it is no choice. She has sold herself for slaughter almost since the day she first came.

Then, she gathers herself and stands. 'Ava is right,' says Wulfrun. 'I will go.'

The crowd disperses. Ava orders most back to their duties, for even when we send a woman to her end, the fires must be lit and the bread must be baked. Tove stalks off back to the infirmary, swearing in Norse and English, cursing them all for cowards and fools.

I go to follow Tove back to the infirmary, pushing through the men and women who have gathered outside, but Sweet reaches out and grips me by my arm.

'I would talk with you,' she says, 'alone.'

We walk a few feet away from the chapter house and stop underneath a huddle of bare trees. Not much cover against prying eyes, but none in the convent mark either of us much. Above, a chill wind runs careless fingers through the branches. There is the taste of coming snow and I know that, tomorrow, we will wake to whiteness.

'What think you?' I ask. 'It was you who told me the tale in the first place. Why was Botwine not enough? He bore no crown, but he led us all.'

'And he was killed,' says Sweet, 'along with his son. You

did not let either of them survive long enough to see what might have come after.'

Her words trail off. I watch the empty sky. What I would give for a gull, a harrier, even a crow. There is a tiredness in me deeper than flesh, deeper than bone.

'I am sorry,' I say. 'You kept the secret so long and now all know of it.'

Sweet sighs. She is so worn these days.

'You did not tell Ava?'

'No,' I say. 'The abbess did, before she died. I asked Ava to not speak of it, but . . .'

Sweet's lips tighten. 'She has never been afraid of turning friends to enemies, that girl,' she says, 'especially when it comes to tending the convent.'

'I cannot hate her for it,' I say and find it is the truth.

'I can,' says Sweet. 'Wulfrun is not the saint others believe her to be, but nor has she earned this. A lonely end.'

I see it in her, then. The fear she has carried with her for four decades, ever since she herself was chosen to go to the marsh. She has spent her whole life fighting never to be in that place again and now she watches as another is sacrificed. Sweet is meant for movement, for always looking for what must be done next, even if she will grumble as she does it. But today, she is still, and she is ashamed of it.

'I have something I would ask of you,' I say.

Her pale face grows paler. 'No,' she says. 'I will not let you.'

'I am not yours to order about,' I say, gently. 'Not any more.'

She spits on the ground. 'I knew this house would twist you. A whole life ahead of you and you would choose suffering over it all. Christ-followers, all the same down to the bone, desperate to throw yourselves away.'

I take her hand in my own. It is trembling, so hard, so calloused. All those hours spent growing herbs, pounding cures. For those with wealth she charged a heavy price. For those without, sometimes no price at all. 'It was not the abbess that taught me generosity,' I say. 'Nor mercy.'

She pulls me into an embrace, then. Clings to me, like she might gather back all the years apart like so much wool. Like anything might be undone between us. I stiffen and then sink into her arms, letting her hold me, letting her brush the back of my head with her hand.

When she pulls away, her eyes are filled with tears. 'There is always a place for you by my hearth,' she says. 'A bowl of pottage, too, if you are fortunate.'

'I have eaten your pottage,' I say and my own voice comes thick, 'and so I will take only the seat.'

'Foolish girl,' she says, cuffing me about the head as if I am a child. 'A swift journey and fair winds to you.'

I find Wulfrun by the gate. She is already dressed for travel, though I think she lingers with her gloves. They are calfskin, hastily mended at the seams. She pulls at them, sighing to herself as if all that stands in her way are these gloves and her clumsy fingers.

She looks up at my arrival. She is dressed almost as I first saw her that late autumn day, Eadwig missing and Sweet's bone-charms whispering above us. Then she was remote, Polaris shining bright and strange and never to be reached. Now, I count the toll of the last three months on her. Her face thinner, though cheeks and arms still plump. Her eyes tired, shining like she is a fevered patient.

There are few people at the gate. They have said their farewells in the chapter house. Only Ava and Tove, stood apart from us, still arguing in low voices.

Wulfrun goes to embrace me and then hesitates.

'I am glad,' she says, 'that you came to say farewell.'

'I am sorry,' I say and close the two steps between us easily. I kiss her on her lips, her cheek, her cold nose. Every part of her open to me, I find and I adore.

'How long had you known?' she asks.

'No,' I say. 'No, I did not know. It was a passing thought and I think I am wrong. Only, Ava heard it and believed it truth and now the whole convent—'

'How long had you believed, then?' asks Wulfrun, firm but not unkind.

'Since that day in the church,' I say. 'When I fell, I saw something about you. And you spoke so often of wanting to be crowned.'

Wulfrun sighs. 'That was a few days ago,' she says. 'I might have gone earlier and this convent would already be saved.'

'Or you might have been devil-sick all the longer,' I say. 'And you are not listening. I do not think this will work. You throw your life away for nothing.'

Wulfrun's dark eyes have tears in them. 'Do not,' she whispers, 'please, do not try and talk me from this. You will only make it harder.'

'Good,' I say.

Wulfrun opens her mouth to reply, but is interrupted by Ava and Tove. They have finished their argument and come to us, each holding something. Tove has her cloak in her

Mere

arms and Ava holds a wrapped box. Two Magi, come in devotion, bearing gifts.

'If you feel that you must go,' says Tove, each word forced through a tightened jaw, 'then I cannot stop you. But, if at any point you decide that you would return, we would welcome you.'

'Unless—' begins Ava, but Tove holds up her hand.

'We would welcome you,' she says.

Then, she presses the cloak into Wulfrun's hands. 'You will need this,' she says, 'for it will be a bitter day and an even colder night.'

'Thank you,' says Wulfrun and again I see her with no words at Tove's kindness.

'No need for thanks,' says Tove, gruffly. 'You give far more than I could ever.'

She looks between us both and for a moment I am sure she will say something more. But she only shakes her head and there is every one of her eight decades in her face and then she leaves us.

Ava steps forward next, her body held stiffly.

'We do not have much in the way of provisions left,' she says. 'A month or two, if spring does not come late. But I thought this might help in your journey.'

She thrusts the box into Wulfrun's hands. Wulfrun unwraps it slowly, but does not recognize it at first. I am the one to laugh, to turn to Ava.

'The abbess's dates?' I ask.

'I have been saving them,' says Ava. 'But they are best with you.'

Wulfrun opens the box, picks up one of the dates and stares at it. This, more than anything, breaks through her resolve.

'You know,' says Wulfrun, 'what I go to? For what purpose I leave? How will this help me?'

'Please,' says Ava, weakly, 'take it.'

For a heartbeat, I think Wulfrun will refuse. An ox led down a path might buck, if only to feel free for that heartbeat where the yoke is hanging in the air away from its neck. But Wulfrun looks at Ava, so rigid, so desperate.

'I will,' says Wulfrun, placing the box in her own bag. 'Thank you also.' There is not much space left and so she bends over the bag, unpacking and repacking, fussing. She would stretch these few moments to a day, if she could.

While she wrestles with the gift, Ava turns to me.

'You have your path, then,' I say.

'I obey what I think to be good,' says Ava, 'no matter what follows.'

She will not ask for forgiveness, for there is none to be had. In the end, Wulfrun does this of her own will. Ava has always been a distaff, the water to my flame, and today I feel it the keenest of all. I am but a few choices away from her.

'I keep Ethel in my prayers,' I say. 'With Mildred. With Alwin and Botwine.'

'That is good of you,' says Ava. 'I still pray for you. I always have. Or, at least, most days, if you have not been stubborn or disobedient or prideful.'

'And I you,' I say. 'If you have not been mulish or tight-fisted or rule-bound.'

'Well,' she says. 'We must take even the smallest graces when they come our way.'

She glances at Wulfrun.

'I will leave you both,' she says, 'to your farewells.'

*

Mere

Then, it is only Wulfrun and I, two small figures in the cold. Wulfrun's breath billows out in front of her as she stands, newly unsure. In stained glass and manuscripts, martyrdom is always glorious, sky blue, sun shining. Or else beneath a roiling storm, dark clouds and lightning flashing gold and silver. It does not happen on days like this, damp, dreary, a cold mist settling that is so thick that we cannot see beyond a few paces in front of us.

She will not even be able to find her way out of the convent grounds.

'Well,' says Wulfrun and she is brave again. She has practised these words, her farewell to me. 'Hilda, meadowsweet, dear heart. I could not have asked for a better friend. You have—'

'Be quiet,' I say. 'Please, I do not want to hear this.'

'No,' says Wulfrun. 'No, you must listen. I do not know how I could have lived these last months without you. I do not know how I did not know you before, for it seems as if I have had you at my side my whole life. Kind, brave, a—'

'Yes, yes,' I say. 'I am the heart of you. I know this. Come, we have more urgent matters to speak of.'

Wulfrun frowns. 'More urgent?' she says. 'How?'

'The path to take out of the convent,' I say. 'How many rushlights to take along.'

'I do not understand,' says Wulfrun, 'I have already all that I need.'

'Well, you shall have to tally again,' I say. 'For another.'

'Another?' she asks. She is slow to understand, because she does not wish to.

I look behind her shoulder. Sweet is returning from the infirmary, laden with my cloak, my small satchel of herbs and salves. Her every step is slower than the last but I do not care because, for the first time in my life, I know what I must do and find the courage to do it. I feel still Wulfrun's girdle tight around my upper arm, an unending circle, binding me to her for now and for ever.

'I am coming with you,' I say.

Chapter 29

The first part of our journey is in silence. Wulfrun is angry, so angry she will not speak to me but instead stalks on, leaving me to hurry in her wake. It is as if she thinks that by outpacing me, she might convince me to turn back. The cloak that Tove gave her is about her shoulders, the hours and hours she spent repairing it already coming undone in the roughness of our journey.

But the snowstorm has arrived now and any path back towards the convent is long gone. She holds the torch in front of her and I must call out, tell her to slow.

'Or else,' I say, 'I shall be lost and all of this will be for nothing.'

'It is for nothing anyway,' says Wulfrun. She glances to the sky. It cannot be more than an hour past midday but the dark is already crowding in, impatient, hungry. She wears, still, her crown, reflecting the flickering rushlight.

We stand, water to our ankles. I thought I knew the path that we followed, out of the convent and through the marsh towards Gipeswic. We turned right at the old yew tree, past the sunken boats, followed a path on raised earth. There should be a causeway soon, wooden slats bound to posts sitting a foot or so above the water that would lead us through the mere and out. But the flood is still with us, making old land unfamiliar and, somewhere, we turned off the path.

'There is yet time,' says Wulfrun. 'You might turn back.'

'That was a mile ago,' I say. 'I am with you in this now.'

Her face twists. 'And how will you help? Does the mere-devil perhaps have a cut that needs treating? A flux that must be soothed?'

'No,' I say. 'But you might. Here.'

I reach into my bag, pull out some mugwort and place it in her spare hand. 'Put it in your boots,' I say. 'It soothes the feet and brings luck for good journeys.'

Wulfrun looks at it. Something has broken free within her in the past hour and she does not know how to tame it. It is behind her eyes, in the throb of her pulse and the catch of her breath. Terror.

She lifts her hand and throws my mugwort to the water.

'That is as much help as you will be,' she says.

I smile. She thinks herself cunning.

'You know,' I say, 'nothing will make me leave you now.'

'You are a poor infirmarian,' she says. 'Your cures do not work as they should.'

I stare at her, then shake my head.

'Is this an insult?' I ask.

'One of many,' she says, defiance in her voice. 'You are far too rough when you bleed. A skilled leech should prick, not slash.'

'True enough,' I say and I cannot keep the laughter from

Mere

my voice. I have heard her spit venom about her enemies, have seen her topple my convent from the inside out. But here she is again, this fool I see only sometimes. The maid who cannot even think of anything truly evil to say to me.

Wulfrun stares, hopeless. 'We go to a battle,' she says, 'one we will not win.'

I look about me. I cannot tell where the fog ends and the water begins. The first snow falls, flakes aligning on empty branches and shining there for a breath, before melting into nothing. Branches above grasping like hands, fellow sisters embracing like roots. We are in a world without boundaries. The edge-land. I have always found the rarest herbs here, the most potent cures.

Sweet told me, an age ago, that this place was not kind to border-walkers. I thought her wise then, but now I think it nothing but foolishness. She was bound by her fear, too bound to think clearly. My cunning, wounded mother.

'I begin to think,' I say, 'that there was never a battle to be fought at all.'

The silence that follows is a cloak wrapping around us both, smothering and total.

'Then what is there?' says Wulfrun. 'Nothing but defeat?'

She looks at me as if I must have some answer. But I have none, not yet.

'You do not seem afraid,' she says, almost an accusation.

'I am,' I say. 'But it feels far away. A clear head for fair healing, so Sweet always tells me.'

In the days before I must cut out some tumour or lance some boil, I am nearly sick with worry, not eating, not sleeping, whetting my every tool so that they would cut just to look at them. But on the day, I am calm. Not because that is how I feel, truly, but because it is what I must feel.

'I did not think this would be easy,' says Wulfrun, dully, 'but I did not think I would be so full of doubt. Catherine on the wheel, Daniel in the lion's den, even poor Edmund against the heathen arrows: did they fear so?'

'I do not know,' I say. 'They are not alive to tell us.'

'I feel no good in this,' says Wulfrun. 'Is that wrong?'

I look about. The snow begins to fall thicker around us. It is beginning to settle, picking out the lines of the marsh in white like an illuminator adding silver to a page. We still cannot see beyond the few paces ahead of us.

'No,' I say. I think back to what Sweet told me of the crowning. Of how it was an honour once, a service given. It has rotted, I think, this gift. Men and women grew fearful of losing what they had, turned it into a curse to be borne by others.

'What they have sent you to do, there is no good in it.'

Wulfrun does not reply. Her gaze is on a trembling branch, bare but with the memory of buds upon its tips. A spring that neither of us will likely see.

'I am glad,' she says after some time, 'that you are here with me. How selfish, to feel so.'

I reach across, adjust the knot of her cloak to keep her throat from the cold. Kiss her cracked lips, press myself against her. I can feel her heartbeat, as fast as a new-caught hare's.

'Let us be selfish, then,' I say.

We hold each other under the smudged sky, until the cold creeps into our bones, until it makes even our teeth ache. Even then we do not part but stay, hand in hand, looking at each other like new-found jewels.

Wulfrun rubs some warmth into my hands, but she is not looking at me any more. Something beyond has caught

Mere

her. 'We must go on,' says Wulfrun, 'or else we will freeze to death here. If there is shelter . . .'

She is right, but I do not want to stir myself from her. Every step we take is into greater uncertainty.

'There should be some trees,' I say, 'further along the path. We might light a fire there, if fortune favours us.'

Wulfrun laughs, then, bitter. 'I would not trust in it,' she says.

We walk on, hand in hand. I do not know how long for. The sun is gone, and our bearings with it, and so the path is a slow and difficult one. Several times we think we have found a way, a trail of pressed earth, only for it to end in a mere-pool or another crossroads. There is no sign of any causeway. We might be miles from the convent, or we might only be a few hundred feet and walking in circles. I have heard of travellers, frozen to death in the cold, a few feet from their threshold, not knowing how close they were to home.

The knot of trees I spoke of does not appear. But we do see a shape in the water, a pale tunic blooming outwards. Both Wulfrun and I stop and for a heartbeat I think there is a body beneath, another poor drowned soul. But as we grow closer, we see it is only filled with water.

'That is Alwin's,' says Wulfrun, dully. I peer down, see the fine embroidery at the neck. 'Why would he have taken it off, in this cold?'

I have no answer and so I only say, 'We cannot linger here.' I do not want to think of Alwin, lost and alone in this murky place. His body surely not far. Perhaps it is good that he was lost before he could learn of Mildred's death.

We continue on. My teeth are the first to stop chattering. Wulfrun does not hear it at first, too wrapped in her own footsteps, her own breath. Then, her face pale, she turns to me.

'You are quiet,' she says.

Each word feels as if it is dragged up from deep below me. 'Yes,' I say. 'I am no longer feeing the cold. The first sign.'

She does not ask what of. I have seen it perhaps a handful of times in my life. A child, out playing too long and lingering in the chill. An old woman, unable to light her fire and too proud to ask another to do it for her. A man forced by his master to sleep outside as punishment. Each of them unable to warm themselves, even in front of a fire.

'We should stop,' she says, beginning to remove the cloak that Tove gave her. I take it, gratefully, wrap it around me.

'It is too bare here,' I say. 'A fire will not last.'

She looks about, as if some bowed oak or ancient cave or even fisherman's hut will present itself. But we stand, the tallest shapes for what seems like miles, lashed by every passing wind and shivering squall.

'I see the path,' she says, suddenly. 'A post, over there. Let us hurry.'

She pulls me along before I can protest. She does not pick out the path any more but wades through and though there are half a dozen pools she might fall into, none claim her. Good fortune, at last, but there is something beneath this and I want to urge caution, want to call out. My lips are slow, my tongue heavy.

And she is right. For as we draw closer I see the post also, the beginning of a long stretch of wooden slats. The wood of each is from a different tree. Ash and yew, oak

Mere

and birch, so that with a single step we might cross an entire forest. Willow woven through, knotting and securing. There is no iron in it, no nails.

It is ancient, also. Moss reaching out from water, from gaps between slats, to glisten like fat on new-cooked meat. Brilliant green. Should be rotting, falling apart, but no sign of that here. No human hands, either, have touched it, have tended it. It was built a long time ago and has stayed the same.

Two souls have found this path before and both grew devil-sick and both are now dead.

'The path to Gipeswic?' asks Wulfrun, though she must know she is wrong.

I try to gather my slowing thoughts. Tove's cloak helps a little, for I am beginning to feel the chill in my bones.

Then, I sense it. There is something in the air. Impossible, a wonder, and it is there all the same. Spring blossom. Warmth.

'I think we must follow it,' says Wulfrun.

She pulls me up, holds me close to her. Still so warm, even with both her cloaks on me instead. They are far too long, in the sleeve and the hem. I see redness creeping up her hands and her cheeks.

'Our journey's end,' she says, her eyes shining and this is the end, I have not stopped it I have not saved her and I must watch only watch and I do not know if I can bear it and we follow this strange path towards the warmth towards the sweet smell. My eyelids grow heavy and Wulfrun is ahead of me

behind me

at my side her hand pulling me on urging me

there is water in my eyes in my mouth soaking my lungs

Danielle Giles

winding about my throat and I thrash and reach out for
Wulfrun but there is nothing to hold onto only
  a great maw
  an empty belly
  a relief to rest

Chapter 30

I open my eyes, in sudden sunlight. There is birdsong in the trees, the hum of flies and bees and beetles. Life that has not announced itself for days in the convent is all about here. Softness beneath me, damp moss covering the ground.

I push myself to my elbows. Wulfrun's cloaks fall off me, a blanket that she has placed on me when I was asleep. We are in a clearing, embraced on all sides by fog. It is different to anywhere we have passed before, full of pools and ridges, rushes and sedges and ferns, tufts of grass, splintered trees and sodden earth and great swathes of moss, running from water to earth and back again and all of it as green as any I have ever seen, the green of a bud before it blooms, the green of an oak in full majesty.

I turn and see a shape next to me. For a moment I think it is Wulfrun but I am wrong, so wrong, for it is Botwine that is laid out beside me and he is dead.

He is bloated. Flies swarm above his head, maggots crawl

through his flesh, determined as apostles. His skin has stretched and darkened and the blood at his temple and cheek has grown solid. The dark stain in his belly where Alwin struck his blow has also hardened, the cloth of his habit held in place there by the wound. His eyes are closed and he might look peaceful if not for all the life that feasts within him.

He reeks, almost sweetly, and I turn and retch. I have not eaten much in so long, that all that comes out is bile. The wound at the back of my head aches, almost in fellow-feeling with poor Botwine's suffering.

'I think he came here to be warm,' says Wulfrun. I start at her voice, turn around. She is crouched a few feet from me, inspecting something I cannot see. 'And then died from his wounds.'

There is gold glinting at his feet. His rings, his chain, his torque. He must have taken them off towards the end, piled them all and left them for gross vanity and nothing more. Only a wooden cross still about his neck, his Pater Noster cord. Nobody to shrive him, nobody to take a vigil over his body living or dead and perhaps even now he suffers, his smallest sins heavy around his neck, a millstone keeping him from heaven.

Swallowing down more bile, I reach and press my hand against his chest, mutter a prayer. I think of the pelican he once told me of, thin and dying and holy no more.

'I hope the next kingdom is what you hoped for,' I say, 'for Christ knows you have earned it.'

Wulfrun watches us both. She does not cross herself. Perhaps she has no grace to spare, not when we are so wretched ourselves.

'He is here, of course,' she says. 'A reminder of my sins.'

Mere

'You did not drive the spear into his gut,' I say, 'nor drive him away.'

'No,' says Wulfrun. 'But I called him coward. And when a woman names a man so, there is only one thing she wishes from him. Some heroic act. Well, here it is.'

'I think Botwine was lost to us as soon as Eadwig found that firesteel in the storeroom,' I say.

Wulfrun considers this gift of mine, this forgiveness. Then, she stands, brushes dirt from her skirts. She is blocking something from me with her body.

'Your crown,' I say, for I can see that it is gone. Its imprint remains still in the wimple on her head. A memory of power.

She shrugs. 'I lost it in coming here,' she says. Vagueness passes her face. She does not remember the journey here any more than I do.

'Well, I shall never give you anything,' I say. I reach to my arm, check that the girdle she gave me is still there. It is, soft and warm and tight. 'I kept your gift for weeks and you have had that crown for less than a day and you lose it.'

I mean to pull a smile for her, even at the end. But her face remains serious. 'I am glad you are awake and warm,' she says. 'Come, let us carry on.'

I look about. Fog on all sides and paths out, yet there is a strange, embraced feeling about this place. I think of Botwine and Eadwig, talking of a trap sprung on them, of a hunger that could not be sated and a thirst that would not be quenched.

'Might we rest?' I ask. 'I am still weary.'

'I do not wish to linger here,' says Wulfrun. 'This is an evil place.'

But I feel no evil in it. No good either. It is vast and old and slow.

I stand and walk over to her. There is still coldness in my limbs, making my steps stiff. Wulfrun puts her hands out to support me and I see, then, what she was trying to hide from me.

A small spring, clear and deep. There are skulls at its bed, half a dozen or so. Teeth and jawbones, scattered like jewels. Other pieces of the bodies elsewhere, scraps here and there. A finger a few feet away, a segment of spine half-submerged by the pool. Tatters of fur, glass beads decorated in a style I have never seen before. It is an odd sight, as if the bodies are sinking into the mere and rising from it all at once.

And, on the crown of every skull, a circle of moss. Spreading in a ring and reaching downwards, worming through eyes and nose and jaw. The green about from which all other green is drawn.

'Oh,' I say, for there is little else in my mind.

'I have never seen clothing like this,' says Wulfrun, looking anywhere but the skulls in the spring, 'nor jewellery. They must be from the age of giants.'

'On their head—' I begin, but Wulfrun pulls me away.

'Come,' she says, 'we have to go now.'

I might tell her it is hopeless, but she knows that already. So instead I stumble after her, picking a route through the fog. We hold hands the whole time and every time we pass a tree, Wulfrun scores into it with her knife.

'If we become lost,' she says, 'we might mark our steps.'

'If,' I say and I feel like laughing. I have never been as lost as we are now, fog still thick about us but not cold any

Mere

more. Still, I watch as she cuts into the yew, the birch, the willow, leaving raw white in our wake.

And then we push aside bramble, we part reeds and scrub that reaches our chest and ahead there is fog and beyond that fog there is

clearing

The first time, Wulfrun falls to her knees as she sees it, cursing and wrathful, pulling up the moss in great fistfuls as if she wishes to tear into the heart of the marsh itself.

The second time she only sets her jaw and carries on. If we see a score in the bark, a path-marker, she adds a sideways cut, so that we follow the way of the cross.

The fourth time she blames me. The seventh she blames God, then me, then herself.

The twelfth time she stops, asks if I am not tired.

'I would carry on,' she says, 'but if you must rest . . .'

She is swaying, her feet dragging. Her entire body pulling her rest-wards but she waits instead for my word.

I look up at the sky. We cannot see the sun, but I would have expected nightfall by now. Instead the grey light has remained.

'The day passes wrong here,' I say. 'Botwine said he had been away only a day, but he returned after a week. And Leogifu looked starved as if she had not eaten for an age.' Sweet's tales, of kingdoms beyond man's knowledge. I think we have fallen into such a place.

'We have been here three hours or so,' says Wulfrun, 'by my reckoning.'

'Then let us rest,' I say, 'for it will have been a day or two already, back at the convent.'

We collapse together, as far away from the skulls as we can. There is water about us, but it does not quench us.

Nor does the ale in our leather pouches, nor the abbess's dates. We pluck sweet honeyed darkness and swallow it down but our throats are dry still, our stomachs still empty.

'Botwine spoke of this,' I say. 'He said he was hungry and thirsty and that there was but one choice for him.'

Wulfrun looks about at the fog, the endless marsh. She does not look at the spring, the water cool and bright.

'So we are trapped,' she says.

'I hoped for a miracle,' I say. 'It is always when souls are most desperate that one occurs.'

Wulfrun turns the last of the dates about in her fingers. They are sticky with the feast, glistening like fresh-gilded pages.

'No,' she says. 'No more miracles.'

It is strange, now that we are here. A place I have dreaded for months and yet I find a peace settling. No end could be better and maybe I am glad to be done with it all.

Wulfrun takes a date and flings it as far as she can. In the distance, I hear a soft splash.

'To eat and drink, but not be sated. We are in hell.'

'I do not think they have dates in hell, Wulfrun,' I say.

'Of course they do,' she says. 'To show the poor sinners what they might eat, had they not strayed so from the path.'

'You truly think so?' I ask. Some of Wulfrun's vision-work bleeds through into her mind. It makes her full of fancy and magic, turns shadows into devils and candles into holy flame. 'I think the Devil does not like dates. They remind him too much of heaven.'

Wulfrun looks at me, then laughs. I remember her the night that we feasted in the infirmary, the careless girl she might have been in another life. Here, at the end, perhaps she does not have to worry so much.

Mere

I sit beside her and press her hand in mine. For a while we remain in silence. There are birdcalls in the trees, sparrows protesting, starlings in all their mimicry. The tilt of the cuckoo, the keen, far off, of some harrier. Mice and rats and voles slipping easily between water and bank, stick-legged boatmen hovering on the surface of the spring, at the very edge where water becomes air. It is all that has been lost to us, ever since Eadwig came stumbling from the marsh.

I take a breath. Richer than any brew I could ever make, full of damp and rot and life. I press my fingers into the moss and they sink, so I cannot tell where I end and where the green begins. And Wulfrun's hand in my own, her pulse an answer to the call of my own heartbeat.

'I wish we could stay here,' I say. 'With no hunger, no thirst. It would be our Eden.'

'Two Eves,' muses Wulfrun. 'One too many.'

She tilts her head towards me. The dates are sweet on her breath. I bite her lip as I feel her fingers press at the back of my neck, hard enough to bruise. The last marks we will leave on each other. Then, slowly, she pushes me away.

'I cannot,' she says and I only nod. After a while, she pulls herself across to me, lies her head on my lap. Together, we turn our faces heavenwards and watch the fog weave and unravel above us.

'We cannot stay here,' says Wulfrun. 'We would die. We would leave all those at the convent to die.'

'I know,' I say. 'How would they live without their saint?'

'They would live well,' says Wulfrun, a little bitterness in her voice. 'Saints are always best dead anyway. They will miss their infirmarian far more.'

I can see the spring, still, from the corner of my eye. All those skulls beneath.

'One mouthful,' says Wulfrun 'That is what Botwine said. Only a drink from the spring and we would be free.'

I know her look. I saw it before the whipping and I hated it then as I hate it now.

I pull myself to my feet and shuffle over to the water. The crowns around the skulls have grown greener, so verdant and thick now that it seems impossible, as if it leeches all the colour from our convent and blots it about itself. There are marks, where other souls have knelt, considered the two paths ahead of them. Those who did not drink, did they refuse? Leogifu and Oswy and Edwin, too full of fear or perhaps too full of courage. Or perhaps they never found this place.

Wulfrun crouches beside me.

'I thought that this mere-devil would show himself,' she says, 'that he would appear a beast, a revenant, a wicked spirit. The abbess spoke of him as if we might battle him, the ceorls spoke of giving gifts as if to a greedy thegn. But he is not here, is he? At least, not in a way that we might touch.' She looks again at the skulls in the water. 'We made a devil from nothing more than some old bones.'

'Botwine said he found no demon here,' I say. 'Only a choice.' I regret this as soon as I speak it, for I see the words take hold of Wulfrun. An easy sacrifice, full of glory and martyrdom.

I am thinking of what I might say to convince her otherwise when her hand darts forward and there is the flash of bright water and she is crouched over now, shielding it from me and swallowing and I scramble across but
   already her mouth empty

Mere

teeth clean
eyes shut tight so she does not have to see me
and I fall upon her, scrambling, shouting, trying to force my fingers down her throat but her jaw is tight her fingers sharp and she scratches me, hard, across my face and I fall back, my hand reaching for the wound and she stops, horror in her look.

'I'm sorry,' she says softly.

The clearing is quiet. We thrashed and fought and drove life away and now it is only us. I taste blood in my mouth from a split lip, feel the sting of the cut on my face. But that is for another time, another Hilda. These little pains cannot hurt me.

'You could not have waited?'

She swallows, then shakes her head. 'I had to do it,' she says, 'while I had my courage.'

I reach over, brush my fingers on her lips, unpick strands of hair from her forehead, kiss her cheek, her brow.

'You fool,' I whisper and she gives a small smile. Like some kitchen oblate who has spilt the pottage one too many times. Eadwig, Botwine and now Wulfrun. All three charged to my care, all three failed. I knock her hand away.

'They will not let you pass,' I say. 'They will see your devil-sickness and bar you, as they did Botwine.'

'I will spin a vision,' she says, tilting her chin. I see her as she was of old, proud and bold, knowing neither weakness nor fear.

'They will not care. They wanted you to sacrifice yourself for them, not to return.'

'I shall tell them the truth, then.'

'As Botwine did. They will hear only a devil-sick woman, or worse.'

Wulfrun turns her gaze downwards, then. 'Perhaps,' she says. 'Hilda, I know you are angry—'

'I do not wish to hear your apologies,' I say.

'Good,' says Wulfrun, 'for I am not sorry.'

We stare at each other and then, slowly, she tilts into me, lays her head in my lap. I stroke her hair, murmur that British song for which I still only know half of the words. Wulfrun closes her eyes. I can feel the quick beat of her heart, the fever in her brow. She gives a moan and reaches for her head.

'Oh,' she says, 'there is so much. So much, so tight.'

A crown of another sort.

I count every mark on her skin. The blemishes, the freckles, the ebb and flow of her scar. That false tooth. Her eyelashes and the lines about her eyes. I have been so foolish not to have committed all of her to memory, because now she is leaving me and there will be a day, maybe not far away, where I will think of her and not be able to recall for certain which of her fingers was unusually long, and whether her smile was slightly crooked on the right side of her mouth or the left.

'I should have gone with you,' I say, 'that first night. If we had found Eadwig, this all might be different.'

'He was already taken by then,' says Wulfrun. 'I should—'

For a moment her body tenses and she is in pain, my sweetness is being torn somewhere and she does not make a sound but only breathes faster, as if preparing for childbirth.

'It pains you?' I say, but she shakes her head. Slowly, too slowly, it passes and she is herself again.

'I am well,' she says, 'I am with you.'

I cannot, too much to give and it is not fair, to have

Mere

known her only a few months. I had thought myself beyond hope but I understand now that I had thought we would both somehow live through this. That we had a thousand nights ahead of us and a thousand more mornings.

'Spin a vision for me,' I say. 'Tell me how this might have been, in a better world.'

She smiles, weakly. 'You ask for the stars themselves.'

'So you cannot do it?' I say.

She takes another deep breath and I worry that I have pushed her too far, asked something that will only cause her more pain. And then, she speaks.

'*I long to be about my maid's waist.*
Sometimes I am soft, other times hard and thick.
A husband gives it to his new wife.'

I stroke her brow, shaking my head. 'I cannot believe you so sinful,' I say and her eyes dance.

'It is not that,' she says. 'It is only your mind that follows such wicked paths.'

'Ah yes, I forget. You have never lusted in your life.'

'You know, though? What I speak of.'

'I do,' I say. 'It is a girdle.' It is about my arm still, as I lean forward to kiss her. 'The finest gift I have ever had. The fairest future we might have been given.'

It is there for that shimmering moment, a life shared, our souls each the other's and bound together

an end and then an end and then an end

and her lips are on mine and mine on hers and there is something wet and rich between us and there are tears on my cheek hers mine I cannot tell and

her heart an echo in my jaw and through her I feel
the sweep beneath earth
unfolding eggs in sediment waiting for spring

Danielle Giles

fish soft beneath ice

I give a shout of laughter and she flinches away mouth open and I sense no longer those ice-bound fish those patient eggs

it has been easy all along even Christ Himself did not carry the cross all the way alone there are many paths and many people to take them and

even as we end and we end it continues a loop the golden thread forged and then woven and it is not meant to belong to one soul alone but to be shared to be given as a gift

her and I so close already

'Both of us,' I say, 'we both drink.'

She tries to stop me but she has made herself weak and I am finished before she can even reach me, a great mouthful all at once. It is bitter going down, bitter in my stomach, my throat and there is a pain behind my eyes and about my temple and I fall back giggling for

delicious

a feast

nobody told me

Interlude

the marsh has fingers and it reaches out above water below water and all those places that are both at once and it shelters those fat clotted leeches dreaming of springblood and beneath them trembling beetle eggs one day to be snapped up by pike sharptooth and there are eels knotted with blacksmith muscle and they could take a man's hand if they wished
    past a sheepskull long dead
    her heart mine
    not a crown but a girdle and
    we must only return
    the burn on her face bright as she shouts across the flood and hears our answer
    one day there will be sundew flowers feasting on flyflesh
    one day there will be pike tough as shields
    one day frogs will sing their songs of love
    bitterns drumming out
    sparrow fledglings trembling their wings in hunger calling yes more as much as there is I will take it
    and a tremble through me too and it is painful yes but lovely

Danielle Giles

also and Ava shines a saint of shields and Tove shines a saint of pity and Sweet crossing over and lifting me on her shoulders no saint she only rough hands and
    fleas in the mattress
    a blanket and warm fire and
    as much as there is we will bear it

Chapter 31

Three weeks later

I wake to the call of the Matins bell. For a heartbeat I think it is for me and then I remember. A wet dawn this morning, but with most of the chill taken from it. Even so, I stay under my blankets, warm, shielded, until Sweet walks by and, seeing my eyes open, kicks my feet.

'The fire's lit,' she says. 'But we've geese to feed. Then, we will eat, then I must go to the hives.'

She hurries on without waiting for a reply, for there is much for her to do in this long-awaited spring of ours.

I sigh, but do as she bids, throwing a cloak over my tunic, hose and long skirts. Though Sweet is the poorest of the ceorls, the material is still softer than my old habit. I pity the poor sister who has taken my clothes, until I remember that they burnt what Wulfrun and I returned in.

I duck out the door and

a harrier hanging in the air a hare beneath it then the drop and the scream lifeblood dark on claws on beak seeping into the soil where worms feel the stomp of feet and think it rain and it is Wulfrun a mile or so away already awake calling my sisters to worship the blood in her wrist jumping as she says hurry hurry and there are tiny creatures in her eyebrows that none know of none see but we two and my breath catching how brilliant how endless

I stumble and shake my head.

It grows easier with every passing day. My first night at Sweet's, I awoke thinking that I was a fox pouncing, a seed sprouting, a bird puffed up against winter. It took me until midday to find myself again.

Now, three weeks later, I can place it beside me, a pool that I can dip into when I must.

And I am glad for this, for when I go to release the geese, their sheer outraged life would be enough to topple me, if I was not careful. They swagger at my feet, calling in their aggrieved voices as I throw what vegetable scraps we have kept back for them. Only when they are sure that I have none left do they turn to nipping at the grass and bugs.

I can see other figures in the dawn, tending to beasts and fowl, collecting wood for smouldering fires, collecting water from the stream. The flood is gone, the ice melted, but the land is not how it was before. Most of the ditches have collapsed and the mere has reclaimed much of the land that we once hoped to till.

Many still live in the convent bounds, not yet able to begin the slow work of reclaiming their homes. There is no justice in which buildings survived. Some built deep and stout were swept away entirely. Yet Sweet's home, its mudpacked walls so close to the marsh, was spared. She tells me it was a reward. I think it was because her land is softer, wetter than the cut-channel, crumble-dry earth that many of the others farmed. Rather than fighting the floodwaters with shovel and ditch, it embraced them.

Mere

I cannot linger long on these thoughts, though, for Sweet calls me into breakfast in the same way she has every day for the last three weeks, by telling me that if I am slow she will eat it all and that I shall have to find some other kind soul to take me in and feed me.

There has not been a single morning where she has made good on this threat and today is no different, for I find her serving my own portion before hers, grumbling the whole time.

Though the pottage is bitter, I eat it quickly and in gratitude. Too many long days with an empty stomach. Not much grain in it, but plenty of nettles and reed-roots and acorns. Blackberries, sweet in the brew. Fish, slices of eel. There are even a few lumps of meat in it, from a sheep that returned, baffled, from the marsh, not drowned after all but only lost and followed soon after by a dozen or so more.

The eels, too, made their hidden way back into our traps, and fish began to spring out of ponds where no fish sprang before. As if bidden by some hidden master, beets and parsnips pushed out from banks where they had remained sleeping and safe through the frost and flood.

A miracle, a miracle they all cried, returning to a land that had been dried out once more. Nearly half of us dead, but half of us alive, hungry, joyful. All this in the first few days after Wulfrun and I came stumbling from the mere's jaws, though I remember none of it. Only a great release, as if a held breath had been, at last, let out.

'So,' says Sweet, watching me over her bowl, 'I had Fair Alfred coming to me last night.'

I raise my eyebrows at her, but she shakes her head and laughs. 'No,' she says, 'he is far too young and I far too old for that. And anyway, he came for, ever since the curse was lifted, he has found his manhood shrivelled. His poor wife has coaxed it, has prayed over it and even cast some charms herself, but nothing has worked. They think it some wicked spell cast by a former lover.'

'Well,' I say, 'that might have been the case for half of the women and a fair few of the sisters in the convent.'

'I told him to mix ginger, turnip and cow's milk,' says Sweet. 'But he would have it made by your hands. Believes there is power in a cure from Hilda the Wise.'

'There is not,' I say, quickly. 'No more than before.'

'No,' says Sweet, tilting her head. 'So you say.'

The last few mornings have been this way, Sweet bringing me a list of complaints to cure. Plenty come to her, still too wary to speak to me directly, petitioning me through my mother. Not just those outside the convent, but a few sisters, too. There is still no infirmarian behind the walls and so Tove and Ava do what they can. When the fog cleared, a messenger was sent to Gipeswic and there will be a handful of girls and women returning, one of whom might take the post of infirmarian.

There is a test in these morning talks, as well. She watches for the beginnings of devil-sickness on my tongue. Poor Botwine and Eadwig, their heads bowed from the weight of it all, their thoughts painful and bright. It was not meant to belong to one soul alone and they didn't know, couldn't know how it might be shared, diluted as it passes from one to another, unending. Not the lonely crown but a sweet-given girdle.

Perhaps, we are not the first to find this. Perhaps, once, more bore it together, a dozen souls all bonded. There were many skulls in the water.

Mere

But there is much else to think of today, for Matins is not at its end and Wulfrun is picking her way down the path to this home at the edge of the marsh.

'Thank you for the pottage,' I say. 'When I return, I will make that salve for Fair Alfred, but you must not tell him that it was I who made it.'

'I will not,' says Sweet. 'But I cannot stop what he believes.'

A familiar reply already. I have already awoken twice to a fresh-baked loaf on our doorstep, a basket of gleaming goose eggs nestled beneath our eaves. Heathen worship, I worry, but Sweet only waves away my fears and tells me a gift is a gift and not to think too much on it. And if it means our bellies are full, I think she does not much care the reasons behind it.

Each soul in this place has taken the tale of mine and Wulfrun's survival and turned it to their liking. In the convent, devout sisters tell how we fought a great battle against the mere-devil and only won because of our shared faith. In it, they see our convent restored once again: piety, sacrifice, the power of prayers redoubled in community. Wulfrun has not told them otherwise and I think she half believes it herself.

The others, like Fair Alfred, see dominion in it. They sent us out, crowned, as in the old ways. But we were not like the others in their weakness. We were strong, where Botwine and Eadwig were not, and our Christ-magics have now been made more powerful by marsh-cunning.

As was always in this place, many of the souls here have both on their tongues at once.

'Take care at the convent,' says Sweet at the door. 'If they sour with you, flee. You understand?'

'I will not need to,' I say, but Sweet shakes her head.

'No,' she says. 'Twice now, I have let you go. It will not happen again. Swear to me.'

I look at my mother. Her life full of trials that would best a lesser woman. Every path a treacherous one, every choice one between two evils. And still, she went up to the convent for me and talked Ava into returning to me the most basic of my tools, at least until a new infirmarian is found. She sought Tove and asked that I be held in the convent's prayers, at least once a day, for she knows that if they forget my name, it is an easy path to forgetting that they must show mercy towards me. All of it a risk to her, though she might sit fat and happy with her new hides of land.

'I give you my word,' I say and her grey eyes soften.

Eluned greets me on the path. She, out of all, has not treated me as any other than I was. She knows, surely, how I might now drift when talking, or how I might know of a bird's flight before it has yet taken wing, but she says she has heard of similar in Wealh tales, of enchantresses who might turn themselves to a hare, then a hawk, then a hound, all in the span of a day.

'Fair morning,' she says. Her cheeks are flushed but she keeps her skirts pulled down about her hose, wears tight the hair covering that was not permitted to her before as a slave. She goes early to her work, settling land that has been left ruined. The old owner was one of those who was swept away in the flood and she sleeps in his old bed. There were mutterings that it was ill-fated to take the house of a dead man, but Eluned has had it thrice-blessed. Every passing day she grows stronger, brighter.

Mere

'Tell me,' she says, nodding at a corner that she has turned over, 'what of this soil? Will it bear crops well?'

I stop. It teems, beneath, but only weakly. I point a little further along. 'There,' I say, 'it is richer there.'

She does not ask how I know, only nods. 'I knew I should have waited to ask you before starting,' she says. 'A morning's strain, for nothing. And why are you here so early?'

'I go to the convent,' I say.

'Good,' she says. 'You have been away too long, they suffer without you.'

'Are you not glad to have me here, with you all?'

Eluned shrugs. 'You were often down here before. Where you sleep makes little difference.'

I do not feel the same carelessness, hear in every bell that rings from the convent a beckoning and a punishment all at once. But perhaps that was how it always was and it is only now that I understand it.

'If you see Ava or Tove at the convent, ask them about this manumission. They must talk of it now, before they forget their gratitude.'

A show of thanks by the households who survived, to release all those bonded to them as an act of faith. I do not know who first spoke of it, though I suspect Sweet and her quick tongue, but it has taken hold. And it is not only out of mercy. The households are poorer, less able to feed another mouth and there is more land than hands to till it.

'I shall,' I say.

She looks at me with doubt. 'And if they do not listen to you,' she says, 'Wulfrun tells me she will have a vision and that will spur them all on.'

She speaks so simply, so easily of turning a holy miracle

to her own ends. It seems an age ago that I was with her in Sweet's dwelling, giving her yet another potion and listening to her despair. Nothing would ever change for her, back then. Now, I think she is ready to overturn Christendom itself.

'And,' she says, leaning closer, 'I think there will be pilgrims coming soon, to see Wulfrun, she who defeated this devil. When they come, will the men stay within the convent or without?'

'Within,' I say. 'Why?'

'And the rich men,' she says, 'will they stay somewhere else?'

I laugh. 'I am sure,' I say, 'you will find them, wherever they are.'

'Good,' she says, 'I am fair now, but it will not last. You must tell me which of them is the most biddable. I have never been to Gipeswic, but I have heard many things of it. From there, I might even go west. To Wealh, maybe. If there is anybody left to find.'

She glances up, beyond me. 'But I keep you,' she says. 'She is waiting for you.'

Wulfrun sits on a fallen bough further along the path, carven and content. She feels the devil-sickness differently, I know, suffers from it less. What it stirs up in me, settles deep in her. I do not know why.

I lean down and kiss her. Again
tiny creatures in her skin our lips brushing fleas in her habit which will grow to a terror if she is not careful a worm in my gut a worm in her gut the taste of sheep's meat in my mouth fish in hers the creak of muscles as she pushes close to me and kingdoms rise and fall between us if we were to both stay here the reeds would rise up through our bones and

Mere

Laughing, she pushes me away. I blink, smile.

'Careful,' she says.

It is strange, for looking at Wulfrun, no soul would see the mark of the past few months on her. Now that we eat, her face has grown plump again, the darkness under her eyes receding. Even her burn has faded, a little, or perhaps that is only the dawn light.

But she no longer wears much of her finery. Her fur she has given to Tove, her embroidered wimple to Ava. Her girdle I wear still about my arm. Only the gold ring on her finger shows that she was ever anything other than a sister of this convent.

'How goes the triumvirate?' I ask, as we begin to walk.

Wulfrun shakes her head. 'We talk and talk and come to our decision and then talk on it again. This manumission, for one. I am glad that Tove is abbess, but she needs a firmer hand.'

'Be careful,' I say, 'for she might turn that hand on you as well as Ava.'

'Surely not,' says Wulfrun, 'I speak only good sense and nothing else.'

An odd election, in the end, for Ava would not stand for the position out of guilt and Wulfrun, newly returned, was not yet trusted enough to be considered. Tove did not wish for the position but she was the first choice and so there was little to be done. But she rules in a council of sorts, Ava thinking always of smallness, details, ledgers, and Wulfrun turning to the sky, the water.

Tove wears her power uneasily, will often begin to start speaking and then must change her words to that of an abbess. But she has spent a lifetime learning the ways of this place and has a fine memory for all the sins of her fellow sisters. The abbess punished us for them, but Tove has her own ways. Novices who are full of spirit but slow at learning are set at busywork, so that they are too tired in their lessons to cause trouble. The kitchen sisters have long been hoarding food, knowing that they sit at the lowest place in the table and will not eat enough otherwise, but Tove has allowed them greater portions. And if there is a sister who is slothful or greedy, Tove chides them only lightly, knowing that the displeasure of the others will soon correct her faster than any whipping. She is still only able to walk twenty paces at a time, but that is all that she needs, for Tove rules with a cunning that feels like mercy.

When Tove eventually dies, I am sure the election between Wulfrun and Ava will be fierce. But I hope for many long years before that.

As we come to the bridge, we both stiffen. It is new repaired and there are none guarding it, but still I remember Botwine reaching for us all and finding a spear in his gut.

That first day when we returned, she told them of a victory. I was still half-mad and it was all that she could do to convince them not to stone me there and then. I had seen the demon, she told them, watched her defeat it, but my mind had unravelled with fear. In the end, Tove came to the gate and chided every soul there until Wulfrun was let inside. Tove began to fight for me also, but Sweet offered to take me in until I was well. If this devil was defeated, she told them, there was no reason why she might not return to her hut and care for me.

'All will be well,' says Wulfrun, as we step across the threshold together.

So strange, to fear the convent. I had thought my path

Mere

set at the end of autumn, another long year in duty and quiet, and now I am half-outcast.

'I don't know how they bore it alone,' I say, softly. 'Eadwig, Botwine.'

'No,' says Wulfrun and I can hear her heart and how fast it beats.

In my absence, the orchard has grown bold. Tenacious daffodils push pale green shoots from dark soil, daphne flowers unfold pink-tinged and poisonous, and there is even a pear sapling I thought killed by the frost that is showing its first bud. In a few weeks, spring will have laid claim to this place, beckoned dormant green to wake once more for another season.

We are not followed to the orchard, for none would admit their curiosity in me and I know that both Ava and Tove have instructed that I am to be left in peace. But there are more sisters who find that they must pass by on some errand or another, craning their necks to see if I shall suddenly froth at the mouth and set a fire in some building.

Wulfrun leads the way through the garden, though I know the path well enough. Still, I am glad to be led along.

'It is Shrove Tuesday tomorrow,' says Wulfrun. 'Will you come? We will have confession and feasting. The other sisters have seen that you are not devil-sick, as Eadwig and Botwine were, and with every day you are absent, their need of you grows.'

'I do not know,' I say. I think, still, of my fellow sisters. How they kept Mildred away, alone in those dark stables. How they bayed at Botwine, and fell upon Alwin and then dared rejoice when Wulfrun stood to be sacrificed in their place. I do not know I can ever forgive them that, nor myself for standing by so long.

'In time, maybe,' I say. 'I must think on it.'

'You must think on forgiving them, you mean,' says Wulfrun. How easily she knows me.

'I do not know how you do it,' I say.

Wulfrun shrugs, serene. 'It is simpler than you think,' she says. 'A moment's mercy, that is all.'

She has always known when to be hard and when not to. Her weakness turned strength, her suffering turned victory. But there is more of Sweet in me than I thought. That bitter seed in me that cannot turn a cheek.

'My duties grow more and more,' says Wulfrun. 'I may not have as much time to visit you.'

How strange, for her to try to lie when I can feel the spark of her pulse, the tautness of her shoulders. She urges me back to the convent before I am ready. She realizes it too, for she begins to smile.

'I am sure you can find a way,' I say.

'You are missed,' she says. 'Not only by me.'

'Another infirmarian and they will forget all about me,' I say.

Wulfrun's expression becomes pained and she is about to say something when she looks ahead and stops. We have reached the end of this small pilgrimage.

Many markers in this orchard. The post I carved for Mildred is still there and then there is one of a warrior-priest, all fire and judgement, beside her. Alwin's body washed up the day after we were cast out. Here they rest together, at last.

Oswy and Edwin, too, given a plot near Cellarer Leogifu.

Mere

Abbess Sigeburg, and Ethel, and all those others who died in my infirmary.

Some have not been so fortunate. Botwine lies still deep within the marsh. Even if I returned to that spring, I would not have the strength to bring him back. He will sink into that hidden place and rest there instead. We could not find Eadwig, the flood having upended heaven and earth and left him without a place to rest.

Each of these missing and found is marked and remembered.

We kneel together in front of the graves and pray, voices weaving over each other until we have a devotion strong and soft as the finest wool. I watch as a redbreast flutters down onto Mildred's marker and begins a hunt for worms and beetles, heedless of our presence.

'Portress Ava is here most days,' says Wulfrun. 'At Ethel's grave, mostly. She has still not spoken to you? Begged forgiveness?'

'For what?' I ask. Of all the souls left alive, she I cannot blame, for there was no hatred in it. Only duty.

'She feels some guilt, I am sure,' says Wulfrun. 'Or else she would come see you, as Tove did.'

A strange visit in the end, Sweet offering meat and bread and Tove waving it away, saying she could not stay for long. I was still in bed, then, still uncertain of what was myself and what was the devil-sickness. But she came all the same, pressed her hand against mine and found no strangeness. I feared, back then, that any touch would spread it, as it did with Botwine and Eadwig. But I think as mandrake root might poison if eaten directly but cure if mixed with wine and water, so between us Wulfrun and I dilute the worst of it.

Both Ava and Tove have guessed, I think, the truth. They see beyond Wulfrun's holy tale, remember the riddle and its answer.

'Tove has been asking me,' says Wulfrun, lightly, 'what will happen to the convent if one or the other of us dies.'

'They will mourn and call you saint.'

She smiles, but in truth it is something I have been thinking on myself. I think others will have to go, a pair perhaps or more. We cannot hope, as before, that it will slumber in the marsh for decades.

'I have been speaking,' says Wulfrun, 'of how we found a holy spring on our way to defeat this mere-devil, which gave us strength. One that might be drunk from, but only in Christian fellowship, or else all will turn to ruin.'

'And you think that will be enough? To rouse some brave souls?'

'It is just as when we break bread in worship,' she says, 'we who are many are one body.'

She sees divinity in the gift and I cannot deny that it feels sacred. But for me, it is the slow glory of lichen across old stones. A bloom, across edge-lands.

And yet, I do not think her wrong to tell this tale, for it is nothing more than she has always done. She pulls holy future from our unsteady days and now she plans for the safety of sisters that we may never even meet.

'Tove and Ava believe your tale?'

'Tove takes nothing as truth without first unpicking every stitch,' says Wulfrun. 'But she sees the use in the tale. Ava scorns it, though not where others can hear her.'

'She will follow it,' I say, 'in time. She has always longed for her path to be shown to her. It is only that now she does not like her guide.'

Mere

We reach the end of words and sit, instead, in silence, on a fallen bough from a tree where
a dozen feet away a sister reaches down and scratches at a swelling bite, then shoos away a creeping spider which skitters back, retreats to the humming threads of its web where a trapped fly twitches, still half-alive.

Both Wulfrun and I flinch.

'Eadwig's mother will know by now,' says Wulfrun, her head bowed. 'If the messengers arrived to Gipeswic. I gave her my word that I would care for him and instead I bring her the tale of his death.'

'And gold,' I say. 'Far more than his weregild, if you were to reckon it.'

'And if I were her, I would throw it down a well and curse my name,' says Wulfrun.

'I know,' I say. I cannot offer comfort where there is none. We failed Eadwig, us both, in body and soul. Mildred, too, for I still wake sometimes and think that I will see her gathering herbs out on the slopes of our convent, or else stopping on the path with laundry in her arms, turning her face to the sun as if she might drink in all its warmth.

Our repentance will last a lifetime and longer.

'I will not say thank you,' says Wulfrun at last, 'for I am still angry that you came. That you exile yourself away from me. Away from us all.'

'But?'

'But,' she says, 'it is a good thing that you were there with me, at the end.'

She reaches across, runs her fingers over the fabric of my sleeve where, beneath, the girdle is tied fast.

'So strange,' she says, 'to be saved by such a small thing.'

Danielle Giles

'The old ways had it wrong,' I say, 'by sending out a single crowned soul. It was always meant to be shared.'

Beside me, Wulfrun takes a deep breath. She smiles. That single false tooth, darker than the others.

'It is good to live,' she says.

I place my hand in hers. A bee, lulled a little early from its wall-nest, drones about us and

a few feet away hellebore spreads white welcome and witch hazel spider's legs tracing scent in the air and larvae still wrapped tight in deep water and there is her pulse jumping the girdle still tight about my arm and shared always between us my darling there are even tiny mushrooms in the folds between our skin and we breathe in and taste each other taste cooking smoke a water-vole darting across open ground the snap of a pike the hammer of hooves far away men full of sweat and pride and ale bringing with them cattle sheep women pilgrims and

We leap up together. Wulfrun's eyes are bright.

'The messengers are back from Gipeswic,' she says. 'The path is opened.'

I see the fear in her and I feel it myself. Perhaps they bring tales of fresh disaster, of some royal proclamation against us or the Ealdorman hearing of the abbess's death and disbanding this place. Perhaps they come not with gold and help but with tales of northman raiders and a kingdom in ruin.

'Come,' I say. 'There is much left to do, with life still in us.'

She looks at me and

above a seagull wheeling inland crying out not pain but delight an open sky

beneath roots reaching and taking and giving

kingdoms unfolding

Acknowledgements

Books are made by communities, and *Mere* is no exception.

A massive thank you to my agent Jess Lee, who found my stories about worms and prawns and asked me if I was working on anything else. I could not ask for a steadier, more insightful or more passionate advocate. Many thanks as well to everyone at A. M. Heath.

My editor, Madeleine O'Shea, whose guidance has been warm, astute and utterly invaluable. Thank you for asking all the important questions and helping me find the answers (even if that answer is to add more goat sacrifice).

The whole team at Mantle at Pan Macmillan is extraordinary, and special thank you to Maria Rejt, Kinza Azira and Michael Davies for their incredible welcome. Thanks also to Rebecca Needes and Tamsin Shelton, who helped me cull my many errant commas, and to Kimberley Nyamhondera for her tireless creativity in publicizing this book.

I am in particular debt to my readers: Katharina Matthews,

Acknowledgements

Grace Hawkins, Laurie Kent and Jen Russell. You gave me many of your hours and you are all in every chapter of this book. Thanks also to Lily Bland, who provided company, cups of tea and an unparalleled view of visiting songbirds during my edits.

I have been lucky enough to be supported by a number of teachers. Ms Morgan, Ms Langton and Ms Boardman, in particular, encouraged early forays into fiction, and Tricia Wastvedt at Bath Spa showed me the value of precision.

Thank you also to all the experts and historians whose work helped put together the world of *Mere*. There are too many to mention them all, but I am especially grateful to Danièle Cybulskie, whose masterclass was a revelation.

I'm thankful for everyone who has provided me with places of refuge (if not always quiet): Janet and Mark Loftus and Charlotte and Jack Sykes in particular. Thank you, also, to all the other members of my sprawling extended family, who are continually a source of joy and courage.

My mother Margaret gave me tenacity, and my father John showed me patience. Alexej, my brother, is a consistent fount of good humour, and Katharina never ceases to inspire me with her hard work (and her beautiful cat). My nan, Margaret, terrified me wonderfully with tales of banshees and my grandad Harry told me stories of the Bristol docks that were earthier but no less magical.

And finally for Jethro, whose patience, kindness and love are truly without end. He sees and encourages the best of me.